Wrong Place
Wrong Time

Wrong Place
Wrong Time

A Novel

GILLIAN McALLISTER

WILLIAM MORROW
An Imprint of HarperCollins*Publishers*

WRONG PLACE WRONG TIME. Copyright © 2022 by Gillian McAllister. Excerpt from JUST ANOTHER MISSING PERSON copyright © 2022 by Gillian McAllister. All rights reserved. Printed in the United States of America. No part of this book may be used or reproduced in any manner whatsoever without written permission except in the case of brief quotations embodied in critical articles and reviews. For information, address HarperCollins Publishers, 195 Broadway, New York, NY 10007.

HarperCollins books may be purchased for educational, business, or sales promotional use. For information, please email the Special Markets Department at SPsales@harpercollins.com.

Published in the UK in 2022 by Michael Joseph.

FIRST US EDITION

Library of Congress Cataloging-in-Publication Data has been applied for.

ISBN 978-0-06-325234-9 (hardcover)
ISBN 978-0-06-327527-0 (international edition)

22 23 24 25 26   LSC   10 9 8 7 6 5 4 3 2 1

For Felicity and Lucy: in any multiverse,
I'd want to be agented by you.

Day Zero, just after midnight

Jen is glad of the clocks going back tonight. A gained hour, extra time, to be spent pretending she isn't waiting up for her son.

Now that it is past midnight, it is officially the thirtieth of October. Almost Halloween. Jen tells herself that Todd is eighteen, her September baby now an adult. He can do *whatever he wants*.

She has spent much of the evening badly carving a pumpkin. She places it now on the sill of the picture window that overlooks their driveway, and lights it. She only carved it for the same reason she does most things – because she felt she should – but it's actually quite beautiful, in its own jagged way.

She hears her husband Kelly's feet on the landing above hers and turns to look. It's unusual for him to be up, he the lark and she the nightingale. He emerges from their bedroom on the top floor. His hair is messy, blue-black in the dimness. He has on not a single piece of clothing, only a small, amused smile, which he blows out of the side of his mouth.

He descends the stairs toward her. His wrist tattoo catches the light, an inscribed date, the day he says he knew he loved her: spring 2003. Jen looks at his body. Just a few of his dark chest hairs have turned white over the past year, his forty-third. "Been busy?" He gestures to the pumpkin.

"Everyone had done one," Jen explains lamely. "All the neighbors."

"Who cares?" he says. Classic Kelly.

"Todd's not back."

"It's the early evening, for him," he says. Soft Welsh accent just barely detectable on the three-syllable *ev-en-ing*, like his breath is stumbling over a mountain range. "Isn't it one o'clock? His curfew."

It's a typical exchange for them. Jen cares very much, Kelly perhaps too little. Just as she thinks this, he turns, and there it is: his perfect, perfect arse that she's loved for almost twenty years. She gazes back down at the street, looking for Todd, then back at Kelly.

"The neighbors can now see your arse," she says.

"They'll think it's another pumpkin," he says, his wit as fast and sharp as the slice of a knife. Banter. It's always been their currency. "Come to bed? Can't believe Merrilocks is done," he adds with a stretch. He's been restoring a Victorian tiled floor at a house on Merrilocks Road all week. Working alone, exactly the way Kelly likes it. He listens to podcast after podcast, hardly ever sees anyone. Complicated, kind of unfulfilled, that's Kelly.

"Sure," she says. "In a bit. I just want to know he's home okay."

"He'll be here any minute now, kebab in hand." Kelly waves a hand. "You waiting up for the chips?"

"Stop," Jen says with a smile.

Kelly winks and retreats to bed.

Jen wanders aimlessly around the house. She thinks about a case she has on at work, a divorcing couple arguing primarily over a set of china plates but of course, really, over a betrayal. She shouldn't have taken it on, she has over three hundred cases already. But Mrs. Vichare had looked at Jen in that first meeting and said, "If I have to give him those plates, I will have lost every single thing I love," and Jen hadn't been able to resist. She wishes she didn't care so much – about divorcing strangers, about neighbors, about bloody pumpkins – but she does.

She makes a tea and takes it back up to the picture window, continuing her vigil. She'll wait as long as it takes. Both phases of parenthood – the newborn years and the almost-adult ones – are bookended by sleep deprivation, though for different reasons.

They bought this house because of this window in the exact center of their three-story house. "We'd look out of it like kings," Jen had said, while Kelly laughed.

She stares out into the October mist, and there is Todd, outside on the street, at last. Jen sees him just as Daylight Saving Time kicks in and her phone switches from 01:59 to 01:00. She hides a smile: thanks to the clocks going back, he is deliberately no longer late. That's Todd for you; he finds the linguistic and semantic back-flipping of arguing a curfew more important than the reason for it.

He is loping up the street. He's skin and bones, doesn't ever seem to gain weight. His knees poke angles in his jeans as he walks. The mist outside is colorless, the trees and pavement black, the air a translucent white. A world in grayscale.

Their street – the back end of Crosby, Merseyside – is unlit. Kelly installed a Narnia-style lamp outside their house. He surprised her with it, wrought iron, expensive;

she has no idea how he afforded it. It clicks on as it detects movement.

But – wait. Todd's seen something. He stops dead, squints. Jen follows his gaze, and then she sees it, too: a figure hurrying along the street from the other side. He is older than Todd, much older. She can tell by his body, his movements. Jen notices things like this. Always has. It is what makes her a good lawyer.

She places a hot palm on the cool glass of the window.

Something is wrong. Something is about to happen. Jen is sure of this, without being able to name what it is; some instinct for danger, the same way she feels around fireworks and level crossings and cliff edges. The thoughts rush through her mind like the clicking of a camera, one after the other after the other.

She sets the mug on the windowsill, calls Kelly, then rushes down the stairs two at a time, the striped runner rough on her bare feet. She throws on shoes, then pauses for a second with her hand on the metal front doorknob.

What – what's that feeling? She can't explain it.

Is it déjà vu? She hardly ever experiences it. She blinks, and the feeling is gone, as insubstantial as smoke. What was it? Her hand on the brass knob? The yellow lamp shining outside? No, she can't recall. It's gone now.

"What?" Kelly says, appearing behind her, tying a gray dressing gown around his waist.

"Todd – he's – he's out there with . . . someone."

They hurry out. The autumn cold chills her skin immediately. Jen runs toward Todd and the stranger. But before she's even realized what is happening, Kelly's shouted out: "Stop!"

Todd is running, and within seconds has the front of this stranger's hooded coat in his grasp. He is squaring up to him, his shoulders thrust forward, their bodies together. The stranger reaches a hand into his pocket.

Kelly is running toward them, looking panicked, his eyes going left and right, up and down the street. "Todd, no!" he says.

And that's when Jen sees the knife.

Adrenaline sharpens her vision as she sees it happen. A quick, clean stab. And then everything slows way down: the movement of the arm pulling back, the clothing resisting then releasing the knife. Two white feathers emerge with the blade, drifting aimlessly in the frozen air like snowflakes.

Jen stares as blood begins to spurt, huge amounts of it. She must be kneeling down now, because she becomes aware of the little stones of the path cutting round divots into her knees. She's cradling him, parting his jacket, feeling the heat of the blood as it surges down her hands, between her fingers, along her wrists.

She undoes his shirt. His torso begins to flood; the three coin-slot wounds swim in and out of view – it's like trying to see the bottom of a red pond. She has gone completely cold.

"No." Her voice is thick and wet as she screams.

"Jen," Kelly says hoarsely.

There's so much blood. She lays him on her driveway and leans over, looking carefully. She hopes she's wrong, but she's sure, for just a moment, that he isn't here any more. The way the yellowed lamplight hits his eyes isn't quite right.

The night is completely silent, and after what must be several minutes she blinks in shock, then looks up at her son.

Kelly has moved Todd away from the victim and has his arms wrapped around him. Kelly's back is to her, Todd facing her, just gazing down at her over his father's shoulder, his expression neutral. He drops the knife. It rings out like a church bell as the metal hits the frozen pavement. He wipes a hand across his face, leaving a smear of blood.

Jen stares at his expression. Maybe he is regretful, maybe not. She can't tell. Jen can read almost everyone, but she never could read Todd.

Day Zero, just after 01:00

Somebody must have called 999, because the street is suddenly lit up with bright blue orbs. "What . . ." Jen says to Todd. Jen's "What . . ." conveys it all: Who, why, what the fuck?

Kelly releases his son, his face pale in shock, but he says nothing, as is often her husband's way.

Todd doesn't look at her or at his father. "Mum," he says eventually. Don't children always seek out their mother first? She reaches for him, but she can't leave the body. She can't release the pressure on the wounds. That might make it worse for everyone. "Mum," he says again. His voice is fractured, like dry ground that divides clean in two. He bites his lip and looks away, down the street.

"Todd," she says. The man's blood is lapping over her hands like thick bathwater.

"I had to," he says to her, finally looking her way.

Jen's jaw slackens in shock. Kelly's head drops to his chest. The sleeves of his dressing gown are covered in the blood from Todd's hands. "Mate," Kelly says, so softly Jen isn't sure he definitely spoke. "Todd."

"I had to," Todd says again, more emphatically. He breathes out a contrail of steam into the freezing air. "There was no choice," he says again, but this time with teenage finality. The blue of the police car pulses closer.

Kelly is staring at Todd. His lips – white with lack of blood – mime something, a silent profanity, maybe.

She stares at him, her son, this violent perpetrator, who likes computers and statistics and – still – a pair of Christmas pajamas each year, folded and placed at the end of his bed.

Kelly turns in a useless circle on the driveway, his hands in his hair. He hasn't looked at the man once. His eyes are only on Todd.

Jen tries to stem the wounds that pulsate underneath her hands. She can't leave the – the victim. The police are here, but no paramedics yet.

Todd is still trembling, with the cold or the shock, she's not sure. "Who is he?" Jen asks him. She has so many more questions, but Todd shrugs, not answering. Jen wants to reach to him, to squeeze the answers out of him, but they don't come.

"They're going to arrest you," Kelly says in a low voice. A policeman is running toward them. "Look – don't say anything, all right? We'll –"

"Who is he?" Jen says. It comes out too loudly, a shout in the night. She wills the police to slow down, please slow down, just give us a bit of time.

Todd turns his gaze back to her. "I . . ." he says, and for once, he doesn't have a wordy explanation, no intellectual posturing. Just nothing, a trailed-off sentence, puffed into the damp air that hangs between them in their final moments before this becomes something bigger than their family.

The officer arrives next to them: tall, black stab vest, white shirt, radio held in his left hand. "Echo from

Tango two four five — at scene now. Ambo coming." Todd looks over his shoulder at the officer, once, twice, then back at his mother. This is the moment. This is the moment he explains, before they encroach completely with their handcuffs and their power.

Jen's face is frozen, her hands hot with blood. She is just waiting, afraid to move, to lose eye contact. Todd is the one who breaks it. He bites his lip, then stares at his feet. And that's it.

Another policeman moves Jen away from the stranger's body, and she stands on her driveway in her trainers and pajamas, hands wet and sticky, just looking at her son, and then at her husband, in his dressing gown, trying to negotiate with the justice system. She should be the one taking charge. She's the lawyer, after all. But she is speechless. Totally bewildered. As lost as if she has just been deposited at the North Pole.

"Can you confirm your name?" the first policeman says to Todd. Other officers get out of other cars, like ants from a nest.

Jen and Kelly step forward in one motion, but Todd does something, then, just a tiny gesture. He moves his hand out to the side to stop them.

"Todd Brotherhood," he says dully.

"Can you tell me what happened?" the officer asks.

"Hang on," Jen says, springing to life. "You can't interview him by the side of the road."

"Let us all come to the station," Kelly says urgently. "And —"

"Well, I stabbed him," Todd interrupts, gesturing to the man on the ground. He puts his hands back in his pockets and steps toward the policeman. "So I'm guessing you'd better arrest me."

"Todd," Jen says. "Stop talking." Tears are clogging her throat. This cannot be happening. She needs a stiff drink, to go back in time, to be sick. Her whole body begins to tremble out here in the absurd, confusing cold.

"Todd Brotherhood, you do not have to say anything," the policeman says, "but it may harm your defense if you do not mention when questioned . . ." Todd puts his wrists together willingly, like he is in a fucking movie, and he's cuffed, just like that, with a metallic click. His shoulders are up. He's cold. His expression is neutral, resigned, even. Jen cannot, cannot, cannot stop staring at him.

"You can't do that!" Kelly says. "Is this a —"

"Wait," Jen says, panicked, to the policeman. "We'll come? He's just a teen . . ."

"I'm eighteen," Todd says.

"In there," the policeman says to Todd, pointing at the car, ignoring Jen. Into the radio, he says, "Echo from Tango two four five — dry cell prepped, please."

"We'll follow you, then," she says desperately. "I'm a lawyer," she adds needlessly, though she hasn't a clue about criminal law. Still, even now, in crisis, the maternal instinct burns as bright and as obvious as the pumpkin in the window. They just need to find out why he did it, get him off, then get him help. That is what they need to do. That is what they will do.

"We'll come," she says. "We'll meet you at the station."

The policeman finally meets her gaze. He looks like a

model. Cut-outs beneath his cheekbones. God, it's such a cliché, but don't all coppers look so young these days? "Crosby station," he says to her, then gets back into the car without another word, taking her son with him. The other officer stays with the victim, over there. Jen can hardly bear to think about him. She glances, just once. The blood, the expression on the policeman's face . . . she is sure the man is dead.

She turns to Kelly, and she will never forget the look her stoic husband gives her just then. She meets his navy eyes. The world seems to stop turning just for a second and, in the quiet and the stillness, Jen thinks: Kelly looks how it is to be heartbroken.

The police station has a white sign out the front advertising itself to the public. MERSEYSIDE POLICE – CROSBY. Behind it sits a squat sixties building, surrounded by a low brick wall. Tides of October leaves have been washed up against it.

Jen pulls up outside, just on the double yellows, and stops the engine. Their son's stabbed somebody – what does a parking ticket matter? Kelly gets out before the car is even stationary. He reaches – unconsciously, she thinks – behind him for her hand. She grasps it like it's a raft at sea.

He pushes one of the double glass doors open and they hurry in across a tired gray linoleum foyer. It smells old-fashioned inside. Like schools, like hospitals, like care homes. Institutions that require uniforms and crap food, the kind of places Kelly hates. "I will never," he'd said early on in their relationship, "join the rat race."

"I'll talk to them," Kelly says shortly to Jen. He is trembling. But it doesn't seem to be from fear, rather from anger. He is furious.

"It's fine – I can lawyer up and do the initial –"

"Where's the super?" Kelly barks to a bald officer manning reception who has a signet ring on his little finger. Kelly's body language is different. Legs spread widely, shoulders puffed up. Even Jen has only rarely seen him drop his guard like this.

In a bored tone, the officer tells them to wait to be seen.

"You've got five minutes," Kelly says, pointing to the clock before throwing himself into a chair across the foyer.

Jen sits down next to him and takes his hand. His wedding ring is loose on his finger. He must be cold. They sit there, Kelly crossing and uncrossing his long legs, huffing, Jen saying nothing. An officer arrives in reception, speaking quietly into his phone. "It's the same crime as two days ago – a section 18 wounding with intent. That victim was Nicola Williams, perpetrator AWOL." His voice is so low, Jen has to strain to hear.

She sits, just listening. Section 18 wounding with intent is a stabbing. They must be talking about Todd. And a similar crime from two days ago.

Eventually, the arresting officer emerges, the tall one with the cheekbones.

Jen looks at the clock behind the desk. It's three thirty, or perhaps four thirty. She doesn't know whether it's British Summer Time in here still. It's disorientating.

"Your son is staying with us tonight – we'll interview him soon."

"Where – back there?" Kelly says. "Let me in."

"You won't be able to see him," the officer says. "You are witnesses."

Irritation flares within Jen. This sort of thing – exactly *this* – is why people hate the justice system.

"It's like that, is it?" Kelly says acidly to the officer. He holds his hands up.

"Sorry?" the officer says mildly.

"What, so we're enemies?"

"Kelly!" Jen says.

"Nobody is anybody's enemy," the officer says. "You can speak to your son in the morning."

"Where is the superintendent?" Kelly says.

"You can speak to your son in the morning."

Kelly leaves a loaded, dangerous silence. Jen has seen only a handful of people on the receiving end of these, but still, she doesn't envy the policeman. Kelly's fuse usually takes a long time to trip but, when it does, it's explosive.

"I'll call someone," she says. "I know someone." She gets her phone out and begins shakily scrolling through her contacts. Criminal lawyers. She knows loads of them. The first rule of law is never to dabble in something you don't specialize in. The second is never to represent your family.

"He has said he doesn't want one," the officer says.

"He needs a solicitor – you shouldn't . . ." she says.

The officer raises his palms to her. Next to her, Jen can feel Kelly's temper brewing.

"I'll just call one, and then he can –" she starts.

"All right, let me back there," Kelly says, gesturing to the white door leading to the rest of the station.

13

"That cannot be authorized," the officer says.

"Fuck. You," Kelly says. Jen stares at him in shock.

The officer doesn't even dignify this with a response, just looks at Kelly in stony silence.

"So – what now then?" Jen says. God, Kelly has told a copper to fuck himself. A public order offense is not the way to defuse this situation.

"As I've already told you, he'll remain with us overnight," the officer says to her plainly, ignoring Kelly. "I suggest you come back tomorrow." His eyes flick to Kelly. "You can't force your son to take a solicitor. We have tried."

"But he's a kid," Jen says, though she knows that, legally, he isn't. "He's just a kid," she says again softly, mostly to herself, thinking of his Christmas pajamas and the way he wanted her to sit up with him recently when he had a vomiting bug. They spent all night in the en suite. Chatting about nothing, her wiping his mouth with a damp flannel.

"They don't care about that, or anything," Kelly says bitterly.

"We'll come back, in the morning – with a solicitor," Jen says, trying to ameliorate, to peacemake.

"Feel free. We need to send a team back with you to the house now," he says. Jen nods wordlessly. Forensics. Their house being searched. The lot.

Jen and Kelly leave the police station. Jen rubs at her forehead as they go to the car and get in. She blasts the heat on as they sit there.

"Are we really just going to go home?" she says. "Sit there while they search?"

Kelly's shoulders are tense. He stares at her, black hair everywhere, eyes sad like a poet's.

"I have no fucking idea."

Jen gazes out of the windshield at a bush glistening with middle-of-the-night autumnal dew. After a few seconds, she puts the car in reverse and drives, because she doesn't know what else to do.

The pumpkin greets them on the windowsill as she parks up. She must have left the candle burning. Forensics have already arrived in their white suits, standing on their driveway like ghosts by the police tape that flutters in the October wind. The puddle of blood has begun to dry at the edges.

They're let in, to their own fucking house, and they sit downstairs, watching the uniformed teams out front, some on their hands and knees doing fingertip searches of the crime scene. They say nothing at all, just hold hands in the silence. Kelly keeps his coat on.

Eventually, when the scene of crime officers have gone, and the police have searched and taken Todd's things, Jen shifts on the sofa so that she's lying down, and stares up at the ceiling. And that's when the tears come. Hot and fast and wet. The tears for the future. And the tears for yesterday, and what she didn't see coming.

Day Minus One, 08:00

Jen opens her eyes.

She must have come up to bed. And she must have slept. She doesn't feel like she did either, but she's in her bedroom, not on the sofa, and it's now light outside beyond their slatted blinds.

She rolls on to her side. Say it isn't true.

She blinks, staring at the empty bed. She's alone. Kelly will already be up, making calls, she very much hopes.

Her clothes litter the bedroom floor as if she evaporated out of them. She steps over them, pulling on jeans and a plain rollneck sweater which makes her look truly enormous but that she loves anyway.

She ventures out on to the hallway, standing outside Todd's empty room.

Her son. Spent the night in a police cell. She can't think about how many more might await him.

Right. She can sort this. Jen is an excellent rescuer, has spent all of her life doing just that, and now it's time to help her son.

She can figure this out.

Why did he do it?

Why did he have a knife with him? Who was the victim, this grown man her son has probably killed? Suddenly Jen can see little clues in Todd in the recent weeks and months. Moodiness. Weight loss. Secrecy.

Things she had put down to teenagehood. Just two days ago, he had taken a call, out in the garden. When Jen had asked who it was, he told her it was none of her business, then threw the phone on to the sofa. It had bounced, once, then fallen to the floor, where they'd both looked at it. He had passed it off as a joke, but it hadn't been, that small temper tantrum.

Jen stares and stares at the door to her son's bedroom. How had she come to raise a murderer? Teenage rage. Knife crime. Gangs. Antifa. Which is it? Which hand have they been dealt?

She can't hear Kelly at all. Halfway down the stairs, she glances out of the picture window, the window that she stood at only hours ago, the moment everything changed. It is still foggy.

She is surprised to see the road below bears no stains – the rain and the mist must have washed the blood away. The police have moved on. The police tape has gone.

She glances up the street, the edges peppered with trees ablaze with crunchy autumn leaves. But something is strange about what she sees. She can't work out what. It must just be the memories of last night. Rendering the view sinister, somehow. Slightly off.

She hurries downstairs, through their wooden-floored hallway and into the kitchen. It smells of last night in here, before anything happened. Food, candles. Normality.

She hears a voice, right above her, a deep male register. Kelly. She looks at the ceiling, confused. He must be in Todd's room. Searching it, probably. She understands that impulse entirely. The urge to find what the police couldn't.

"Kell?" she calls out, running back up the stairs, out of breath by the time she reaches the top. "We need to get on – which solicitor we should –"

"Three score and Jen!" a voice says. It comes from Todd's room and is unmistakably her son's. Jen takes a step back so massive it makes her stumble at the top of the stairs.

And she's not imagining it: Todd emerges from the confines of his room, wearing a black T-shirt which says *Science Guy* on it, and jogging bottoms. He has clearly just woken, and squints down at her, his pale face the only light in the darkness. "We haven't done that one yet," he says with a dimpled grin. "I even – I must confess – went on a pun website."

Jen can only gape at him. Her son, the killer. There is no blood on his hands. No murderous expression on his face, and yet.

"What?" she says. "How are you here?"

"Huh?" He really does look just the same as he did. Even in her confusion, Jen is curious. Same blue eyes. Same tousled, black hair. Same tall, slim frame. But he's committed an unforgivable act. Unforgivable to everyone, except maybe her.

How is he here? How is he home?

"What?" he prompts.

"How did you get back?"

Todd's brow flickers. "This is weird, even for you."

"Did Dad get you? Are you on bail?" she barks.

"On *bail*?" He raises an eyebrow, a new mannerism. For the past few months, he's looked different. Slimmer in the body, in the hips, but bloated in the face. With the pallor somebody gets when they are working too much, eating too many takeaways and drinking no water. None of which Jen is aware Todd is doing, but who knows? And then along came this mannerism, acquired just after he met his new girlfriend, Clio.

"I'm about to meet Connor."

Connor. A boy from his year, but another new friend, made only this summer. Jen befriended his mum, Pauline, years ago. She is just Jen's sort of person: jaded, sweary, not a natural mother, the kind of person who implicitly gives Jen permission to mess up. Jen has always been drawn to these types of people. All of her friends are unpretentious, unafraid to do and say what they think. Just recently, Pauline had said of Connor's younger brother, Theo: "I love him, but because he's seven, he often acts like a twat." They'd laughed like guilty loons at the school gate.

Jen steps forward and looks closely at Todd. No mark of the devil on him, no change behind his eyes, no weapons in the room beyond him. In fact, it looks untouched.

"How did you get home – and what happened?"

"Home from where?"

"The police station," Jen says plainly. She finds herself keeping a distance from him. Just a step more than usual. She no longer knows what this person – her child, the love of her life – is capable of.

"Sorry – the police station?" he says, evidently amused. "Question mark?" Todd's expression twists, nose wrinkling up just like it did when he was a baby. He has two tiny scars left over from the worst of his teenage acne.

Otherwise, his face is still childlike, pristine in that beautiful peach-fuzz way of the young.

"Your arrest, Todd!"

"My *arrest*?"

Jen can usually tell when her son is lying, and at that moment she registers that he is definitely not. He looks at her with his clear twilight eyes, confusion inscribed across his features. "What?" she says in barely a whisper. Something is creeping up her spine, some tentative, frightening knowledge. "I saw . . . I saw what you did." She gestures to the mid-landing window. And that's the moment she realizes what's the matter. It isn't the scene outside: it's the window itself. No pumpkin. It's gone.

Jen's teeth begin to chatter. This can't be happening.

She tears her eyes away from the pumpkin-less windowsill.

"I saw," she says again.

"Saw what?" His eyes are so like Kelly's, she finds herself thinking, for at least the thousandth time in her life: they're identical.

She just looks at him and, for once, his gaze holds hers. "What happened last night, after you got back."

"I wasn't out last night." The banter, the pretension, the posturing are all gone.

"What? I was waiting up for you, you were late, but then the clocks changed . . ."

He pauses, maintaining eye contact. "The clocks go back tomorrow. It's Friday today?"

Day Minus One, 08:20

Some internal elevator plunges down the center of Jen's chest. She pushes her hair off her face and heads to the family bathroom at the back of the house, holding up a finger to Todd for just a second. She shivers as she turns her back on him, like he is a predator she wants to keep an eye on.

She is sick into the toilet, the sort of sick she hasn't been in years. Hardly anything comes up, just a sticky yellow stomach acid that sits right at the bottom of the water. She thinks of her pregnancy, when she told a doctor she was vomiting so much that only bile was coming up, and he apparently felt the need to say, "Bile is bright green and signals real trouble. You mean stomach acid."

She stares and stares into the acid lining the bottom of the toilet. It might not be bile, but she thinks she might be in real trouble.

Todd does not know what she is talking about. That is clear. Even he wouldn't deny this. But why? How?

The pumpkin. The pumpkin is missing. Where is her husband? She can't think straight. Panic rises up through her body, a great pressure with nowhere to go. She's going to be sick again.

She sits on the cold checkerboard tiles.

She gets her phone out of her pocket and stares at it, bringing up the calendar.

It is Friday the twenty-eighth of October. The clocks do indeed go back tomorrow. Monday will be Halloween. Jen stares and stares at that date. How can this be?

She must be going mad. She gets up and paces uselessly. Her body feels like it's covered in ants. She's got to get out of here. But out of where? Out of yesterday?

She navigates to her last text message with Kelly and presses *call*.

He answers immediately. "Look," she says urgently.

"Uh-oh," he says, languid, always amused by her. She hears a door close.

"Where are you?" she asks. She knows she sounds crazed, but she can't help it.

A beat. "I am on planet Earth, but it sounds like you might not be."

"Be serious."

"I'm at work! Obviously! Where are *you*?"

"Was Todd arrested last night?"

"What?" She hears him put something heavy down on a hollow-sounding floor. "Er – for what?"

"No, I'm asking you. *Was* he?"

"No?" Kelly says, sounding baffled. Jen can't believe it. Sweat blooms across her chest. She starts to rub at her arms.

"But we sat – we sat in the police station. You shouted at them. The clocks had just gone back, I was . . . I had done the pumpkin."

"Look – are you okay? I need to finish Merrilocks," he says.

Jen sucks a breath in. He said he finished there

22

yesterday. Didn't he? Yes, she's sure he did. He was at the top of the landing, wearing only a tattoo and a smile. She can remember it. She *can*.

She puts a hand to her eyes as if she can block out the world.

"I don't know what's going on," she says. She starts to cry, water lacing her words. "What did we do? Last night?" She leans her head back against the wall. "Did I do the pumpkin?"

"What are you –"

"I think I've had some sort of episode," she says in barely a whisper. She rolls her pajamas up over her knees and stares at her skin. No impressions where she knelt on the gravel. Not a single speck of dirt on them. No blood under her nails. Goosebumps erupt up and down her arms fast, like a time-lapse.

"Did I carve the pumpkin?" she asks again, but, as she speaks, some deep realization is dawning all around her. If it didn't happen . . . she might have lost her mind, but her son isn't a murderer. She feels her shoulders drop, just slightly, in relief.

"No, you – you said you couldn't be arsed . . ." he says with a little laugh.

"Right," she says faintly, picturing exactly how that pumpkin turned out.

She stands and stares at herself in the mirror. She meets her own eyes. She is a portrait of a panicked woman. Dark hair, pale complexion. Hunted eyes.

"Look, I'd better go," she says. "I'm sure it was a dream," she says, though how can it be?

"Okay," Kelly says slowly. Perhaps he is about to say

something but decides against it, because he says only "Okay," again, then adds: "I'll leave early," and Jen is glad he is this, a family man, not the kind of man who goes to pubs or plays sport with friends, just her Kelly.

She leaves the bathroom and goes down to the kitchen. Mist shrouds the garden beyond their patio doors, erasing the tops of the trees to nothing. Kelly built this kitchen for them a couple of years ago, after she had said – drunk – that she wanted to be "the kind of woman who has her shit together, you know, happy clients, a happy kid, a Belfast sink."

He presented it to her one evening. "Expect to imminently have your shit together, Jen, because you've got the sink of dreams here."

The memory fades. Jen always advises her stressed trainees to take ten deep breaths and make a coffee, so that's what she will do herself. She's trained for this. Two decades in a high-pressure job does give you some skills.

But as she approaches their marble kitchen island, her footsteps slow. A whole, uncarved pumpkin sits on the side.

She stops dead. It may as well be a ghost. Jen thinks she might be sick again. "Oh," she says to nobody, a tiny slip of a word, a giant syllable of understanding. She approaches the pumpkin as though it is an unexploded bomb and turns it around, but it's whole underneath her fingertips, firm and unharmed, and Jesus Christ last night didn't happen. It didn't fucking happen. Relief laps over her. He didn't do it. He didn't do it.

She listens to Todd in his room. Opening and closing drawers, footsteps back and forth, the sound of a zipper.

"Back in the real world yet?" he says, arriving in the hallway at the bottom of the stairs. His arch tone makes Jen jump. She stares at him. His body. He is slimmer than he was a few weeks ago, isn't he?

"Almost," she says automatically. She swallows twice. Her back feels shivery, like she's ill, adrenaline burning a kind of feverish panic.

"Well, good . . ."

"I guess I had a horrible dream."

"Oh, bummer," Todd says simply, as though something could explain her confusion so easily.

"Yeah. But – look. In it – you killed somebody."

"Wow," he says, but something shifts, just slightly, beneath the surface of his expression, like a fish swimming deep in an ocean, unseen, apart from the ripples created by it. "Who?" he says, which Jen thinks is a strange initial question. She is accustomed to seeing clients not tell the complete truth, and that is what this looks like to her.

He reaches to pull his dark hair back from his forehead. His T-shirt rides up, exposing the waist she used to hold when he was tiny and wriggly, just learning to sit up, to bounce, to walk. She'd thought motherhood was so boring at the time, so unrewarding, the hours and hours dedicated to the same tasks in a variety of orders. But it wasn't, she now knows; to say so is like saying breathing is boring.

"A grown man. Like, a forty-year-old."

"With these puny limbs?" Todd says, holding a slim arm up theatrically.

Kelly once said to her, late at night, "How did *we* come to raise an over-confident geek?" and they'd had to muffle their giggles. Kelly's dry wit is the thing Jen loves the most about him. She's so glad Todd has inherited it.

"Even with those," she says. But she thinks: *You didn't need muscle. You had a weapon.*

Todd shoves his bare feet into a pair of trainers. Right as he does it, Jen remembers this taking place on Friday morning. She'd marveled at how he didn't feel the October chill, worried his ankles would get cold at school. Worried, too – shamefully – that people would think she was a shit mother, that she was – what, exactly? Anti-socks? Jesus, the things she stresses over.

But she *had*. She remembers.

A frisson moves across her shoulders. Todd grabs the door handle, and Jen recalls the déjà vu. No. She's fine. She's fine. Don't worry about it. Forget it. There's no evidence any of it happened.

Until there is.

"I'm going straight to Clio's after school. If she'll have me. I'll eat there." His tone is short. He's telling her, not asking her; the way it's been lately.

And that is when it happens. The words are on Jen's lips, as natural as a spring bubbling from the earth, the exact same sentence she uttered yesterday. "More oysters in buckets?" she says. The first time Todd went to Clio's for dinner they'd had actual oysters. He'd sent her a photo of one, its entrance pried open, balanced on the tips of his fingers, captioned: *You said I needed to open up more?*

She waits for Todd's reply. That he's pretty sure they will have something low-key like foie gras.

He flashes her a grin which cuts through the tension.

"I'm pretty sure we'll just have something low-key, like, you know, foie gras."

She cannot. She cannot deal with this. This is madness. Her heart feels like it's going to pound itself into a cardiac arrest.

Todd picks up his bag. Something about the movement of it thumping on to his shoulder unnerves her further. It looks heavy.

The thought arrives, fully formed, right then. *What if the weapon is in that bag?* What if the crime is *going* to happen? What if it wasn't a dream, but a premonition?

Jen goes hot and then cold. "Was that your computer I heard?" she says, eyes to the ceiling. "It made a noise."

It's laughably easy to make a teenager go to check a device, and Jen feels a guilty pathos, for just a second, as she watches his feet trip over each other in his rush to go and investigate. It's habitual, a residual sympathy she's always felt for Todd – too much, at times, getting involved with school-gate drama when he was left out of any social occasion – but, today, it feels misplaced. She's seen him kill.

Whatever it is she feels, it isn't enough to stop her looking.

Front pockets, side pockets. It's a good distraction to be taking action. She hears Todd humming upstairs in that way that he does when he's impatient. "'Sake," he says.

Two chemistry textbooks, three loose pens. Jen puts them on the hallway floor and continues searching.

"No notifications," he shouts. His tone is irritated again. Just recently, she's felt like a nuisance around him.

"Sorry," she calls, thinking, *Give me one fucking minute, just one, just one.* "Must've misheard."

The bottom of the bag is lined with the crumbs from a thousand sandwiches.

But what's this? Right in the back? A sheath, a leather sheath. It's as cold and hard as a thigh bone, sitting right there against the back of her son's rucksack. She knows what it will be before she pulls it out.

A long leather pouch. She exhales, then unbuttons the top and slides a handle out.

And – inside it . . . a knife. *The* knife.

Day Minus One, 08:30

Jen stands there, staring at it, at this betrayal in her hand. She hadn't thought what she would do if she found something. She never thought she would.

She holds the long, sinister black handle.

The panic begins again, a tide of anxiety that goes out to sea but always, always returns. She wrenches open the under-stairs cupboard. Shoes and sports equipment and canned goods they can't fit in the kitchen crowd out and she fumbles past them, pushing the knife right to the back. She can hear Todd on the landing. She leans the knife against the back wall and retreats out of the cupboard, tidying up the rest of his things back into the bag.

Todd – disgruntled smile, young Kelly written across his features – picks up the bag. He doesn't seem to notice the difference, the lightness of it. Jen stares at him as he opens the front door. Her son, armed, so he thinks, and with intent. Her son who thrust that knife with such force it split another person's torso right open in three places. He throws a look over his shoulder, suspicious, and Jen thinks for a second that he might know what she's done.

He leaves, and Jen climbs the stairs and watches his car from the picture window. As he drives off, she's sure she sees his eyes flick up to the rear-view mirror and meet hers, for just the briefest of moments, like a butterfly landing and leaving before you even notice, flapping its wings only once.

"I found a knife in Todd's bag," Jen says, the second her husband arrives home. She doesn't explain the rest, not yet. She's spent the day swinging between panic and rationalization. It was nothing, it was a dream, it's something, it's a living nightmare. She's mad, she's mad, she's mad.

Kelly's face shuts down immediately, as Jen expected it might.

He approaches her, picking the blade up and holding it across his hands as if it is some kind of archaeological find. His pupils have gone huge. "What did he say? When you found it?" His tone is frosty.

"He doesn't know."

Kelly nods, staring down at the long, sharp blade, not saying anything. Jen remembers his angry behavior from last night and thinks that, now, he just looks withdrawn instead.

"It's a brand-new knife," he says now, flicking his eyes to her. "I'm going to fucking kill him."

"I know."

"Unused."

Jen laughs, a hard, unhumorous laugh. "Right."

"What?"

"It's just – I mean, I saw Todd stab somebody with this last night."

"What . . ." he says, the word not lilting upward, not a question, just a statement of disbelief.

"Yesterday, I waited up for Todd and he – he knifed someone, on the street. You were there, too."

"But . . ." Kelly rubs a hand over his chin. "But I wasn't. You weren't. You said that was a dream." He flashes her a quick smile. "Have you gone to madtown?" he says, their abbreviation for neuroses.

Jen turns away from him. Outside, their neighbor walks his dog past. Jen knows his phone is about to ring, remembers it from yesterday, but it does so before she can say it to Kelly. She needs to think of something else that's about to happen to prove it to Kelly, but she can't, she can't think of anything except how has she woken up here, in some alternative, scary universe.

"I was awake," she says, turning her gaze from the neighbor, thinking of all of the items that would be considered circumstantial evidence that yesterday didn't happen: the smooth, uncut pumpkin, her son's presence in the bedroom, the absence of any blood or police tape on the street outside. But then she thinks of the knife. That knife is the only piece of tangible proof she has.

"Look, I didn't see anything last night. We'll just ask him about it. When he gets back," Kelly says. "It's a criminal offense. So . . . we can tell him that."

Jen nods, saying nothing. What can she possibly say?

"Get out from under my feet," Kelly says. He is addressing their cat, Henry VIII, so called because he has been obese from the day they rescued him.

Jen, lounging on the sofa in their kitchen, winces. Kelly said exactly the same thing on Friday night. The first Friday night. He gave in then, fed Henry, said, "Fine, but know that I am judging you."

31

She gets to her feet and paces past Kelly. She can't. She can't just sit here and let a day play out that she's already lived.

"Where you off to?" Kelly says to her, amused. "You look so stressed you actually just created a breeze as you came past me." Then, to the meowing cat: "Fine, but know that I am judging you." He opens a packet of Felix. Heat travels up Jen's chest. She can feel a panicked blush rise through her neck and to her cheeks.

"This all happened," she says. "This has all happened before. What's going on?" She sits down on the sofa and pulls uselessly at her clothes, trying to escape her own body, trying to express something impossible. If she hadn't already lost her mind, she certainly looks as though she has now.

"The knife?"

"Not the knife, I only found the knife today," she says, knowing that this won't make any sense to anyone but her. "Everything else. I have experienced everything else that's happening. I have lived this day twice now."

Kelly sighs as he finishes feeding Henry and opens the freezer door. "This is mad even for you," he says sardonically. Jen tilts her head, looking up at him from her position on the sofa.

They'd argued the first time they lived this night, about holidays. Jen always wanting to go on them, Kelly refusing to fly. A plane he was on once dropped five thousand feet during turbulence, he told her early on in their relationship. He's not flown since. "You're not remotely an anxious person," Jen had said. "Well, I am about this," he'd said, before getting a Magnum out of the freezer.

"I know you're about to eat a Magnum," she says now, but Kelly's hand is already on the freezer.

"However did you guess that?" he says. "She's a psychic," he says to the cat.

Kelly leaves the kitchen. She knows he will go upstairs to shower.

As he walks past her, he trails his fingers so lightly along her upper back that it makes her shiver. She meets his eyes. "You're fine," he says. She wishes she hadn't been so anxious in the past. She raises her hand to grasp his just as he's leaving, as she has a thousand times before. His hand is her anchor, a woman alone, out at sea. And then he's gone. If he is worried about the knife, or what she's been saying, he doesn't say. It isn't his style.

Jen puts on *Grey's Anatomy* and leans back on the sofa, alone, trying to relax.

Jen and Kelly met almost twenty years ago. He walked into her father's law firm asking if they wanted any decorating done. Jeans slung low on his waist, a slow, knowing smile when his eyes landed on Jen. Her father had turned him down, but Jen had gone for lunch with him, more by accident than anything else. He'd walked out with her, at twelve o'clock, and they'd seen the rain-slicked pub opposite had a two-for-one offer on. All through the lunch, then pudding, then coffee, Jen kept saying she ought to get back, but they seemed to have so much to say to each other. Kelly asked her interested question after interested question. He's the best listener she knows.

She remembers almost everything about that date. It had been late March, absurdly cold and wet, and yet, as Jen sat there, at a little table in the corner of a pub with

Kelly, the sun had come out from behind the dense cloud, just for a minute or two, and illuminated them. And, right then, it had felt, suddenly, like spring, even though it began to rain again only minutes later.

They'd shared an umbrella from the pub back to the office. She'd let him leave with it, a totally deliberate act, and when he brought it into the office the following Monday, he left his keys on her desk.

That date has come to define Jen's sense of time. Each March, she feels it. The smell of a daffodil, the way the sun slants sometimes, green and fresh. An open window reminds her of them, in bed together, their legs entwined together, their torsos separate, like two happy mermaids. Each spring, she's back there: rainy March, with him.

Jen finds comfort, now, watching *Grey's Anatomy*, as she has many times, in the cardiothoracic wing of the Seattle Grace Hospital, and in taking off her bra. Maybe this is her fault, she thinks, watching the television but not really watching it, too. She always found motherhood so hard. It had been such a shock. Such a vast reduction in the time available to her. She did nothing well, not work nor parenting. She put out fires in both for what felt like a decade straight, has only recently emerged. But maybe the damage is already done.

It's a dream, that's all, she tells herself. Yes. Conviction fires up through her chest. Of course it was a dream.

She turns *Grey's Anatomy* off. The news replaces it automatically. She remembers this segment, about Facebook privacy settings being reviewed. The next one will be about an epilepsy drug being tested on laboratory mice. It's hardly proof of time travel but, nevertheless, it pops up.

"A new trial of a drug in the . . ."

Jen turns off the television, leaves the kitchen and goes into the hallway. Upstairs, the shower is running, just like she knew it would be. She's got to be able to use this stuff to convince somebody. Surely?

She gets the knife out of the downstairs cupboard and inspects it. Unused, just as Kelly said.

She sits on the bottom stair, waiting for Todd, the knife across her lap. Waiting up for him once more. But this time, she's waiting for an explanation. Waiting for the truth.

"I found this," Jen says, and something small and spiteful within her is glad to be having a new conversation, and not one she has lived before. She extends the knife out to Todd. He doesn't take it.

There are a million tells: his brow drops, he licks his lips, he shifts his weight on his feet. He says nothing and everything. "It's a mate's," he says eventually.

"That is the oldest lie in the book," Jen says. "Do you know how many times lawyers have heard that?" She swallows down more stomach acid. His shiftiness has confirmed it for her. It happens. It happens, tomorrow.

"What are you doing, gulping like that?" Todd says with an indolent shrug. This is how he has been lately, Jen finds herself thinking as she stares at the floor and tries not to be sick again. A boy full of secrets. She finds his shrugging presence sinister now, tonight.

"I'll speak to him," Kelly says from the top of the stairs.

She thought they'd got away without this stuff happening, this teenage stuff. Todd was an easy baby, a happy child. The only drama they'd had over this last summer was when a girl, Gemma, dumped him for being *too weird*. He'd come home heartbroken, not spoken for a full twenty-four hours, leaving Jen and Kelly guessing. He'd sat on Jen's bed the next evening, when Kelly was out, crossed his legs, told her what happened, and asked if she thought it was true. "Absolutely not," she'd said, while guiltily wondering if there was a way to tell him . . . well, maybe? Not too weird, but definitely nerdy. He'd shown her some of the messages he'd sent. *Intense* was the word for them. Long missives, science memes, poems, text after text after text without a reply. Gemma had clearly been cooling off – *thanks for that, chat tomorrow, nah bit busy today* – and Jen had winced for her son.

But now this: knives, murders, arrests.

Kelly is silently appraising his son, his head tilted slightly backward. Jen wishes he'd blow up, escalate things somehow, but evidently, he decides not to. Todd looks suddenly angry. His jaw is fixed.

He holds his palms up but says nothing more.

"So if I check your bank statements – you didn't buy it? It won't appear there?" Kelly asks.

Todd calls his bluff, looking levelly up the stairs. After a few seconds, he breaks eye contact with his father, shrugs himself out of his coat. He kicks his trainers off, feet bare on the floorboards. "That's right," he says, his back to Jen as he hangs his coat up, something he never usually does.

"We understand, you know – wanting to feel . . . protected," Kelly says. "Look – come with me. Take a walk."

"Do we? Understand that?" Jen says. She looks up at him in surprise.

Todd turns violently away from her, running the rest of the way up the stairs and pushing past Kelly.

"What do you think I'm going to do, kill you?" Todd says, so softly Jen wonders if she's misheard. Her whole body heaves.

"Unless you tell me where you got it – and why – you won't be going anywhere. Not for days. Not even to school," she says.

"Fine!" Todd shouts.

He goes into his bedroom, the door slamming so hard it shakes the whole house. Jen stares at Kelly, feeling like she's been slapped.

Kelly runs a hand through his hair. "Fucking hell," he says to her. "What a mess." He swipes at the cabinet that stands at the top of their stairs. A piece of paper falls off it which he picks up, rubbing at his forehead. That piece of paper is an offer of a big job, one Kelly refused because they wanted him to go on their payroll rather than stay self-employed, and he'd said he'd never do that.

"What's happened to him?" she says.

"I don't know," Kelly snaps. He shakes his head. "Let's fucking leave it." He isn't directing the anger at her, Jen knows. It's his temper, sudden and volatile when it eventually goes. He once exploded at a man in a bar who touched Jen's arse. Said he'd be happy to see him outside, which Jen couldn't believe.

She nods, now, too choked up to speak, too panicked with what she fears is to come.

"We can deal with" – Kelly waves a hand – "*all this* tomorrow."

Jen nods, happy to be directed. She takes the knife upstairs with her and puts it underneath their bed.

She and Todd cross paths later that evening, he coming down for a drink, she about to go upstairs for the night. She'd ordinarily be in a whirlwind of laundry and other banal tasks, but she isn't, tonight. She's just watching him across the kitchen without the busyness of normal life surrounding them.

He fills a glass from the tap, downs it in one, then fills it again. He pulls his phone out and scrolls on it while sipping, half smiles at something, then puts it back in his pocket.

She pretends to occupy herself. Todd strides past, glass of water still in hand, but just before he goes upstairs, he checks the lock on the front door. He gets one step up the stairs, turns around, then checks it again. Just to be sure. It looks like a check undertaken out of fear. Her skin feels chilled as she watches.

As she falls asleep, she finds herself thinking that Todd is here, safe in their house, grounded. And she has the knife. Perhaps it has been stopped. Whatever it is. Perhaps she will wake and it will be tomorrow. The day after. Anything but today again.

Day Minus Two, 08:30

Jen wakes up, sweat gathered across her chest. Her phone is lying on the bedside table, but she doesn't check it. A perverse impulse to keep hope alive resides within her.

She pulls on Kelly's dressing gown, still damp in places from his shower, and heads downstairs. The wooden floors are lit up by the sun, glossy with it. The honey light warms her toes and then her feet as she steps forward.

Please don't let it be Friday again. Anything but that.

She peers into the kitchen, hoping to see Kelly. But it's empty. Tidy, too. The counters clear. She blinks. The pumpkin. It isn't here. She walks into the kitchen, then spins around uselessly, just looking. But it's nowhere. Maybe it's Sunday. Maybe it's over.

She brings her phone out of the dressing-gown pocket, holds a breath, then checks it.

It is the twenty-seventh of October. It is the day before the day before.

Blood pounds in her forehead, hot and stretched, like somebody's turned a heater on. She must be mad – she must be. The pumpkin isn't here because it hasn't yet been purchased by her.

Apparently, it is Thursday, eight thirty in the morning. Todd will be on his way to school. Kelly will be at Merrilocks. And Jen – Jen should be at work. She looks out at their garden, the grass gilded by the early-morning sun.

She makes and gulps a coffee that only jangles her nerves further.

If she's right, tomorrow will be Wednesday. Then Tuesday. And then what? Backward forever? She's sick again, this time into the kitchen sink, spewing up sweet black coffee, panic and incomprehension. Afterward, she rests her head briefly on the ceramic edge and makes a decision. She needs to talk to someone who understands her: her oldest friend and colleague, Rakesh.

The street outside Jen's work is often blustery, caught in a wind tunnel in Liverpool city center. The October air gusts her coat up and around her thighs like a bawdy dancer's. Later, it will begin to rain, huge, fat drops that turn the air frigid.

Jen had wanted to live closer to town, but Crosby was as close as Kelly said he'd get. He hates the noise of cities, doesn't like the mess, the bustle. Also Scousers, except you, he had said once, she thinks in jest. Kelly left his hometown behind when he met Jen. Both parents dead, his schoolfriends all wasters, he says, he hardly goes back. The only connection he has to it is an annual camping trip with old friends, on the Whitsun weekend. He'd wanted to live out in the wilderness, he said, but she made him move back to Crosby, with her. "But the suburbs are full of people," he'd said. He is often this way. Dark humor crossed with cynicism.

She pushes open the warm glass door, the foyer ablaze with sunlight, and heads down the corridor to Rakesh's. Rakesh Kapoor – her biggest ally, and longtime friend – was a doctor before he became a lawyer. Ludicrously overqualified, logical to a fault. Jen thinks he's the kind of man Todd might become. The thought hits her with a wave of sadness.

She finds him in the kitchen, stirring sugar into a tea. The kitchen is a small, soulless dark purple space with a stock image on the wall of a sunset. Jen remembers her father choosing this burgundy color when they took the lease here three years ago, eighteen months before he died. The paint had been called Sour Grapes. "Perfect for a law-firm foyer," Jen had said, and her father – usually serious – had exploded into sudden, beautiful laughter.

Rakesh greets her with only a raise of his dark eyebrows and a lift of his full mug. He, like Jen, is not a morning person. "Do you have a minute?" she says. Her voice trembles in fear. He'll never believe her. He'll cart her off somewhere, section her. But what else can she do?

"Sure." She leads him down the corridor and back to her office, where she perches on the edge of her messy desk. Rakesh hovers in the doorway but closes the door when he sees her hesitate. His bedside manner is excellent. Kind but jaded, he favors sweater vests and poorly fitting suits. He left medicine because he didn't like the pressure. He says law is worse, only he doesn't want to leave a second career. They became friends the day she hired him, when, in his interview, he said his biggest professional weakness was office doughnuts.

Jen's office faces east and is lit with morning sun. One wall is lined with haphazard files in pink, blue and green, their ends sun-bleached – a sure sign they ought to be archived, something Jen finds far less interesting than seeing clients.

"How do you feel about giving a medical consult?" she asks Rakesh with a small laugh, followed by a deep breath.

"Unqualified?" he says lightly, as quick as ever.

"Your disclaimer is safe with me."

Rakesh takes his suit jacket off and drapes it over the back of the dark green armchair Jen has in the corner. A proprietary gesture, but a fitting one, too. Jen and Rakesh have spent almost every weekday lunchtime together for a decade. They buy baked potatoes from a van which calls itself Mr. Potato Head. Rakesh collects the loyalty stamps – in the shape of potatoes – all year and, at Christmas, he gets them tons of free ones. He blocks it out in their calendars as CHRISTMAS SPUDDING.

"What disease would you have if you were in a time loop? As in, what does Bill Murray have in *Groundhog Day*?" she asks, thinking it's been so long since she watched it. "I mean – mental-illness-wise."

Rakesh says nothing initially. Just stares at her. Jen feels herself blush with both shame and fear. "I would go for . . . stress," he says eventually, steepling his hands together carefully. "Or a brain tumor. Er – temporal lobe epilepsy. Retrograde amnesia, traumatic head injury . . ."

"Nothing good."

Rakesh doesn't answer again, just communicates an expectant, doctorly pause to her across her office.

She hesitates. If tomorrow will be yesterday, does anything matter, anyway? "I am pretty sure," she says carefully, not looking directly at him, "that I woke up on the twenty-ninth of October, then the twenty-eighth again, and now the twenty-seventh."

"I'd say you need a new diary," he says lightly.

"But something happened on the twenty-ninth. Todd – he – he commits a crime. The day after tomorrow."

"You think you've been to the future?" Rakesh says.

Jen's fear has simmered down to a kind of burning, low-level panic. She feels exhausted. "Do you think I'm mad?"

"Nope," Rakesh says calmly. "You wouldn't ask that if you were."

"Well, then," Jen says with a sigh. "I'm glad I did."

"Tell me exactly what happened." Rakesh crosses her office and stands closer to her, by her window, which overlooks the high street below. Jen loves that old-fashioned window. She insisted it be openable when she chose this room. In the summer, she feels the hot breeze and hears the buskers. In the winter, the drafts make her cold. It's nice to be aware of the weather, rather than a sterile sixty-five-degree office.

He folds his arms, his wedding ring catching the sunlight. He is looking closely at her, his eyes scanning her face. She is suddenly self-conscious under his gaze, as though he is about to uncover something awful, something deadly. "Start at the beginning."

"Which is this Saturday."

He pauses. "Okay, then." He spreads his hands, like, *So be it*, his face in the shade of the low sun.

He stands in silence for over a minute when she has finally finished speaking, telling him every detail, even the strange things: the pumpkin, her naked husband. In the anxiety of it, she has lost all dignity, not caring what he thinks of her.

"So you're saying today has happened before, and now it is happening again, in mostly the same ways?" he says incisively, capturing the logic – or otherwise – of Jen's situation completely.

"Yes."

"So, what did we do? The first time you experienced today? On the *first* twenty-seventh?"

Jen sits back in her chair. What a smart question. She looks at his face properly for a few seconds. She needs to relax to be able to work this out. She puffs the air from her lungs, eyes closed, for just a second. Something comes to her, drifting from the back of her brain to the front. "Do you have weird socks?" she says. "I think – maybe . . . we might have laughed at your socks when we went for potatoes. Pink."

Rakesh blinks, then slips the leg of his trousers up. "I do indeed," he says with a laugh, showing her a pair of cerise socks that say *Usher* on them. That's right. He attended a wedding last weekend, got them as a gift.

"Hardly foolproof, is it?" she says.

"Look. It's stress, probably," Rakesh says quickly. "You're coherent. You do *know* the date. I'd go with something – I don't know. Anxiety. You're a bit prone that way anyway, aren't you? . . . Or depression can make days feel the same, like you're getting nowhere . . . This isn't psychosis."

"Thanks. I hope not."

"I mean – I have to say," Rakesh says, humor laced through his voice, "I have absolutely no fucking idea."

"Me neither," she says, feeling lighter for having spoken to somebody, nevertheless.

"Maybe you just got confused," he says. "Happens to me all the time in small ways. I couldn't remember driving here the other day. Could not tell you for the life of me which way I went. It isn't dissociation, is it? It's life. Get more sleep. Eat some vegetables."

"Yeah." Jen turns away from his gaze and wrenches up the sash window. It isn't that. That is forgetfulness. Not this.

And this isn't *stress*. Of course it isn't.

She looks down at Liverpool below her. She's here. She's in the here and now. Autumn woodsmoke drifts in. The sun warms the backs of her hands.

"My friend did something about time travel for his PhD," Rakesh says.

"Did he?"

"Yes. A study on whether getting stuck in a time loop is possible. I proofread it. He did – what was it?" Rakesh leans against the wall, arms folded, his suit bunched at the shoulders. "Theoretical physics and applied maths. With me – at Liverpool. And then he went on to study . . . God, something nuts. He's at John Moore's now."

"What's his name?"

"Andy Vettese." Rakesh reaches into his suit trouser pocket, pulls an open packet of cigarettes out. "Anyway. Take these off me, please. I'm slipping back."

"Call yourself a doctor," Jen says lightly, holding her palm out for the box. She smiles at Rakesh as he turns to leave, but she is thinking about how she really, truly, is here: on Thursday. She feels calmer, having discussed it with somebody she trusts, more able to assess it objectively.

45

So how has it happened? How did she do it? Is it when she sleeps?

And what does she have to do to get out of it?

She stares down at the battered cigarette box. It must be that she has to change things: to change things in order to stop it. To save Todd, and to get out of it.

"If I remember, I'll wear different socks. The next time we meet," Rakesh says, with an enigmatic smile, one hand on the doorframe.

He leaves, and she waits a second, then calls out, "Quit!" into the corridor, wanting to change something – anything – for the better. "It's so unhealthy!"

"I know," Rakesh says, his back to her, not turning around.

Jen fires up her computer and begins googling time loops. Why not research them? It's what any good lawyer would do.

Two scientists, called James Ward and Oliver Johnson, have written a paper on *the bootstrap paradox: going back in time to observe an event which, it turns out, you caused.* Jen writes this down.

To enter into a time loop, they say you would need to create a *closed timelike curve.* They provide a physics formula. But, helpfully, they break it down underneath. It seems to happen when a huge force is exerted on the body. Ward and Johnson think the force would have to be stronger than gravity to create a time loop.

She scrolls down. The force would need to be one thousand times her body weight.

She sinks her head into her hands. She doesn't understand a single word of this. And one thousand times her weight is . . . a lot. She breaks into a grim smile. An amount not worth contemplating.

She goes back to Google and clicks – desperately – on an article called "Five Easy Tips to Escape a Time Loop." Is this just – is this a thing? There truly is something for everybody on the internet. The five tips are mixed: find out why, tell a friend and get them to loop with you (sure), document everything, experiment . . . and try not to die.

The last one unsettles Jen. She hadn't thought of it at all. Something eerie seems to arrive in the room as she thinks of it. Try not to die. What if that's where this is headed? Some place even darker than that first night, some maternal sacrifice, bargaining with the gods.

She switches off her monitor. There must be a way to make Kelly believe her: her biggest ally, her lover, her friend, the man she is her most silly, unpretentious self with. She will try to prove it to him. And then he can help her.

Her trainee, Natalia, walks by, wheeling a trolley of lever-arch files past Jen's office that Jen has already seen arrive once before. She is about to steer the trolley accidentally into the closed doors of the lift. Jen closes her eyes as she hears the thump for the second time.

She's got to get out of here.

Ten minutes later, she's smoked four of Rakesh's cigarettes outside the back of the building herself, health be damned.

She knows, deep down, somewhere she can't name, that it's her job, isn't it? To stop the murder. To figure out why it happens, and to prevent it.

As though the universe agrees with her, it begins to

rain as she's finishing her fifth cigarette. Huge, fat drops that turn the air frigid.

Jen is slumped, back on the blue kitchen sofa. She left work early. Shouldn't taking the knife have stopped the murder, and therefore ended the time loop?

Is there an alternative reality where it still happened? Is there another Jen, one who didn't go backward, but who is still moving forward?

Todd is out. *With friends*, he said, the same as last time; more short texts, more distance between them.

Jen is googling Andy Vettese. He is indeed a professor in the department of physics at Liverpool John Moore's University. He is easy to find. On LinkedIn, on the university's own page, and he runs a Twitter account called @AndysWorld, his email address in his bio. She could write to him.

She sits up as she hears the front door.

"Can't stop," Todd barks, bursting into the kitchen in a blur of cold air and teenage movement, disturbing Jen's hesitation over a message box.

"Okay," she says. It isn't what she said last time. Last time, she asked if there was a reason why he never wanted to be at home.

She's surprised to see the softer approach works.

"Been to Connor's, now off to Clio's," Todd explains, meeting her eyes. He bounces from foot to foot as he fiddles with a portable phone charger, full of verve, full of the optimism of somebody for whom life truly is only just beginning. Not the behavior of a killer, Jen finds herself thinking.

Connor. Pauline's eldest. There is something about him that Jen isn't quite sure of. Some edge to him. He smokes and he swears – both things Jen does, from time to time – but, nevertheless, both offensive when seen through the ruthless lens of motherhood.

She props herself up on her elbow, looking at Todd. She missed him coming home, the last time. She'd been at work.

A case had taken over, for the last few weeks, meaning Jen had missed more of her home life than usual. She is often this way when a big ancillary relief case is heading to trial. The neediness and heartbreak of her clients invades Jen's already poor boundaries, leading her to take constant calls and practically sleep at the office.

Gina Davis was the client who had kept Jen busy during October, but not for the usual reasons. She had walked into Jen's office for the first time in the summer, with a divorce petition from her husband, who'd left her the week before.

"I want to stop him ever seeing the kids again," Gina said. She had curled her blonde hair carefully, worn an immaculate skirt suit.

"Why?" Jen had said. "Is there some concern?"

"No. He's a great father."

"Okay . . . ?"

"To punish him."

She was thirty-seven, heartbroken and angry. Jen felt an immediate kinship with her, the kind of woman who doesn't hide her emotions. The kind of woman who speaks the taboo. "I just want to hurt him," she said to Jen.

"I can't charge you for this," Jen had said. It wasn't the

right thing to do, she thought, to profiteer off this. Soon enough, Gina would come to her senses and stop.

"So do it for free," Gina said, and Jen had. Not because her late father's firm didn't need the money, but because Jen knew, eventually, that Gina would drop it, accept the decree nisi, accept the residency split, and move on. But it hadn't happened yet, not after Jen told Gina to go away and think about it over the summer, and advised against it in the many meetings during the autumn. They'd chatted, too, about all sorts – their kids, the news, even *Love Island*. "Gross but compelling," Gina had said, while Jen laughed and nodded.

Jen looks at Todd now and wonders, suddenly, if he's in love, like Gina is. Wonders who this Clio really is to him. What she means. The madness of first love cannot be overlooked, surely, given what he does in two days' time.

Jen has not met Clio. After Gemma dumped him over the summer, Todd became automatically secretive about his love life, embarrassed, Jen thinks, that it didn't last. Embarrassed about that evening when he'd showed her all those unanswered texts.

Just as he's getting ready to go out again, he glances, just once, at the front door. It isn't a quick, curious glance. It's something else. Some wariness, like he's expecting somebody to be there, like he's nervous. Jen never would have noticed it had she not been scrutinizing him. It's so quick, his expression clearing almost immediately.

"What's that?" Todd says, looking back at her and gesturing to her screen.

"Oh, I was just reading this interesting thing. About time loops, you know?"

"Love that," Todd says. He's gelled his hair upward in a kind of quiff, has on a retro-looking snooker shirt. He's recently into it, says he likes the maths of potting the balls. Jen looks at him, her damningly handsome son.

"What would you do – if you were caught in one?" she asks him.

"Oh, it's almost always about some tiny detail," Todd says casually.

"What do you mean?"

"You know, the butterfly effect. One tiny thing to change the future." Todd reaches down to stroke the cat and, just for a second, looks like a child again. Her boy who believes unquestioningly in time loops. Perhaps she will tell him. See what he says.

But, for now, she can't. If this is really, truly, happening, it is Jen's job to stop the murder. To figure out the events leading up to it, and to intervene. And then, one day, when she manages that, she will wake up, and it won't be yesterday.

And so that is why she doesn't tell Todd.

He leaves, and Jen checks that nobody *is* waiting for him, or following him. And then Jen follows him herself.

Day Minus Two, 19:00

Jen is two cars behind Todd, and is paradoxically relieved to find that he is an incompetent driver: not once, so far as she can tell, has he checked his rear-view mirror and spotted her.

He slows down on a road called Eshe Road North. It would be described by an estate agent as *leafy*, as though plants don't grow on housing estates. There are pumpkins on some of the steps to the houses, carved early, lit up, grotesque reminders of everything that's to come.

Todd parks his car carefully. Jen drives to a side-street, a few houses down, unlit, so she is hopefully unseen, and gets out, drawing her trench coat around her. The night air has that early-autumn spooky feel to it. Damp spiderwebs, the feeling of something coming to an end before you're truly ready to leave it.

Todd walks purposefully down the road, white trainers kicking up the leaves. It is so strange for Jen to witness this; the things that happened while she was lawyering, while she was busy caring too much about work and – clearly – not enough about home.

She stands at the junction of the side-street and Eshe Road North until Todd disappears abruptly inside a house. It is large, set back from the road, with a wide porch and a loft conversion. These kinds of places still intimidate Jen, who grew up in a two-bed terrace that had windows so rickety the breeze wafted her hair around in the evenings. Her father, widowed, didn't notice the draft, and anyway took on too much legal aid work and not enough private to fix it even if he did.

She rounds her shoulders against the cold, a woman in a too-thin coat on a rainy street, looking at the trees covered in their burnt-orange jackets, just thinking. About Todd and about her father and about today, tomorrow and yesterday.

She paces down the street. Todd's inside number 32. She googles the address while she waits, her fingers so cold she can't type easily. It's listed as the registered office of Cutting & Sewing Ltd., which is owned by Ezra Michaels and Joseph Jones. It was set up recently and has never submitted any accounts.

As Todd is swallowed up into the house, someone else leaves.

She's right in the way.

The figure comes through the garden gate just as she passes and, suddenly, she is face-to-face with a dead man. No, that's not right. A man who dies in two days' time. The victim.

Day Minus Two, 19:20

Jen would recognize him anywhere, even though he – currently – has light in his eyes, color in his cheeks. This very much alive man, with mere days to live, looks like somebody who was perhaps once attractive. He is mid-forties, maybe older. He has a full dark beard and elfin ears that point out at their tips.

"Hi there," Jen says spontaneously to him.

"All right," he says warily. His body goes completely still except his black eyes, which run over her face. She tries to think. She needs as much information as possible. Isn't honesty by far the best policy? With clients, with opponents at work, and with your son's enemies, too.

"Todd is my son," she says simply. "I'm Jen."

"Oh. You're *Jen*, Jen Brotherhood," he replies. He seems to know her. "I'm Joseph." His voice is gravelly, but he talks in an authoritative kind of way, like a politician.

Joseph Jones. It must be. The man whose company is registered here.

"Nice kid, Todd. Dating Ezra's niece, isn't he?"

"Ezra is . . ."

"My friend. And business partner."

Jen swallows, trying to digest this information. "Look. I just wondered. I'm a bit worried about him. Todd. Sorry to just – drop by," she says lamely.

"You're worried?" He cocks his head.

"Yeah – you know. Worried he's got in with a bad –"

"Todd's in safe hands. All right now," he says. An instant dismissal by a pro. He motions to her, a kind of *Which way are you going?* gesture. No mistake about it, it means: *Choose, because you are going, whether you like it or not.*

She does nothing, so he brushes past, leaving her there, alone, in the mist, wondering what's happening. Whether the future has continued on without her. If there's another Jen somewhere. Asleep, or too shocked to function? In the world where Todd is probably currently remanded, arrested, charged, convicted. Alone.

She decides to ring the doorbell. The depressing lack of tomorrow has made her fatalistic. And thinking of Todd in police custody has made her desperate.

"I just wanted to know that he's okay," Jen says to the stranger at the door. He must be Ezra. Slightly younger than Joseph. A thickset man with a bent nose.

"Mum?" Todd says from somewhere deep in the house. He emerges into the gloom of the hallway. He looks pale and harassed.

Jen thinks the house was once nice but is now the shabby side of shabby-chic. Worn Victorian quarry tiles. A few offcuts of carpet overlap in the hallway like old papers. "What . . . ?" Todd says to her, making his way past all this. He communicates his bewilderment to her with a tense smile.

A beautiful young woman emerges out of the living room at the end of the hallway, opening the door with her hip. It must be Clio. Jen can tell by the way she moves toward Todd that they are a couple.

She has a Roman nose. A very short, cool fringe. Faded jeans, rips across the knees, tanned skin. No socks. A pink T-shirt with cut-outs. Even her shoulders are attractive, two peaches. She's tall, almost Todd's height. Jen feels a hundred-year-old fool.

"What's wrong?" Todd says. "What's happened?" His voice is so assertive, so irritated. He talks down to her. How had she not noticed?

"Nothing," she says lamely. "I just – er . . . I had a text from you. You sent – your location?" she lies. She looks beyond him again, to the rest of the house. Clio and Todd's tanned skin and white smiles look out of place against the walls – bare plaster – and the living-room door: grubby, with a loose handle. Jen frowns.

Todd gets his phone out of his pocket. "Nope?"

"Oh – sorry. I assumed you wanted me to come."

Todd squints at her, waving his phone. "I didn't. I didn't send anything. Why didn't you call?" As he moves his arm in that way, she is reminded of the precise stabbing motion he made. Forceful, clean, intentional. She shudders.

"You're Jen," Ezra says. Jen blinks. Recognition: the same way Joseph said her name. Todd must talk about her.

"That's right," she tells him. "Sorry – I won't make a habit of dropping by . . ."

Jen is trying to gather as much information as possible before she is imminently expelled by Todd. She casts her gaze about, looking for evidence. She doesn't know what she's looking for; she won't know until she finds it, she guesses.

Ezra is standing with his back against a cupboard.

"Mum?" Todd says. He's smiling, but his eyes communicate an urgent dismissal.

The house doesn't smell like a home. That's what it is. No cooking smells, no laundry. Nothing.

"Sorry – before I go, would you mind if I just used your toilet?" Jen says. She just wants to get *in*. To have a look around. To see what secrets the house might hide.

"Oh God, *Mum*," Todd says, his whole body a teenage eye-roll.

Jen holds her hands up. "I know, I know, I'm sorry. I'll be just a second." She gives Ezra a wide smile. "Where is it?"

"You're five minutes from home."

"This is middle age, Todd."

Todd dies on the spot, but Ezra indicates the living-room door wordlessly. *Yes*. She's in.

Jen squeezes past Todd and Clio and emerges into a room at the very back of the house, a combined kitchen/lounge. It's square, with another door off to the right. There are no photographs on the walls. More bare plaster. A large, printed piece of material hangs over the far wall with a sun and moon stitched on to it. She peers behind it, looking for – what? A secret cupboard? – but of course she doesn't find one.

Jen opens the door to the downstairs toilet and runs the tap, then walks a slow circle around the kitchen. It's mostly bare. Worn tiles underfoot. Crumbs along the kitchen counters. That musty smell, the smell of old and empty dwellings. No fruit in the fruit bowl. No reminder letters on the fridge. If Ezra does live here, he doesn't appear to spend much time at home.

A large TV is affixed to the left-hand wall. An Xbox

sits underneath that. On top of the console rests an iPhone, lit up and blessedly unlocked. Jen picks it up, scrolling straight to the messages. In there, she finds Todd's texts to, she assumes, Clio:

Todd: I am attracted to you like covalent bonds, you know?

Clio: You make me LOL.
You are a nerdarino.

Todd: I am YOUR nerdarino. Right?

Clio: You are mine xx forever.

Jen stares at them. She scrolls further up, feeling guilty as she does so, but not enough to stop.

Clio: This is your morning update.
One coffee consumed, two croissants,
a thousand thoughts about you.

Todd: Only a thousand?

Clio: Now one thousand and one.

Todd: I've had a thousand croissants and only a few thoughts.

Clio: Sounds perfect tbh.

Todd: Can I say something serious?

Clio: Wait, you weren't being serious?
Have you had TWO thousand croissants?

Todd: I literally would do anything for you. X

Clio: Same. X

Anything. Jen doesn't like that word. *Anything* implies all sorts. It implies crimes, it implies murder.

She wants to read further, but she hears footsteps and stops. She replaces the phone on the console. Clio really likes him. Possibly loves him. She sighs and scans the room, but there's nothing else.

She flushes the toilet, turns the tap off, then leaves.

Jen pulls up Andy Vettese's details in the car. She needs help. She emails him on a whim, having been sent away by her embarrassed son.

Dear Andy,

You don't know me, but I'm Rakesh Kapoor's colleague, and I really would like to speak to you about something I'm experiencing which I believe you have studied. I won't say any more for fear of sounding unhinged, but do email me back, please . . .

Best
Jen

"How was work?" Kelly says as she walks in through the door. He's sanding down a bench he's restoring for them. The sort of solitary activity Kelly enjoys. Jen knows what the finished product will look like – he sprays it sage green in two days' time.

"Bad," Jen says, semi-honestly. She needs to try to tell him again.

Kelly wanders over and absentmindedly takes her coat off, the sort of thing she will never get used to, she loves it so much; the simple care and attention he brings to their marriage. He kisses her. He tastes of mint chewing gum. Their hips touch, their legs interlock. It's seamless. Jen feels her breathing automatically slow. Her husband has always had this effect on her.

"Your clients are nutcases," he deadpans, his mouth still next to hers.

"I'm worried about Todd," she says. Kelly steps back. "He's not himself."

"Why?" The heating clicks on, the boiler firing up with a soft flare.

"I'm worried he's in with a bad crowd."

"*Todd?* What bad crowd is that, *Warhammer* lovers?"

Jen can't help but laugh at this. She wishes Kelly would show the outside world this side of him.

"Life's too long for this worry," he adds. It's a phrase of theirs, spanning back decades. She's sure he started it, and he's sure she did.

"This Clio. I'm not sure about her."

"He's still seeing Clio?"

"What do you mean?"

"I thought he said he wasn't. Anyway, I have something for you," he says.

"Don't spend your money on me," she says softly. Kelly is always paid cash in hand, and frequently buys her gifts with it.

"I want to," he says. "It's a pumpkin," he adds.

This distracts Jen entirely. "What?" she says.

"Yeah – you said you wanted one?"

"I was going to buy it tomorrow," she whispers.

"Okay? Look – it's in here."

Jen peers around him, looking into the kitchen. Sure enough, there it is. But it isn't the same one. It's huge and gray. The sight of it chills her skin. What if she changes too much? What if she changes things that don't relate to the murder? Isn't that what always happens in the movies? The protagonists change too much; they can't resist, they get greedy, play the lottery, kill Hitler.

"I'm supposed to buy the pumpkin."

"Hey?"

"Kelly. Yesterday, I told you I was living days backward."

Surprise breaks across his features like a sunrise. "Hey?"

She explains it the same way she did to Rakesh, the same way she already has to Kelly. The first night, the knife in his bag, everything.

"Where is this knife now?"

"I don't know – his bag, probably," she says impatiently, wanting to not revisit conversations they have already had.

"Look. This is fucking ridiculous," he says. She can't say she's surprised by this reaction. "Do you think you should – like – see a GP?"

"Maybe," she says in a whisper. "I don't know. But it's true. What I'm saying is true."

Kelly just stares at her, then at the pumpkin, then back. He goes into the hallway and finds Todd's school bag. Empties it theatrically on to the hallway floor. No knife falls out.

Jen sighs. Todd probably hasn't bought it yet.

"Forget it," she says. "If you won't believe me."

She turns to walk away. It's pointless, even with him. She concedes, as she ascends the stairs, that she wouldn't believe him either. Who would?

"I don't –" she hears him say at the bottom of the stairs, but then he stops himself. Jen is most disappointed in that half-uttered sentence. Kelly likes an easy life at times, and this is clearly one of them.

She showers in a rage. Well, then. If sleeping might be what makes her wake up in yesterday, then she simply won't do it. That's her next tactic.

Kelly falls asleep immediately, the way he always does. But Jen sits up. She sees the clock turn eleven and eleven thirty, when Todd comes back. At midnight, she stares and stares at her phone as 00:00 becomes 00:01 and the date flicks, just like that, from the twenty-seventh to the twenty-eighth, the way it should.

She goes downstairs and watches the rolling BBC news, which segues into the local news, about a road traffic accident that happened on the junction of two roads nearby at eleven o'clock last night. A car rolled over and the owner escaped, unhurt. She sees the clock strike one, then two, then three.

Her eyes become gritty, the adrenaline and the irritation at Kelly wearing off. She does laps of the living room. She makes two coffees and, after the second, she sits on the sofa, just for a second, the news still rolling. The accident, the weather, tomorrow's papers today. She closes her eyes, just for a second, just for one second, and –

Ryan

Ryan Hiles is twenty-three years old and he is going to change the world.

It is his first day at work, his first day as a police constable. He has suffered through the application and interview process. He has endured the police regional training center – twelve weeks in dreary Manchester. He has queued with the other officers on a herringboned floor, waxed and polished, and been given his uniform in a clear plastic bag. A white shirt. A black vest. His police number – 2648 – on his shoulders.

And finally, here he is, in the foyer. His hair wet from the relentless rain, but otherwise ready. He put the uniform on last night, in his bathroom, having waited and waited to do it. He stood on the toilet to see his body in the mirror. And there he was: a policeman. On the toilet, admittedly – but a policeman nevertheless.

More than the uniform, though, Ryan now has what he has always wanted: ability. Specifically, the ability to make a difference. And he is – right now, right this very second – waiting in the station to meet his tutor police officer.

"You're assigned to PC Luke Bradford," the enquiry officer on the front desk says to him, her tone bored. She is older, maybe mid-fifties, though Ryan has never been very good at guessing ages. Hair the color of a piece of slate.

She indicates the row of pale blue bolted-together chairs and he takes a seat next to a man who he assumes is either a criminal or a witness: a young lad with a ponytail, staring at his hands.

Outside, rain batters the police station. Ryan can hear it running off the windowsills. It's rained so much it's been on the news. The wettest October on record. Trains not running, parks and gardens a sodden mess of leaves and water.

PC Luke Bradford arrives after twenty minutes. Ryan takes three deliberate breaths in and out as he approaches. This is it. The beginning.

Bradford crushes Ryan's hand in a shake. He's maybe five years older than Ryan – he is still a police constable, so he must be youngish. And yet he has sallow skin, eye-bags, smells of coffee. His dark hair is salted at the temples and above his ears. Ryan is athletic – if he does say so himself – and he swallows as he looks at Bradford, takes in the small paunch clearly protruding over his black trousers.

"All right, welcome. God, is it still fucking raining?" Bradford glances out at the car park. "First up, parade, then 999 jobs." He turns away from Ryan and leads him into the bowels of the place he will call work.

Parade. Bradford uses old-school language. But still, his first briefing. Ryan feels a dart of excitement like pins and needles in his stomach.

"Kettle on," Bradford says to him.

"Oh, sure," Ryan says, hoping to sound willing.

"Tea round's on the newbie." He indicates the briefing room. "Find out what everyone wants." He claps him on the shoulder as he leaves.

"Okay, then."

It's fine, Ryan tells himself. He can make tea.

But tea, it turns out, is complicated. Fifteen cups. Different strengths, different sweetnesses, different fucking milks. Canderel, proper sugar – the works. Ryan's hands are trembling by the time he's ferried the last few mugs out, his knuckles burning. When he reaches the briefing room just as parade begins, he realizes he hasn't made one for himself.

The sergeant, Joanne Zamo, is in her late forties, has the kind of wide smile that takes over a face. She begins to run through the list of active jobs, none of which Ryan understands. He is the only new PC here; the rest have been dispersed across the north. He gazes around the room, looking at the fifteen coppers and their fifteen cuppas. He'd hoped to find a mate here, someone his age.

Ryan left school at eighteen, worked office jobs with friends for the last few years. He had a great gig ordering stationery where nobody actually expected him to do anything productive but still wanted to pay him. He'd thought it was great, for a while, but it turns out ordering rulers and A4 lined paper is not enough for Ryan. He woke up one Monday morning, six months ago, and thought, *Is this it?*

And then he'd applied to join the police.

Zamo is giving out the list of call jobs. "Right," she adds. "Okay, who have we got here in new recruits? You." Her brown eyes light on Ryan. "Your tutor is Bradford?"

"That's right," Bradford says, before Ryan can.

"Okay – you're Echo." She looks straight at Ryan. "And Mike."

"Mike?" Ryan says. "Sorry, no. I'm Ryan. Ryan Hiles."

A flutter of Bradford's eyelashes. A frisson that Ryan fails to understand. A beat. And then the room erupts.

"Echo Mike," Bradford says, laughing, as though it is a punchline. He has one hand on the doorframe and one hand on his stomach. "Did you not learn about the phonetic alphabet at the Manchester academy, or do they not teach that these days?"

"Oh yes, yes," Ryan says, his cheeks hot. "No, I did, I just – sorry, I thought . . . Mike confused me for just a second there."

"Right," the sergeant says, clearly unimpressed at the unbridled laughter. Just as it stops, it begins again, a wave coming from where CID are clustered. Great.

"Echo Mike two four five," Bradford says, clearly trying to move on. He moves toward Ryan. "I'll do the first response, then let you pick up the second," he adds, hurrying them out of the briefing room. Ryan daren't ask what he means.

They walk down a green-carpeted corridor that smells of hoovering. They reach a locker and Bradford hands Ryan a radio. "All right. That's yours. Calls come in like this: Echo Mike, your vehicle number. You respond with your collar number – yours is 2648, from your shoulder, right?"

"Okay," Ryan says. "Okay." Every officer spends their first two years on 999 calls. Anything could come in. A burglary. A murder.

"Right. Great," Bradford says. "Let's go."

He makes a gesture which says both *This way, please* and *Christ, I hope you're not a fucking idiot*, and Ryan walks back out through the reception and into the rain.

"This is EM two four five, all right, like Zamo said?" Bradford says, gesturing to the police car. The stripes. The lights. Ryan can't stop looking at it.

"Okay," he says. "Sure." He opens the passenger seat and gets in. It smells of old cigarettes.

"Echo Mike two four five, two four five from Echo," says the radio.

"Echo from Mike two four five, go ahead," Bradford says tonelessly back. He hasn't turned the engine on yet, is still twanging the gear stick. Next, he checks the lights work, hits a huge button on the dashboard which bathes them in blue. Ryan sits with his legs crossed in the foot-well, listening to the radio.

"Yes, thanks. We've got reports of an elderly male who appears drunk and is being offensive to passers-by."

Ryan checks his watch. It's five past eight in the morning.

"Echo from Mike two four five, that's received, on our way." Bradford finally starts the car's engine and puts it into gear. "It'll be Old Sandy," he remarks.

Ryan, terrified that there is also a letter of the police alphabet hidden in this sentence, says nothing.

"Homeless guy, nice guy," Bradford says, checking his rear-view mirror as he pulls out. "We'll just probably give him another warning. Call an ambo if he's in a really bad way. Vodka's his thing. Drinks pints and pints of it. Amazing constitution, really."

Ryan watches the traffic as they wait at a set of lights. It is a totally different experience to driving his civilian car. You'd be forgiven for thinking everyone was an exemplary driver; it's like something from *The Truman*

Show, everyone acting. Hands at ten and two. Eyes straight ahead.

"Amazing how well behaved everybody is," Ryan says, and Bradford says nothing. Ryan keeps thinking about Old Sandy and his vodka. And, of course, about his own brother. "What's his history?" Ryan says. "Old Sandy's?"

"No idea."

"Wonder if we could ask."

"Ha," Bradford says, his eyes looking straight ahead. "Yeah – if we did that for everyone, we'd be fucking heroes, right?"

"Right," Ryan says softly. The rain has smudged the lines outside to a soft blur, the streets reflecting brake lights and the white skies.

"First rule of the job: almost all 999 calls are boring or involve idiots. Usually both," Bradford says flatly. "You can't save idiots."

"Okay, great," Ryan says sarcastically.

"Second rule: the new recruits are always far too soft."

They arrive at the beach and Bradford parks neatly in a space. Ryan doesn't dignify his remarks with an answer.

"Come on then, Mike," Bradford says as he gets out. Ryan blushes again. The nickname will stick, he knows it will. This is how it works. He once attended a stag do where one of the stags was called First-floor Wanker the entire weekend only because of where his hotel room was compared to theirs. Ryan never even learned his real name.

Old Sandy isn't that old. He has the pink, bruised face of an alcoholic but a lithe body. He is ranting about God as they approach, the whipped-up ocean an apocalyptic background, the eeriness of the seafront in off-season.

"All right, Old Sandy," Bradford says. Sandy stops and pulls his coarse hair back from his forehead in recognition.

"It's you," he says sincerely to Bradford. "I hoped it would be you."

It turns out, later, that his name is Daniel, not Sandy. The police call him Sandy because he sleeps at the beach.

Ryan looks up at the rain on the way to the next call-out and sighs.

Six incidents later. One domestic violence – the four-teenth call-out made by the wife, who can never bring herself to press charges. That was the most depressing but also – inappropriately – the most interesting. The rest . . . well. A man who urinated through the letterbox of a funeral parlor. A fight between two dog-owners about littering. An ATM that had eaten a ten-pound note. Seriously. Mundane is the right word for it.

Ryan arrives back at the police station with Bradford at six o'clock, his police uniform soaked through, as ex-hausted as if he hasn't slept.

"See you in the morning, Mike," Bradford says, chuck-ling to himself as they head inside. But Ryan can't clock off: he's got to fill in a training record about each call-out before he can go home. He is actually looking forward to the quiet of a little meeting room, the chance to re-flect, to get his thoughts in order. To have a fucking cup of tea at last. His brain feels like a shaken snow globe. He thought it would be . . . he thought it would be differ-ent to this.

He walks into the foyer, past the enquiry officer – a

different one, but with the same bored expression – and through a quiet corridor with a panic strip along the side. He is hoping to catch a glimpse of a suspect being interviewed, or of the cells, of anything, really. Anything except 999 calls. Six calls a day. Four days on, three off. Forty-eight weeks a year. Two years. Ryan can't be bothered to work out how many calls that is, but he knows it's a lot. Maybe today was just an anomaly, a bad day. Maybe Bradford is just jaded. Maybe tomorrow will be interesting. Maybe, maybe.

He pushes open the door to an empty meeting room. It has two doors, for soundproofing. He pulls a chair up at a cheap metal table, the kind you'd find in a village hall. He gets a notebook out of his vest pocket and takes a pen from a red plastic pot in the corner of the table and scrawls the date along the top. He was supposed to make these notes at the time, but Bradford told him that was training-school bollocks.

He begins to write about Sandy, then stops, wanting to think, instead. Wanting to think about how he can make a difference.

Looking back, his brother had started to go *wayward*, as his mother used to say, when he was in his late teens. It started with nicking cars, which escalated to selling drugs. All the way from puff to gear as fast as naught to sixty. What would Bradford have to say about that? He'd probably have thought his brother was wasting police time, too. A predictable set of affairs – no male role model, no prospects. Their mum had tried her best, but she wasn't always there, she had two jobs. His brother, in a funny sort of way, wanted to help with the finances.

That's all. And he did, for a while, he did bring the money in, though they all wondered where from.

Ryan upends the pen against the notebook. Maybe he *is* making a difference to people like his brother. Old Sandy was pleased to see them – seemed to know Bradford well, anyway. Maybe they are helping him, just not in the way Ryan expected.

Bugger it, Ryan thinks. He'll do the notebook tomorrow. He's not in the right mood now.

He opens the door to the meeting room. A big guy is walking past. He's wearing a suit. CID, maybe. Ryan feels something positive bloom across his chest. Yes, yes, yes, there's still plenty of opportunities here. To do interesting things and to make a difference. That's all Ryan wants to do. Isn't that all anyone wants to do?

"All right," Ryan says to the man. He's tall, well over six feet, and thickset, too. Looks kind of like a computer-game villain.

"First day?"

Ryan nods. "Yeah – on response."

"Fun, fun, fun." The man laughs. He holds a warm hand out. "Pete, but everyone calls me Muscles."

"Nice to meet you," Ryan says. "You're CID?"

"For my sins." He leans against the magnolia-painted wall. He takes a stick of gum out and offers one to Ryan, who takes it. Mint explodes in his mouth. "Any good jobs for you today? Who's your tutor?"

"Bradford."

"Ouch."

"Right," Ryan smiles. "No good call-outs yet."

"No, I bet not. So, you're not local? The accent . . ."

"No – commuting across from Manchester," he says.

"Yeah? What brought you here, then – the pull of non-stop fascinating 999 calls?"

"Something like that," Ryan says. "And, you know, *wanting to make a difference*." He uses air quotes.

"You'll soon regret that." Muscles pushes himself off the wall, then wanders down the corridor. Ryan follows him out. Just before they come to the door that leads to the enquiry office, Muscles turns back.

"You know, it can be a good thing not to know the lingo," he says. "You'll find out why."

"You heard the Mike thing," Ryan says.

"Exactly," Muscles says, barely hiding a smile.

"Well, yeah – I'm not that up on the lingo, but I'm going to be," he says.

"Well, don't get too good, Ryan," Muscles says, enigmatically. He chews the gum for a few more seconds, staring at the door, thinking. "Not all good policemen talk like them."

Day Minus Three, 08:00

Jen's eyes open. She is in bed. And it's the twenty-sixth.

It's Day Minus Three.

She goes to the picture window. It's raining outside. Where is this going to end? Cycling back — what, for ever? Until she ceases to exist?

She needs to know the rules. That is what any lawyer would do. Understand the statute, the framework, and then you can play the game. All she knows so far is that nothing has worked. She can only infer from traveling backward that she hasn't managed to stop the crime. Surely. Stop the crime, stop the time loop. That *must* be the key.

She hastily refreshes her email, looking for a reply from Andy Vettese, but there's nothing. She goes downstairs to find Todd hunting for something.

"On the top of the TV unit," Jen says. She knows he will be looking for his physics folder. She knows because she's his mother, but she also knows because this has already happened.

"Ah, thanks." He throws her a self-conscious grin. "Quantum today." God, he towers over her. He used to be many feet shorter than her, would reach his arm right up vertically when he was on the school run, his warm hand always finding hers. He'd get frustrated if she couldn't take it, when she was fussing with her handbag or reaching to press the button on the traffic lights. She had felt guilty each time. It's crazy the things mothers feel guilt over.

And now look, over a foot taller than her and refusing to meet her gaze.

Maybe she had been right to feel guilty, she thinks hopelessly. Maybe she should have never done anything except hold his hand. She could come up with a thousand maternal crimes: letting him watch too much television, sleep-training him – the lot, she thinks bitterly.

"Do you know who Joseph Jones is?" she says quietly, watching him carefully. Not to see if he tells her, but to see if he lies about it, which she thinks he will. A mother's instincts are better than any lawyer's.

Todd puffs air into his cheeks, then plugs his phone in the charger on the kitchen island. "Nope," he says, a studied frown crossing his features. He's never once charged his phone there before school. He charges it overnight. "Why?" he asks.

Jen appraises him. Interesting. He could have easily said, "Clio's uncle's friend," but he chose not to. Just as she expected.

She hesitates, not wanting to do something big, wanting to plan her moment. "Doesn't matter," she says.

"Alrighty. Mysterious Jen. More a question than an axiom. Shower time." Todd leaves his phone charging. Jen stands there in the kitchen, without a theory, without a hope, and with the only person who might be able to help lying to her.

She glances at the stairs. She's got between five and twenty minutes. Todd sometimes takes long and contemplative showers, sometimes quick ones, rushing so much to get dressed afterward that his clothes stick to his wet skin. She tries to get into his phone but fails the PIN request twice.

She dashes upstairs. She'll search his room instead. She's got to find something useful.

Todd's room is a dark cave, painted bottle green. Curtains closed. A double bed with a tartan cover on it sits underneath the window. A television faces the bed. There is a desk in the corner, underneath the stairs that lead up to her and Kelly's bedroom. It's neat but not cosy: the way many men keep their spaces. A black lamp and a MacBook sit on the otherwise empty desk; an exercise bike leans against the far wall.

She opens his laptop, and fails that password log-in twice, too. She looks around his bedroom, thinking how best she can use the time.

Frantically, she opens his desk drawers and the ones in his bedside tables and looks under the bed. She pulls the duvet back and feels around in the bottom of the wardrobe. She just knows she's going to find something. She can feel it. Something damning. Something she can never forget.

She ransacks the room. She'll never be able to get it straight again, but she doesn't care.

She's already wasted six minutes. One unit of legal time: an hour divided into tenths. Her gaze lands on his Xbox. He's always on it. He must talk to some people on there. It's worth a shot.

She powers it up, listening out for the shower, then navigates to the messenger section. It's a dark world in

75

there. Messages with random people about spooky games, fighting games, games where you earn enough points to buy knives to stab other players with . . .

She goes to the recent sent items, which has two messages in. One to User78630 and one to Connor18. The first says: *okay*. The one to Connor says: *11pm I'll drop it off?*

She will ask Pauline about Connor. See if he's wrapped up in anything. It seems too much of a coincidence that they have started spending time together just as Todd goes off the rails. And 11 p.m. drop-offs . . . that doesn't sound good.

She turns off the console and leaves Todd's room. Seconds later, he opens the bathroom door.

They meet on the landing. He has only a towel around his waist.

She meets his eyes, but he doesn't hold her gaze for long. She can't gauge his mood. She recalls his facial expression from the night of the murder. There wasn't any remorse on it, not anywhere, not even a bit.

What's the point in going to the office if, when she wakes up tomorrow, it will be yesterday? There is, for the first time in Jen's adult life, no point in working at all. She muses on this while feeding Henry VIII.

She tries calling a number she finds listed for Andy Vettese but gets no answer. She googles him again. He won some science award yesterday, for a paper on black holes. She emails two more people who have written theses on time travel.

She thinks about how to convince her husband of what is happening.

Jen sighs and eventually finds a legal pad full of notes on a case that doesn't seem to matter much right now. All she can hear is the soft hum of the heating.

In the notebook, she writes *Day Minus Three*.

What I know, she writes underneath that.

Joseph Jones's name, his full address
Clio may be involved
Connor drop-offs?

It isn't a lot.

For the first time in years, Jen is on the school run. The green school gates are clotted with parents. Cliques, loners, people dressed up, people very much dressed down – the lot. Jen would usually spend her time at the school gate paranoid everybody was talking about her but, today, she wishes she had done this more often. For starters, it's fascinating.

She spots Pauline immediately. She is alone, has lately been insisting on collecting Connor so she knows he's been to school – he was recently told off for skipping – and then goes on to get her youngest, Theo. She is wearing a denim jacket and a huge scarf, is staring down at her phone, her legs crossed at the ankles.

"I thought I'd try one of these school-run things," Jen says to her.

"I'm genuinely honored," Pauline says, looking up with a laugh. "Everyone here is a dick. Honestly – Mario's mum has a Mulberry handbag with her. For the school run."

Pauline is one of Jen's easiest friends. Jen did her

divorce, three years ago, separating her neatly from her cheating husband, Eric. Pauline had turned up at Jen's firm for an initial consultation, screenshots of Eric's infidelity in hand. Jen had known of her from the school but had never spoken to her. She made Pauline a tea and very professionally looked at the damning texts, sent from Eric to his mistress, and said she'd take Pauline's case on.

"Sorry you had to see them," Pauline had said in Jen's office, pocketing her phone and sipping the tea.

"Yes, well, it's good to have the – er – evidence," Jen had said. And, despite herself – her stiff suit, the corporate surrounds – she felt her expression falter. "However – um . . . graphic."

Pauline met her eyes for just a second. "So do you attach dick pics to the court petition?" she had said and, right there in Jen's office, they had exploded into laughter. "That was the first time I'd laughed since I found them," Pauline had said sincerely, later. And, just like that, a friendship was born, out of tragedy and humor, as they often are. Jen had been so pleased when Connor and Todd had become friends, too. Until now.

"Well, you've got me, here, unwashed," Jen says.

Pauline smiles and scuffs a Converse shoe on the floor. "You not working today?"

Todd appears in the distance, loping along with Connor, one of the only students who is taller than him. Thicker set, too, a unit of a kid.

"No."

"How's things? How's your enigma of a husband?"

"Listen," Jen says, skipping past the small talk.

"Uh-oh," Pauline says. "I don't like that lawyerly *listen*."

"Nothing to worry about," she says lightly. "Todd is, I think – maybe – caught up in something . . ."

"In what?" Pauline says, suddenly serious. For all her humor, she is a formidable mother where it matters. She will tolerate smoking and swearing, Jen thinks, but nothing worse. Look at her here: checking Connor has made it to school.

"I don't know – I just . . . Todd is acting strangely. And I just wondered – has Connor?"

Pauline tilts her head back just a fraction. "I see."

"Exactly."

More parents begin to gather around them by the gates. Eleven-year-olds and fifteen-year-olds greet their parents and Jen thinks how she's only done this a handful of times, instead choosing to sift through disclosure at the office, appraising trainees, making bundles of documents. Earning money. She wonders, now, quite what it was all for.

"He seems fine . . ." Pauline says slowly, and Jen is so thankful, suddenly, here, for her friend, who has understood the subtext and chosen not to take offense. "But let me do some digging," she adds, right before Connor and Todd arrive.

"All right," Connor says to Jen. He has a tattoo that looks like a necklace, rosary beads maybe, disappearing into the neck of his T-shirt. Tattoos are personal choice, Jen tells herself. Stop being snobby.

He takes his cigarettes out of his pocket, which Jen is relieved to see Pauline wince at. He flares the lighter while still staring at Jen. The flame illuminates his face for the briefest of moments. He gives her a wink, so fast you'd miss it if you weren't looking for it.

It's been a difficult evening. Todd left as soon as he got home; "Going to Clio's," he said. He had been irritated by Jen's appearance at the school pick-up, and annoyed with Kelly, too. "Can either of you two get hobbies?" he'd said, when they were all at home by four o'clock.

After he left, Jen looked up Clio on Facebook. She is a couple of years older than Todd, but in education still. An art college nearby. Her page is meticulously curated. Model-like shots of her, a strangely high number of political memes, a lot of bunches of flowers. Pretty innocuous teenage stuff. Jen is going to go and see her, soon, she has decided. To talk to her.

She tidies up, thinking about what Pauline might find. It's useless to clean, she acknowledges, as she scrubs at the kitchen countertops and stacks the dishwasher. When she wakes up, yesterday, none of this will have been done, but isn't that kind of always the way housework feels?

Pauline calls her twenty minutes later. "I have spoken to Connor," she says. She always speaks without any introduction at all, always gets straight to the point. "And I've done some digging."

"Shoot." Her arms feel chilled as she draws the curtains across their patio doors.

"I've checked Connor's phone. Nothing suspicious. A few unfortunate photographs. Takes after his father."

"Jesus."

"What's going on with Todd?"

"He seems to know these older men – an uncle and friend of his new girlfriend. There's a weird vibe at their house. Plus, they own a company called Cutting & Sewing Ltd. It's brand-new, no turnover, no accounts. I think it's got to be a front. Pretty unusual for two blokes to set up a sewing company, right?"

"Right. That . . . all?"

Jen sighs. Obviously not, but the rest is unbelievable. A dark underworld ending in a murder that she's got to crack open. She turns away from the patio doors, spooked.

And that's when it comes to her. Just like that. The news story she watched yesterday, the road traffic accident. It happens tonight, is on tomorrow's news. She can use it. She can use it to convince the person she needs to confide in the most. If she can convince Kelly, maybe it will break the cycle, break the time loop, and she'll wake up on tomorrow.

"I'll be in touch," she tells Pauline. "Don't worry. It's – it's nothing, probably," she adds, wondering why she has always felt the need to do that. To be easygoing, not to worry people, to be *good*.

"Hope so," Pauline says.

Kelly wanders into the kitchen, much later, after ten at night.

"What?" Kelly says curiously, catching her expression. "What's up?"

"Will you come somewhere with me?" she says.

"Now?" he asks. He looks at her for a beat. "You in full madtown?" he says with a small, wry smile. After they first met, and went traveling around the UK in a little camper van, they lived for years in the Lancashire countryside, just the three of them, in a little white house with a gray slate roof at the bottom of a valley that caught the mist in the winter like a candyfloss hat. Jen's favorite ever house. Kelly had coined this term back then, when she used to come home and download her entire working day to him. She'd never needed anybody else.

"Totally," she says.

"Come on then. We can walk."

Their gazes meet, and Jen wonders what she might be about to set in motion, wonders whether the future is different, now. Wonders if, together, they might make it worse, if there is some alternative future unspooling as she stands here, motionless, in her kitchen, where Todd himself is murdered, where he runs away, where he attacks more than one person.

Jen pushes open the front door. She's excited for it. To present him with actual, tangible proof.

The night air is chilly and damp, the same as it was on that first night. It smells of the mildew of autumn.

"I have something to say to you, and I know how you're going to react, because I've already told you," she says. Kelly's hand is warm in hers. The road is slick with rain. Jen's getting better at this explanation.

"Is this about work?" Kelly is used to Jen asking him about work, theorizing at him, though mostly all he does is listen. Just last week, she asked him about Mr. Mahoney, who wanted to give his ex-wife his entire pension, just to save the battle. Kelly had shrugged and said avoiding pain was priceless to some.

"No." And there, in the darkness, she tells him everything in total detail. Again. She tells him about the first time, and then the day before it, and then the day before that. He listens, his eyes on her, the way he always has.

He doesn't speak for a few moments after she's finished. Just leans there, against the road sign, close to where the accident is due to happen, appearing to be lost in thought. Eventually, he seems to come to a conclusion, and says, "Would you believe this, if it were me?"

"No."

He barks out a laugh. "Right."

"I promise," she says, "on everything we stand for, all our history – that I am telling you the truth. Todd murders somebody this Saturday – late. And I'm moving back in time to stop it."

Kelly is silent for a minute. It begins to drizzle again. He pushes his hair off his forehead as it gets wet. "Why are we here?"

"For me to prove it to you. A car's going to come along here, soon," she says, gesturing to the dark, quiet street. "It'll lose control and flip on to its side. It was just on the news last night. My tomorrow. The owner escapes, totally unharmed. It's a black Audi. It flips over there. It won't go near us."

Kelly rubs a hand along his jaw. "Okay," he says again, dismissive, confused. Together, they lean back on the road sign, side by side.

Just as she is beginning to think the car won't come, it does. Jen hears it first. A distant, speeding rumble. "Here it is."

Kelly looks at her. The rain has intensified. His hair begins to drip.

And then it rounds the corner. A black Audi, fast, out of control. The driver clearly reckless, drunk, both. Its engine sounds like gunfire as it passes them. Kelly watches it, his eyes fixed on it. His expression inscrutable.

Kelly pulls his hood up with one hand, against the downpour, just as the car flips. A metallic crunch and skid. The horn goes.

Then nothing. A beat of silence while the car smokes, then the owner emerges, wide-eyed. He's maybe fifty, ambles across the road to them.

"You're lucky to be out of that," Jen says. Kelly's eyes are back on her. Disbelief, but also a weird kind of panic seems to radiate from him.

"I know," the man says to Jen. He pats his legs, like he's unable to believe that he's really fine.

Kelly shakes his head. "I don't understand this."

"A neighbor is about to come out, to offer help," Jen commentates.

Kelly waits, saying nothing, one foot against the leg of the street sign, arms folded. A door slams somewhere.

"I've called an ambulance," a voice says a few houses down.

"Do you believe me yet?" she says to Kelly.

"I can't think of any other explanation," he says after a few seconds. "But this is – this is *mental*."

"I know that. Of course I know that." She squares herself in front of him so she can look directly into his eyes. "But I promise. I promise, I promise, I *promise* it's true."

Kelly makes a gesture, down the street, and they walk, but not home. They stroll aimlessly, together, in the rain. Jen thinks he might believe her. Truly. And won't that do something, surely? If Todd's other parent believes it. Maybe Kelly will wake up with her, yesterday for him, too. It's a long shot, but she has to try it.

"This is completely batshit," he says. His eyes catch the overhead lights as they move. "There is no way you could've known about that car. Is there?" She can see him trying to work it out.

"No. I mean – literally, no."

"I can't see how . . ." His breath mists up the air in front of him. "I just don't . . ."

"I know."

They take a left, then walk down an alleyway, past their favorite Indian takeaway, then start a slow loop back toward home.

Eventually, he takes her hand in his. "If it's true, it must be horrible," he says.

That *if*. Jen loves it. It is a small step, a small concession from husband to wife. "It is horrible," she says thickly. As she thinks over the past few days of panic and alienation, her eyes moisten and a tear tracks its way down her cheek. She stares at their feet as they walk the streets in perfect sync. Kelly must be watching her, because he stops and wipes the tear away with a thumb.

"I'll try," he says simply, softly, to her. "I'll try to believe you."

When they get in, he pulls up a stool at the breakfast bar, sitting at it with his knees spread, his elbows on the counter, his eyes on her, brows raised.

"Do you have a theory? On this – Joseph?" Kelly says.

Henry VIII jumps on to the kitchen island and Jen

gathers him to her, his fur soft, his body so fat and yielding, and puts her hands around him, like cupping a bowl. She's so glad to be here. With Kelly. Sharing the same spot in the universe together, confiding in him.

"I mean – no. But the night Todd stabbed him. It's like he sees this Joseph, then just – he just panics. And does it."

"So he's afraid of him."

"Yes!" Jen says. "That's exactly it." She looks at her husband. "So you believe me?"

"Maybe I'm humoring you," he says languidly, but she doesn't think so.

"Look – I made these notes," she says, jumping up and grabbing the notepad. Kelly joins her on the sofa in their kitchen. "They're – I mean, they're pretty scant."

Kelly looks at the page, then laughs, a tiny exhale of a sound. "Oh dear, oh dear. These are *very* scant."

"Stop it, or I won't tell you the lottery numbers," Jen says, and it's so nice, it's so nice to laugh about it. It's so nice to be back here, in their easy dynamic.

"Oh yeah – all right. Look. Let's write down every possible reason he could have for doing this. Even the mad ones."

"Self-defense, loss of control, conspiracy," Jen says. "Working as a – I don't know, a hitman."

"This isn't James Bond."

"All right, cross that one out."

Kelly laughs as he scratches a line through *hitman*. "Aliens?"

"Stop it," Jen says, through laughter.

They make more and more and more lists as the night

draws on. All his friends, all his acquaintances that she could speak to.

On the dimly lit sofa, Jen's body sags. She leans into Kelly, whose arm immediately snakes around her.

"When will you – I don't know. Go?"

"When I sleep."

"So let's stay up."

"Tried that one."

She stays there, listening to his breathing slow. She can feel hers slowing, too. But she's happy to go, today. She's happy she got today, with him.

"What would you do?" she asks, turning to look at him.

Kelly folds his lips in on themselves, an expression on his face that Jen can't read. "You sure you want to know that?"

"Of course I do," she says, though, for just a second, she wonders if she really does. Kelly's sense of humor can be dark but – just sometimes – his very core self can seem this way, too. If Jen had to describe it, she'd say she expects the best of people, and Kelly expects the worst.

"I'd kill him," he says softly.

"Joseph?" Jen says, her jaw slack.

"Yeah." He pulls his eyes away from whatever he's looking at and meets her gaze. "Yeah, I'd kill him myself, this Joseph, if I could get away with it."

"So that Todd couldn't," she says in almost a whisper.

"Exactly."

She shivers, totally chilled by this incisive thought, this edge her husband sometimes exhibits. "But could you?"

Kelly shrugs, looking out at the dark garden. He doesn't intend to answer this question, Jen can tell.

"So tomorrow," he murmurs, pulling her back close to him, against his body. "It'll be yesterday for you, tomorrow for me?"

"That's right," she says sadly, but thinking privately that maybe it won't be, that maybe telling him has avoided that fate, somehow. Kelly's quiet; he's falling asleep. Jen's blinks get longer.

They are here, tonight, together, even if they might part again tomorrow, like two passengers on two trains going in opposite directions.

Day Minus Four, 09:00

Four days back.

And, worse, the notebook is blank.

Jen lets a scream of frustration out in the kitchen. Of course it is. Of course it fucking is. Because she hasn't written in it yet. Because she's in the past.

Kelly walks into the kitchen, biting into an apple. "God," he says, wincing, "these are tart. Here – try. It's like eating a lemon!"

He holds it out to her, his arm extended, his eyes happy, crinkled. "Do you remember our walk last night?" she asks him desperately.

"Huh?" he says, through a mouthful. "What?"

He clearly doesn't. Telling him achieved nothing. Just twelve hours ago they sat here, together, and made a plan. The car crash, the conviction on his features as he turned to her. All gone, consigned not to the past, but to the future.

"Never mind."

"You all right? You look like shit," he says.

"Ah, married life. So romantic."

But, inside, her mind is racing. If the notebook is blank, then – of course – the phone calls and emails to Andy Vettese haven't yet been made, either. She checks her sent items: nothing. Of course! No wonder he hasn't replied. It is so hard to get used to a life lived backward.

Even when she thinks she understands it, she doesn't. It trips her up.

She needs to leave, get away from this Kelly who knows nothing about tomorrow, and the next day, and everything that follows. She needs to get away from disappearing notebooks and knives in school bags, and from the scene of the crime that stands silently, waiting.

She needs to go to work. Back to Rakesh, and to Andy Vettese, too.

Ten o'clock in the morning. A sweet black coffee, her desk, and Rakesh. He has stood here thousands of times over the years, often swings by early and complains that he doesn't want to start work. That was the foundation they built their friendship on: moaning.

"Can you try to contact Andy for me?" Jen says to Rakesh now.

She has just told Rakesh, again, what's happening to her. Jen rushed through her explanation to Rakesh, appearing inauthentic and haphazard. She's told it so many times, she has become tired of the tragedy of it, like somebody who's seen so much death and destruction that they are immune.

Still, Rakesh seemed to believe that she really thinks this is happening to her, the same way he did last time. Passively, serious, perhaps internally diagnosing her with something, but not saying what.

"I can't get hold of him, and I need to," Jen says sincerely but urgently. She needs to speak to Andy *today*: it's all she has.

Rakesh steeples his fingers together in that way he

does. "I'm sure I've never told you about Andy," he says with a small smile.

"You do – in a few days."

"I see," Rakesh says, looking at her directly, his brown eyes on hers. He's wearing a sweater vest, today, in purple, and holding a coffee. The rectangular outline of a box of cigarettes is visible in his trouser pocket. Some things don't change.

Jen can't help but smile back at him. "Please call him. He's nearby, isn't he? John Moore's? I can go to his office – whatever."

"What's it worth?" Rakesh leans on the doorframe.

"Oh, are we negotiating?"

"Always."

"I'll do your costs schedule on Blakemore."

"God, deal," he says immediately. "You're so easy. I would've done it for a potato."

"And I'll take your cigarettes so you can get back on the wagon." She points to his pocket. He blinks, then pulls them out.

"Wow. Okay. I see." He retreats back down the corridor. "I'll call him now." He raises a hand, a parting gesture. "Let you know."

"Thank you, thank you," Jen says, though she doesn't think he can still hear her. She rests her elbows on the desk she's worked at for the past two decades, feeling momentarily relieved to have instructed an expert.

The sunlight warms her back. She'd forgotten this little warm spell. A few days in October that felt, for a second, just like summer.

*

Gillian McAllister

Andy says he will come to Liverpool city center in two hours' time. Jen – like a mug – does Rakesh's costs schedule for him.

Jen and Andy arrange to meet in a café that Jen likes. It is unpretentious, cheap, the coffee good and strong. She finds romance in the retro quality it has: tea that costs pence, not pounds, ham sandwiches on the menu, torn vinyl benches to sit on.

As she walks there, weaving between shoppers and past off-key buskers, all the ways she's ineffectually mothered Todd crowd into her mind. Feeding him too much so he slept more, upending the bottle while watching daytime television, bored, no eye contact. That time she shouted in frustration when he wouldn't nap. How early she went back to work because her father put pressure on her; enrolling Todd in nursery so young, too young. Has she planted these seeds here? Was she a shit mother, or just a human? She doesn't know.

Andy is already there, at a Formica-covered table: Jen recognizes him from his LinkedIn photo instantly. About Rakesh's age, unruly hair woven black and gray. A T-shirt that says *Franny and Zooey* on it. J. D. Salinger, is that?

"Thanks for seeing me," Jen says quickly, taking a seat opposite him. He's already ordered two black coffees. A miniature silver milk jug sits on the table, which he gestures wordlessly to. Neither of them uses it.

"Pleasure," Andy says, though it doesn't sound like it. He sounds jaded, like how she gets when pushed into giving free legal advice at parties. It's fair enough.

"This must be – I mean, this must be unorthodox," she says, adding sugar to her coffee.

"You know," he says, sitting back with a small shrug. He has just a trace of an American accent. "Yes." He makes a lattice with his hands and rests his face on it, just looking at her. "But Rakesh is a good friend."

"Well, I won't keep you long," she says, though she doesn't mean it. She wants him to sit with her all day: ideally, into yesterday.

Andy raises his eyebrows, not saying anything.

He sips his coffee then replaces it on the table, calm hazel eyes looking at her. He motions wordlessly, the kind of gesture you'd make when letting somebody through a door.

"Go ahead," he says crisply.

Jen begins to speak. She tells him everything. Every last piece. She talks fast, gesticulating, insane amounts of detail. Every last part. Pumpkins, naked husbands, Cutting & Sewing Ltd., the knife, how she tried to stay up, the car accident, Clio. The lot.

A waitress silently fills their coffees up from a steaming percolator, and Andy thanks her, but only with his eyes and a small smile. He doesn't interrupt Jen once.

"I think that's everything," she says, when she has finished. Steam dances around the overhead fluorescent lights. The café is near empty on this day – whatever day it is – in the mid-morning, mid-week. Jen is so tired, suddenly, with somebody else temporarily in charge, she thinks she could sleep right here at the table. She wonders what would happen if she did.

"I don't need to ask you if you believe you are telling me the truth," Andy says after what looks like a moment's consideration.

The somewhat passive-aggressive *if you believe* rattles Jen. The parlance of doctors, legal opponents, passive-aggressive relatives, Slimming World leaders . . .

"I do," she says. "For what it's worth."

She rubs at her eyes for a minute, trying to think. Come on, she tells herself. You're a smart woman. This isn't so hard. It's time as you know it, only backward.

"You win an award in two days," she says, thinking of the story she saw about him when he hadn't answered her. "For your work on black holes."

When she opens her eyes, Andy has paused, his coffee halfway to his mouth, the Styrofoam cup made elliptical by the pressure of his grip. His mouth is open, his eyes on hers. "The Penny Jameson?"

"I think so? I saw it while googling you."

"I win?"

Jen feels a petty, triumphant little spark light within her. There. "You do."

"That award is embargoed. I know I'm shortlisted. But nobody else does. It isn't –" he gets his phone out and types quietly for a second, then replaces it, face down, on the table. "That information is not in the public domain."

"Well, I'm glad."

"All right then, Jen," he says. "You have my attention."

"Good."

"How interesting." Andy sucks his bottom lip into his mouth. He drums his fingers on the back of his phone.

"So: is it scientifically possible?" she asks him.

He spreads his hands wide, then repositions them around his cup. "We don't know," he says. "Science is much more of an art than you'd think. What you say

94

violates Einstein's law of general relativity – but who's to say his theorem should control our life? Time travel isn't proven to be *im*possible," he says. "If you can get above the speed of light . . ."

"Yes, yes, a gravitational force a thousand times my body weight, right?"

"Exactly."

"But – I didn't feel anything like that. Can I ask – do you think I went forward, too, in time? So, somewhere, I'm living the life where Todd was arrested?"

"You think there may be more than one of you?"

"I guess so."

"Hang on." He takes the knife from the cutlery pot sitting next to them. "Can you use this?"

"Use it?"

"A tiny papercut." He leaves the rest implicit.

Jen swallows. "I see. Okay." She takes the knife and makes – quite honestly – the most pathetic shallow cut along the side of her finger. Barely a scour.

"Deeper," he says.

Jen directs the knife further into her cut. A bead of blood escapes. "Okay," she says, blotting it with a tissue. "Okay?" She looks down at the wound, a centimeter long.

"If that cut isn't there tomorrow . . . I'd say you're waking up in yesterday's body, each day. You move from Monday to Sunday to Saturday."

"Rather than time-traveling?"

"Right. Tell me." He sits forward. "Did you experience any kind of – compressing sensation when this happened? Or only the déjà vu?"

"Only the déjà vu."

"How curious. The panic you felt for your son . . . do you think it caused that feeling?"

"I don't know," Jen says softly, almost to herself. "It's mad. It's so mad. I don't understand it. I haven't yet telephoned you. I do — later in the week. I leave loads of messages."

"It seems to me," Andy says, finishing his coffee, "that you do, actually, already understand the rules of the universe you are unwillingly in."

"It doesn't feel like it," she says, and he allows a smile to escape again.

"It's theoretically possible for you to have somehow created such a force that you are stuck in a closed time-like curve."

"Theoretically possible. Right. So — how do I — get out of it?"

"Physics aside, the obvious answer would be that you will reach the inception of the crime, wouldn't it? Go back to what made Todd commit the crime?"

"And then what? If you had to guess?" She raises her hands in a gesture of non-confrontation. "Nothing at stake. Just a guess. What do you think would happen?"

Andy bites his bottom lip, eyes to the table, then looks at her. "You would stop the crime from happening."

"God, I so hope so," Jen says, her eyes wet.

"Can I ask a question that might seem facetious?" Andy says. The air seems to quieten around them as Andy's gaze meets hers.

"Why do *you* think this is happening to you?"

Jen hesitates, about to say — indeed, facetiously — that

96

she doesn't know: that is why she has forced him to meet her. But something stops her.

She thinks about time loops, about the butterfly effect, changing one tiny thing.

"I wonder if I – alone – know something that can stop the murder," Jen says. "Deep in my subconscious."

"Knowledge," Andy says, nodding. "This isn't time travel, or science or maths. Isn't this just – you have the knowledge – and the love – to stop a crime?"

Jen thinks about the knife she found in Todd's bag, and about Eshe Road North. "Like, on every day I have relived, so far, I've learned something, by doing some-thing different . . . following someone or witnessing something I hadn't the first time. Even just paying more attention to small things."

Andy fiddles with his empty cup on the table, turning his mouth down, still thinking, eyes on the windows behind Jen. "Well, then, is it fair to say that each day you're land-ing in is somehow significant to the crime?"

"Maybe. Yes."

"So as you go backward – maybe you'll skip a day. Maybe you'll skip a week."

"Perhaps. Then I should be looking for clues on each one?"

"Yes, maybe," he says simply.

"I hoped you'd – you know. Give me a hack. To get out. I don't know, two sticks of dynamite and a code, or something."

"Dynamite," Andy says with a laugh. He rises to his feet and reaches out to shake her hand. Her eyes close as he does it, just for a second. It's real. His hand is real. *She* is real.

"Until we meet again," she says, opening her eyes.

"Until then," Andy says.

Jen leaves the café after him, deep, deep in thought about what it might all mean. She calls Todd, wanting to know where he is. Wanting to know if there is something he is doing that she missed the first time she lived this day, feeling a renewed kind of vigor for working out how to change things, for saving him.

"All right?" he answers. It's quiet in the background. Jen, caught in a Liverpool wind tunnel, turns her body away from the gust.

"Just wondering where you are," she says to him.

"Online," he says, and Jen can't help but smile. At just him, lovely him.

"Online – in our house?" she says.

"I have a free period. So I am in our house, on our VPN, on my bed in Crosby, Merseyside, UK," he says, a laugh in his voice.

She looks at the sky and thinks, *Well, I'll see.* She might see August before November. But she'll get to the beginning of the problem, whenever that is.

The moon is out, an early lunchtime moon, hanging above both of them, whichever versions of themselves they are. She, in the past. And Todd, undergoing whatever changes that lead to him killing somebody in four days' time.

"I'll be home soon," she says.

"Where are *you*?"

"The universe," she says, and he laughs, a noise so perfect to her it may as well be music.

*

Jen is back at Eshe Road North, hoping to find Clio. She assumes she doesn't live with her uncle, but perhaps he can direct her to Clio's address.

Jen believes the key rests with Clio. Todd met her a couple of months ago – as far as Jen knows, but you can add at least a few weeks for teenage secrecy. It can't be a coincidence that that is when it began, along with his friendship with Connor. *It* being an amorphous, hard-to-describe change. Sullenness, secrecy, that strange pallor he has at times.

And so here she is, knocking. Almost immediately, a female form appears in the frosted glass. Jen's heart rises up in her chest.

The door opens, and Jen can't help but marvel at Clio's beauty. That short, chic fringe, her close-together eyes. Her hair is snarled, undone, but it looks good for it, rather than the insane way Jen would look if she tried the same.

"Hi," Jen says.

Clio glances over her shoulder, a quick, automatic move, but Jen spots it and wonders what it means.

"Todd's mum," Jen says, realizing after a second's hesitation that although Jen has met Clio, Clio has not met Jen.

"Oh," Clio says, her striking features slackening in surprise.

"I just wondered . . ." Jen says. She glances down. Clio has stepped back slightly. Not to let Jen in, but as if she is about to close the door. Jen thinks of her open, curious expression the first time she saw her, when she was in those ripped jeans at the end of this same hallway. Clio's face now, when Todd isn't here, is totally different. "I just wondered if we might have a bit of a chat?" She gestures to Clio. "It's nothing to do with – it's nothing to do with you, really. I'm fine with your – with your relationship. Can I come in . . . just for a sec? Is this where you live?" she gabbles.

"Look – I can't . . ." Clio says. Jen looks around the hallway. Clio's coat is hanging up, thrown over the door to the cupboard that Ezra closed. Over the coat is a Chanel handbag, Jen thinks a real one. They're worth at least five thousand pounds, aren't they? How can she afford one? Unless it's a fake?

"It's nothing bad," Jen says, her eyes still on that bag.

Clio's brows knit together. Her mouth begins to scrunch up into a delicate kind of apology. "I really . . ." she says, her hands wringing together. She takes another step back. "I'm so, so sorry. I really – I just really can't . . ."

"You can't what?" Jen says, totally bewildered.

"I really can't talk about it with you."

"Talk about what?" Jen says, suddenly remembering that Kelly thought they'd broken up. "You haven't fallen out?"

Something seems to pass over Clio's features that Jen can't name. Some understanding, but Jen isn't privy to what. "Please explain," she adds pathetically.

"We broke up, but then we got back together yesterday – it's . . . complicated."

"How?"

Clio shrinks back from Jen, drawing her arms around her stomach, folding in on herself, like somebody frail or feeling ill. "Sorry," she says, barely audibly, taking another step back. "I'll see you soon – okay?" She closes the door, leaving Jen there, alone.

It latches with a soft click, and through the frosted glass Jen watches Clio retreat.

She turns to leave. As she does so, a police car circles past. Very, very slowly. It's the pace of it that makes Jen look up at it. The windows are up, the driver looking straight ahead, the passenger – who Jen is sure is the handsome police officer who arrests Todd – looking straight at her. As she walks to her car, defeated by Clio's reaction, bewildered by the mystery facing her, the car circles back, going the other way.

Jen thinks about what Andy said as she drives away. About her subconscious, about what she knows, about things she might have seen and dismissed as insignificant, and about what she's here to do. There's nothing else for it, she thinks, as she drives away. She's got to ask her son.

"I have something I want to run by you," Jen says conversationally, walking to the corner shop with Todd. He will buy a Snickers. Last time, she bought a bottle of wine, but she's not in the mood, tonight. They take this walk often. Todd because of his insatiable teenage appetite and – well, the same for Jen, actually.

There will be somebody in the corner shop wearing a trilby, and this trilby is Jen's trump card. Unpredictable, vivid, true. She is glad she has remembered it. She can use it to convince Todd and then – if nothing else – find out what *he* would do in this situation. Her brainiac son.

"Shoot," Todd says easily.

They turn down a side-street. The night air smells of other people's dinners, something Jen finds endlessly nostalgic, reminding her of holidays with her parents to campsites when she was little. She will always remember the distant orange lights of other static caravans, the chink of cutlery, the swirling smoke of barbecues. God, she misses her father. Her mother, too, she guesses, though she hardly remembers her.

"What would you do if you could time travel? Would you go forward, or back?" Jen says, and he looks at her in surprise.

"Why?" he asks.

Typically, before she can answer, he does: "I'd go back," he says, his breath blowing smoke rings out into the night air.

"How come?"

"So I could tell past me some stuff." He smiles, a private smile at the pavement. Jen laughs softly. Inscrutable Gen-Z-ers.

"Then," he says, "I'd just email myself. From past me to future me. Sent on a timer. You can do that on some sites."

"Email yourself?"

"Yeah. You know. Find out whose stocks and shares are going to go through the roof. Then go back in time, do a timed email, from me to me, saying: in September 2006, or whatever, buy shares in Apple."

I'd just email myself.

Well, it's something to try. An email, sent, timed, to be received at one o'clock in the morning on the day it happens, on the twenty-ninth, heading into the thirtieth. She will write it so it contains instructions. Get outside, stop a murder. Surely if she had advance warning, she could physically stop Todd?

"You're so smart."

"Why thank you."

"You might wonder why I'm asking," she says.

"Not really," he says cheerfully.

She begins to explain traveling backward, omitting the crime for now.

She is glancing at him all the time as they walk and talk. If she had to predict his response, she would say he will need no convincing. She knows him. She *knows* him. He – still a kid in so many ways – believes unquestioningly in time loops, in time travel, in science and philosophy and *cool maths* and exceptional things happening in his life, which he still, in his young mind, believes to be extraordinary.

Todd says nothing for a few seconds, staring at his trainers as they walk through the cold, his features wrinkled. He raises an eyebrow to her. "You for real?" he asks.

"Completely. Totally."

"You've seen the future?"

"I have."

"All right then, Mother. So what happens?" he says jovially, and she's pretty sure he thinks she's joking. "Meteors, the next pandemic, what?"

Jen says nothing, debating how honest to be.

He looks at her and catches her expression. "You're not actually serious."

"I really, really am. You're about to buy a Snickers. There will be someone in the corner shop wearing a trilby."

". . . Okay." He nods, just once. "A time loop. A trilby. You're on." Jen smiles at him, unsurprised he's isolated the element of the future that he cannot control, that belongs to someone else: the hat.

This is exactly what she thought he would do. He is a much easier person to convince than Kelly.

"Do you know why?" he says.

"Something happens in four days. That I think I need to stop."

"What?" he says again.

"I – I . . . it's not good, Todd. In four days' time, you kill someone," she says. This time, it's like lighting a bonfire. A tiny spark and then a rush. Todd's head snaps up to look at her. Jen goes as hot as if she's standing right by it. What if she *makes* this happen, by telling him? Surely the knowledge that you can kill is damaging to a person?

No. She has decided to do this and she needs to see it through. He can take it, her son. He likes facts. He likes people to be straight with him.

He doesn't speak for over a minute. "Who?" he says, the same question he asked the last time.

"He was a stranger to me. You seemed to know him."

He doesn't react. They reach the lit-up shop, next door to a Chinese takeaway, and they stand outside it. Eventually, his eyes meet hers. She's surprised to see that they're wet. Just the slightest damp covering. It could be nothing. It could just be the lights of the shops, the cold air. "Well, I'd never kill anyone," he says, not making eye contact with her. She spreads her arms wide.

"But you do. He's called Joseph Jones." Her eyes are wet, too, now. Todd runs his gaze over her face, holds a finger up, and goes into the shop. He's right, of course, he wouldn't kill someone, unless he had no other choice. She *knows* him: he would ameliorate, confess. He would do a whole long list of things before killing. This is perhaps the most useful piece of information Jen has landed on.

Seconds later, he's out, and his body language has completely changed. It's infinitesimal. As though somebody momentarily pressed pause on his movements, then started him up again. Only a stutter.

"Trilby," he says. A beat. "Present and correct."

"So you believe me now?"

"You saw the trilby from down the street, I assume."

"I didn't – Todd, you know that I didn't."

"I would never kill someone. Never, never, never." His eyes look up, to the heavens, and Jen is sure – as sure as she can be – that she sees disappointment but also understanding cross his features. Like somebody who's been told something. Like somebody who's been told the ending, when they're right at the beginning. She is blindsided by his reaction. It isn't time travel that has outsmarted her: it is parenting.

He turns away from her. Jen knows him. He closed up as soon as she told him the details. "Why'd you break up with Clio?"

"None of your business. Back together now, anyway."

Jen sighs. They walk back in stony silence.

Kelly answers the door before Jen can get out a key. Todd brushes past him without speaking to him, going upstairs. Interestingly, he doesn't tell Kelly what Jen just told him. Ordinarily, she's sure they would take the piss together.

Kelly is cooking a pie. When she sits down at the breakfast bar in the kitchen, he pours the sauce into the pastry-lined dish and opens the oven. The heat and the steam from the oven shimmer so violently he seems to disappear right in front of her.

That night, Jen googles how to send a timed email and then fires it off, hopeful, into the ether. As she falls asleep, she prays it works. She prays a future her, somewhere, stops the crime, and breaks the time loop.

Day Minus Eight, 08:00

The email didn't work. The cut she made with the knife is gone.

And, for the first time, Jen has skipped back more than one day. She's moved four days. It is the twenty-first. She sits up in bed and thinks about Andy. It seems he was right.

Or perhaps it's speeding up and, soon, she will leap back years at a time, and then cease to exist entirely.

No. Don't think this way. Concentrate on Todd.

As if on cue, she hears him slam his bedroom door. "Where are you going?" she calls out to him.

She hears him ascend the stairs to the top floor where Jen and Kelly's bedroom is, and then he appears, a wide smile across his face. He looks full of the lols, as he would say. "Dad is making me come running," he says. "Pray for me."

"You're in my thoughts," Jen says as she listens to them go. She's glad to see him like this. Pink-cheeked and happy.

Within minutes, still in her dressing gown, she's back in Todd's room. Searching his desk drawers again, the ones in his bedside tables, under his mattress. Under his bed.

As she searches, she recites to herself what she knows. "Todd meets Clio in late summer. Kelly said, *He's still seeing Clio? I thought he said he wasn't,* in the days before the crime. Todd confirmed a few days earlier that they broke up and got back together."

Plates, cups, reams and reams of school stuff printed from the internet. Behind the wardrobe, a piece of paper about astrophysics.

"Clio is frightened to speak to me," she adds, thinking it must be significant. "Plus – that weird circling police car."

Finally, finally, finally, after twenty minutes, she finds something that feels a lot more tangible than listening to her own ramblings.

It's on top of his wardrobe, right at the back, but not covered in dust, so not old.

It is a small gray oblong bundle held together by an elastic band. Jen climbs down from his desk chair and holds it in the flat of her hand. Drugs – she thinks it might be drugs. Her hands shake as she undoes the elastic, then peels open the bubble wrap.

It isn't drugs.

The package contains three items.

A Merseyside Police badge. Not the full ID, just the leather wallet with the Merseyside crest on. On it is em- broidered a number and a name: Ryan Hiles, 2648.

Jen fingers it. It's cool in her hands. She holds it up to the light. How does a teenage boy come to have a police badge? She doesn't chase that thought down the alley it wants to go down, though it's obvious that it's nothing good.

Next, folded into four neat squares, is a dog-eared A4 poster with a photograph of a baby on it, maybe four months old. Above him or her is written *MISSING* in red, blocky letters. There is a pinhole in the corner.

Jen blinks in shock. Missing. Missing babies? Police IDs? What is this dark world Todd's been plunged into?

The final item is what looks like a pay-as-you-go phone. It's off. Jen's finger trembles as she presses the *on* button and watches it spring to life, its screen a neon green. No passcode. It's an old-style flip phone, not a smartphone. It was clearly never meant to be discovered. She looks at the contacts. There are three: Joseph Jones, Ezra Michaels, and somebody called Nicola Williams.

She goes to the text messages, listening out for Todd and Kelly.

Times for meetings with Joseph and Ezra. 11 p.m. here, 9 a.m. there.

But, with Nicola, it's different:

> Burner phone 15/10: Nice to chat.
> See you on 16th?

Nicola W 15/10: I can be there.

> Burner phone 15/10: Happy to
> help tomorrow?

Nicola W 15/10: Happy to help.

> Burner phone 17/10: Call me.

Nicola W 17/10: PS. It's in place
but see you tonight.

Nicola W 17/10: Nice to meet. Happy to
do it, but you need to work for it.
Given what's happened.

Burner phone 17/10: Yep. Understood.

Nicola W 17/10: Get back in there.

Burner phone 17/10: Baby or no baby.

Nicola W 18/10: All in place.
When we have enough, we can move in.

Jen stares at them. A goldmine. Actual, date-stamped messages arranging something. Jen must be able to work out what. She must be able to follow her son on these days, to insert herself into proceedings.

She turns the rest of the items over, looking for more, but there's nothing.

She sits back on Todd's desk chair. Catastrophes crowd into Jen's mind. Dead policemen. Dead kids. Kidnaps. Ransoms. Is he some sort of foot soldier, a minion sent to undertake a gang's bidding?

She stands on the chair and puts the bundle back, exactly where it was, then sits in her son's ransacked bedroom. Her knees tremble. She watches them, shivering just slightly, thinking that it's all her fault. It must be.

Nicola Williams. Why is that name familiar to her?

She looks up Joseph, Clio, Ezra and Nicola on Facebook. All are there except Nicola, and all three are friends with the other. Joseph's profile is new, but he looks like a perfectly ordinary man. An interest in horse-racing and opinions on Brexit. Ezra's is more established, his profile pictures dating back ten years, but it's otherwise locked.

She tidies up, then makes Todd's bed, her hand

smoothing over his pillow, but it's lumpy, something underneath it. She never checked there. Checked only under the mattress, like in the movies. She reaches for the bulge, hoping to find information, but actually, she just finds Science Bear. The teddy Todd's had since he was two, the one who holds a blue fluffy Bunsen burner and a test tube. He must still sleep with it. Her heart cracks for him, here in his bedroom, thinking of that night with the norovirus and wiping his mouth with that hot flannel, and the other night, the one with the murder. Her son, the half child, half man.

Crosby police station foyer looks the same, as it did that first night, tired, smelling of canteen dinners and coffee. Jen arrives at six, looking for Ryan Hiles. It seems to her that this is the next logical step. Todd and Kelly think she's at the supermarket.

She is told to wait and she sits on one of the metal chairs, staring at the white door to the left of the reception desk. At the end of a long corridor behind it, she can see a tall, slim police officer moving around, on the phone, laughing at something, pacing slowly this way and that.

The receptionist is blonde. She has chapped lips, the line between skin and mouth blurred and sore-looking in that way it is when people have a habit of wetting their lips.

The automatic doors open, but nobody comes in.

The receptionist ignores the doors. She's typing quickly, her gaze not moving from the screen.

It's twilight outside; to anybody else, it looks like a normal day at six o'clock in October. Woodsmoke comes in on the breeze as the glitchy automatic doors open and close for nobody again. Jen folds her hands in her lap and thinks about normal life. The continuity of one day following another. She stares at the doors sliding open, hesitating, and then closing, and tries not to wonder if Todd is proceeding somewhere, in the future, without her. Facing life in prison. Not even the best lawyer would be able to get him off.

"Can I just take your name?" the receptionist says. She seems content to conduct this conversation across the foyer.

"Alison," Jen says, not yet ready to reveal her identity without knowing where Ryan Hiles is and why Todd has his badge. The last thing she wants to do is make things worse for Todd in the future. "Alison Bland," she invents.

"Okay. And what's the . . ."

"I'm looking for a police officer. I have his name and badge number."

"Why is it you want to see him?" The receptionist dials a number on the desk phone.

Jen doesn't say she has the badge itself – doesn't want to hand over evidence, link Todd's fingerprints to something heinous. To something *else* heinous.

"I just want to speak to him."

"Sorry, we can't have civilians coming in to give names and ask to speak to coppers," the receptionist says.

"It isn't – it isn't a bad thing. I just want to talk to him."

"We really can't do that. Do you need to report a crime?"

"I mean . . ." Jen says. She goes to say *no*, but then hesitates. Maybe the police can help her. Just because the murder hasn't happened yet doesn't mean that no crimes at all have been committed. The knife . . . buying a knife is a crime. It's a gamble – he might not yet have bought it – but it's one she is prepared to take. If Todd is investigated for something smaller, perhaps that would stop the larger crime?

Something ignites in Jen. All she needs is change. To blow out one match in a whole line of them. To keep a domino standing that would otherwise fall. And then, perhaps, she will wake up, and it will be tomorrow.

"Yes," she says, to the receptionist's obvious surprise. "Yes, I'd like to report a crime."

Twenty-five minutes later, Jen is in a meeting room with a police officer. He's young, with pale blue eyes like a wolf. Each time they meet hers, Jen is struck by how unusual they are, a dark blue rim, light blue pools in the center, tiny pupils. Something about the color makes them look vacant. He's freshly shaven, his uniform a little too big for him.

"Right, tell me," he says. They have two white plastic cups of water in front of them. The room smells of photocopier toner and stale coffee. The setting seems so mundane for the reaction Jen hopes to set off.

"I'll just keep a note," he adds. She doesn't want this. A young officer who takes meticulous notes and won't answer questions. Jen wants a maverick. Someone who goes off the record, who has a dead wife and an alcohol problem: someone who can help her.

"I'm pretty sure my son is involved in something," she says simply. She skims over the alias she gave, hoping he won't question this, and goes to the heart of the matter: "His name is Todd Brotherhood."

And that's when it happens. Recognition: Jen is sure of it. It passes across his features like a ghost.

"What makes you say that he's involved in something?"

She tells the officer about the cutting and sewing business, about her son meeting Joseph Jones, and about the knife. She hopes that, if Todd has armed himself already, they will find that weapon, arrest him and stop the crime.

The police officer's pen stalls, just slightly, at the mention of the knife. His iced eyes flick to hers, the color of a gas fire on low, then back down again. Jen can feel it in the air, the change, even in here. She has lit the touchpaper. The butterfly has flapped its wings.

"Right – where is the knife? How do you know he bought one?"

"I'm not sure right now, but I have seen it in his school bag once," she says, omitting that this happens in the future.

"Has he ever left the house with it?"

"I assume so."

"Okay then . . ." the officer says, upending the pen. "All right. Looks like we need to speak to your son."

"Today?" Jen asks.

The policeman finishes writing and looks at her. He glances at the clock on the wall.

"We'll make enquiries with Todd."

She shivers, there in the warm police interviewing room. What if there is some unintended consequence of this action she's just taken? Maybe Joseph Jones *should* die, if he's got something to do with something terrible, and she only needs to help Todd get away with it. How is she supposed to know which it is?

"Okay – well, I can go and get Todd for you," she says, wondering quite how she's coming across. How strange it must sound. Even now, in this chaos, Jen still worries about being judged as a parent.

"Just your address is enough," the officer says. He stands up and extends the flat of his palm toward the door. An instant dismissal. *Just arrest him, please arrest him, so he can't do anything more*, Jen thinks.

"Nothing you can do today?" she probes again. She needs him taken in tonight, before she sleeps, if she has even a chance of stopping the crime. Tomorrow doesn't exist, not to her, anyway.

The policeman pauses, looking at his feet, that palm still extended. "I'll try my best. You know – usually, young men carry knives because of gangs."

"I know," Jen whispers.

"We'll talk to your son, but in order to get kids out of this you have to work out the why."

"I'm trying," Jen says. She stops just there, on the threshold of the meeting room, then decides to just ask. "Have any babies gone missing in the area? Recently?"

"Sorry?" the officer says. "Missing babies?"

"Yes. Recently."

"I can't discuss other cases," he says, giving nothing away.

She leaves then, and as she exits through the glass doors etched with a finely threaded grid and steps outside, she smells it. Not what she was expecting: petrichor.

Rain on pavements. Summer's coming back. That smell, that intangible smell – lawns being mowed, cow parsley, hot, packed earth – always reminds her of the house they had in the valley, the little white bungalow. How happy they were there, away from the city. Before.

On the way home, she thinks about Ryan Hiles, and about the missing baby. She can still see the poster. There is something she recognizes about that baby. An instinctive familiarity, as though they may be a distant relative, someone she now knows as an adult . . . someone she has perhaps met, but she can't think. Jen has never been good with babies.

She got pregnant with Todd accidentally, only eight months after she met Kelly. It was a shock, but he used to joke they'd had a decade's worth of sex in that year, which is true. The little camper van and their clothes strewn across the floor are her only memories of that time. His hips against hers, how he'd said to her wryly one night that everybody would be able to see their van rocking. How she didn't care.

They'd been in their early twenties. She'd been on the pill, and most of the time they used condoms. Something about the impossibility of the pregnancy was what made her keep the baby. That, and a single sentence Kelly had said: "I hope the baby has your eyes." Right away, as with millions of women before her, she had thought, *But I hope he has yours.* Sperm had met egg, and each of their thoughts had met the other's, and she felt immediately ready. Like she'd grown up in the space of a two-minute pregnancy test, looking to a future generation instead of to herself.

But she hadn't been ready, not at all.

Nobody had warned her of the car crash that was labor. At one point she had been sure she was going to die, and that conviction never really left her, even after she was fine. She couldn't believe women went through that. That they chose to do it again and again. She couldn't believe pain like that actually existed.

She had begun her motherhood journey with pain, but also in fear: of the judgment of health visitors, of GPs, and of other mothers.

Todd hadn't been what anybody would call *a difficult baby*. He'd always slept well. But an easy baby is still difficult, and Jen – a fan of self-recrimination anyway – was thrust into something that would in other circumstances have been described as torture. And yet to describe it as such was taboo. She'd looked down at him one night, and thought, *How do I know if I love you?*

Jen can see that she was susceptible to *wanting it all*. A woman working in a job that took as much as you were able to give. Having a repressed father. Vulnerable to people's judgment, to reading huge amounts into the small things people say. That vein of inadequacy running through her that led her to say yes to banal networking events and taking on more cases than she could realistically run led – in parenthood – to misery.

She'd wanted to sleep in the same room as Todd, for him to hear her breathing, she'd wanted to breastfeed, she'd wanted, wanted, wanted to do it perfectly, and maybe that was compensation for what she should have felt but didn't.

She'd tried to tell a health visitor about all this, but

they had only looked uncomfortable and asked if she wanted to kill herself.

"No," Jen had said dully. She hadn't wanted to kill herself. She had wanted to take it back. She'd driven to work to see her father, walked around the office like a zombie. In the foyer, her father had hugged her extra tightly, but hadn't said anything. Hadn't been able to say anything: that she was doing a good job, did she need help? A typical man of his generation, but it had still hurt.

Like all disasters, it ebbed away, and the love bloomed, big and beautiful, when Todd started to do things: to sit up, to talk, to smear Bourbon biscuits over his entire head. And, until recently, when his friends had descended into teenage sullenness, he hadn't. Still full of puns, of laughs, of facts, just for her. At the beginning, the love she had felt for him had been eclipsed by how hard it had been in the early days, and it wasn't any longer. That was all. An explanation as big and as small as that.

But she'd been too afraid to have any more children. She looks at the road unfolding in front of her, now, and thinks that the baby in the poster is a girl. She finds a little hard stone of regret in her stomach that she didn't have that other child. A sibling for Todd, somebody he could confide in, somebody who could help him now, more than she can.

She can't let it happen. She can't let the murder play out. She can't have him lose everything. Her easy little baby who unknowingly witnessed his mother crying so often, she can't bear for this to be his end. She can't bear for him to be bad. Let him, let him, let him – and her – be good.

Day Minus Eight, 19:30

"Ready?" Kelly says to Jen when she arrives home. He's standing in their kitchen, trainers and parka on, a smile on his face. He doesn't notice her misty eyes.

"For . . ."

"Parents' evening?" he says, a question in his voice. Henry VIII is winding his way around Kelly's feet.

Parents' evening.

Perhaps it's this. Perhaps this is why she's skipped back more than one day. Like Andy said. This must be an opportunity, of some kind or other. She remembers dreading this but, tonight, she feels ignited by it. Bring it on, let me notice the thing, let me figure this out, and let it *end*.

"Sure," she says brightly. "Yeah, forgot."

"I wish," he says. "Let's just not go." Kelly hates these sorts of things too, though for different reasons, his relating to *the Establishment*. The last time, she took a selfie of them in the car, wanting to put it on Facebook, and he stopped her.

He holds the door open for her now. "How was the office?"

Jen looks down at her jeans and T-shirt. "Yeah – had a meeting with an old client, second divorce," she says glibly as they leave, as though she does much repeat business. Kelly doesn't seem to mind enough to ask.

*

The school hall is set up with tables spaced so evenly it looks like something from the military. At each one sits a teacher, two empty plastic chairs in front of them. Jen thinks of Todd, at home alone, playing Xbox, unknowingly waiting for his arrest for possession of a knife he might not even have.

The first time she lived this evening, all of the reports were glowing, to her relief. Mr. Adams, the physics teacher, described Todd as *a joy*. Jen had been distracted by work, she remembers, considering what to do about Gina's divorce, and how to convince her to allow her soon-to-be-ex access to their children, but that single word had pierced through the membrane of busyness, and she'd grinned as Kelly said drily, "Just like his parents."

Jen is sitting here opposite the same man now. The hall is brightly lit, the floors shining.

Jen and Kelly sent Todd here, to *a good comprehensive*. They didn't want Todd to go to private school, to become part of the institution. They settled on this, Burleigh Secondary School, a place full of well-meaning teachers but with terrible, dated classrooms and grotesque bathrooms. Sometimes, today in particular, Jen wishes they'd chosen somewhere else, someplace where a parents' evening would provide Nespresso coffees and comfy chairs. But, as Kelly had once said, "He'll get decked later in life if he spends his formative years in a choir singing hymns with a load of knobs."

"Yes, sharp, engaged," Mr. Adams is saying. Jen's attention is firmly on him. He's an avuncular sort of man, big ears, white hair, a kind face. He has a cold, smells

distinctively sweet; the scent of Olbas oil on a handker-
chief. She missed this last time. It doesn't *matter*, but she
still missed it. Along with what else?

"Anything we should know about?"

Mr. Adams looks up in surprise. "Like what?"

"Is he – you know, hanging out with anybody new,
working less hard, doing anything out of character?"

"Perhaps lacking common sense at times in the lab."

Kelly laughs softly under his breath, the first noise
he's made since they arrived here, her introverted husband. He reaches for Jen's hand, fiddling with her wedding ring. After this session with Mr. Adams, he will go
to the table serving tea and coffee, get them two teas, but
drop one. The absurdity of this knowledge.

"Oh, but the brightest minds are," Mr. Adams says.
"Honestly, he's a joy." Jen's heart is full of sunbeams for
the second time. You can never hear enough that your
children are good. Especially not now.

They scrape their chairs back and walk over to the
trestle table along the back. Jen debates taking the tea
from Kelly before he drops it. She watches his hands.

"These things are so fucking pointless," he says to her
under his breath as he faffs with teabags. "So dystopian.
Like being in some sort of crazy evaluation system."

"I know," Jen says, passing him the milk. "Judgment
ahoy."

Kelly smiles a pained sort of smile at her. *How long
until we can leave?*

"How long until we can leave?"

"Soon," she promises him. "Do you think he is a good
kid?" she asks. "Honestly."

"Huh?"

"Do you think we're out of the woods? You know – teenagers going astray."

"Not Todd going astray?" a voice says at Jen's shoulder.

She turns around and there's Pauline, in a bright purple dress and a cloud of perfume. "Who knows?" Jen says with a sigh. She'd forgotten this interaction. Totally forgotten that they met here.

Kelly wanders off in the direction of the bathroom. Pauline raises her eyebrows. "Wonder if your husband hates me," she says. "He always disappears."

"He hates everyone."

Pauline laughs. "How's Todd, then?"

"I don't know," Jen says to Pauline. "I think we're heading toward some – some rebellion."

"Connor's teacher just said he's not handing in any homework," Pauline says.

"None?" Jen says, thinking: *Is this relevant?* This small piece of information, so small Pauline obviously forgets to relay it in a few days' time when Jen asks.

"Who knows? Teenage boys. Laws unto themselves," Pauline says. "Theo's the only one with an unblemished record. Right – geography calls. Prayers appreciated."

Jen touches her shoulder as she leaves. Kelly comes back, resumes making the tea. As he passes it to Jen, it falls straight on to the floor, an eruption of beige liquid, teabag and all. Jen stares at it bubbling away there.

They see Mr. Sampson next, Todd's form tutor. He looks barely older than Todd. Side-parted dark hair, a kind of eager-to-please expression.

"All good," he says quickly, crisply, while Jen sips the

tea. She thinks suddenly, horribly, of what Mr. Sampson will say in the future. The day after the crime, the day after that. Day Plus One. Day Plus Two. Each one an equal and opposite reaction to Day Minus One, Day Minus Two. "Good kid, never knew he'd have it in him," he will say sadly. Jen can just see it now. "Must've been unhappy in some way."

"You've not noticed anything?" Jen asks Mr. Sampson now.

"Perhaps he is ever so slightly more withdrawn?"

"Is he? He's not – he's not involved in anything, is he?" she asks. "Anything – I don't know . . . I sometimes wonder if he's gone off the rails a bit."

Kelly turns to her in surprise, but Jen isn't focusing on him. Mr. Sampson is hesitating, just a little. "No," he says, but it contains an invisible ellipsis that streams out into the air after he's finished speaking. He sips a coffee. He winces as he swallows. "No," he says again, more firmly this time, but he doesn't meet Jen's eyes.

Ryan

It's Ryan's fifth day at work, Friday, and five minutes ago everything changed. He arrived at the station and this man, this *Leo*, told him he wasn't working on response today. He walked Ryan into the large meeting room at the back of the station, more of a boardroom, and Ryan had watched curiously as he locked the door behind them.

Leo is maybe in his late forties, slim but jowly, his hairline receding. He speaks with a jaded kind of brevity, as though he's never not talking to idiots. Similar to Bradford, but not at Ryan's expense. Not yet, anyway. Unlike Bradford, whose reputation Ryan now knows to be that of an embittered junior, Leo's generally regarded as a crazy genius. Much worse, in many ways, but much more interesting, too.

They have just been joined by Jamie, who is maybe thirty. These men are not only in plain clothes but in actual scruffs: Jamie is in jogging bottoms, a stained T-shirt and a black baseball cap. Leo looks like he is about to go and coach a football team.

Ryan is feeling fairly uneasy at this point, sitting opposite these men, a giant table between them. "Sorry — what is this . . . ?" he starts to ask.

"We'll get on to that," Leo says. He has a cockney accent, a signet ring on the little finger of his left hand

124

which clinks against the wooden table. "Where did you say you're from, Ryan?"

"Manchester . . ." Ryan says, wondering if he's about to get sacked. "Can I just ask —"

Next to him, Jamie takes his baseball cap off and rubs at his hair. He puts the cap on the table, very deliberately, it seems to Ryan, over the recording equipment. Ryan's eyes track to it. "Nine nine nine response is pretty boring, isn't it?" Leo asks.

"For sure."

"Look. How do you fancy doing something more interesting? We can call it research."

"Research?"

"We need information about an organized-crime gang operating around Liverpool."

Day Minus Nine, 15:00

That it is Day Minus Nine makes sense to Jen.

She has come to the school. She's here, the day before parents' evening, to see if she can get any insight into what was underneath Mr. Sampson's hesitation last night, in private. People are always more confessional in private.

"He has mentioned a falling-out, I seem to remember," he is saying to Jen.

Mr. Sampson teaches geography. Behind him there is a wall that seems to be a tribute to the features of the world he likes the most – the white desert in Egypt, a cave of crystals in Mexico. He is leaning back against his desk, facing Jen.

"When? And with who?" Jen says. She looks around this classroom which must greet Todd every morning but that she has never seen herself, never had time to, because of her job. Green speckled carpets. White desks that seat two students. Blue plastic chairs. She found out her mother died when she was in a classroom just like this. Called out by the head teacher. She hadn't returned for several days afterward. Her father had hardly talked about it. "Can't change what's happened," he'd said once. Repressed, unhappy at times, a very typical lawyer. Jen had been so determined to parent differently. Openly, honestly, humanely, but maybe she'd fucked it up as much as he had. Isn't that what Larkin says?

Her phone rings in her handbag on the chair. Mr. Sampson's eyes stray to it. Jen checks it. "Just work," she says, declining the call. It instantly rings again.

"Do answer," he says with a wave of his hand.

Jen picks up reluctantly. This is not what she is here to do. "I've got someone here for you," Jen's secretary, Shaz, says. Mr. Sampson busies himself at his desk.

"I'll be in late," Jen says.

"It's Gina. What shall I tell her?"

Jen blinks. Gina. The client who doesn't want her husband to have access to their children. Some memory is coming to Jen, some small detail of Gina's life. "Uh," she stalls, trying to think. That's it: the last time Jen saw Gina, she'd turned to Jen, on the threshold of her office, and said, "I should've seen it coming. It's literally what I do for a living. Personal investigator. For my sins." Jen had nodded slowly in recognition.

It cannot be a coincidence that Jen has woken up on this day, the day Gina is in her office. Maybe this isn't about seeing Mr. Sampson at all. "I'll come in," she says. "Tell her to wait." She hangs up and turns back to Mr. Sampson. "Sorry, sorry," she says hurriedly. "When was this falling-out?"

"A week ago, maybe? He said he'd had a domestic. That's all . . ."

"With who?"

"He didn't say. He was talking to someone – I just overheard."

"Who was he talking to?"

"Connor."

The same names. The same names keep coming up over and over. Connor, Ezra, Clio, Joseph himself.

"He also said something about a baby?"

"What?"

"I'm not sure – it just came to me. Something about a baby."

"Right. It would have been good to know before now," Jen says, one of the very first times she has said exactly what she thinks to somebody like this, to somebody outside her immediate family or colleagues. How liberating it feels. Next, she will be telling clients to go fuck themselves.

"Right . . ." Mr. Sampson says awkwardly.

She stares out of the window. It's foggy out, but still mild. Summer still feels just within reach. She watches as the shallow mist moves like a tide back and forth over the playing fields.

She gives a friendly but helpless shrug, saying nothing, the kind of stony silence Kelly would impart. It is so therapeutic, not having to deal with the consequences of her actions. This meeting is contextless, like a dream, like a conversation with a drunk person who will not remember.

"I'll check in with him tomorrow," Mr. Sampson says, and Jen hopes maybe that'll help, somewhere, in the future.

The mist becomes drizzle becomes rain as Jen heads to her car. She looks absentmindedly for Todd's and spots it immediately. As she watches, Connor arrives, too. He's late. She stands there with one hand on her car door, looking, hoping to see something.

But nothing happens. He locks his car and smokes a cigarette on his way into the building. His tattoo is hidden, today, under a round-neck sweater. At the door, he turns to Jen, raises a hand in greeting. Jen waves back, but she's surprised: she didn't know he'd seen her.

The police badge, the missing-baby poster and the phone were not on Todd's wardrobe when Jen went home just now. She searched and searched for them, but they were gone. She assumed at first that he has not yet acquired them, but the texts on the phone date back to the fifteenth of October. Nevertheless, they're nowhere to be found, and so she has nothing to show Gina, who she is now well over an hour late to see.

Gina is sitting in the chair in the corner of Jen's office wearing a beige trench coat and a muted expression.

"I'm so sorry – I'm so sorry," Jen says. "I'm having a family drama."

She puts down her umbrella, leaving damp droplets on the carpet. "That's fine, don't worry," Gina says cordially. Jen had been wary of crossing the boundary from professional to friend with clients, but she has, in these past few weeks, with Gina. They've even texted a bit. It doesn't matter – Jen is the business owner, after all – but Jen now wonders if all of that happened for a reason.

She tries to remember what she said in this meeting the last time. "Can I just ask," she says, removing her coat and powering up her computer, trying to step back into Jen the professional adviser, "what your plan is if you succeed in preventing your ex-husband's access to the children?"

"He'd come back to me, wouldn't he?" Gina says. "So he could see the kids."

Jen bites her lip. "But – Gina. It doesn't work like that."

Gina looks around Jen's office with panicked eyes. "I know I'm being mad." She drops her head. "You've helped me to see that."

Jen feels choked up, despite herself. God, she relates to this, now. This desperation, this denial. This urge to exert some kind of crazy control, somehow.

"That's what I'm here for," Jen says thickly. "But – you know. It's better to move on, isn't it? Forward."

"God, I'm getting all anxious again," Gina says, wafting her hands at her eyes.

"The reason I'm doing this for free," Jen says gently, "is, really, because I don't plan on doing it."

"Right," Gina says. She crosses and uncrosses her legs in the chair. She has on wrinkled clothes. "I know. I know. I realized when we were" – she wipes her eyes – "when we were talking about fucking *Love Island*. I thought – those girls would never beg. How sad is that, taking lessons from a bloody TV show?"

"It's very informative," Jen says drily.

Gina looks down at her lap. "I just need to . . . I don't know. I just need a bit of time. Okay?"

"Okay – good," Jen says. "Good." This has gone better than it did the last time.

"Fancy distracting me with your family drama?" Gina says wanly.

"Maybe?" Jen says with her own wobbly smile. She glances at Gina as she straightens up in the chair.

"Hit me," Gina says.

Jen hesitates. This is both unethical and, perhaps,

dangerous. And yet . . . so useful. Here she is, on this day, at this meeting. Surely, surely, for a reason.

She's already decided to ask Gina about the poster, the badge, and the texts on the burner phone. *Baby or no baby*. What does that mean? She isn't supposed to know Gina's occupation – she hasn't been told yet – but she breezes past that, and Gina doesn't seem to notice.

Jen explains how Todd has been behaving strangely, and then she found the bundle containing the police badge and the poster.

"And you don't have them with you now?" Gina asks. Her eyes – alert now – are on Jen.

"No. Sorry. My son had them, but he doesn't any more." Jen licks her lips. "I'm pretty sure he's mixed up in something dark. I need someone to find out what."

Gina meets her eyes and blinks just once. Her mobile phone starts ringing, but she ignores it. "All right. Me."

"Yes."

"So – to be clear – you want me to find out what I can about the police officer, Ryan, and the missing baby? And Nicola Williams?"

"Exactly," Jen says, marveling at Gina's upright body language. How different we are at work to how we feel inside.

"Leave it with me," she says, and Jen could kiss her. Finally. Some help. Gina meets Jen's eye. "And thank you. For – you know. For *Love Island*."

"No problem," Jen says, her eyes damp.

"You need the info asap?"

"Ideally today," Jen says. "Is that okay? I'll pay whatever you need to get it by this evening."

Gina waves a hand. "What is it you say . . . pro bono?"

"Right," Jen says. "Yes, pro bono. For the public good." After all, isn't that what stopping a murder is?

Jen stays in the office, using the various tools at her disposal to pillage information.

She emails the firm's librarian, asking her to find details of any babies who have gone missing in Liverpool recently. She sends back a few articles: court battles, people who've lied about their children being kidnapped, a woman whose baby was snatched outside a supermarket then returned to a doctor's surgery.

Jen makes her way methodically through them. None look like the missing baby. There is something base about her recognition of it, something familiar. It must be a maternal instinct.

She looks up Nicola Williams next, but the name is so common, and she has nothing else to go on. She should've taken down the number. Memorized it.

Nicola. Nicola Williams.

Wait. That first night. In the police station. Was Nicola Williams the name she heard in the police station the night of Todd's arrest? The name of the person who'd been stabbed two nights previously?

Jen sinks her head into her hands at her desk. Was it? She feels sure it was, but she can't go forward . . . only back. And it's no use googling it: it hasn't happened yet.

Say it *was* Nicola who was injured . . . the thought chills Jen. Where was Todd? What did he do on Day Minus Two? Is he connected to that? She can't remember. It's all a blur.

She doesn't know. She just doesn't *know*.

Jen leaves the office and drives aimlessly. The rain has intensified. She doesn't want to go home. Doesn't want to go back to the scene of the crime, doesn't want to sit in the house failing to work everything out. She drives slowly toward the coast. She knows it's mad to go to the beach in the rain, but then Jen feels mad. She wants to stand there and feel it, each cold drop of water on her skin. She wants to remind herself that she is still here, still alive, just not in the way she's accustomed to.

She parks up at Crosby beach. It's deserted. Rain snakes down the path leading to the sea in stripes, already a few inches deep. Jen's hair is slicked to her scalp within seconds. It smells of cold brine. The wind whips the grit of the sand into her face.

She walks past a homeless man sitting by a parking meter. He's soaked through, and Jen feels so guilty she passes him a wet five-pound note.

The beach has the Antony Gormley exhibition on it. *Another Place*. Dozens of bronze statues looking out to sea. Jen approaches them, the noise of the downpour around her as loud as a train. She is the only human on the beach.

Her feet sink into pale sand that compacts like snow.

She stands by one of the metal figures, shoulder to shoulder, and looks at the blurred and rainy horizon, spending time with a statue instead of another person. If only. If only she could work this through with some-body. She'd figure it out much more easily, she's sure, if she wasn't always alone. The statue's body is freezing cold against her palm, its mouth wordless. Together, they look at every single metal figurine, each in a different time, in a different place, alone, looking out to sea for answers.

That evening, late, Jen heads out, back to Eshe Road North, just hoping to observe something. Bad, criminal things only happen at night, so she may as well sit and watch the house.

She still hasn't heard from Gina.

At a quarter past ten, Ezra leaves the house, and gets into his car, wearing a uniform of some sort – dark green trousers, green jacket, hi-vis waistcoat.

Jen follows him, keeping well back, her headlights on, just a normal driver, just a coincidence. They drive like this for a while, down a track road and crossing a staggered junction.

She follows him all the way to Birkenhead port. He gets out and takes a clipboard from another man there, looping an ID around his neck with one hand and fumbling for a cigarette with the other. He takes up a position to check cars in and stands there, doing nothing except smoking.

Jen's shoulders sink in disappointment. So he only works here.

She leaves the engine idling, watching as a Tesla appears. The port is blustery, leaves tossed on the breeze. It's busy, too, cars coming and going, but the Tesla does something different: it flashes its lights, then disappears slowly down a side-street. Ezra follows it on foot. She puts the car into gear and is just behind them. She parks randomly on a drive, hoping to look like a resident, and switches her lights off.

A boy – only Todd's age, but shorter and blond – gets out of the Tesla with an oblong-shaped package under his arm. Ezra greets him, shaking his hand and, together, they crouch in front of the Tesla. It takes Jen a few minutes to work out what they're doing: they are removing the plates from the Tesla and putting different ones on.

The kid leaves, and Ezra drives the Tesla back through the parking barrier and leaves it waiting to be loaded on to a ship.

So Ezra is a bent port worker, then. Taking stolen cars, plating them and shipping them somewhere to sell, no doubt for cash given to him on the side. She supposes the blond boy is a foot soldier of sorts, paid a pittance to steal the cars from people's driveways with the promise of gang advancement ahead. What if Todd is working for Ezra and Joseph, too? It goes wrong, somehow, and Joseph ends up dead. Jen doesn't want to believe it, but that doesn't mean it isn't true.

She waits a minute before leaving. She passes the boy, walking by the side of the road. She looks carefully at him. His gaze is fixed ahead. He can't be more than sixteen, a teenager, a baby, burning bright, with no idea of the damage he is doing to his mother, waiting at a window back home.

It's almost midnight, and Gina has sent across photos of twelve babies who have gone missing in England in the past year. None from anywhere near Merseyside. And none that looks exactly like the baby in the poster. Some have lighter hair, some larger eyes, though it's hard to know for sure that they're different. Jen is suddenly struck by the terrifying thought that the baby may not yet be missing.

She scrolls up through Gina's texts. She missed them all while she was distracted at the port.

> Nothing on Nicola. Name too common.
> I have something on Ryan though – he's dead.

Panic flashes across Jen's body as if she has been doused in hot oil. She calls Gina immediately, but there's no answer. She rings again and again and again. But Gina doesn't pick up today; it's gone. They'll have to start from scratch tomorrow, tomorrow, tomorrow, yesterday.

Day Minus Twelve, 08:00

Twelve days back and Jen opens her eyes on the exact day Nicola Williams texted Todd's burner phone saying, *It's in place but see you tonight.* Jen is therefore determined to follow Todd today, not to let him out of her sight. Personal investigators be damned. This has got to be the better way. Jen can't start over again with Gina today. It's too disheartening to lose it all when she sleeps.

She follows Todd to school and intends to wait outside, all day, in the car park. As long as it takes. She has absolutely nothing better to do. The only requirement of today is that Todd has zero opportunity to meet Nicola alone.

She sends some work emails while she waits, eyes on Todd's car, and on the school doors. She researches local missing babies, and goes deeper into the probate registers, looking for Ryan, but she uncovers nothing.

It begins to rain around eleven o'clock, fat drops that land like falling pennies that disappear to nothing on her windshield. She stares out as the car park becomes a moving, shivering river. She'd forgotten this. Mid-October had been unseasonably wet.

Jen stares up at the rain striking the windshield, thinking about the weather, her son, and the ripple effects that can spread from a single raindrop.

She thinks about what the implications are for the changes she makes today. She wishes she understood it.

Maybe she can. It'll just take a tedious explanation first.

She dials Andy's office and is surprised when he answers straight away.

"You won't know me," she starts hesitatingly.

"No, clearly not," he says, deadpan.

She explains her predicament as briefly as she can while he communicates a baffled and judgmental silence down the phone to her.

"And that's about it," she finishes.

A beat. "Okay," he says. "I do get these calls from time to time, so I can't say I'm surprised."

"No. Pranksters, usually, right?" Jen says. She's seen them about, too. She read another thread on Reddit this morning from somebody claiming to have time-traveled to 2022 from 2031. She didn't believe it, despite experiencing much the same thing herself. This guy couldn't even prove it. Says there's a nuclear war in 2031, and nobody can disprove that anyway.

"Yes, exactly. Hard to know who to believe, isn't it?" he says. She can't bear it; she can't bear for anyone – even this virtual stranger – to think her mad or needy or a malingerer, someone who calls up professors and bullshits them.

"Yeah. Look – later on in October you're shortlisted for – and win – an award," she says. "The Penny Jameson. This won't help me much today, but – well. There you are. You win."

"That award is –"

"Embargoed. I know."

"I don't know I'm shortlisted. But I do know I'm in for it. But you shouldn't."

"Yes," Jen says. "It's all I've got, my proof."

"I like your proof," he says succinctly. "I'm happy to accept it." The clarity of scientists. "I've just googled that award. It isn't anywhere online."

"That's what you say the next time."

Another beat of silence while Andy seems to consider things. "Where? Do we meet?" His tone is noticeably warmer.

"In a café in Liverpool city center. I suggest it. You wear a T-shirt that says *Franny and Zooey* on it."

"My J. D. Salinger," he says in surprise. "Tell me, are you outside my office window?"

"No," Jen says with a laugh.

"This must be infuriating, then. To have to go through these – ah – these security questions – with me each time."

"Yes, it is," Jen says honestly.

"How can I help?"

"When we meet in Liverpool in a week's time, you talk about the power of my subconscious landing me on certain days."

". . . Yes," Andy says, and Jen is struck, there in her rainy little car, that it isn't his expertise that matters, only somebody sympathetic actively listening on the end of the line. Some safe space to hold her thoughts up to the light: isn't that what everybody needs, anyway? Gina; Todd, even?

"Well, that is definitely happening. I'm skipping multiple days now. And I think the ones I end up on are significant – in some way."

"Well, good. I'm glad you're working it out, within the

framework available to you," he says. She hears bristling, a hand across a beard. "So . . . you have more questions?"

"Yes. I wanted to ask . . . let's say in a few days, a few weeks, I work this out."

"Yes."

"I just want to know, really, the extent to which the things I've already done will 'stick,' so to speak? Like, I told Todd, on one of the days, that he kills someone in the future. But I'm now back before that conversation has taken place? So – has it?"

Andy pauses, which Jen is glad about. She needs somebody who considers things. Somebody who doesn't speak to fill silences, to make wild guesses. Eventually, he speaks. "It's the butterfly effect, isn't it? Let's say you win the lottery on Day Minus Ten, and continue to go back through time, to Day Minus Eleven, Day Minus Twelve, and so on. If, at some point, you solve the crime, and wake up on Day Zero, are you still the lottery winner from Day Minus Ten?"

"Exactly, that's what I want to know."

"I don't think so. I don't think the things you're doing now will stick. I think you will go onward from the day you solve it, and only changes from that day forward will remain. They will wipe the rest. That's just my feeling."

Tap, tap, tap go the drops of rainwater. Jen watches them land and then spread, forming rivulets. She opens a window and extends her arm out, just feeling it, real rain, the same rain she's experienced once before, on her skin. "And – just say if I don't solve it."

"I think it'll become clear. Have faith, Jen. There's an order to things that we sometimes don't even know."

This man, this kind, smart man on the end of the phone, becomes a guru to Jen. A wise old professor, a Gandalf, a Dumbledore. "But – like . . . what if I just cycle back forty years, to oblivion, and then that's it?" she asks. Now perhaps her greatest fear. She swallows as she thinks this horrible, catastrophic thought. Oh, to have a brain that does not torture itself.

"Well, that's all any of us is doing, only in the other direction," he says, which does nothing to ease Jen's anxiety whatsoever.

"Do you mind if I just tell you everything I know? Just to . . . see if you can spot anything?" she asks him.

"Shoot. I even have a pad and paper. And I am soon to be crowned one of the great physics minds in Britain, if your premonition is correct."

"Oh, it is," she says. "Okay – so."

And she tells him. She tells him about the missing-baby poster, the dead policeman and about the burner phone and the texts to Nicola Williams. She tells him about the port worker and how she suspects it's organized crime. She tells him about Nicola Williams maybe having been stabbed, too. She tells him every date, every time she knows. As she speaks, she hears the sound of a pen being uncapped. Probably a fountain pen, a distinctive, hard click. "And that's all," she says, breathless with having divulged everything.

"So, putting that into chronological order . . ." he says.

"Okay, yes. Todd meets Clio in August. Her uncle is running some sort of – I don't know. Crime ring."

"Okay, so then – into October." She hears him leaf through papers. "You say Todd appears to ask somebody called Nicola Williams for help. Perhaps setting her up – to meet, and then she's harmed?"

"Yes. And at this point, the seventeenth of October, the baby is likely already missing, and the policeman is also probably dead, his ID taken."

Jen sits back. What was a stormy ocean is now so clear she can see the bedrock beneath it. "That's that."

"Well, then. Seems like Nicola is the missing piece. She's the one you know the least about. And a person who seems to be directly connected to Todd, and who was injured, too, two nights before the crime."

"Okay. Yes. I need to find Nicola," Jen agrees.

At three thirty, Jen follows Todd home and arrives at the door two minutes after him.

He turns to her, his face perhaps a little pale, but otherwise looking pretty cheerful, and says, "Did you know that a flea can accelerate faster than a rocket?"

"I'm fine, thanks, had a half-day," she says sarcastically.

"Well, then, Mother, look at this." He puts his bag down and begins rooting through it, a clear, sunny expression on his face. Not a sniff of organized crime, of gangs, of violence, dead policemen, of anything. "Look." He passes her an essay, grade A+, his fingers just brushing hers, as light as a feather.

Jen stares down at it, a biology essay. She vaguely remembers this. Last time, in the evening, she had issued a perfunctory *well done*. Todd's A+s are the rule and not the exception. This time, she reads it properly. "It's amazing," she says after a few minutes. Todd blinks in surprise, and that blink – it cracks her heart open just a little. She's tried so hard, but look at his shock. "How long did it take you?" she asks.

"Oh, you know, not long."

"Well, I couldn't do it. I don't even know what photo-synthesis is."

"Yeah." A soft laugh. "It's plants, Mother."

His eyes are on his own essay, reading it back, a sketch of a smile across his features. He's so confident. She has done one thing right, at least. Hopefully Todd will never sit up at night and doubt his own parenting, his intellect, his self.

"What're you going to do tonight to celebrate?" she asks.

He looks at her.

"Absolutely nothing?"

"You've no plans?" she asks again.

"Am I in a court of law?" Todd says, holding his hands up.

"You're not seeing anyone? Clio? Connor?"

"Oh, curiosity beckons, does it? I wondered when you'd get nosey about Clio."

"Consider that day today," Jen says weakly.

Todd turns away from them, heading into the kitchen. "Meh."

"Meh?"

"Not sure it's a runner."

"What? She was your – your proper girlfriend."

"No longer." Todd's jaw is clenched as he says it, staring down at his phone.

Kelly arrives in the kitchen. His gaze tracks Todd. He appears to be deep in thought, though he doesn't say as much. "I have a job on," he says. He's pulling his coat on.

"Sure," Jen says vaguely. "What's happened with Clio?"

"It's off limits," Todd says tightly. Kelly clatters some cans in their cupboards, then swears. "They are my Cokes," Todd says to him.

"Well, later, then," Kelly says. "I'll get my own Coke."

"Adieu," Todd says to Kelly, perhaps somewhat sharply. "I think I'm going to celebrate my essay by melting my brain on the Xbox," he says to Jen.

He grabs an orange from the fruit bowl and throws it to her with a laugh so loud it thrums in her heart like a bass drum. *I love you, I love you, I love you*, she thinks as she catches it. "Is this photosynthesizing, right now?" she says, holding the orange up.

"Don't use words you don't know the meaning of," Todd says, coming over to ruffle her hair. *Whatever it is you've done*, Jen thinks, *I'll never not love you*.

The entire evening, he doesn't leave the house. Jen checks on him at midnight, and he's sleeping. She stays up until four, just to make sure, then goes to bed herself. There is no way that, today, he has seen Nicola Williams. None at all.

Ryan

The best part of Ryan's recreational training in Manchester was the hint of what was to come in this interesting, long and varied career he had ahead of him. Hostage negotiation, terrorist prevention training, undercover work ... there were so many ways to develop as a police officer. They'd had a talk from an officer who trained people under the reasonable-force legislation and he'd stood there, at the very front of the lecture theater. The officer said one of the most interesting sentences Ryan had ever heard in his life: "Coppers, when it comes down to it, can be pretty neatly divided into two types: those who can kill when they need to, and those who can't."

The hairs on Ryan's arms had raised up. Which was he? Could he do it, pull a trigger, if the situation dictated it?

And so, today, thinking about that interesting lecture, it is doubly disappointing to be told by Jamie that not only is he being taken off response calls to do research but also that there are no spare offices for him: they have set a desk up in the cleaner's cupboard for him, will that be okay? Ryan is happy to work in a cupboard, yes, but doing *what*?

He looks around it. It's freezing. No heating, and it's cold outside. Gray linoleum floor. Rows of shelving, a desk moved in temporarily with a letter rack on it. A corkboard and a mop bucket lean against the wall. That's it. To be fair, they did remove the rest of the cleaning stuff.

Leo arrives in the cupboard, looking harassed. "God, how small is this room?" he says. "None of the cells free?" He carelessly grabs a sheet of paper sitting in the letter rack. It's lined, and he turns it over to the plain side. "All right. Shut that door," he says to Jamie, who steps away from it.

Finally, Ryan is going to get an explanation. "So –" he begins to say.

"This is what we know." Leo talks over him in that way that he does. "There are two different organized-crime operations trading in this area, right? They overlap but, roughly speaking, one is nicking cars and one is importing drugs. The money from both is then funneled." He dots a ballpoint pen on the paper, then draws an arrow upward. "We have the names from surveillance of three suppliers who we haven't yet arrested. But we're looking for the importers – one rung above them."

Ryan nods eagerly. "Yep, I understand all that."

"Right, anyway, next," Leo continues. "The gang consists of two arms – drugs and thefts. The drugs come in, but the same port workers turn a blind eye to what goes out, which is the other arm: stolen cars. Other men, we think" – he draws a box away from the arrows, the pen dragging across the paper – "are stealing cars. They take them overnight, get them to the port, then they're gone, before the owners are even awake, to the Middle East. They then launder the money. The two ops never cross."

"Obviously," Ryan says.

"Is it – obvious?"

"My brother . . ."

"Yes, the brother," Leo says. "Tell us more about the brother." He sits forward, his eyes shining strangely.

"I did disclose him to HR and vetting," Ryan says, panicking.

Leo makes an impatient gesture. "I know. I waved it through. I'm not suspicious. It's *helpful* to us – your brother. Who better to work out the who's who of a gang than someone who's witnessed how these people operate?"

"I see . . ." Ryan says slowly.

"So – would his ops be separate, too?"

"Yes, always. Like, you'd never use a stolen car to import drugs. You'd get nicked immediately."

"Right," Leo says. "Right. Can you tell us more about him? He was quite a lot older than you – right? But same dad?" Question after question after question.

"Don't mind Leo," Jamie says drily. "He has a one-track mind when he gets going."

"Answers, please," Leo says.

"Yes," Ryan says. "Okay, well . . . a fair bit older than me, yes. He got mixed up in some stuff. I don't know, we were quite . . . we were quite angry, I guess. He's always – we both always – have had this ambition. But his became a bit misguided. He needed money, and he started dealing drugs."

"What drugs? Just so we can talk – you know. Skill sets."

"Well – he just . . . er, he just progressed in a totally clichéd way. Puff, then coke, then gear."

"Did he bring the gear home?" Leo watches Ryan intently.

"Sometimes."

"Did you see it?"

"I mean, yeah," Ryan says, blinking.

"If we had some gear now, how would you open it?"

"Like a cracker," Ryan says, without even having to think about it.

"Exactly!" Leo exclaims. He thumps the table. Leo frightens Ryan. He might indeed be one of those crazy-genius types. Or he might just be mad.

"I helped him a lot. It invades your life, gear, doesn't it? I was curious. In the end" – Ryan gives a despairing laugh – "I was fucking cutting it with him."

"Good. Good knowledge to have."

Ryan says nothing, about as confused as he's ever been.

Leo glances at Jamie, then speaks. "We'll have a job for you, after your research," Leo says. He picks his tea up and finishes it in three noisy gulps. He places it on the table. "If you're interested."

"Very," Ryan says, looking directly at Leo.

"We need someone brainy. Know why? This gang has probably got a nerd in it. Right? Someone who's working stuff out for them. Some sort of foot soldier."

"Okay."

"So we need our own nerd," Leo says, reaching over to touch Ryan lightly on the shoulder, "to analyze that information. Not only that, we need a nerd who actually knows how this shit works. We know three of the dealers, but none of the car thieves. We need their names, faces, how they relate to each other. A big old family tree of crime. You up for that?" He gestures to the corkboard. "So your task is to watch every minute of that CCTV and see who brings the cars. Okay?"

"Oh right, yeah," Ryan says. He becomes aware of his heartbeat. A strong, clean, excited thudding in his chest.

"Then when we know who they are and their movements, we'll catch them in the act. You know — as close to entrapment as we can while staying legal," he says easily.

Even Ryan's arms and legs feel excited, as if he could get up and do star jumps. Finally, something that fucking matters. Something that he might be good at. Something where he could change the world.

Leo grabs the corkboard and sets it on the desk. Ryan loves the drama of it. The cut and thrust of policing. Here he is: home. Leo pins the piece of paper on the board and on it he writes a name. "This bloke works at the port. And he's bent. Turns a blind eye and allows stolen cars on. We got him on the very corner of CCTV. Haven't nicked him yet as we want to see what sort of cog he is in the machine. All right?"

Ryan looks at the paper pinned up there: Ezra Michaels.

"See who brings the cars to Ezra. Okay?" Leo says.

"And then . . ." Ryan says, looking up at Leo hopefully. "Once we know a bit more about them . . . I mean" — he gestures to Leo's scruffy clothes, to Jamie's hat — "I've got your department right, haven't I? Covert?"

"Yes," Leo says simply, communicating something that, until now, has remained unsaid. "Undercover."

Day Minus Thirteen, 19:00

A police car followed Todd home today. Jen is sure of it. She thinks of the car that drove past Clio's, twice.

It's the evening now, and Todd and Kelly are sitting opposite each other. The lamp on the breakfast bar is on, the sky a lit-up pewter beyond the doors.

The trees outside have more leaves on them. What just a few days ago was a thick collection on their patio is now a cluster of bright red flags, back in their spots on the trees.

"Good evening, squire," Todd addresses her. "We're talking about Schrödinger's cat."

Jen spent the morning at work, pretending to be normal. She had an initial meeting with a new client, who she knows tells her in a few meetings' time that she doesn't want to leave her husband, after all. Jen took far fewer notes this time.

Todd's eating a Chinese takeaway out of the box, like an American, except it isn't in a kitsch carton with chopsticks in it but a plastic Tupperware container. Bless his heart.

Kelly widens his eyes at Jen across the breakfast bar. "We are not," he says with a laugh. "*You* were. *I* was eating wings."

"I'm not sure Dad is your best audience," Jen says,

and she hears the perfect little amused exhale that is her husband's laugh.

"What happened with the Venus and Mars project?" Kelly asks.

Todd inches his phone out of his pocket and passes it to Kelly. The first time Jen lived this day, she was at work. Didn't know anything about this project.

Kelly reads Todd's phone for a few seconds, then says, "Ah – an A! A for astrophysics prodigy."

"A for Alexander Kuzemsky," Todd says.

"Can you speak English?" Jen asks.

"He is a great physicist," Todd says. "This assignment." He passes her his phone.

"Well done," she says sincerely. She starts to read the assignment with interest, partly wondering if it might contain some science that might help her, but Todd takes the phone off her.

"Really, don't worry about it."

"I'm interested!"

"You never usually are," Todd shoots back.

A guilty stone arrives in her stomach. Maternal guilt, that thing she has tried to work against for much of her life, but that always – always – sits there anyway. *You never usually are.*

"You all right?" Kelly says with a laugh. "You look like the Grim Reaper."

Todd snorts into his takeaway while Jen dishes hers out.

Kelly leaves the counter, his mobile ringing. She stares into the hallway, thinking about Todd.

"What do you mean?" she asks him.

"I mean – you don't usually pay attention to my stuff."

"Your stuff?" Jen says, the world feeling suddenly still. Todd says nothing, reaching for a chicken ball and eating it whole. "Do you think I don't listen to you?" she asks.

A hazy kind of awareness is descending on her, the way cloud cover does: you can't quite see it if you're in it, but you can feel it.

Todd seems to actively consider the answer, looking down at his plate, his brow furrowed. "Maybe," he says eventually.

He is still staring at her. Kelly's eyes. But everything else is hers. Dark, unruly hair, pale skin. Unbearably large appetite. She made him. And look: he thinks she doesn't listen to him. Just says it like it is a plain fact.

"It isn't interesting to you," he adds.

"Oh," she whispers.

"I care about physics," he says. "So it isn't funny that I care about Alexander Kuzemsky. I actually care about him."

Jen experiences the eerie feeling of being wrong in an argument. So totally wrong. Her mind performs gymnastics. This isn't about planets. This is about their relationship.

Todd with his fun science facts and his head in the clouds. Jen with her wry inability to understand what he is talking about. That's how she has always thought of them. She and Kelly couldn't believe they'd made such a cerebral child, clever in a totally different way to them, both so earthy, and Todd so . . . not. But he isn't *something made*. He isn't an object. Here he is, right in front of her, telling her who he is. She's let her own insecurities about being stupid turn his intellectualism into something to be laughed off. Laughed *at*.

"God." She puts her head in her hands. "All right. I see. I'm sorry. It's not – I'm so sorry," she finishes lamely.

"Okay," he says.

"Everything you do is interesting to me," she says, tears springing with the kind of reckless fatalism of somebody who won't be here tomorrow; a deathbed proclamation, a call from a hijacked plane. A woman who can connect and connect and connect with her son, but it doesn't matter, it won't last. "I have never loved any-body as much as I love you. Never will," she says plainly, her eyes wet. "I got it wrong. If I don't show you that. Because it is so true – it is the truest thing."

He blinks. His expression ripples into sadness, like a stone dropped into a pond. "Thank you," he says. "It's just – you know."

"I know," Jen says. "I know."

"Thank you," he says again.

"You're welcome," she says softly, just as Kelly strides in.

"I ate all the balls, because this last one's mine too," Todd says with a smile. The joke's a deflection, armor against their other family member witnessing this pri-vate moment, but Jen laughs anyway, too, though she wants to cry.

"That was a client," Kelly says needlessly. Jen glances back at Todd. He puts the final chicken ball in his mouth and smiles up at her with his eyes. She reaches over to tousle his hair, which he leans into, like a neglected animal.

Todd drops the Tupperware right into the bin, some-thing she would usually complain about but chooses not to, today.

"Where to tonight?" she asks him.

"Snooker." He does a chef's kiss in the air.

Jen nods quickly. "Well, have fun." Then she adds, "I'm going out too. Drink with Pauline."

"Are you?" Kelly says in surprise.

"Yeah, I did tell you." A lie. "Which venue?" she asks Todd, hoping to sound only curious.

"Crosby."

She smiles at him. Because, the reality is, wherever he goes, she will be there too.

The entrance to Crosby sports bar is an anonymous little black door on the high street. A retro neon sign above it. An England flag above that. It is a twenties building with mullioned windows, red bricks and three chimneys along the top.

Jen pulls up in a car park at the back shared by two restaurants, the sports bar and a Travelodge. As she gets out of her car, she smells chargrilled meat, pushed out into the autumn air by a vent somewhere. God, she's had a Chinese, but she could totally eat a burger.

She tries the door at the back of the bar, even though it looks like a fire door. It's jammed shut, locked. She goes to the front, peering through the glass, hands either side of her head. It's dark inside. She can't see anything at all. She could just stay here, she thinks, the glass cool-ing her forehead. She's so tired. She's so fucking tired. Let her just stay here and cease to exist. Let her become part of the snooker club, an ornament. Not a tortured, living, breathing human.

A light flicks on inside, red-toned, dim, illuminating what is right in front of her: stairs, painted black. Shabby, stained, old and, more importantly, empty.

She pushes open the door and ascends as quietly as she can. They lead to an empty landing, two closed doors either side of it. The perfect place to sit and listen. The perfect place to take a risk.

She holds her breath. After a few seconds, she hears the click of the balls. The thump of the end of a cue on to the floor.

A full-length art deco window sits behind her, letting in the glow of the streetlights. The floor is painted black, rickety old wooden floorboards that creak as she moves.

"Next week, for sure," Todd says. A click. He must have taken his shot. Jen leans over toward the hinge of the door and peers through, hoping nobody will see a single eye over here, in the darkness.

"Maybe we can go away next summer," Clio says. It's definitely Clio, her dreamy voice.

Todd moves back and forth in her vision. He holds his snooker cue like a staff, exactly the way a wizard in his favorite computer game holds it, his weight on it, his other hand on his hip. Jen's heart turns over in her chest as she gazes at him, her son. He is acting. She is sure of it.

His hair is coiffed, his trainers bright white, pacing slowly around the snooker table, moving in and out of view. He is in full bravado mode.

"If you're still together," a male voice says. Jen is pretty certain it's Joseph, though she can't see him.

"Sure we will be," Todd says. Nerves thrum in his voice. Jen can hear them, detectable only to her, like the shivering after a piano key is depressed.

"Good shot," another voice says, perhaps Ezra.

"Hope I'm not interrupting." This time, a female voice. Jen shifts so she can see. A woman has entered from a dark door at the other side of the snooker room. She's about Jen's own age, maybe slightly older. She has graying hair scraped back into a tidy ponytail. Her outfit looks casual, jogging bottoms and a T-shirt. She walks in an alert sort of way, full of verve, like an athlete.

"Nicola," Joseph says. "A nice surprise."

Nicola. Jen just about manages not to gasp.

"Long time no see."

"Indeed." Joseph walks into view, leaning on the cue. Nicola follows him. "This is Todd, and Clio. And you know Ezra. Nicola used to work for us."

"Nicola Williams, one and the same," Ezra says.

Jen frowns, sitting there on the steps, listening to this play out. Todd is being *introduced* to Nicola. But Todd has already texted Nicola. Hasn't he? She runs over the dates in the phone messages. Yes, he has. He *has.* He texted her on the fifteenth, saying *Nice to chat.* Today is the sixteenth. But he meets her on the seventeenth. Doesn't he?

Jen shifts as quietly as possible, straining her eyes, looking past the lit-green of the snooker table, and beyond. On the red plush sofa attached to the far wall is Clio. Golden legs, short fringe, the lot. Jen blinks, just watching, waiting for the small talk to end.

"Room for a little one?" Nicola says. She grabs the cue off Todd, who sits down. It seems like a perfectly normal outing. Todd's girlfriend, her family. But Nicola's appearance has set something off, perhaps because Jen knows Todd's lying, perhaps not. There is some sinister undercurrent now, like a shark in the water.

Jen shifts again to look at Todd sitting on the bench with Clio. He isn't as close to her as he was the other night. But, nevertheless, he's with her. So, what – does he end it tonight?

Music kicks in from nowhere. Big, bass-led rap that drowns out their voices. Jen peers and sees that it's coming from a jukebox she hadn't noticed, a red retro-looking one with white lights surrounding the display.

She sits for the duration of the song, hoping it'll stop, but another kicks in. Todd is talking to Joseph, and Clio stands and joins them too, with Nicola, but Jen can't hear a thing. She can only watch it play out. Something that looks like casual conversation, but Todd is uncomfortable, she can tell. She can tell by the way he walks toe to heel around the table, a pacing lion.

Suddenly, Jen realizes the music isn't accidental. It's to drown anyone else out. Any eavesdroppers like her – and others, she thinks, remembering the circling police.

After an hour, Joseph puts on a coat. Todd cleans up, potting the balls effortlessly himself. As Joseph leaves with Nicola, Jen dives through the door on her left, which she discovers leads to the toilets. She stands there in a retro-decorated bathroom alone, listening for footsteps.

The bathroom has vintage wallpaper up, pink clamshells, the texture gone fuzzy with age. Two wooden boxes of toiletries sit between the two sinks, also pink, and a gilded full-length mirror hangs on the wall.

She leans against the sinks and thinks about what she knows:

Todd meets Clio in August.

They're currently still together but, by tomorrow, he's gone off her. But then five days before the crime, they're back together.

Yesterday, he asked Nicola for some sort of help.

Today, Nicola shows up at the snooker club. He pretends not to know her. She clearly knows Clio's uncle, used to *work for him.*

In a few days, a blond kid steals a car for Ezra. Clio's family are clearly criminals. The Chanel bag. And, in a few more days, Nicola is injured. And then Todd becomes a killer.

She stares outside, considering this timeline of events. The window is open, letting in a steady stream of cool night air. She waits at least ten minutes before considering leaving, then hears a low voice, laughter, outside. Without thinking, she climbs on to the unit holding the two sinks, her knees painful on the hard surface, and peers out through the crack. It's Todd. He's on the phone. He has reached his car, parked out the back. He leans his elbows on the roof – he's so tall – as he talks animatedly.

She strains to hear. It's quiet out. She should be able to listen. She reaches to her side to switch the light out, so she can sit here, once again unseen at yet another window.

"I almost called your secret phone. I'm trying to phase Clio out," he is saying. "Don't worry. Your dirty work is safe with me." His tone is acidic, like a lemon.

A pause. Jen stops breathing. "Yeah – I mean, who

knows," he adds. She has no idea who he is talking to, can't gauge it. It isn't a mate. Isn't an equal.

Todd laughs again, a sort of hard laugh, bitter and sardonic. "*No.* That's just what I was trying to say. We're at the end of the line, aren't we?" He tilts his head back, looking up at the heavens. The moon is out, a pale hologram in the sky. The temperature is dropping. Jen is cold, kneeling there on the sinks, listening to her son, who seems to think they're *at the end of the line*. What does that curiously adult expression mean? Is this why, in just under two weeks, he kills?

He moves his gaze down, like he's watching a ball slowly drop, and looks straight at Jen's window. She can't look away, as their eyes meet, but he moves his gaze quickly away. He can't have seen her. The glass is frosted, the light is out.

"Yeah, okay," Todd says.

Another pause.

"Ask Nicola. See you at home," Todd says into the phone.

The world seems to stop, just for a second. See you at home. See you at home. See you at home.

That can only be one person: her husband.

Day Minus Thirteen, 20:40

Todd gets into his car, revs the engine and drives away, leaving Jen alone in the dark bathroom, her knees damp from the water sitting on the side.

See you at home.

The person on the end of that phone is Kelly.

Ask Nicola.

Kelly knows Nicola. Not Todd. Todd wasn't lying when he was introduced to her.

I almost called your secret phone.

It is Kelly to whom the burner phone belongs. It is Kelly who texted Nicola.

"You were just on the phone to Todd," Jen says the second she storms through the front door. Todd isn't home yet. Perhaps he caught up with Clio again. And Jen can't wait. Who cares? She has no tomorrow. She's got to ask him now.

Kelly is wearing faded jeans and a white T-shirt. He is sitting on their velvet sofa. They put it in the bay window in their living room. It fits exactly, not even a centimeter of wiggle room. They had laughed so much as they tried to thump it into place. Kelly had suggested they use lube and Jen hadn't been able to stop giggling.

She drops her handbag on to the wooden floor. The house is quiet, the lamps on low.

Kelly apparently needs a moment to think. Those three seconds break Jen's fucking heart.

"I know he's involved in something dodgy – and so do you," she says.

Evidently, Kelly decides to go for an outright denial. "He's having women trouble." Kelly's eyes don't change at all as he speaks these words, these lies. "Jen?" He reaches for her.

"I heard you," she says.

"We talked about Clio."

"Who's Nicola?"

"What? I don't know a Nicola."

"Kelly," she says, the word exploding out of her. "I know you know them. Who is Joseph Jones?"

"No idea," Kelly says quickly, not missing a beat. He busies himself, standing and turning on the overhead light, her enigmatic husband. Mysterious – or a liar? "Sorry – I don't know what you mean?" he says, turning to her.

As he does, she sees the glimmer of sweat around his hairline catching the light for just a second. "I know you're lying," she says to his back as he begins to retreat again. Now he's putting shoes on, a coat.

"This is not up for discussion," he says. He opens the front door and leaves the house, the frame shaking as he slams it behind him.

Ryan

Ryan is in his element. Ryan is finally good at something.

He has in front of him, just like in the movies, a bigger corkboard that he ordered from Supplies three days ago. It's four feet long by three feet tall (he doesn't yet have authority to put it up). It's resting against the wall and Ryan is sitting, cross-legged, in front of it.

He's been gathering his surveillance information for two months. He began by wheeling a TV into his cupboard. For hours, through bleary eyes, he reviewed the CCTV of the port. Tape after tape after tape, evenings and weekends. He watched carefully, jotting down anybody who visited more than once, anybody who talked to Ezra, or who disappeared with him. Ryan made notes on Post-its and then pinned them to the board.

By the end of the month, he had a list of regulars.

"Can you match these faces to any on the system?" he asked a passing analyst one Friday night. He pointed at the faces he'd freeze-framed and printed.

"On it," the analyst said, just like that.

And now he's got them: his foot soldiers.

The undercover team have provided him with the names of the drugs suppliers now, too. An undercover officer has infiltrated the gang. He went in as a test purchaser. Dressed up scruffy, as Leo put it, asked for gear.

The transaction went ahead, observed by Leo's team, and he reported back with the name of the dealer, who goes now on to Ryan's board.

He did it five more times. Five more test purchases. And then he said he'd moved house, he knew a few people who'd buy, wanted to trial supplying a patch. The dealer introduced him to the supplier, whose name also went on to Ryan's board.

"Ryan," Leo says, striding into his cupboard. "You're a certified genius."

This is the best job Ryan's ever had. The most fun. The most satisfying. And the most autonomous, too. He feels a bubble of pride rise up through him, for him and his corkboard.

"This is just the start," he says to Leo. "It's just part of the picture. The top guy has about ten different ops running."

They look at the corkboard together in silence.

Leo says nothing for a minute, maybe more. One of the other officers walks past the cupboard. "Got a sec?" he says to Leo, poking his head around the door.

"No," Leo barks, closing the door. Life feels good when you're in Leo's sunlight, terrible if you're in his shadow, like so many people in charge.

"On our last job," Leo says thoughtfully, as though this exchange has not taken place, "the guy at the top was so unassuming. So normal. Just normal. Stayed under the radar. You know, didn't have a proper job – was self-employed. Stayed under the tax threshold. Didn't travel."

"Seems impossible," Ryan says.

"Right, anyway, look at this, please," he says. "We have been creating a *legend*." He sits down creakily on the chair as Ryan unpins the various foot soldiers and moves them across. "Maybe we should get you a better office," he says through a laugh.

"That'd be nice . . ."

"Okay, so, legends. Ready for a lesson?"

"Ready."

"When officers go undercover, they step into a persona that we have already created, long ago, right?"

"Okay."

"So if someone was buying gear, the crims *always* suspect the DS. Drugs squad. So we create a legend in advance. He lives here, he drives this car, he works here, he does this. We have *history*, right? It goes anywhere we can get it – online, wherever. Then he steps into it. And so we are working on one now."

He rubs at his jowls, then sips Ryan's tea, which offends Ryan, but he doesn't say anything. Leo does things like this when he's thinking. And Leo is brilliant when he's thinking, so everybody puts up with it.

"Leo," Jamie says, pushing the door open. He looks harassed, his hair standing on end. "Got an issue."

"What?" Leo is fiddling with one of Ryan's pins, which he shoves back into the board. "Can people stop fucking interrup –"

"Last night two of the foot soldiers stole a car on one of the posh estates in Wallasey," Jamie says. "We've had a report in."

"Okay . . ."

"Rumor has it they thought it was one of the unoccupied houses they targeted, but it wasn't . . ."

Ryan swivels his head to look at Jamie.

"There was a baby in the back of the car. They took it. The car is headed for the port – with the baby in the back."

Day Minus Twenty-two, 18:30

Jen is in her sanctuary, the office. She wanted to be here, at work, in this calm, organized environment she is fully in control of, or at least can pretend that she is. The knowledge that Kelly is involved keeps repeating on her. She feels like she's on a boat, the ground underfoot uncertain and slippery. Kelly. Her Kelly. The man she can tell anything to. But, evidently, that doesn't work both ways. How could he have pretended to work this through with her on that night that he believed her?

The street down below is dotted with people shopping, enjoying the last of the summer warmth. Early October looks different to late. Gingerbread light outside. Honey-colored leaves. The last gasp of summer. She opens the window. Only the tiniest bite of cold laces the air: like a single drop of dye in water that will soon spread.

She sighs and wanders down the corridor. She renovated the premises after her father died last spring. What was once his office – the plaque said *Managing Partner*, like he wanted – is now the kitchenette, a decision she made so she didn't have to look at his old door or, worse, work in there herself.

Her father had been a good lawyer. Incisive, cautious, able to accept and confront bad news without kidding himself. Tough, she'd describe him as, with the hindsight of grief. Stoic, too. At the end of a working week, once, she'd found out that he had slept there two nights, to get the job done, and had never said.

She is now much further back than she anticipated. Jen thinks her biggest fear is that she is going to pass the inception of the crime. She wishes she could ask her father what to do. Kenneth Charles Eagles. He'd gone by the name KC. If Jen and Kelly had had a daughter, they would have called her Kacie. KC. He'd have liked that.

He'd died alone, eighteen months ago. An aneurysm, sometime in the evening. He'd sat in his armchair, a bag of peanuts and a bottle of half-drunk beer by his side. Jen, in the early days, had to turn her mind away from his last moments, like trying to steer a ship with a preference for one way only. She is more able to look at it, now, to stand here in the spot where he once did. But, today more than ever, she misses him. He'd have no sympathy for time-travel theories — she'd have been too afraid to tell him, she thinks, fearing judgment — but she still misses him in the way that children will always miss their parents' guiding hands, the way they can hold your problems away from you, if only temporarily.

She makes a cup of tea then leaves the kitchenette. Rakesh walks by her office with another lawyer, Sara.

"The husband asked us to halve her maintenance budget to account for the fact that she only ever wears sweatpants. He's crossed off any allowance for clothing. Plus haircuts, and bras. He's annotated it to say she wears old, graying underwear," Sara is saying.

Rakesh's disbelieving laughter rings out like a church bell.

Jen smiles wanly. She's always felt so at home here with the workaholics and the gallows humor.

She sends a few emails, happily passing on pieces of information, giving advice. The stuff she could do with her eyes closed, the things she's done for two decades.

The soon-to-be-ex-husband of one of Jen's clients couriers over twenty-five boxes of his accounts at seven o'clock in the evening. Jen receives them from a jaded DPD driver with a T-shirt tan. Last time, she'd stayed to start going through them, indexing their contents and stacking the boxes neatly in her office. Rakesh had poked his head around the door and asked if she was building a fort.

He passes now, at the exact same time. But, today, not wanting to sort boxes, but not wanting to go home either, she asks if he fancies a drink.

"For sure," he says, chewing gum. "What's all this? You building a fort?"

Jen smiles to herself. It's getting harder and harder to remember each day, the further she goes back. It's nice to hear her predictions come true, in a funny kind of way.

"I will be on Monday," she says. "Disclosure from the other side. The husband's accounts."

"What does he do, work for the Bank of fucking England?"

"Classic tactics," Jen says, shifting a box just so she can find a path to him. "Send so many boxes he hopes nobody will ever look."

"I'll make sure you're not buried alive under it, on Monday. I need wine in an IV," Rakesh says, grabbing her coat for her.

"Bad day?"

"I sent a petition off to my client today. To sign — nothing more. Next to count four of unreasonable behavior she's written — in pen — *also wanked into socks all the time*. Like this was some urgent addition. I need to re-send them to her now. We can't file that at court."

"A fair complaint," Jen says. "Nice detail on the socks."

"You're not the one who has to see him at the trial."

"Don't follow him into the bathroom."

As they leave, coats slung on arms in the now very, very early autumn, it's so nice to be back here, at work, where people spend some of the most intimate hours of their lives. She's worked with Rakesh for over a decade. She knows he eats potatoes most lunchtimes and gets bogged down in the *Daily Mail* website during his three o'clock slump. She knows he mouths *Fuck off* whenever his phone rings and that he once sweated through his own trousers during a particularly tricky hearing, says he left a mark on the chair.

And so it's nice, too, tonight, to step out of the detritus of her family life. To leave the mystery, and to innocently anticipate a glass of wine with her old friend, to discuss their clients warring over who fucked someone else first, to drink two glasses — no, three — to smoke cigarettes out in the beer garden and laugh about it. It's so, so very nice to pretend.

Jen has had too much wine to drive and so she walks home. It's just after nine o'clock. She is weaving along the pavement, looking up at her lit-up house just ahead, and thinking about her husband, whom she has told she is working late.

She's a divorce lawyer, she is thinking morosely, and yet she missed her own betrayal. Didn't see it coming whatsoever. Not a bit.

She tries to re-jig the events into shape, knowing what she knows now. The wine has helped to loosen her mind. It feels elastic and free in the chilly night. For once, she feels broad-minded and open, not neurotic and closed.

The burner phone belongs to Kelly. So the missing baby poster and the police ID must belong to him, too. But why were they in Todd's room?

She hears voices as she approaches her house. They're coming from outside, somewhere in the open air. They're too loud to be inside. She stops by Kelly's car. It gives off some heat. She places a hand on the bonnet: just been driven.

The voices belong to her husband and son, the very subject of her thoughts, and they're yelling, urgent.

They're in the back garden. Jen hurries as quietly as she can to the gate. She stops there, a finger on the cool black latch, immediately absolutely stone-cold sober.

"Why have you told me this?" Todd says. Jen is disturbed to hear that his voice is laced with panicked tears.

"Because I have to ask something of you," Kelly says. "All right? I wouldn't tell you otherwise."

"What?"

"You have to break up with Clio."

"What?"

"You have to," Kelly says. "I can ask Nicola for help, but you cannot continue to see Clio. Given everything."

Jen's stomach rolls over. She is suddenly nauseous, and it has nothing to do with the drink.

"That will arouse even more suspicion," Todd says. "Let alone fucking break my *fucking* heart."

Jen feels like her knees are going to give way. The pain, the pain, the pain in her baby boy's voice.

"I'm sorry," Kelly says. "I'm sorry – I'm sorry. I'm sorry. How many times can I say it?"

"This is the most fucked-up thing that has ever happened to me," Todd says. Only he doesn't merely say it: it's a scream. A scream of anguish.

Something thumps, a fist on a table, maybe. "I tried!" Kelly says. His voice is hoarse, ragged at the edges with emotion. Jen has heard this side of him only a handful of times. Once in the station, after Todd's arrest. No wonder. He's trying to stop it. And – clearly – doesn't manage. "I tried so hard. Joseph either knows or is about to find out, Todd, and we've got to extract ourselves from him. Without him knowing why."

"Collateral be damned, right?" Todd says. "*Me.*" Jen thinks of how Clio wouldn't discuss the breakup with her, and wonders if, somehow, Todd has told Clio something about this conversation. Something he shouldn't have.

"Right," Kelly says softly, and Jen wants to step away from her position at the gate, cold and alone, and go and shake her husband. That was rhetorical, she'd say. Todd was not offering that up to you, you complete idiot.

"There is no indication that he knows," Todd says.

"The second he does, he will come here, and he will . . ."

"That's a hypothetical. I can't believe you have involved me in this. Lies? Kidnapped kids?"

Jen's entire body goes still, covered in goosebumps. The baby.

"It's this or much, much worse," Kelly says, an inky-black note to his voice.

"Oh yeah, keep it secret at all costs. Sail me and my first love up the river!" Todd shouts. The back door slams. Feet on stairs inside.

Jen stays at the gate, trying to breathe.

It's pointless asking them. Clearly, they will lie. And clearly, too, there is a secret at the heart of their relationship that they will do anything to keep. They will do anything, except tell Jen.

In the cool night air, three weeks before her son becomes a murderer, Jen hears her husband begin to cry in their garden, his sobs becoming quieter and quieter, like a wounded animal slowly dying.

Day Minus Forty-Seven, 08:30

A lot can happen in three weeks. It is the biggest jump back so far.

Eight thirty in the morning, Day Minus Forty-Seven. Nearly seven weeks back in total.

Jen stops at the picture window on her way downstairs. The street looks completely different. The sepia-brown of late summer, grasses parched from lack of rain. The breeze against her arms is warm. She wonders what Andy would make of it.

She went to bed last night with Kelly. He did an admirable job of acting normally. You wouldn't know anything had happened unless you'd overheard it.

He'd been lying on their bed, hands behind his head, elbows out to the side. A caricature of a relaxed husband. "Work good?" he'd said.

"Full of documents. What'd you do?"

"Oh, you know," he had said. "Showered, dinner, scintillating stuff."

She remembers this line from last time. She had thought Kelly was just being dry, but sitting underneath his words last night was a kind of quivering fury. A man who had lost control of a situation.

She'd gone to sleep next to him, her husband the betrayer, because she didn't know what else to do. He'd spooned her as he always did, his body warm. Once he

173

was asleep, she'd looked at the skin on his arms. His – like hers – didn't look any different, but he was made of different stuff to what she had thought.

And now it is forty-seven days back. She feels utterly alienated again, like she did in those first few days. She has pink nail polish on her toes that she remembers getting done halfway through August, to see her through the final, warm, flip-flop days.

It's mid-September. And what does she know? Kelly thinks Joseph is going to find something out, so he asked Todd to stop seeing Clio. He does, but then gets back together with her. Kelly asks Nicola Williams for help. Nicola is injured, and then Joseph shows up and Todd kills him.

Jen knows more than she did but, in many ways, it feels like less, it's so confusing. The doorbell goes, interrupting her thoughts.

She checks the date again. Right – it's the first day back at school, Todd's first in Year Thirteen. She tries to spring herself back into action.

"Who's that?" she calls.

"Clio!" Todd says. Jen leaps back from the window and into her bedroom. Did this happen the last time? Eight thirty . . . she'd have left already. Suited, booted, a typical weekday, latte in hand, divorces at the ready. But here, in the hub of family life, lies the secret. *If he finds out, he'll come here.* That's what Kelly said.

"I'll get it!" Jen calls. Even though she's in a tatty and ancient pair of maternity shorts – fucking hell, couldn't she have worn something nicer to bed back in

174

September? – and a T-shirt through which you can definitely see her boobs, she is going to answer that door. She pulls on a dressing gown and takes the stairs two at a time.

"Hi," Clio says. And there she is. The woman her son has fallen in love with, breaks up with, gets back together with. Is forced to leave by his father. The woman – surely – at the heart of it.

Jen doesn't know what to ask first.

"Jen, right?" Clio says. She – charmingly – reaches out to shake Jen's hand. Her fingers are long and tanned from the summer, her grip loose, her skin dry, but soft, still childlike. She looks, otherwise, the same as in October. That fringe, those huge eyes, the whites of them shining healthily.

"Yes, nice to meet you," Jen says.

"I don't start back until tomorrow, but I said I'd walk with Todd," Clio explains.

"That's quite enough," Todd says. His backpack is over his shoulders just like it was when he was five, eight, twelve. He, too, is tanned. Much healthier-looking than in October. Less burdened. Jen can't stop looking at him, thinking of his tears last night, his fury. An explosive argument, and now this: a huge leap backward. What does it mean?

Kelly emerges out of the kitchen but stops when he sees Jen. "Are you off work?" he says to her. "I didn't want to wake you . . ."

"I think I'm sick," she says spontaneously. "I turned my alarm off. Throat like razor blades."

"Bunk off. Sod the lawyers," Kelly says.

"An astounding lack of work ethic from the Dad there," Todd commentates.

Kelly turns his gaze to Todd. "Work hard enough and, one day, you too can bunk off," he says.

This phrase isn't what makes Jen stop, makes her wish she could press pause to absorb this moment. It's the look that passes between Kelly and Todd. Pure affection. There is nothing barbed under it whatsoever. Their eyes are alight.

When was the last time she saw them interact like this? She can't remember.

Todd reaches out to shove him, a mock shove. Jen's gaze lands on them.

Throughout her entire career she has always looked for the absence of things as well as their presence. Evidence is often in what people don't say. What they take out. The man who fiddles his accounts, trying to bury huge personal profit in twenty-five boxes of disclosure that he hopes the lawyers won't be bothered to go through.

But she missed it at home. The lack of this easy banter. A clue in itself.

That is why she's on this day, she thinks. To observe the contrast. The argument she overheard at the gate changed something for them, fractured it. And here she is, before it. And don't things look completely different?

"Anyway, nice to meet you," Clio says to Jen as Todd ushers her out.

"Nice to see you again," she adds, looking at Kelly. And it's this sentence that turns Jen's attention away from Clio, and on to Kelly.

Her eyes meet her husband's as Todd closes the door

behind him. She doesn't hear his car: they must be walking in the sun together. "Nice to see you *again?*" she asks him.

"Huh?" He's turned away from her, is heading into the kitchen. She reaches out for him. It's legitimate. It's perfectly legitimate to ask this, why Clio would say that to him, she tells herself. But why does she feel the need to think this way? She pauses. Because her husband can be evasive, comes the answer, from somewhere deep within her.

"Have you met Clio before?"

"Yeah, she came for lunch with Todd one day."

"Did she?"

"Only for about five minutes. Think I interrogated her," he says with a charming smile. She can tell he's thinking fast.

"You never said. You never said you'd met her."

Kelly gives a laconic shrug. "Didn't think it was important."

"But you knew it would be important to me," she says. She hardly ever challenges her husband in this way. She's always wanted to be . . . she doesn't know. Easygoing. Easy to live with. "You know I've wondered what she's like." She almost adds that she knows he knows her uncle's friend. That, later, he asks Todd to stop seeing her, but she stops herself. He will only lie.

"She's nice," he says. The more she pushes, the more he dodges. She's never noticed before, this quickstepping of his. Answering a different question. Answering the original question. He goes into the kitchen and opens a can of Coke. The pop of the ring pull sounds like a gunshot, which makes her jump.

*

Jen considers what to do, then gets dressed, pulling her trainers on. "Going to get something for my throat," she calls.

"I'll go!" Kelly says, considerate as ever. "Or wait – don't we have that stuff that –"

"It's fine," she says, slamming the front door behind her before he can object.

She drives to the school then waits in a side-street, watching for Todd and Clio to appear. They do after only five minutes, *Truman Show*–like, holding hands, their long limbs catching the sun. Clio is wearing a khaki boiler suit that Jen would look like a fat janitor in. Todd is in skinny jeans, no socks, trainers and a white T-shirt. They look like a wholesome advert for vitamins or something.

Jen is going to offer Clio a lift home, and try to pretend she isn't insane for having followed them here.

She waits for Clio to see Todd in. But first, of course, they kiss. She shouldn't be looking, a creep in a car, but she can't stop. Their bodies are pressed together from their feet to their lips, right the way up, like somebody has sealed them. She watches for a second, thinking about Kelly. They still do kiss in this way, sometimes. He is good at that. Maintaining their chemistry, holding her interest. But, nevertheless, it isn't the same.

When they finally part, Todd loping off with a smirk and a swagger, Jen leaves the side-street and pulls up alongside Clio.

"I was passing," she says. "You want a lift?"

Confusion crosses Clio's features. "You're not on your way to work?" she says. She has one foot on the pavement, one dangling off the curb as she looks at Jen in indecision. God, Jen feels like some sort of evil perpetrator, picking up her son's girlfriend, but . . . five minutes in the car where she can ask her anything. It's too tantalizing to pass up.

"No, no. Came to drop off something for Todd. Heading back now."

"Well, sure," Clio says happily. Jen is sort of glad to note that Clio is an appeaser, just like Jen herself is. Clio could easily draw a boundary here, but she doesn't. Instead, she gets in beside Jen. She smells of toothpaste – perhaps Todd's, Jen thinks darkly – and deodorant. A wholesome sort of smell. She has the trousers of her boiler suit rolled up, revealing smooth, tanned, slim ankles. Jen looks at them, feeling a wave of nostalgia for *back then*, whenever that is; some unknown time. When she went to pubs, when she kissed boys, when she was slim (never). When she had it all in front of her.

"Where to?" Jen says. She doesn't explain her presence at the gate any further. In some ways, Jen is taking inspiration from her husband, who has been so good at lying that his secrets have been hidden in plain sight. There have been no over-explanations, no details at all, in fact. Only a complete lack of them. The best kind of liar. The smartest.

"It's Appleby Road," Clio says. A road behind Eshe Road North. Makes sense.

"Oh, so you don't live at Eshe Road?" Jen asks lightly as she indicates and pulls away.

"No, no," Clio says, but she looks surprised that Jen knows her address. That's right: Jen has never been there.

Is never supposed to have been there. "Just me and Mum at Appleby." Clio doesn't elaborate, the same as last time.

Jen glances quickly at her as she comes to a stop at a roundabout. Their eyes meet for just a second.

Clio breaks contact, gets her phone out of her jeans pocket, angling her hips up to slide it out. "Kelly must think I live on Eshe Road," Clio says with a laugh.

Jen tries not to react. "Why?"

"I'm always there, aren't I?" She pauses. "Kelly and Ezra and Joseph – they go way back, don't they?"

"Right, right, yes," Jen says. "Sorry – so did he . . . did Kelly introduce you to Todd, then?"

"Yes, exactly," she says. "Well – when I came with Joe to drop something off for Kelly, Todd answered the door . . . and then . . . has he never said?"

"Do you know – Kelly has so many friends," Jen says: a sentence which is the exact opposite of the truth, "I plain forgot."

Clio turns her gaze to the left and looks out of the passenger window, not understanding the significance of the information she's imparted.

Bewildered, Jen spends the rest of the trip in silence. She drops Clio at her mother's house, who comes out on to the drive and waves at Jen. She looks nothing like Clio. Clio must look like her father, just like Todd does.

Two hours later, Jen is doing yoga for the first time in her entire life, a grotesque kind of downward dog in Kelly's car, her head underneath the seats, her arse somewhere near the neighbor's windows, it feels like.

Jen needs to find the burner phone again, the one she

now thinks belongs to Kelly. She wants to use it to call Nicola.

And so this is what she is doing, while he's out running.

But there's nothing in his car. A few old coffee cups, a jack, an unopened bottle of Sprite. In a funny kind of way, she is glad he hasn't hidden the phone in here, under the seats or with the spare tire in the trunk. Kelly is never drawn to cliché, and she likes this, that he is not behaving exactly like every dishonest man before him. Like she still knows him, somewhere underneath the mess.

She shakes her head and walks back into the house, where she continues her search. Tool bags, the airing cupboard, old coats. Anywhere.

He arrives back later and she stops abruptly, trying to tidy away some of the mess she's made. While he showers, she grabs his regular phone and turns on Find My iPhone to track him. She'll have to do it every morning, because she is traveling backward in time, but so be it. She will do whatever it takes.

It's five to eight in the evening. Kelly and Jen haven't eaten yet. Jen is biding her time, waiting to confront Kelly about – well, everything, really. She's just working out what to start with.

Todd is upstairs, on his Xbox. Jen can hear the noises of his games playing out like thunder and lightning above them.

"Do you ever think he's getting a bit – insular?" Jen says. She's sitting on one of the bar stools while Kelly leans his elbows on the kitchen counter, looking at her.

"Nah, no way," he says. "I was the same at his age."

"Computer games?"

"Well – you know. I hate to break it to you, but he will be on porn sites." Kelly raises his hands, palms to Jen. It's so easy. How is it so easy to interact with him in this way, their shared humor that they've always had? In the café, back on that first date, Kelly had been so quiet, so guarded, but by the end of the evening he had laughed her into bed.

"What – while the war rages on in *Call of Duty*?"

"Of course. Headphones in for the porn. *Call of Duty* on as a decoy." He gets up and turns to the cupboards, opening and closing them listlessly. "We have no food."

"I've just lost my appetite."

"Oh, stop. It's perfectly *natural*, Jennifer."

"What, watching women with fake tits have fake orgasms?"

"It taught me well." Kelly turns and raises an eyebrow at her and, despite, despite, despite everything, Jen feels her stomach burn. That dark little look, just for her. He's been a good husband, or so she had thought. Not exactly ambitious, somewhat unfulfilled at times, but interesting, layered, sexy. Isn't that what she always wanted?

"I could go for a curry," he adds, evidently thinking about food as she is deconstructing their marriage in her mind.

She hears a phone vibrate. The kind of noise she would usually tune out, it's so ubiquitous in their house. Kelly unconsciously puts his hand to his front pocket but, as he turns, she sees that his iPhone is in his back pocket. She watches him closely. Two phones. Both on his body. She never would have noticed. Why would she? The burner phone is small, like a pebble. He wears his jeans loose, low slung, always has.

Jen draws her head back in a reverse nod, appraising him. "Sure," she says. The Indian takeaway is a restaurant three streets up from theirs. They love it, even though it is expensive (perhaps because). It is entirely made of wooden cladding, like something from Center Parcs, and is beautifully lit. Jen and Kelly say they can never eat in there because the waiters have seen them pick up takeaway in loungewear (pajamas) so often.

"I'll go," he says.

Yes, this is right, isn't it? He went out, came home carrying joyous scented bags of Indian food. Had he been back later than she'd expected? She doesn't think so. God, not everything is a fucking clue, is it?

"I'll come."

"Nah. I'll go. You relax. Watch some porn," he throws over his shoulder as he leaves. She can hear him laughing as he opens the front door. As though nothing whatsoever is amiss.

He's either taking a call or meeting someone. That's what Jen concludes. And so, right after he's left, she heads to the picture window to watch him go. She leaves the light off. She stands there, invisible, just watching him walk.

Several houses down, somebody is waiting. Kelly raises a hand to him. Jen shifts so she can still watch them, so close to the window that her breath mists it up. She squints, trying to work out who it is.

The sun has only recently set. Jen is much closer to

summertime than she was yesterday. The sky is still silvery behind the black, shadowy houses. It helps to illuminate them. Jen sees Kelly clasp the man on the shoulder. The kind of gesture a teacher might make. A mentor, a therapist.

Or a very old friend.

In an almost-perfect echo of the night this all started, they turn around, and Jen sees that the person being greeted by Kelly is Joseph.

They walk a couple of meters down the road, then Joseph says something. They stop, and a small bag passes from Joseph to Kelly, brown, about the size of Kelly's palm. He doesn't open it or look at its contents. He puts it in the pocket of his jeans, touches Joseph's shoulder again, then raises a hand behind him as he leaves. Joseph heads back, past their house. Jen shrinks to the side to remain unseen. Joseph's eyes look up to the windows as he passes.

Todd emerges from his room just as Jen is thinking it through: so all that talk about no food, that was groundwork being laid, as carefully as an architect. Kelly was waiting for that phone to buzz, to signal Joseph's arrival. How sinister it is to relive your life backward. To see things you hadn't at the time. To realize the horrible significance of events you had no idea were playing out around you. To uncover lies told by your husband. Jen would always have said Kelly was as straight as they come. But don't all good liars seem that way?

"Any danger of some food around here, or do I have to call social services?" Todd says, coming up behind her.

"Do you know who that is?" Jen says, pointing down

to the street. This is surely better, actually, than asking Kelly. Todd is less connected to Joseph than she first thought, and is almost two months from killing him. And so maybe he won't lie.

Todd squints. "That's Clio's uncle's mate's car."

"How does Dad know him? They were just talking."

Todd shifts back from her, barely a step. Jen stares at him. Something significant has happened in his mind, but Jen has no idea what.

"Do they know each other?" Jen asks again. They both look back down at the street. The dark is gathering. Her husband just performed some sort of transaction right there, so brazenly. Jen can feel the significance of this, of the argument Kelly and Todd go on to have, too. Information is rushing toward her. Perhaps an end is in sight.

"I need to know," she says to Todd.

"Look – I . . . I don't want to be causing marital issues here."

"Todd, you are not in a sitcom," Jen snaps.

"Amazingly, I do know that. Yes, Dad knows Clio's uncle and his mate. Asked me not to tell you." Todd scuffs his bare foot on the carpet.

"What? Why?"

"He says they're his old friends and you used to find them irritating. And you wouldn't like that he'd got back in touch with them."

"He asked you to lie to me?"

"Do you not find them irritating?"

"I have no idea who they are." Jen is completely confused. In a few weeks' time, Kelly tells Todd he can no longer see Clio, can no longer associate with any of them. And yet – look. Items passed under streetlights; trades willingly arranged on burner phones.

Kelly has some association with Joseph. Clio and Todd got together and complicated it. And Kelly . . . Kelly thought it would fizzle out, that he could cover it up for long enough, and, when it became apparent that he couldn't, he told Todd to end it. And why.

That *why* is the missing piece. And Jen is fairly sure that, today, Todd doesn't know why. Only Kelly does.

Todd holds his hands up. "I don't know any more than that."

"Is Joseph trouble?" Jen asks curiously while her mind performs a firework display of questions.

"He might be a wheeler-dealer. I don't know. He's a bit of a wide boy."

"How so?"

Todd turns his mouth down. "I don't know. He doesn't work, but he has money. I really don't *know*."

"Does Clio know more?"

"No."

"I'll ask Dad."

Jen grabs a jacket and shoves her feet into trainers, heads out into the mild, soupy night, summer's last exhale. She's glad to do this away from Todd. He already knows too much, clearly.

She hurries along the street to the takeaway, feeling guilty about grilling Todd, feeling guilty in case he's worrying, feeling complicit in her hurt in some way. He's just a fucking kid. Of course he'd lie in order to keep his glamorous girlfriend.

Jen's footsteps ring out as she half walks, half runs along the streets. The air is close, the sunset mono-chrome, rendered gray by cloud cover. The odd September leaf has fallen in the street. Brown, three-cloved, like a child's depiction. More and more and more will gather and fall, and she won't see any of them.

Jen rounds the corner of the street that the takeaway is on and stops when she sees Kelly. He's got his back to her, is leaning on a street sign. His legs are crossed in front of him. He's on the phone. The burner phone she discovered in Todd's room in October. She registers now that that was after their row, so . . . why did the phone end up in Todd's room? Does Todd take it from Kelly?

"I've done it," he says. "So you're going to have to be in play, too."

Jen waits there, saying nothing. She walks a few silent paces back, hidden behind a corner, still able to hear.

"I'll bring it to you. It's a spare key, it's on Mandolin Avenue, not far. I need to go now. Need to put in an ap-pearance at home."

That second sentence kills Jen more than the first.

She gapes, there, her hands flat against a wall while her entire world seems to spin off around her. She's about to charge at him, to ambush him, to yell, when he says, "Thanks. Thanks, Nic."

While Jen's lying husband emerges holding the takeaway, she collects herself. She needs to think. She wants to be sure she gains as much information as possible, rather than confronting him.

His footsteps slow when he sees her.

"Hey?" His smile is easy, but wary. He's no fool. He knows she knows something.

"What's going on?"

He immediately understands Jen, and he knows what a warning those questions are. "That phone call? Nic? No . . ." he says, an educated guess. "You don't think . . ."

"Show me your pockets."

He looks once down the road, back at the Indian take-away. Then at his feet. A bite of his lip, then he sets the takeaway down on the ground and does what she has asked. She walks toward him.

Two phones and the brown package containing the key tumble out into Jen's hands.

She says nothing, merely waiting for an explanation.

"I – this is my client's phone, Nicola. And her car."

"Stop lying!" Jen shouts. Her words echo around the street, bouncing back distorted. Kelly's face slackens in shock. "You're lying to me," she says with a sob that she can't contain. For all her intentions, it has descended into the domestic she wanted to avoid. She can't help being emotional with him.

He runs a hand through his hair then turns on the spot. He's angry.

"Burner phones and illegal transactions, Kelly."

He doesn't say anything, just bites his lip and looks at her.

"All right – yeah. The package. It isn't for a client's car."

"Whose is it then?"

He goes silent again. Kelly often allows pauses to

expand, choosing to say nothing where other people would speak. Somebody else always talks first. But, this time, Jen waits too, just looking at him across the quiet, dark street.

His eyes run across her face. He's trying to figure out what she knows. He's trying to work out how to play his hand. "The car is stolen, but it isn't – what you think," he eventually says.

"What is it then?"

"I can't say that."

"Why?"

He stops speaking again, staring down at his feet, evidently thinking.

"What? Tell me or – we're in trouble, Kelly." She holds a hand up. "I am not joking."

"I know perfectly well that you're not joking," he says tightly. "And neither am I."

"Tell me what the fuck is going on, or I go."

"I . . ." He paces again, another useless circle that seems to serve only to burn off steam. "Jen – I . . ." His cheeks have gone red. She's getting to him, she can tell. Her husband may be calm, but even he has a limit. Just look what he did in the police station on the night that started everything.

"Just tell me who the key goes to. Just tell me who the guy was that you met just now."

"It's . . . I'd tell you if I could."

"You don't want to tell me what you're mixed up in. Isn't it as simple as that? You're giving me a fucking no-comment interview, Kell."

"It isn't even half as simple as that."

"I can't just stand by and have illegal shit happen out-side the house."

"I know, I know."

"Missing babies. Stolen cars."

"Missing babies?" he says. His eyes flash, then meet hers, his expression changing from irritation to panic.

"The missing baby."

He pauses, breathing hard, then looks at her. "If I say something – will you trust me on it?"

Jen spreads her arms wide, right there in the street. "Of course."

Kelly comes over, grasping her shoulders urgently. "Do not look into that baby."

Nothing could have shocked Jen more than this sen-tence. "What?"

"Whatever you've found. Stop."

"Who's Joseph Jones?"

"Do *not* look into Joseph Jones either," he says, his tone as vicious and as sharp as a snake's.

They stand there in silence for a few seconds, Jen still in his arms.

"Kelly – I . . . you're asking me to –"

"Just – stop. Whatever it is you're doing. Stop."

Jen hates this tone of his. It provokes an ancient emo-tion in her. Her body wants to run, she wants to escape: fear.

"Why?" she says, barely a whisper.

Kelly's fuse finally reaches its end. "You're in danger, Jen," he says. She steps back from him in shock. Her shoulders are covered in goosebumps. She begins to shiver, feeling so alone. Who can she trust?

Kelly looks at her. Behind the sorrow, she is sure she can make out an emotion on his features that she hasn't ever seen before on him, that she can't read.

She tells him not to come home with her if he won't tell her anything else, and he doesn't. He leaves. She doesn't know where he goes, almost doesn't care. The takeaway bag sits there, its brown sides buffeting slightly in the wind. She picks it up and takes it home, for Todd. For once, she has no appetite.

Ryan

Ryan is loitering before the emergency briefing led by the sergeant, Joanne Zamo.

Leo, Jamie and Ryan are standing along the back wall of the briefing room. "One for you," Jamie says, right before Zamo starts speaking. "OCG is Organized-Crime Group."

"Thanks," Ryan says. "I knew that."

"All right," Zamo says. She's in a trouser suit, flat black shoes, holding a coffee in her hand. Her weight is on one leg, and she's clearly thinking, staring at the floor but probably at nothing, her brow lowered. "Surveillance are feeding some stuff through to us now. Everybody ready?"

The briefing room is ablaze with adrenaline in a way it isn't usually. A copper whose name Ryan doesn't know is erecting a board, pinning various items on to it. Two others are on the phone, talking more and more loudly.

"Okay," Zamo says. "Surveillance have told us that the OCG were targeting an empty house. Then they saw a BMW idling on the driveway next door, keys in the ignition, engine on. So they took it." She folds her lips in on themselves, dimples appearing either side of her mouth. "What they didn't know is it belonged to a new mother who was intending to go on a nighttime drive to get her baby daughter to sleep. She secured her in the car seat, then left her there for just a few seconds while she dashed in to get her phone . . ."

Something turns over in Ryan's chest. He can see it all. The panic. The terror. The woman seeing the car begin to move. Rushing out after it. The 999 call . . .

"And now it's five hours post. The car hasn't been sighted, but we have eyes on the port, where it was heading."

Ryan thinks of that baby, with criminals. Or on a ship, in international waters, in the back seat of a car, alone.

"We have surveillance looking at ANPR for it, but we suspect they will have swapped the plates. We've put a stop on all ferries. Now let's find baby Eve."

Leo throws Ryan a look he can't read.

It's his job, now, Ryan assumes, to go and get the names off his corkboard, and they're going to dispatch more surveillance officers to watch all of them, to see if they can find the car, and the baby.

Ryan stares at the missing poster pinned to the board. He reaches a finger out to touch it. The paper feels soft and thin.

The baby is beautiful. Ryan has always wanted children. Two, a boy and a girl. He knows that's so passé, but it's always how he's felt. Two kids and a woman who could make him laugh. Building his own family unit again, from the rubble of his upbringing. If those you've left behind don't stack up, create new people, in front of you.

She's four months old. She has the most beautiful eyes, like a soulful little lion. And it's his job to find her.

*

193

"All right, Ryan," Leo says an hour later. "Sorry for the delay. Been getting authorizations for more coverts." He sips his coffee.

Ryan really wants that drink. He's so tired. He worries that he's beginning to prefer it, the station coffee, that he might start drinking from plastic cups at home.

"Where will they take the baby?" Leo asks Ryan. "In your opinion."

"The easiest place. They won't care what happens to her. The baby."

"Right . . . so – the port?"

"They will fulfill the order, whatever that is. That's their priority. They might ditch the baby somewhere on the way. They won't take A roads or motorways because of ANPR. They'll go rural. That's what my brother would do, anyway," Ryan says, the words feeling like a betrayal to him. His older brother. He had always pro-tected Ryan, sort of, but now look. " 'The feds are always watching,' he always used to say."

"You're an asset," Leo says. "Because of the brother thing. You know?"

Ryan shrugs, embarrassed now. "I mean –"

"There's no need for modesty," Leo says. He rises from the chair. "My point being: you know this stuff *and* yet you're here. You grew up there" – he holds his left hand out, far apart from his side – "and you arrived here."

"Thank you," Ryan says thickly. "I mean . . . in some ways, Kelly taught me a lot. I guess the best criminals do."

Day Minus Sixty, 08:00

"Morning, beautiful," Kelly says. He walks into the bedroom, wearing only boxers. Jen startles.

She could scream. The last day she spent with him, she left this man on the street. A domestic. A sinister, dark street corner, betrayals, crimes. Here – thirteen days before – he is greeting her sleepily, his expression as friendly as the August sun outside.

"Morning," she murmurs, because she doesn't know what else to say. Stolen cars, stolen babies, dead policemen, don't look into Joseph Jones, don't try to find the baby. Her son's anguished shouts in their back garden.

And now this. Kelly, here, topless, grinning at her.

He doesn't miss a trick, stops getting dressed, jeans halfway up his thighs. "What's up?"

"No, nothing. Got to go in early. It's the trainee rotation day," she says, a fact she wasn't even aware of until she said it. The power of the subconscious. She knew immediately, from twenty years in the law, the second she saw the date, that it was trainee changeover day.

So what else does she know?

Todd walks into their room, too, and – God. The little things you never notice about living with somebody while they are growing up. He's maybe an inch shorter now than he is in October. Less broad, too, across the chest. He picks a bottle of perfume up from Jen's chest of drawers and sniffs it. Kelly pulls a T-shirt on.

"You look mental," Todd says dispassionately to Jen. "Your poor trainee."

Jen swats him away, but she doesn't mean it. She could stay here with him for ever. And, she is ashamed to admit, with her husband. She could pause it all. Todd sniffing that perfume. Kelly with his head popping out of the neck of his T-shirt. Walk around them like they're statues. Love them, just love them, and never go forward into the darkness and lies that await them, remaining here in blissful ignorance.

Kelly showers and Jen checks his iPhone and turns back on location tracking as perfunctorily as she eats her breakfast.

Some lawyers occasionally, during their careers, have moments of genius. Most of practicing law is mundane: form-filling, costs budgeting, trying to extract everybody with the least damage done possible, but there are sometimes real lightbulb moments, too, and Jen is having hers today. It *is* significant, it turns out, that it is trainee handover day. Because here, in Jen's office, is a brand-new trainee who does not know the name of Jen's husband.

And, on Find My iPhone, Kelly does not appear to be unblocking a chimney nearby but is at the Grosvenor Hotel in Liverpool city center.

Jen's been trying to do the spying herself. But now, she can send a trainee to do it for her.

The one assigned to Jen is called Natalia. She is a classic solicitor-in-training: organized, overly cheerful, neat both in her work and in her appearance. Her hair is slicked back into a piece of elastic so perfectly that Jen takes a second, in her sunlit office, to marvel at it. Like a horse's tail.

Jen knows that Natalia's life will implode in early October. She will get home to find her boyfriend gone, packed up. He won't engage with her over it, practically ghosts her. She will tell Jen about it after several days of tearfulness and unproductivity.

"I have a task for you," Jen says. Her tone is probably too familiar. But she's worked with Natalia for eight weeks already, having shared a pepperoni Domino's pizza while Natalia cried and said she hated Simon. And if her tone surprises Natalia, she masks it well.

Jen pulls up a photograph of her husband on her computer. She has surprisingly few. "All right, this might be somewhat unorthodox," she says.

"Perfect. I'll do anything," Natalia says cheerfully.

"This man is in the Grosvenor Hotel, right this minute," she says, pointing at her screen. "Presumably with somebody. We need to know what they're discussing."

Natalia blinks. Even her eyelids are perfect. Jen knows this is a strange thing to notice but, nevertheless, they are. Smooth and painted with a color just slightly lighter than her skin, enough to make her look alert and awake. "Wow, okay. So, like, surveillance on cheating spouses?" Natalia says.

"Sure," Jen says lightly. "Yes." She bolsters the lie. "The court will be much easier on the wife if we can prove adultery." This is strictly legally correct, though Jen would never usually go to these lengths.

"Great." Natalia takes a pad and pen and goes to leave.

"If you have trouble finding him, call me," Jen says.

Jen struggles to get any work done while Natalia is gone, which she supposes doesn't really matter. She undertakes useless filing and filling in of timesheets instead, while she waits.

Natalia arrives back at one o'clock, over two hours after Jen dispatched her. She is holding a blue legal pad and an Eagles pen bearing the logo that Jen's dad designed years ago. Her hair is still absolutely, completely immaculate. "I bought a Coke, I hope that's okay?" Natalia says.

Jen feels a dart of guilt. God, this is a sordid task to give to a trainee on her first day, and she didn't even brief her on expenses. "Oh my God, of course," Jen says. She gets a ten-pound note out of her purse and hands it to Natalia.

"Shouldn't I put it in the – the system?"

"I am the system," Jen says crisply. "Don't worry."

"All right," Natalia says, and Jen suddenly feels like some kind of psycho, dispatching a completely new trainee to spy on her husband. The kind of desperate behavior of somebody unhinged, somebody abusing their power. She pushes the thoughts away. It's for the greater good.

"Okay," Natalia goes on. "He – Kelly – met a woman. He calls her Nic. I don't think they are having an affair, though."

Nicola Williams. Again and again and again. Even though she knows what she looks like, she still cannot find her online.

"No?"

"It didn't look that way. It was a business meeting."

Jen swallows. "Right," she says. "Shoot."

"They seemed to be starting up some sort of arrangement again? It's hard to say what. Possibly working for someone called Joe – I don't know. Kelly doesn't want to do it. Nic wants him to, she seems to . . . maybe think he owes her something. It sounded very loaded. I don't know . . ."

"Okay. And Joe wasn't there?"

"No – they kept saying he was inside. But I didn't really understand because *they* were inside?" Natalia stops speaking, her pen poised above the pad, leafing through it, flicking through pages and pages of immaculate notes. Fucking hell, Jen thinks, Natalia went to Oxford University, Marlborough College before that. And yet. *Inside.* She doesn't know what that means. These kids. These naïve kids.

"I think that's it. There was a lot of talk around what work they'd do for Joe, but no specifics mentioned," Natalia finishes.

Inside.

Jen holds a finger up and googles *Joseph Jones prison.* The information about him was there all along, hidden away among the common names. He was released last week from HMP Altcourse and was convicted twenty years ago in one of the largest trials of its type.

Possession with Intent to Supply Class A Drugs, Conspiracy to Rob, Conspiracy to Produce Counterfeit Currency, Section 18 Grievous Bodily Harm with Intent. The offenses go on and on. Drugs, money laundering, robbing, stealing cars, burgling people's houses, violence. As many as there are droplets of mist outside when Todd murders him. Jen reads each while Natalia stands there in silence. She gradually becomes numb to them, to what this could possibly mean about her husband, and for her son.

"Thanks," she says softly to Natalia after a second. "Great job."

"Shame he's not cheating," Natalia says. "If it would've helped. He actually mentioned how much he loved his wife."

Jen turns away from her computer, and from Natalia, too, staring out the window, down at the street, her eyes wet. "Did he?" she whispers.

"Yeah. Just said he loved his wife. No context really, in among all the Joe stuff."

Jen nods, turning back to Natalia, wondering what would happen if she imparted some wisdom here, knowing, as she does, what faces Natalia in the future.

But knowing the future is worse than not knowing. Isn't it?

Day Minus Sixty-Five, 17:05

Jen has been finding comfort in heading into the office on weekdays. Undertaking – piecemeal – whatever tasks await her on that specific day. In September, she was doing financial investigations before a trial with Natalia. And into August she has been drafting an advice on child protection – something slightly outside her remit, but enjoyable nevertheless, even though it disappears more with each day that passes. She has a trainee called Chance, who leaves in September for a rival firm, which Jen does her best to forget now.

At five past five, her desk phone rings.

"It's me," Valerie, their receptionist, says. "There's someone in reception. I know, I know, I know you're harassed."

Jen blinks. "Am I?" She doesn't feel remotely harassed. The child protection advice is half written, a hot cup of tea sits on her desk. She's looking forward to going home and seeing Todd, who's been baking cookies, sending her photographs of each flavor. She remembers that they are delicious, so she's extra-excited. A little haven in her fucked-up, backward world.

"Rakesh said you're on the child protection advice yesterday and today – I know . . ."

"Yes," Jen says faintly. She remembers this. The advice had taken her an embarrassing amount of time to get to. Weeks. The client had chased her twice, the second time asking if a simple note was beyond her. It was so hard, in law, to make the time to do large pieces of work. Phone calls, emails, unexpected and horrifying Outlook calendar appointments. Eventually, she'd blocked all calls to get to it. She'd even locked her office door! God, what a diva.

"Who?" Jen says. "Who's in reception?"

"Says he's called Mr. Jones?"

Jen's mouth goes dry. She wets her lips with her tongue. Look. Look what she missed.

It's the twenty-fifth of August. And Joseph Jones is out, and looking for *her*.

Joseph turns in the pale-carpeted foyer when he sees her. EAGLES is written behind the reception desk in blocky lettering. The lights – on timers – have gone off, save for a single one, illuminating just him.

"Looking for Kelly," he says.

Jen pauses, her footsteps slowing as she crosses the foyer toward him.

"Kelly Brotherhood?" she says.

Something seems to break across his features as he meets her eyes, but Jen isn't sure what. He's older than she first thought, that first night, and the night she saw him at Eshe Road North. He's probably older than fifty. Tattoos across the knuckles. Eyes flinty. Body language poised somehow, like a cat about to strike. He's light on his feet with it.

"Yes." He holds both hands up. "He was an old friend." The knowledge is a physical feeling that shivers across her torso. Joseph's sentence was twenty years. So he must have known Kelly *before* it.

"What kind of friend?" Jen can't resist saying. But, inside, she is thinking that Joseph, too, knows *her*. He knew to come to the law firm to find Kelly.

Joseph smiles back at her, so fast as not to be genuine. "An important one."

"Surprised you'd look here?" she says.

"I've been away. No matter. Wanted to re-start something." He turns away from her. He's in a white T-shirt, the material thin and cheap, and, underneath it, Jen can make out a tattoo that spans the entire width of his back: an angel's wings, right across his shoulder blades.

"Re-start what?" she says, but he ignores her, leaving, the foyer door shutting softly behind him. Jen leans her hands on the reception desk, trying to breathe, trying to think.

Joseph was released only days ago. And look: he's come here, almost immediately. It's clear to Jen, on this isolated day in this strange second-chance life, that Joseph Jones's release from prison set something in motion. Somewhere in the future, which she cannot reach at the moment, no matter how hard she tries. Something that involves almost everybody she knows. Todd, Kelly, and now her, too, surely: why else would he come to Eagles? A gruesome cast of dramatis personae. A hit list of betrayals.

Day Minus One Hundred and Five, 08:55

A Saturday in mid-July. It's perfect outside, the sky so blue it looks like a bauble fit to shatter. It's five to nine, and Jen is pulling up outside HMP Altcourse.

As soon as she realized the date and that Joseph would still be inside, she made her excuses to Kelly and Todd, who were taking the piss out of *Saturday Kitchen* – she said she had brunch with a client – and left. To her dismay, nobody was surprised. Jen has spent her entire life doing things for others: seeing demanding clients when she wanted to be watching Todd's swimming lessons. Watching Todd's swimming lessons when she wanted to be lying down with a book. The maternal habit of a lifetime, feeling guilty no matter which she chose.

Todd hasn't met Clio yet, nor started associating with Connor. So, what, were they all red herrings, now that she's gone back past them?

HMP Altcourse looks like an industrial estate, a strange kind of self-enclosed village. Jen's only been here once, as part of her training. Beyond that, she's never practiced criminal law. Her father found the idea of repeat business from criminals so distasteful that they never did it. Jen finds making money from divorces vaguely distasteful, too, but there you go. Everyone has to make rent, and heartbreak is more ubiquitous than crime.

Jen walks into the foyer of the prison, thinking how fortuitous it is that Joseph is back in prison, and that visiting hours are limited and structured on weekdays but unlimited and informal at weekends – any unauthorized visitor can turn up and request to see any inmate on a Saturday. Today.

It's like she knew.

It is raining outside, midsummer rain; the media have named it Storm Richard. Each time somebody enters the reception, the smell of wet grass puffs in. Visitors' shoes leave patterns of water across the floor that a jaded cleaner mops up periodically, one hand on a hip, putting up more and more yellow triangular WET FLOOR signs.

The reception is modern, like a private hospital. A wide and sweeping desk dominates the space. A man clicks a mouse at it, takes softly spoken phone calls.

Behind the reception is a whiteboard with times written on it. Through a door marked CANTEEN (SECURE 2), Jen can hear an argument escalating. "You said I could order smoky bacon, not salt 'n' vinegar," a man is saying.

"I know – but Liam –"

"It was fucking clear!" the man shouts. Jen winces. The power of a packet of crisps.

For a second, just a second, she wants to confess all, right here in the foyer. Shout and scream. Commit a crime. Commit *herself*. Tell them she's time-traveling and be sedated somewhere, meals made, crisp-ordering the height of her control.

"Request here," the receptionist says suddenly. He stands and passes a form to Jen, which she fills in.

"He's happy to see you," the receptionist says after two phone calls and several more minutes. "Visitor center that way." He points inward, through a set of double doors, into the bowels of the building, and hands Jen a temporary pass with no string or safety pin.

She pushes the cold metal panels on the doors and enters a corridor staffed by two security guards. It smells of disinfectant and sweat. The vinyl floors have rubber edges. There are multiple locks on multiple doors.

She is met by a security guard with a name tag on, printed with the name LLOYD. Somebody, in biro, underneath it, has written *Grossman!* He asks to see her handbag, then checks it, a deft hand inside like a doctor performing some grotesque internal, then sends it through an airport-style scanner. He gestures for her to spread her arms wide and as she does so he pats her down, avoiding eye contact.

"Phone in there," he says, and Jen puts it into the blue bank of lockers he indicates.

They go through another set of double doors that he opens with a fob. Underneath an over-the-door heater that momentarily warms the top of her head and shoulders, and then they're in.

The visitor center is a tired room, big and square with public-sector faded blue-and-red carpet, black plastic chairs, tiny tables. The back wall is solely floor-to-ceiling windows. Fat raindrops strike them and the roof above, rattling the skylights. The room is already full.

It's less easy than Jen thought it would be to differentiate between prisoners and visitors. It looks like any other busy meeting room. A couple sits, split, across a table, their hands not quite meeting in the center of it. Steadfastly not touching, but getting as close to the boundary of the rules as is possible. At another table, a child reaches toward her father, hand flexing like a distant blinking star, but the mother stops her, pulls her back into her body.

Jen thinks of her own father. She said goodbye to him in the morgue. She'd been too late. The image of her father lying there for six hours, dead, alone, stayed with her. In the morgue, eventually, the heat from her hand had warmed his, and she'd dipped her forehead to it, pretending, but it was no use.

Jen recognizes Joseph Jones easily. He's sitting alone at a table in the exact center of the room. The elfin ears, the dark hair. The goatee. His skin truly does have the prisoner's pallor she's read about. Not only a lack of suntan; something more. The kind of color people go when they have the flu, when they haven't slept, when they're grieving.

She has been to this man's house. She has seen him die. And now, here she is, about to find out quite who he is, after all.

"Hi," she says as she sits down, her voice shaking. All his crimes. Robbery. Supplying. Assault. Her arms and legs begin to tingle.

The chair shifts underneath her. It's the plastic kind that folds into a single line to stack against a wall.

"Kelly's wife," he says. He pulls the ribbed cuffs of his navy-blue sweatshirt over his hands, playing for time. So he knows her, even though they've not yet met.

Jen sees that he has a gold tooth, right at the back. His

eyes meet hers. "Jen," he finishes, his tongue lingering at his front teeth over the *N*.

She has gone completely cold, and completely calm. The frenzied anxiety of the mystery, of the anticipation, has boiled dry. The fuse has tripped, and she now feels nothing. The room stills around them, like a faded photograph. Quiet and blurred. Something is about to happen; she can feel it.

"I . . ." she says.

"Jen, the love of Kelly's life."

She says nothing, trying to collect herself, but instead thinks about how brazen she's been. Searching belongings, following people, hiding and eavesdropping. But look where it's brought her. Here, a prison, mixed up with criminals, police cars driving by, a missing baby. Her skin burns with fear, like a thousand tigers' eyes are watching her: she's prey.

"How do you know him?" Jen says, swallowing.

"We go way back." Joseph says nothing more. He crosses his legs underneath the table, legs stretched out, his feet underneath her chair. The gesture is deliberately proprietary. Jen wants to move back, but doesn't.

Outside, the light fades, the clouds Russian blue, like somebody has flicked a dimmer switch. Joseph catches her looking. "Storm Richard," he says, passing his thumb behind him. "Going to be a big one."

"Is it?" Jen says faintly.

"Oh yeah. The murderers here love a storm." He gestures expansively around him. "Hypes them up."

How strange that he wishes to differentiate himself from the prisoners, Jen finds herself thinking. She can't help but notice it. "Tell me how you go way back?" she presses.

Joseph leans across the table toward her. "You know, you'll find out when I get out of here. I'm hoping to start it up again," he says, the same thing he said in the law-firm foyer. He makes another gesture, rubbing his thumb across his fingers, a signal for money or maybe just a twitch. Jen can't catch it, perhaps imagined the delicate movement. It lasted less than a second. The rest of his body is completely, eerily still.

"When did you meet?"

"I think Kelly's your man for this one," Joseph says. "Don't you?"

Joseph rubs one of his hand tattoos, his head not moving at all, just looking at her. The wind picks up outside. A plastic bag drifts by like a balloon.

"Jen," Joseph says, repeating her name. Like somebody toying with her. "Jen."

"What?"

"I have one question, before I leave."

"Okay?"

"And that is – Jen . . . how could you not know?" Joseph cocks his head to the side like a bird. He's mad, Jen finds herself thinking. He's totally mad, this man who knows who she is. "Even I thought you knew."

Forked lightning illuminates the sky outside, a split-second flash. Blink and you'd miss it.

"Know what?"

Jen stares and stares at Joseph as the visitors' center seems to narrow around them. As thunder flexes in the sky above, he leans closer to her, gesturing for her to do the same, left hand upturned on the desk like a beetle on its back, fingers making pulling motions toward his body. She leans in reluctantly.

"Ask me what we did."

"What?"

"Burglaries. Supply. Assaults. That's what we did."

Joseph's list of charges.

Jen blinks, darting her head back. "But you're in here, and he isn't?"

"Ah," Joseph croaks. "Welcome to the gang."

Fear, realization and horror blow across Jen's mind like the strong winds outside. Is this what she knows? Somewhere deep and dark inside her?

Kelly.

A family man.

Not many friends.

Keeps himself to himself.

Hard to get to know.

Sometimes dark.

Doesn't travel.

Doesn't like parties.

Doesn't go on payrolls. Lives life under the radar.

Turns away from her friends at parents' evenings.

Always seems to have enough money.

That dark edge. That dark edge he has to him, that sharp-as-lemons humor that prevents intimacy. Isn't that the oldest story in the book? Humor, banter, as defense mechanism.

The way he sometimes will not compromise, will not elaborate. Will not, will not, will not. Would not move back to Liverpool. Will not work for an employer. Will not travel. Will not fly.

Joseph turns his mouth down. "Look, I don't dob," he says. "I'm no grass. Ask your husband." He stands up, now, the conversation over. Jen, not caring who's looking, allows tears to gather in her eyes as she stares at the space he left.

As she sits, trying to collect herself, she feels the slightest, softest touch on her shoulder, and jumps. Joseph has his mouth right next to her ear. "I'm sure you'll find out the extent of it," he murmurs, then is escorted off.

Jen begins trembling as though there's a freezing draft, but there isn't: it is only his breath she can feel, in her ear, in her mind, while the storm rages on outside.

Day Minus One Hundred
and Forty-Four, 18:30

"Oh, it was mad," Todd is saying animatedly to Jen, his words tripping over each other. Jen is sitting on the love-seat in their bay window, thinking that her husband is involved in organized crime. "Fractional distillation didn't come up at all. We did all the prep on it — we thought it would be the main question, and it just totally wasn't?" He fiddles with Henry VIII's collar, the cat lying contentedly on his lap on the sofa. "It never goes the way you'd expect, you know?" He shifts, unable to keep still, and the cat jumps down on to the floor. Three candles are lit along the windowsill.

Jen nods, smiling at her son.

The first thing she noticed this morning was that her phone was different. Her hand closed clumsily around it. It was chunkier, bigger than the slimline one that she got in early July. Shit shit shit, she thought. She knew she'd jumped back further before she checked the date.

It was June. The rose bush in the front garden of the house opposite was in full bloom as she stared out of her bedroom window, fat bundles of fragrant flowers clutched together, about to fall. How could it be June? Where was this going to *end*? In nothingness? In birth, in death? And — an even darker thought — it's too late for Jen to kill him herself, like Kelly suggested, all those days ago. He's inside.

…rst thing that Jen thought, getting dressed in dif-
…es, clothes she throws out in several months'
…Kelly is to Joseph. And how it might have
worked: Joseph gets out of prison, comes to the law
firm to find his *old friend* Kelly, Todd gets involved with
Clio, doesn't like what he finds out Joseph and Kelly are
doing, and kills Joseph? It was plausible, but unlikely, she
concluded. It seems a weak motivation for murder. And
it leaves a lot to be explained: Ryan Hiles, the missing
baby, Nicola Williams, the veiled conversations between
Kelly and Todd. The thing Joseph knows about Kelly.

She looks at Todd, now, sitting in the lamplight with
cat hair all over his trousers. "You'll have aced it," she
says thickly.

"Well, I did actually enjoy it! Jed said I'm mental."
He's giddy. With relief, with the endorphins that follow
stress, and with something else, maybe, too. Something
that is missing in the autumn. Some lightness. "I mean –
am I some sadist? . . . What?" he says, stopping, looking
across the room at her.

"You're not a sadist," she says, but even she can hear
her voice is imbued with sadness. She misses this. Just
normality, not fractured days, everything backward. She
doesn't even know why she's woken up on today, the sev-
enth of June. Todd hasn't met Clio yet. Joseph is inside.
So what is it? She leans her face in the palm of her hand.

"I wonder if I'll get an A," Todd says thoughtfully.
"Maybe just a B."

He gets an A.

Only recently, Todd came home talking so happily
about making *polymer bouncing balls*. "Polymer what?"

Kelly had said. Todd had hesitated, then pulled one out of his rucksack. "Got you one," he'd said lightly, confident enough to steal from school. They hadn't minded, thought it was funny. He was overly interested in chemistry, so what if he shouldn't have been allowed to take it? Maybe it's that sort of thing that causes Todd to go wayward. Jen never gave much thought to what sort of parent she'd be, but maybe she was too relaxed, favoring banter over discipline. Fooled, by his intellect, into thinking he'd never rebel. But all kids rebel, even the good ones: they just rebel differently.

Jen looks at her handsome son and thinks about everything that future-Todd will miss out on. University, marriage, some graduate scheme with other geniuses. But instead, what faces him? Remand, a trial, prison. Out by the time he's thirty-five. The knowledge, for ever, that he has taken a life, for whatever misguided reason.

"Are you going to order, or shall I?" Todd says, waving the Domino's app at her on his phone.

They must have agreed to get a takeaway. "Yeah – let's just wait for Dad." Henry VIII pads over and leaps up on to Jen's lap. He is slimmer, too, she thinks ruefully.

Todd makes an over-the-top puzzled face, a cartoon double-take. "Oh-*kay*," he says. "Dad's away, but sure. You do that, Jen."

"Is he?" she asks sharply. "At risk of being accused of being old," she adds, rictus grin in place, "remind me where he is?"

"It's Whitsun."

"Oh," Jen says. She can feel her mouth make the shape, a round, significant O. Kelly goes away every Whitsun

"Pizza for two then," she says to Todd, but, in fact, she's thinking: That's why. That's why today. Out of all of the days that have come before.

Thank God. Thank God she turned on Find My iPhone this morning on Kelly's phone, the same way she does each morning now. When she checked earlier, he was in Liverpool, but she'll look again.

"Let me think," Jen says, getting her phone out, ostensibly ordering pizza but, really, looking at Find My iPhone. Kelly goes camping in the Lake District. Lake Windermere. Same spot every year.

But look. Here is his blue spot. Not in the Lake District at all. At a house in Salford.

Jen looks back up at her son, who is staring down at his phone, an expression of concentration on his face.

"Todd," she says, cringing as she says it. Her baby, post exam, looking forward to pizza with his mother; he deserves better. He looks up at her in surprise. "How bad would it be if I had to pop to the office? Just quickly – we can have the pizza afterward."

Todd's eyebrows rise in surprise, but then he waves a hand. "Yeah, fine," he says. "Don't worry. I shall go immerse myself in H_2O. Also known as a bath to mere mortals."

Jen laughs softly to herself, then rubs at her eyes as he stands and leaves the living room. Is this the right thing to be doing? More neglect of Todd, not less, in search of answers? But she's got to know for sure.

She decides to get a taxi so that she can arrive incognito.

"Won't be long," she calls to Todd. She hears the sound of the bath running, doesn't catch his reply. She hesitates at the bottom of the stairs, torn, torn between duties. But it's all for him, she decides as the Uber app vibrates to say her car is a minute away. It's all to save him, wonderful him.

"Get extra bacon on mine," Todd calls.

"Sure thing."

She waits out on the street for the taxi.

It's the height of summer. Geraniums, sweet peas, roses in her neighbors' gardens. It smells like a perfumery. The air is soft. It's raining lightly, warm drizzle, but Jen doesn't mind. It's humid, like a steam room.

She reaches to pluck off the petal of a peony at the very corner of her driveway, in the only tiny patch of soil they can be bothered to maintain. Once white, it's now a deep brown around the edges, like an old newspaper, but it still smells of delicious, pungent vanilla.

She looks up at their sleeping house, one light on in the frosted bathroom window, thinking of her son and his pizza. He'll understand one day.

As the Uber pulls up, she thinks suddenly of how much she trusted her husband. She trusted him so much. Camping with people she's never met. She never thought, never thought once.

She tugs on the cool plastic handle of the Uber and is greeted by Eri, a middle-aged man with a beard wearing

er
dr
says.

"Oh." Eri considers the notes, then eventually takes them.

"I'll pay whatever I owe on the app, too. We need to keep an eye on this." She shows him the phone. "If the blue dot moves, we might need to . . . redirect."

"Okay then," he says. "Like in the movies," he adds, his eyes meeting hers in the rear-view mirror.

"Mmm." Jen sits in the back, leaning her head against the cold window, watching her street rush by. A woman in a black cab following her husband. The oldest story in the book, with a twist. "Like in the movies," she repeats.

Call of Duty awaits you, Todd texts Jen.

God, isn't it funny, Jen thinks, the lights of Merseyside rushing by like scattered colorful stars, how you can forget entire phases of your life? The PS5 phase, *Call of Duty.* Two controls they had to charge all the time, they'd played so much. They had been so addicted. When they weren't playing it, they would shoot at each other around corners of the house. "This is Black Ops," Todd would say to her, walking into the kitchen, holding an imaginary walkie-talkie.

Jen wonders now, as they race down the motorway, lit-up blue signs passing above their heads like they're flying, whether she had been irresponsible to let her son play that game, ignoring the warnings about violent computer games. It wouldn't happen to them, she had thought. She had been too lax. She must have been. Raised by a lawyer, she'd wanted to teach a kid how to relax and have fun – but had she gone too far?

Kelly's spot is at the end of a track road, just a little way off the motorway junction at Salford. Eri drives dutifully, not saying anything.

As Jen is considering whether this is a good idea, he says: "You don't look very happy."

"No. I'm not."

Eri turns the radio off completely. The air is warm, the car a lit-up cocoon. "Are you following your husband?"

"How do you know?"

Eri catches her gaze in the mirror, then helps himself to a second stick of powdery Wrigley's. He holds one up for her, and she declines. "Usually is," he says.

Jen turns her mouth down, pleading the fifth. She'd usually make small talk, try to make the taxi driver feel okay about being nosey, but she doesn't today.

They come off at a roundabout, take the second exit, then head out into the country. The track road is unlit, not even tarmacked. Just mud. The hairs on Jen's arms rise as they travel down it. The smells of the countryside in summer drift in through the air-con. Hay bales. Rain on hot pavements after a long drought.

"Maybe I should get a role in the films," Eri says cheerfully. "Following husbands."

"Maybe."

They head up what looks like a private drive, an unmarked hairline fracture on Google Maps.

"Should we go all the way up?" Eri asks. He takes his baseball cap off. His hair was perhaps once thick but has now thinned out, fine strands still curling like a baby's after a bath.

Eri brings the car to a stop when Jen doesn't reply. They are about three hundred feet from Kelly's dot. Jen should get out, but she hesitates. Wanting to enjoy these last few moments until . . . until something.

With Eri's headlights now off, Jen's eyes adjust to the twilit drive. It winds to the left, then to the right. The sky is a bright mother of pearl, close to the summer solstice. The trees are full, shaggy, the leaves of one meeting the other.

Headlights sweep the skies like laser beams. "He's driving," Eri says. He reverses quickly backward and out on to the main road. Jen glances at her phone as the blue dot begins to move.

Kelly drives past them and into the distance, not seeming to notice them. "Shall we follow?" Eri asks.

"No. Let's . . . I want to see where he was, what's at the end of this drive."

Eri heads wordlessly all the way to the top. It winds this way and that, the bends obscuring what lies at the end of it. Jen is expecting to see a wedding venue, a castle, a stately home, but instead a small and shabby housing development slides into view, one building at a time. Seven houses dotted around a shingled driveway. Eri pulls the car to a stop. The houses are old stone. The windows are illuminated in four of them; the others in darkness.

One is untidier than the rest. Roof tiles missing. An

old-fashioned wooden front door that looks rickety, near rotten. One bay window on the first story is boarded up, *QAnon* looped on it in pink spray paint. Eri sits in silence while Jen gazes up at it. That's the house. She's sure of it. It's the only one without a car outside.

"I have no idea what this is," she says.

"Looks dodgy."

Jen's mind is spinning in overtime. A place to deal. A hideaway. A place to cut drugs. A place to kill people. A place to keep missing children, dead policemen . . . it could be anything. Nothing good.

"He said he was going camping," she whispers to Eri instead of all this.

"Maybe he is. Looks pretty outdoorsy," he adds with a laugh.

"In the Lake District."

"Oh."

"Will you wait here?" she asks, easing the door handle open. "I need to go and look."

"'Course," he says, but his facial expression has become more wary. Her fleeting friend the Uber driver, the person she has confessed the most to. She glances back at him as she goes. He's lit up by the interior light, a snow globe in the dimness.

She walks tentatively across the gray shingle. The air outside is holiday air. Summertime smells, the sound of crickets.

And suddenly, she wishes to be back there, on the landing with the pumpkin, watching Todd kill a man. She'd just let it happen. Accept it. He'd do his time. He'd be able to have a life afterward. She wants, for the first time, to re-cover this wound she has discovered. Stop discovering its depths. Move on.

She walks through the darkness, up to the house, and tries the front door, but it's locked. It sits slightly apart from the other houses. None of them are boundaried, no fences, no front or back gardens. The neighbor has manicured their lawn up to an arbitrary straight line. After it, the wildness of this garden begins – nettles, weeds, two giant pink lupins which nod and sway in the breeze.

Jen pushes the letterbox open. It reminds her of the one they had growing up. It's stiff and cold underneath her fingertips, and she thinks of her father and the day he died and how she didn't get there in time.

Through the letterbox she can see an old-fashioned hallway. Uneven quarry tiles. She presumes Kelly has picked up the post from the floor and stacked it on the hallway table there.

The sign on the plaster to the side of the door says *Sandalwood*. The next cottage along says *Bay*. It's tiny, two rooms deep. Jen walks a clockwise loop around it. At the back are two old-fashioned sliding patio doors, the glass stained with a blush of moss.

A dark-wood dining table sits in a teal-carpeted room inside, like a doll's house. No chairs. An empty kitchen-ette to the left, nothing out on the work surfaces, not even a kettle. She presses her hands around her forehead to lean against the patio doors, peering in, and her fin-gers come away green. It's uncared for, but not derelict, maybe recently emptied.

She circles back around to the front. The windows to

the living room are mullioned, every other square a distorted circle of blown glass. The living room is preserved, like a museum or a set. A pink three-piece suite sits in the center, its arms covered in what were once white pieces of lace. A remote control rests on an empty coffee table at a diagonal angle. A full bookcase, nothing she can make out. Two dusty champagne flutes on the top. She's about to stop looking when she notices something right in the front of her field of vision: the distinctive black velvet back of a double photo frame, right here on the windowsill that's littered with dead flies on their backs. The distorted glass meant she almost missed it. She shifts against the window to get a closer look.

The air seems to soften and still as it comes into focus, the molecules of the universe settling around her. This is not a wild-goose chase. This is not madness.

Here it is.

It's a photograph of Kelly – clearly Kelly – that guarded, small smile. He's much younger, maybe twenty, standing next to somebody else. A man with a shaved head. Their arms around each other. The frame is thick with dust, and she's a foot away from it, but she can see that they look like each other. Their eyes. And something intangible, too. The way families sometimes bear resemblances that aren't obvious. Bone structure, the shape of their foreheads, the way they stand: the way they seem to hold potential in their bodies, like runners on the starting blocks.

So who is he? This stranger who looks like her husband? Kelly says he has no living relatives: another thing she'd always believed. She considers this as she stares at the figures in the photograph. It's one thing to lie about knowing an acquaintance who's been in prison. It's quite another to lie about your family, about where you came from.

And why would her husband have a photo of himself if this house is in any way the site of something dodgy? He wouldn't. Surely he wouldn't. He's not stupid.

She walks back to the Uber. He has Kelly's eyes. He has Todd's eyes. That's all she keeps thinking. Three sets of navy-blue eyes. Her husband, her son, and somebody else. Somebody she doesn't know, won't be able to find. Even if she breaks in, takes the photograph with her, she won't have it tomorrow.

Eri is playing some platform game on his phone, holding it horizontal, pressing at the screen as tinny music plays. "Sorry," he says, then locks the screen. Jen gets in the front, next to him.

"What . . ." he says, in the tone of voice of somebody who feels that they have to ask.

"I don't know. It's empty."

Jen opens the app and looks back at Find My iPhone. Kelly now looks to be heading to the Lake District, where he always said he was going. But via here, this abandoned house.

"Who owns it?"

"Hang on," Jen says. You can find out who owns any property from the Land Registry for three pounds.

She downloads the title and scrolls to the registry. The proprietor is the Duchy of Lancaster. That's the Crown. Unclaimed property reverts to the Crown. The first thing any property lawyer learns. Jen holds her lit-up phone in her lap and stares up at the house.

"Mind if I smoke?" Eri says as he winds his window down.

"Go ahead." He rasps at the lighter, two flares, and the car is briefly illuminated. He smokes, and she thinks. His cigarette smells of the past: summer evenings outside wine bars, standing at train stations, the docks at night.

"We should go," Jen says.

"Will you confront him?" Eri says, his cheekbones jutting out as he sucks on the cigarette.

"No. He'll only lie."

They travel in silence, Jen thinking about the two men in the photograph. Her husband, and somebody else. Somebody who looks like him. What does it all mean?

When Jen arrives home, two pizza boxes sit on the counter. One empty, one full. Todd had his without her. He must have ordered it himself, alone.

Ryan

Ryan is doing push-ups on a grimy living-room floor. Bits of fluff and dirt keep sticking to his palms. He's working out for two reasons: one, he can no longer go to the gym, and two, because he cannot, cannot, cannot get the missing baby out of his mind.

The gym aside, Ryan can do hardly anything he usually can. He can't go home to see his family. He can't go out with his friends. He can't even go back to his old *place of abode* . . .

It happened so fast.

He moved here last night, to a bedsit in Wallasey. He's to live here, eat here, sleep here. It's two rooms: a bathroom and everything else in one space. Pretty economical, really, he thinks. A sofa that folds out into a bed. A row of kitchen cabinets against the far wall. A television, a landline. What more could he need? He doesn't mind. It's exciting. And, even better, it's temporary.

He arrived here at one o'clock in the morning, last night, made sure he wasn't followed, let himself into the bedsit with the key he was given at the station. As he swung his rucksack off his shoulder and on to the grim carpet, he'd let a breath out and thought: *I am here.*

Leo had finally spelled it out the other day in the cupboard. "We want you to go undercover in this group, Ry, now," Leo said. "Today." He held eye contact, not breaking away for even a millisecond, not blinking, nothing. "The legend we set up is . . . well. It's you."

"Right," Ryan said with a gulp. All became clear. Just like that. The corkboard. The corkboard was a way in. All the questions about his history, his brother, what he knew . . .

He wanted this, he tried to tell himself. He wanted an interesting career. But – wow – undercover work. Intercepting a *gang*. He suddenly wanted to know the fatality rate of undercover police. The odds. His chances.

"You know, you don't talk like a police officer," Leo said. And then he clarified: "That's what we wanted."

"I see," Ryan said, not knowing whether to laugh or cry. Jesus, so he was an undercover candidate because he was nothing like a policeman? He'd even fucked up the police alphabet. Ryan bit his lip. A sad, soft feeling came over him, like he had swallowed a hot and melancholic drink.

"No – I mean, a police officer would say, *Can this gent procure me some high-class cocaine?* You would say, *Got any beak, lad?*"

Ryan barks a laugh out.

"You know. I exaggerate for comedic effect. You're fucking great at intel, though. That corkboard. Golden," Leo says warmly.

"Thank you."

And now, Ryan is to be introduced to the OCG by a colleague who's already in, their inside man.

His phone rings.

"All set?" says Leo.

"Yeah, think so." He looks out at the cold estate. It's

the very tail end of winter now. The trees have been re-
duced to stickmen. The skies are bleak, white, no color
to them at all. The weather is lackluster, can't be bothered to do anything at all; no sun, no rain, nothing.

"Remember, three pieces of advice."

"Okay?" Ryan turns back to face the living room.

"One: stay in character at absolutely all times, even if
you think your cover has been blown. It's better for
people to suspect you're a bobby than for you to confirm it."

"Right." Ryan swallows. He is nervous. He can admit
that much. It might be cool and stuff, but – what happens if they guess? What if they get ready for the big
entrapment and he blows it?

"Two: at every turn, crims suspect drugs squads. You
should, too. You should be mortally offended if accused
of being DS, and accuse others, too."

"I will. I'm fine with all that," Ryan says truthfully.
They're sending him in quite high up, to try and infiltrate
the people who tip off the gang that the houses will be
empty. Not into the drugs ring, but the theft ring, instead.

"Three: never fucking tell anyone."

"Noted. I mean – that should be number one, really,"
Ryan says.

Leo laughs loudly, which makes Ryan's chest feel full
and happy.

In his hand Ryan has his phone, containing a text which
he checks and checks again: 2 Cross Street. He's dressed
all in black, as directed.

The text came just as Ryan's inside man, Angela, said it

would. From a blocked number. And this is what they're trying to figure out: who gets the addresses, and how?

Ryan had not met Angela before, as is protocol within the force: nobody meets the active undercover officers. Angela has been on a four-month-long project to get to know the arm of the gang involved in the thefts, and she's done a good job so far. She's stolen four cars and got to know Ezra at the port. In that time, she has never once set foot inside the station, in case somebody saw her.

Ryan met Angela a few nights ago, facilitated from afar by Leo. They exchanged a few words outside a One Stop shop. Angela is organized and serious, resists his jokes, as though they inconvenience her. Yesterday, she introduced Ryan, her "cousin" and "experienced thief" to the gang to bolster her own worth, but also to try to get Ryan to go in higher up. To get to know the person behind the intel, rather than just the foot soldiers.

And Ryan's first task to prove himself is this: to go to the address written here on the phone and rob the car.

As easy and as difficult as that.

It's after two o'clock in the morning. The moon is up, a luminous ball thrown into the sky that stays there for just a night before it falls again.

The house in front of him is sleeping. The owners are away, in the Lake District. The hallway light is the only one on; an obvious timer. If that wasn't clear enough, the lawn is unruly: a clear tell people are on holiday.

Ryan doesn't think about it. Just does it. Letterbox open. He's in luck: this one will be simple, the keys left within reach. He gets the long black pole out, fishes the keys out and pockets them. He unlocks the car with a gloved hand, slides in and reverses it off the drive without the engine on. If the police ever find this car and run forensics on it, that is when the undercover unit will disclose him: that this is Ryan, actually. One of the good guys; immune from prosecution.

On an unlit road nearby, he starts the next task. His hands are shaking. He's never plated a car. The police assumed he'd know how to do it, but he's always been rubbish at mechanics, DIY, anything like that. He can't figure out how things go together. He drops two tiny screws, which roll around on the pavement, blending easily into the tarmac. "Shitting hell," he says, kneeling down to try and find them with his fingertips.

It takes him forty minutes to plate the car and he cuts his hand, right across the palm, with the sharp edge of the number plate. But it's done. Another crime committed.

Ryan drives to the port, where he waits, as instructed, for Ezra to be free, then coasts up to him, getting out and handing him the keys.

"Perfection," Ezra says. Right there, at the cold port, Ryan loses his nerve. *Imagine, imagine, imagine,* is all he can think. Imagine if Ezra realizes who he is. Ryan may not be in danger of getting arrested, but he is definitely in danger of getting fucking murdered.

"Great," Ryan says. His hand is trembling as he reaches to clap Ezra on the shoulder. He disguises it, lets his jaw swing, a common symptom of being on cocaine. Let Ezra think it's that, that he's coked up, like his brother's associates.

Ryan looks just beyond Ezra, to the cargo ships, the brightly colored cranes against the night sky.

Ezra meets his eyes. Something seems to pass between them, though Ryan doesn't know what. His knees begin to weaken, and he disguises it by hopping from foot to foot.

"First one?" Ezra asks carefully.

"Yeah. First of many." Ryan rocks back on his heels. They will kill him. No matter the police protection, the safe house he will go to if his cover is blown: these people will kill Ryan if they discover him. Stop thinking about it. Just stop it.

"We've done forty this week," Ezra says.

"Forty cars?"

"Mmm."

Wow. Ryan blows air out through his mouth. The scale of this is bigger than even he realized.

"You hurt your hand?" Ezra asks.

"Yeah, no big deal," Ryan says. "Just the number plate."

"I did the same with DIY earlier!" Ezra says, showing Ryan his own palm.

"Ha," Ryan says, his mind spinning.

"You should get Savlon on that," Ezra says casually, like they're two kids, not men in an organized-crime gang. Fucking Savlon.

Day Minus Five Hundred and Thirty-One, 08:40

It's May, but May the previous year. This isn't right, how far back she is. She's got to speak to Andy. To ask what to do. To stop it. To slow it down.

Jen descends the stairs and can tell just from the light and the noise of the house – Kelly cooking, Todd chattering away – that it's a weekend. She stops on the penultimate step, just listening to her husband and her son's easy banter.

"That would be *uninterested*," Todd is saying. "*Disinterested* means impartial."

"Why, thanks, *OED*," Kelly says. "I actually did mean impartial."

"No you didn't!" Todd says, and they both explode with laughter.

Jen walks into the kitchen. "Morning, beautiful," Kelly says easily. He flips a pancake. The scene looks so normal. But . . . the photograph. He has some relative, out there, that he's never told her about.

It's painful to look at him, like looking at an eclipse. Jen can feel herself squinting. "What?" he says again.

Her gaze goes back to Todd. He is a child, a kid, an adolescent. Huge feet and hands, big ears, goofy teeth that haven't yet settled and straightened. Four spots on his cheeks. Not a sniff of facial hair. He's short.

She drifts over to where Kelly is flipping the pancakes.

"So you were saying you are *impartial* to my computer game?" Todd asks Kelly.

Kelly's black hair catches the sunlight as he adds more pancake batter to a pan. "Yeah – that's what I meant."

"I smell bullshit."

"All right, all right," Kelly holds his hand up. "Thanks for the lesson. I meant *uninterested*. You shitbag."

Todd giggles, a high, childlike giggle, at his father. "Just think – you could've had two of me, if you'd had another. A double pain in the arse," Todd says.

"Yeah," Kelly says, something old and whimsical crossing his features for just a second. He always wanted another child.

"You're more than enough," Jen says to Todd.

"Hey, we're all only children," Todd says, reaching for a banana and unpeeling it. "I never thought of that before." Jen watches Kelly closely. Is it this conversation? Is that why she's here?

He says nothing, busying himself in the kitchen. "We are," he says casually after a second or two.

Jen looks out at the garden. May. May 2021. She cannot believe it. Early-morning sunbeams funnel down, like shafts from heaven. Their old shed is still out there, the one they had before they got the little blue one. Jen is wondering if anybody else could tell two Mays apart, just from the way the light hits the grass.

"Right, I need to shower," she says.

She goes to the very top of the house, where she sits on the exact center of their double bed and uses a phone she had too long ago to google and dial Andy's number.

"Andy Vettese."

Jen goes through the usual spiel hurriedly. The dates, the conversations they have already had. Andy keeps up in the way that he does, his silence somewhat misanthropic, but avid, Jen thinks. She tells him about the Penny Jameson in the future. He says he was being put forward for it.

He seems to believe her. "Okay, Jen. Shoot. What do you want to ask?"

"I just – it's *eighteen months* before," she says, trying to turn her attention back to the task at hand.

"Do the days you're landing on have anything in common?"

"Sometimes . . . I always learn something. But . . ." She cradles the phone between her shoulder and her ear and rubs her hands down her legs. She's freezing cold. She has very old nail polish on, an apricot shade she went through a phase of loving but dislikes now. "So many things ought to have worked to stop it that haven't."

"Maybe it isn't about stopping it."

"Huh?"

"You say he's bad, right? This Joseph? Maybe it's not about stopping his murder."

"Go on."

"Well, if you stop it, seems like you have another problem."

"Huh?"

"Maybe it isn't about stopping it but about understanding it. So you can defend it. You know? If you know the *why*, then you could tell a court that."

Jen's ears shiver after he's finished speaking. Maybe,

233

maybe. She is a lawyer, after all. "Yes. Like, it was self-defense, or provocation."

"Exactly."

Jen wishes she could go back to Day Zero, just once, to watch it again, knowing everything she knows now.

"I don't know if I told you this in the future, but I always tell my wannabe time travelers the same thing: if you seek me out in the past, tell me you know that my imaginary friend was called George, at school. Nobody knows that. Well – apart from the travelers I've told. So far, nobody has ever come to tell me."

"I'll tell you," Jen says, moved by this personal piece of information. By this clue, by this shortcut, by this hack.

She thanks him and says goodbye.

"Any time," he says. "Speak to you yesterday."

Jen smiles a wan, sad smile, hangs up, and thinks about today. It's all she has, after all.

Today. May 2021.

May 2021. Something is creeping toward her consciousness, like a fine mist gathering on the horizon.

It hits as some thoughts sometimes do. It arrives without warning. She checks her phone. Yes. She's right. It is the sixteenth of May 2021.

That's when it lands.

Like a sucker punch, so violent it knocks her off her feet momentarily: today is the day her father dies.

Jen pretends to resist the urge to do it. She's not traveling back in order to see her father, to right one of the big wrongs in her life, she tells herself as she straightens her

234

hair. She's not doing this to say goodbye to him. She's here to save her son.

But all morning she thinks of that morgue goodbye, just her and his dead body, his hand cold and dry in hers, his soul someplace else.

She watches Todd play *Crash Team Races Nitro-Fueled* – their game *du jour* – while fiddling madly, crossing and uncrossing her legs. Eventually, Todd goes, "*What?*" to her, and she wanders off, leaving him to it.

She googles Kelly on her phone while standing in the hallway. There is nothing, no online footprint at all. She puts his surname into an ancestry site, but it throws up hundreds of results around the UK. She finds a photograph of Kelly and reverse-image searches it, but nothing comes up.

She drifts upstairs. Kelly is doing his accounts. "I'm being patronized by Microsoft," he says to her. Cup of coffee on a coaster. Small smile on his face. As she approaches, he angles the computer just ever so slightly away from her. She catches it this time. Must have missed it the first.

Maybe he has another income stream somewhere. Drugs, dead policemen, crime. Does he have more money than a painter/decorator ought to? Not really. Not a lot, she doesn't think. Nothing she's ever noticed – and wouldn't she have? A memory springs up from nowhere. Kelly having given money to charity, a couple of years ago. Buckets of it, several hundred pounds. He hadn't told her, and when asked he had explained it as anonymous philanthropy thanks to a good job that had come in. It had bothered Jen in that intangible way it does when your husband lies to you, even about something benign. The lie hadn't been bigger than what it was, but, nevertheless, it had been one.

"Hey, strange question," she says lightly. "But do you have any living relatives? You know, a cousin, once removed . . ."

Kelly frowns. "No? Parents were only children," he says quickly.

"Not even a very distant relative, up another generation maybe?"

". . . No. Why?"

"Realized I'd never asked about the wider family. And I got this – this weird memory of seeing an old photograph of you. You were with this man who had your eyes. He was thicker set than you. Same eyes. Lighter hair."

Kelly appears to experience a full-body reaction to this sentence, which he disguises by standing up abruptly. "No idea," he says. "I don't think – do I even have any old photographs? You know me. Unsentimental."

Jen nods, watching him and thinking how untrue this is. He is not at all unsentimental.

"Must've made it up," she says. They're just eyes. Perhaps it's only a friend in the photograph.

Jen meets those blue irises and suddenly feels as alone as she ever has in her entire life. She is supposed to be forty-three, but, here, she is forty-two. She's supposed to be in the autumn, but she's in a spring, eighteen months before. And her husband isn't who he says he is, no matter what time zone she's in.

And her father is alive.

Her father who loves her unconditionally, even if that

is in his own way. Just as Jen feels she must examine her own parenting in order to save her son, she wants, now, to turn to the person who raised her.

"I'm going to go see Dad," she says. It comes from nowhere. She can't resist. She needs to feel his warm hand in hers. She needs to watch him lay out the beer and the peanuts that he dies beside. She won't stay. She'll just – she'll just tell him she loves him. And then leave.

"Oh, cool," Kelly says. "Have fun," he calls, as she races down the stairs. "Say hi from me."

Kelly and her father have always had a cordial relationship, but never close. Jen thought Kelly might search for a father figure, adopt hers willingly, but, actually, he did the opposite, always keeping Ken at arm's length, the way he does with most people.

She calls her dad from the car, part of her brain still thinking he won't answer.

But, of course, he does. And this proves to Jen, above almost anything else, that this is really happening. It really is.

"A nice surprise," Jen's father says to her. And there he is, on the end of the line. Back from the dead. His voice – posh, reserved, but mellowed into humor with age. Jen leans into it like a captive animal feeling a breeze after so long, too long.

"Up to much? Thought I'd come over," Jen says, her voice thick.

"Sure. I'll put the kettle on."

She closes her eyes into the phrase she has heard a hundred thousand times, but not for eighteen long months.

"Okay," she says.

"Great." He sounds happy. He is lonely, old, dying, too, though he doesn't know it yet.

Everything Jen knows tells her that she shouldn't be here. All the fucking movies would agree. She should only change things that might stop the crime, right? Not get too eager, so selfish that she tries to alter other things, too. To play God.

But she can't resist.

He lives in a double-fronted Victorian house, three stories high including the loft conversion. Double sash windows either side of the front door, dark-wood frames. Old-fashioned, but charmingly so. Like him.

She stares at him in wonder as he steps back, gesturing to let her inside. That arm. Full-bodied, warm-blooded, actually attached to her father's alive body. "What . . . ?" he says, a mystified expression crossing his features.

"Oh, nothing," she says, "I . . . I'm having a strange day is all."

Her father remained in the matrimonial home after her mother died. He'd insisted, and she had nobody to help her convince him. The life of the only child. He told her the stairs would be fine, that he would still keep the gutters clear himself. And neither the gutters nor the stairs killed him, in the end.

"How so?"

"It's nothing," Jen says, shaking her head and following him down the hallway that seems smaller, somehow, now that she is an adult. A very specific feeling settles over Jen when she comes here. A kind of just-out-of-reach nostalgia, covered in a fine film of dust, as though she might be able to grasp hold of the past if only she could try hard enough. And now here she is, right here, the spring of the year before her son becomes a murderer, the day her father dies, but it doesn't feel like it.

"You sure?" he says to her. A backward glance as they move through the tired lounge. Sage-green carpets, hoovered carefully, but nevertheless gray-black at their edges. She'd never noticed that before. Perhaps she inherited her disdain of housework from him.

A round gray rug with geometric shapes on it. Ornaments he's had for decades sit on various dark-wood shelves that jut out above fireplaces and radiators.

He switches on the kitchen light even though it's the middle of the day. A striplight. It hums to life. "Did *Morris vs. Morris* settle?" he asks, a raise of his eyebrows. He pronounces the *vs.* as *and*, the way all lawyers do.

"I . . ." She hesitates. She can't remember at all, obviously.

"Jen! You said it would!"

She tilts her head, looking up at him. This. She'd forgotten. Don't all familial irritations get subsumed by grief, in the end? This sort of exchange would have annoyed her then, but it doesn't today. She's just pleased to be here, in the arena, not cast out by death.

"Sorry – I'm tired."

"You've got four days before they take it off the table," he says. Suddenly, with the benefit of hindsight, she can see precisely where some of her insecurities have come from: here. In adulthood, she gravitated away from people like her father, made friends with misanthropic types like Rakesh, like Pauline. Married Kelly. They allow her to be the real, true her.

"I know – it'll be fine. We'll settle it on Monday," she says.

"What does the client think about the offer?"

"Oh, I can't remember." She waves a hand, wanting the conversation to be over. It wasn't an idyll, was it, working together? It was hard sometimes, like this. Her father, driven, devoted, a stickler for detail. Jen, driven too, but more to help people than anything else.

She vividly recalls attending an important joint-settlement meeting with her father, who huffed when she didn't have one form or other and she'd texted, *My dad is a twat*, over and over to Pauline, who sent back emojis. She almost laughs, now, it's so bittersweet. The children we are with our parents.

"Sorry – not sleeping well," she says, meeting his eyes. "I'll be better on Monday. I promise."

"You look like – I don't know. Yes – you look like when Todd was tiny and you never rested."

Jen smiles a half-smile. "Remember those days."

"You can sleep anywhere when you have a baby, you're so tired," he says wistfully. Just like that, a prism held to the light, he shows another facet of himself. He had always been competitive, repressed, but in the years leading up to his death he had mellowed somewhat, began to allow himself to feel, to reveal an oozing, doughy version of himself; a better grandfather than he was a parent. They got so little time together.

"When I had you, I fell asleep at some traffic lights, once."

"I never knew that," she says.

An eerie sensation settles across Jen's back, like a window's open somewhere letting in cold air. What is she doing here? She shouldn't be doing this. Finding out things she can never forget.

"I've never said," he explains. "You never want your child to feel like they were a burden." He says this second sentence with evident difficulty, biting his lip as he finishes and looks at her. They're standing in his dining room, in between his living room and kitchen. The light outside is beautiful, illuminating a shaft of dust in front of his patio doors.

"No, I'm the same with Todd."

"It's hard to have a baby. Nobody says." Her father shrugs, seemingly pleased to be passing what he regards as a normal day with his daughter.

"Was I in the car with you?"

"No. No!" he says with a laugh. "I was on the way to work. God, it was – something else, those newborn days. Sometimes I wanted to call the authorities up and say, *Do you know how hard it is to have a newborn?*"

"I thought Mum did it all."

He turns his mouth down and shakes his head. "I'm afraid to say that Little Jen took over the house with those screams."

She blinks as she watches him walk into the kitchen, where he painstakingly boils his stovetop kettle in that way that he always has. Full to the brim – damn the planet – the lid replaced carefully with a shaking hand. She hasn't seen that kettle for so long. They sold this house a year ago. She hardly kept anything from it.

The kitchen smells antiquated. Of tannin and musk, a caravan sort of smell.

"Why the lack of sleep?" he asks.

"A fight with Kelly," she says, which she supposes is true. She waves a hand as tears come to her eyes. She's still thinking about the traffic lights. God, the things we do for our kids.

Her father doesn't say anything, just allows Jen to speak, there, standing on the worn tiles. She meets his eyes, exactly like hers. Todd doesn't even have these eyes, these brown eyes. Todd has Kelly's. That's the deal you make when you have children with someone.

"What happened?" her father says. Not a sentence he would've uttered twenty years ago. The kettle begins to bubble, rocking gently on the hob. Her father keeps his eyes on hers, ignoring it, like it is a distant tremor.

"Oh, just the usual marital fight," she says thickly. What else could she say? Tell the whole vast story, from Day Zero to here, Day Minus Five Hundred – or thereabouts?

He leans against the counter opposite her. It's the same kitchen it always was. Eighties-style, off-white Formica, fake oak. There's a comfort in the tired quality. Cabinets containing crystal glasses he no longer uses. A floral plastic tea tray that will house a ready meal each night.

"Kelly has been lying to me," she says.

"About what?"

"He's involved in something dark. Maybe always has been."

Her father waits a beat, then makes more of a noise than utters a word. "Huh." He brings a hand to his mouth. Age spots. Jen's relieved to see them, to still be here, in the relative present. "What kind of thing?"

"I don't know. He's meeting a criminal, I think," she says.

Her father's eyes darken. "Kelly is a good person," he says firmly.

"I know. But you're never – you know."

"What?"

"I don't feel like you – you really ever liked each other?"

"He is good to you," her father says, sidestepping her question.

Jen laughs sadly. "I know."

She thinks of the house and the photograph again. She can't figure it out, and neither can she figure out how to figure it out. It's a locked mystery to her.

"Remember that first day he came into the firm?"

"For sure," Jen says immediately, but that's all she wants to say. March belongs to her and Kelly, even if the memory has been eroded now. It means so much to them he inked it on his skin only a few months later. He hadn't told her he was going to get the tattoo done. Had disappeared in the middle of the day, come home without saying anything. It was only when she undressed him that she discovered it; their shared legacy.

"Remember all the scrappy work we did back then?" she says.

It had been the early days of the firm when her father had taken Jen on as their trainee – a recipe for dysfunction if ever there was one. He had trained at a Magic Circle firm in the City but wanted to run his own firm, so moved home to Liverpool, head full of mergers, acquisitions and ambition. After her mother died – cancer, in the nineties – he had set up Eagles. Why he hadn't called it Legal Eagles, Jen had never understood.

In those early days they had taken any work going, had stretched themselves to the limits of their expertise to avoid being late on the rent. They'd do powers of attorney alongside residential conveyancing alongside personal-injury claims. "Drafting codicils with the textbook under the desk across my knees," he says with a laugh.

Jen smiles sadly. "Do you remember the timeshare conveyances we did?" she adds, happy to reminisce.

"What's that?" her father says, but there is something strange about his tone. Something performative, as though somebody is watching.

"Yeah – remember we did timeshare conveyances, and we had to keep that mad list of whose slot was when?"

"Did we?"

"Of course we did!" Jen says, momentarily confused. Her father has a phenomenal ability to recall events from the past. She must have misunderstood, the memory not quite what she thought.

"I don't think so. But weren't those the days, anyway?" he says. "Pizzas in the office . . ."

Jen nods. "Sure were," she says, though it's a lie.

"And then it kind of all tipped over, didn't it?"

"Yeah." She remembers the spring when she met Kelly. The firm had finally started earning money. A few big client wins. They hired a secretary, and Patricia in Accounts. And now look at it. A hundred employees.

"Stay for dinner?" he says to her, pouring out two cups of tea.

She hesitates, looking at him. It's four o'clock. He has between three and nine hours to live. Their eyes meet.

She takes her steaming mug wordlessly from him and sips it, buying time. She knows she shouldn't do it. Don't change other things. Stick to what you are supposed to be doing. Don't play the lottery. Don't kill Hitler. Don't deviate.

But her mouth is opening to answer on her behalf. "Love to," she says, so quietly she hopes the universe might not hear if she says it under her breath, just to him, no witnesses, a private communication from daughter to father. She wants to stop being alone, just for a while, to stop figuring out all the incomprehensible clues, never moving forward, only backward, backward, backward, a game of snakes and ladders with only snakes.

"What're we having?" she adds.

Her father shrugs, a happy shrug. "Whatever," he says. "Another person just sort of makes life feel official, doesn't it? Even if we just have beans on toast."

Jen knows exactly what he means.

It's five past seven. Jen and her father have put a fish pie he'd had frozen for "God knows how long" in the oven. She should be leaving, she should be leaving, she keeps thinking, her rational brain imploring her with a kind of panicky reasoning, but his feet – in slippers – are crossed at their ankles and he's put *Super Sunday* on, and he's so close to it, and she can't leave him, she can't, she can't.

"Might put a garlic bread in the oven, too," her father says. "I can eat for England these days. You know, your mum hated garlic. Says she ate too much of it in pregnancy."

"Did she?" Jen says, getting up. "I'll put it in."

"God, I hate *Super Sunday*. Vacuous." He begins channel-hopping.

"Let's watch *Law and Order* and criticize the procedure," Jen says over her shoulder.

"Now you're talking," her father says, navigating to the Sky menu. "Get me a beer, too," he says. "And some peanuts for while we wait."

The hairs on the back of Jen's neck rise up, one by one, like little sentries.

"Sure," she says. She walks into the quiet of the kitchen and puts the garlic bread in the oven. The interior lamp illuminates her socked feet.

The beer is already chilling in the door of the fridge.

"Help yourself to whatever," he calls through.

Jen finds the peanuts in a cupboard which seems to contain just about everything – orange squash, two avocados, chocolate-covered raisins, teabags, Mint Club biscuits – and brings them through for him.

"I didn't know Mum ate garlic when she was pregnant."

"Oh yes, tons of the stuff. Even raw, sometimes. She'd stick a few cloves in a roast chicken and eat them one by one," her father says. Jen can just imagine it. A woman she lost too soon, eating garlic cloves at the kitchen counter, greasy fingers, Jen inside her body. Todd inside Jen's. Todd's potential, anyway.

"She said she overdid it. We always said" – he takes the beer and peanuts from her in one hand, one deft movement. God, he is so healthy – "she wouldn't eat her favorite foods in pregnancy if we had another, so she didn't get put off."

He leans forward and lights the fire. He wasn't found with the fire on, a garlic bread and a fish pie in the oven. These are all changes Jen has made. It lights easily, zipping along from left to right, like words appearing on a typewritten page. The room is immediately filled with the soft, hot smell of gas.

Jen sits down next to it on a stool her mother embroidered the top of that her father has kept, no snack or drink for her, just watching him. Waiting.

What do you say to somebody when you know they will be your last words to them? You just . . . you don't, you don't leave, do you? Anxiety rushes over Jen like the fire her father has just lit, making her hot. She was never going to leave. How could she possibly leave him all alone?

And what if this could stop it? Somehow?

"But you didn't have another child," she says to her father, instead of cutting short the conversation, instead of leaving, instead of finding a way to say goodbye to him, now and also for eternity.

"Never a right time, and then too late," he says simply. He opens the bottle of beer with a hiss. "The law – it takes so much, doesn't it? You give it an inch . . . I always thought Kelly had the right idea, never letting work in so much."

"Who knows what ideas Kelly has," Jen says tightly, and her father looks embarrassed.

"He's got the right idea," he says softly. A strange and prescient feeling settles over Jen. Almost like . . . almost like, if her father knew he was going to die, he might tell her something. A key. A piece of the puzzle. A slice of deathbed wisdom that she could use. A side of the prism currently still in darkness.

They lapse into silence, the gas fire the only noise, a kind of rushing, like distant rain. It pumps out such a fierce heat, the air above it shimmers. She could stay here for ever, in her father's quaint old living room, while a garlic bread cooks.

And that's when it happens. Jen watches it pass over her father like a storm cloud. Peanuts and beer right next to him, just like they said. Sweat is the first sign, a milky dusting of it across his forehead, like he's been out in drizzle. "Oh, wow," he says, puffing air into his cheeks. "Jen?"

Jen feels hot with panic. She didn't think it would be like this. She thought it would be sudden.

He brings a hand to his stomach, wincing, eyes on her. "Jen – I don't feel good," he says, his voice anxious, like Todd's when he was little and fell over, looked to her first to see how he felt; his maternal mirror. And now here she is, at the end of her father's life, their roles reversed.

"Daddy," she says, a word she hasn't uttered for decades.

"Jen – call 999, please," he says. His eyes are brown, just like hers, imploring her. She gets her phone out. There is no question. There is absolutely no question. She has only the illusion of choice.

Day Minus Seven Hundred and Eighty-Three, 08:00

Jen is in September, the previous year. She orients herself, thinking of last night, of her father, of the way he looked at her in the hospital bed. Warm and alive. And now it's before that again, and he's alive again now, too, but not because she saved him. She wonders if, somehow, when she goes forward again, she will have still saved him, and he will be there, in the future, alive.

A pile of blue-and-white-striped presents sits in the corner of their bedroom. Oh. It must be Todd's birthday, his sixteenth. What could be hidden on his birthday that might explain why he commits a crime? She thinks about what Andy said, about how maybe it isn't about stopping it, but about defending it instead.

She stares at the pile of presents, wrapped last night somewhere in the past; in a yesterday she might never get to. The gifts are PlayStation games and an Apple watch. Too expensive, but she'd wanted to get the watch for him, couldn't wait to see his face. They will go out for dinner, just to Wagamama's, nowhere special. It's cold. The weather turned early that year, becoming autumn almost overnight.

She begins sorting through Todd's presents, on her hands and knees on the floor. These two squishy presents are socks. This rectangle is the Apple watch . . . she sets the others out on the wooden floor, looking at them, mystified. That little round one looks like lip balm. Surely not. She has no idea. She can't remember.

She hopes he will like them, nevertheless.

She stacks up the presents and walks down the stairs to knock on Todd's door. "Er, come in?" he says in a baffled voice. Right. Of course. Jen only started knocking last year. Next year. Whatever.

"Happy birthday!" she says, nudging the door handle down with the stack of presents.

"Wait, wait, wait for me," Kelly says, rushing up the stairs with two coffees and a squash on a tray. At the picture window, beyond him, the sky is a perfect, high autumn blue. Like nothing untoward has ever happened, will ever happen.

When she walks into Todd's bedroom, he's in pale green pajamas, sitting up in bed, hair mussed up just like Kelly's. Jen pauses at the door, gazing at him. Sixteen. A kid, really, nothing more. So perfectly, perfectly innocent, it hurts her heart to look at him.

Despite his birthday, Todd has to go to school and, while he's getting ready, Jen sees that she has a trial today; a rare event in any divorce lawyer's calendar is a full-scale trial. It's *Addenbrokes vs. Addenbrokes*, a case that took over her life for the past year. A couple who'd been married for over forty years, who still laughed at each other's jokes; but the wife couldn't get past Jen's client's infidelity. Andrew regretted it so much it was painful. If he was in Jen's position, it would be the first and only thing he would change about the past.

She heads downstairs, the house empty again, thinking

that she can't attend a trial. It won't matter. She won't wake up on tomorrow, anyway. What are the odds?

Just as she's thinking this, her phone rings. Andrew.

"You on your way?" he says to her. Her chest tingles. It isn't that, in line with Andy's theory, she is living without consequences, but rather that she isn't directly witnessing the effects of her actions. Not today, at least.

"I . . ." she starts to say. She can't bear to do it to him.

"It's – I mean, it's the day?" he says. And it isn't that she might get sacked, in the future somewhere, if she misses today. It isn't that she knows the outcome – Andrew loses. It is that she knows him to be heart-broken, and that he sounds so flat and sad, like all her clients, like her. And so Jen, as she has a thousand times before with a thousand other clients, tells him she will be there in ten minutes.

Liverpool county court is municipal-looking but never-theless imposing. Jen hardly ever comes here – like most solicitors, she tries to settle early, and settle often, before acrimony and court fees set in. But Andrew and his wife wouldn't. Their primary argument was about a substan-tial pension fund, due to reach maturity next year. Jen remembers being surprised Andrew wouldn't give it up, but most people who have betrayed or have been be-trayed are irrational. It's the single most important les-son she's learned in her career.

"Look," she says to Andrew, after she's greeted the barrister – thank God, somebody who can remember the case is conducting the hearing. "We're going to lose this."

She would never usually say something like this. So

bold, so pessimistic. But they are: of course, she knows they are. "If I were the judge, I would find in favor of your wife," she tells him.

"Oh, well, great, nice to know now that you're on my side," Andrew says acidly. He's approaching sixty-five but still young with it, plays squash three times a week, tennis on the other nights. He's most certainly lonely, hasn't seen the other woman since it happened, after which he issued a full confession to his wife. Jen sometimes wonders, if she were Dorothy, whether she would have forgiven Andrew. Probably, but it's easy for Jen to say, having been so privy to her client's heartbreak, his dysfunction, the way he's left all the photographs of Dorothy up all around his house.

She guides Andrew into one of the meeting rooms that flanks the corridor into the court. It's dusty and cold, feels like it hasn't been opened for at least a few weeks. The lights hum as she flicks them on. "I think you should offer something up," she says to Andrew.

He takes some convincing but, finally, after Jen's insistent, dispassionate arguments that he is going to spend more on barrister's fees than he's trying to save, he offers up seventy-five percent of the pension fund. Jen takes the offer to the meeting room, where his wife is sitting. She thinks it'll be enough.

Dorothy is with her lawyers. She's a diminutive-looking woman, good posture and even better makeup, her physique hinting at a kind of wiry strength, the kind of sixty-five-year-old who walks ten miles on a bank holiday.

"Seventy-five percent of the Aviva," Jen says to the

solicitor, a man called Jacob whom Jen went to law school with. Back then, he ate the same lunch every single day – chicken nuggets and chips – and got forty-nine percent in the family law exam. Jen wouldn't want him representing her, and it strikes her that most professions are probably full of these people.

Jacob raises his eyebrows at Dorothy. Evidently, a threshold of acceptability has already been agreed, because Dorothy nods, her hands clasped together. She signs the consent order Jen drafts carefully, feeling pretty pleased with how much easier she has made this day for everybody. When she brings it back into their meeting room, at not even ten in the morning, she sees that, next to her signature, Dorothy has written a small note. Andrew looks at it, the paper conducting the trembling of his hands as he holds it. Jen tries not to look like she's reading it, too, but she does. It says only: *Thank you x.*

Jen wonders as she walks back to her office if this will help, somehow, in the future, both her and them. This small, small change that she's made. It probably won't – how could it, when she will wake up next before she's made it?

Just as she arrives at her desk, her phone pings with a text from Kelly. *How's the trial? x.* She reads it but doesn't reply. A photo comes in next. *Coffee for one*, it says, a Starbucks takeaway cup held in his hand, his wrist tattoo on show. But blurred into the background – she recognizes it. It's a tiny corner of the house, the abandoned house he visited at Whitsun. It's the same shingle on the drive and the brickwork. He's there again, now. So brazen: he thinks she won't notice; he thinks she's never been there.

So here she is. In the office while receiving this text, rather than in court. It must be for a reason.

Eventually, she wanders down to Rakesh's room without her shoes on, feet in tights, the way she has a hundred times before. He looks younger, still smells of cigarette smoke.

She recites the address to him. "This house, Sandalwood, went *bona vacantia*," she says. Property passing to the Crown. "Is there any way we can find who owned it before that?"

"Ooh, *bona vacantia*, now you're testing me," he says with a flash of a smile. His teeth are whiter.

"I think you can look at the epitome of title with *bona vacantia* – hang on," Rakesh says, clicking quickly at his mouse. Jen is glad to be here, with him, in his office in the past. He's always been so much better than her at legal theory. She should have asked him ages ago.

"Looks like they're trying to check who to pass it to because the beneficiary is dead," Rakesh says. "Hiles. H-I-L-E-S."

An explosion occurs in Jen's chest. Hiles. Ryan Hiles. It must be. The policeman. The dead policeman. Already dead, even now, even this far back. What does it mean? She thinks wildly of what the connection could be between Todd, a dead policeman, and killing Joseph Jones. Maybe Joseph killed the policeman, and Todd avenged it. Maybe that's his defense: seeking justice. It all sounds mad, even to Jen. She's so far back now.

"But . . . I looked recently and couldn't find it. His death isn't registered on the general births, marriages and deaths register."

Rakesh types fast, his eyes scanning. "No, it isn't. But he's definitely dead. The Land Registry insist on the death certificate."

"When did he die?" she asks, crazy theories running around her mind.

"Doesn't say. You can buy the death certificate for three quid – shall I do it? What file shall I put it on?"

"Don't bother," Jen says, jaded. "It'll take too long."

"It takes two days, that's all."

"Honestly, don't."

As she leaves Rakesh's office, she walks past her father's. He's on the phone, his door ajar. She pokes her head around it, and he raises his hand in a wave. He's wearing a white shirt and a gray waistcoat, doesn't look like a man who has only six months to live. The last time she saw him, he was at the hospital. She can't stop looking at him now, healthy and tanned. She hears him say into the phone, "Sorry, our accounts only start in 2005. We had a flood."

God, that's right. The 2005 floods. Jen had been on maternity leave, hadn't even gone in to help him. Her eyes mist over with it. Her fingers linger on the doorframe for just a second too long, and he waves her away impatiently, which is so *him* that it makes her give in to a watery, bittersweet laugh.

Todd is eating edamame beans with garlic and chili salt. He deftly shells them, popping the innards into his mouth, talking through his food. Kelly is reclining in his chair, just listening.

"The thing is," Todd says, swallowing one of the

beans, "Trump is actually just insane – as opposed to merely Republican."

Jen's heart feels both full and light, a pink candyfloss whorl in her chest. She gazes at her son. She knows the man he becomes, at least up until the murder, can see the seeds of him just here. He learns a lot more about American politics in the two years that follow this birthday, totally eclipses her understanding of it. They watch *The West Wing* together next year. He stops it to explain the electoral process to her; she stops it to explain the love interests to him. She'd totally forgotten that, too. The past disappears into the horizon like fog, but here she is, able to live it again, to sift through it.

"Obviously, he will get voted in again," Todd says, stuffing another bean into his mouth. "It's the whole fake-news thing, isn't it? Anything negative about Trump is now fake news. Genius, in a way." He reaches down underneath the table to fiddle with his laces – bright green ones. That is what was in the small circular box. Jen was as surprised as he was.

"He's not a genius. He's a pig," Kelly says dispassionately. "But I agree, he will get a second term."

Jen hides a smile. "Bet you a hundred quid he doesn't get in," she says. "And that Biden does."

"*Biden?* Joe Biden?" Todd blinks. "The old guy?"

"Yep. Deal?" Jen says.

Todd laughs. His hair falls in his face. "Sure, deal," he says.

"So," she says to her son. "What're you going to wish for when the cake comes out?"

He puts his head in his hands, looking at her over his

fingers. She remembers when she used to trim his nails when he was a baby. He was frightened of the nail clippers. She did hers, first, to show him it was fine, even though they didn't need doing. "No, no cake or ceremony," he says, blushing, but he's delighted, she can tell that, too, as though his emotion is hers also. They, mother and son, are a zipper, slowly separating as the years rush by. And so here they are, closer than in 2022.

"Only if you tell us your wish," she says.

"You can't tell anyone a birthday wish," he says automatically. God, his skin. He has no facial hair at all. His emotions still bubble near the surface, that blush, that embarrassed, delighted grin, the superstition about wishes. It is before he has learned to bury it all, to be so male.

"What?" he says curiously, looking at her.

"Just – you look so old," she says, the sentiment the exact opposite of what she is really thinking.

Todd waves a hand, but he looks chuffed. Jen's eyes moisten.

"Oh, not the waterworks," he says casually.

"It's so weird in here," Kelly says, ever the evasive diplomat. Jen looks at his eyes. That navy blue. They are so distinctive. But maybe the person in the photograph . . . maybe they didn't have them, not quite like this. Maybe Jen is mistaken. Kelly leans back and spreads his hands wide. "It feels like a . . . I don't know. Like a school hall. Why are we so close to everybody?"

Their mains come. Katsu chicken curry for Jen, the only thing she likes on the menu. "I wish you could tell me your wish," she says to Todd.

"If you promise it'll still come true," Todd says, spearing a dumpling with a chopstick. He insisted on using the chopsticks, she remembers now. In the past iteration of this day, Jen had laughed at him. But she doesn't today, thinking of what he said to her about science the other night at the dining table. The things that matter to him.

"I promise," she says.

"Just – for things to go well," Todd says simply. "To get the GCSEs. Keep working hard. To become something."

"What's that?" she says softly, holding his eye contact under the harsh lamplight. He looks pale. The air smells of the kiss of garlic hitting the pan and Jen immediately thinks of her father and the garlic bread in the oven.

He shrugs, a child bathed in the glow of parental interest, content to be witnessed thinking, dreaming, wishing. "Sciencey," he says. "Something sciencey. I'd like to come to the Earth's rescue in the future, you know? I'd like to change the world."

"I know," Jen says quietly. How could she ever have laughed at this?

"I think that is laudable," Kelly says. "Really cool."

"I'm not trying to be *cool*," Todd says.

"I just meant it in the old sense of the word."

"Of course," Todd snorts, and Kelly laughs easily. As he looks up, distracted by something behind them, his expression changes completely.

"Oh sorry, got to take this," Kelly says, jumping to his feet. He raises his phone to his ear, and his T-shirt rides up, exposing his slim waist. He walks to the other side of the restaurant, where they can't hear. She stares at the phone in his hand, at his face as he talks into it. She's sure it didn't ring, didn't light up.

She looks behind her.

Nicola Williams is sitting two rows behind them. Jen is sure it is her, even though she looks completely different, her hair down, a glamorous top on. She's sharing a bowl of noodles with a man, and laughing.

Something hot flashes up and down Jen's back. That's right. That's *right*. Kelly left. He left the birthday meal. Something urgent for work, he'd said. Her gaze lands on him again, as he approaches the table after a phone call that lasted only ten seconds. "Work," he says. He's hunched over, not quite looking at them. And certainly not looking at Nicola. "I'm so sorry – a client is back early, wants to discuss a job . . . do you mind if I . . . ?"

"No, no," Todd says, always reasonable, always affable, until he kills. He waves a hand, suddenly looking like a man again, in the hinterland between childhood and adulthood. "'Course not. Go. I'll eat yours."

"It's his birthday!" Jen cries, stalling for time.

"I don't mind."

"Remember me when you win the Nobel," Kelly says to Todd, raising a hand in a parting gesture to both of them.

Jen jumps to her feet. She's got to do something.

"Nicola," she says loudly. Nicola doesn't look at her, doesn't do anything at all, keeps feeding the man noodles. "Nicola?" Jen says again, directing it to her table. Kelly has stopped walking and is turning around slowly on the spot, watching Jen.

Nicola turns her mouth down in bafflement and shakes her head. "You know my husband?" Jen prompts, pointing to Kelly.

Nicola and Kelly's eyes meet, but there's nothing. No recognition whatsoever. They are either master-class liars, they haven't met yet, or this woman isn't Nicola. Jen steps closer to her. God, it isn't. She only saw her through the door of the snooker club. And now, looking at this woman, she's sure it isn't her. She is much more groomed, her hair different, her makeup and clothes much tidier.

"Sorry – sorry. Thought you were someone I knew," Jen says in embarrassment.

Kelly comes back to their table. "What's going on?" he says in a low voice, his palms flat on the table. There is something just the wrong side of assertive about this. He crosses over into menacingly angry.

"Sorry – I thought you used to know her," she says, though she has never met any of Kelly's friends.

"No?" he says, waiting for her to say more. When she doesn't, he leaves. Jen must be mistaken. Nicola must not be the reason he was leaving after all.

"You sad he left?" Jen asks Todd.

Todd shrugs, but it isn't dismissive. She thinks he is genuinely unbothered. "Nah," he says.

"Good."

"It's usually you leaving," he adds lightly. Jen's head snaps up in surprise. Perhaps she isn't here to observe Kelly's behavior at all.

She looks closely at Todd. He's staring at the table. She starts to consider what Andy says about the subconscious. About how clues aren't always the most obvious thing.

Their conversation about Todd's science project pops into her mind. What was it he said to her? *You don't usually pay attention to my stuff.* She thinks of the pizza boxes, one empty, one full, the other night. How she left him. How maybe this is all deeper, deeper, deeper than organized crime, than lying husbands, than murders. Maybe Kelly is a red herring. She's here, on Todd's birthday, when she's been absent so often. What makes somebody commit a crime? Well, maybe it's about her mothering of him. After all, does every action a child performs not begin with their mother?

Jen and Todd have been at the table for two further hours, clearly annoying the waiting staff, who keep asking if they want anything. Outside, the sun has set, the sky a deep plum. Todd's eaten two puddings, ordered one after the other. "When can you, except on your birthday?" he'd said hopefully, and Jen had let him.

"You're growing," she says, slipping seamlessly back into the role of the mother of a younger child. It's innate, she was always told. It lived within her. Only she had never thought it had. It had taken her so long to adjust. The birth had been such a mess, the baby years so fraught, so busy Jen felt like she was in a vortex, always something to be doing. The clichés were all true: cups of undrunk tea left dotted around the house, friends neglected, career botched.

Jen buried it. The shame of it, of not falling head over heels for her baby, who arrived in her life like a detonated grenade. She lived alongside it, that inadequacy, got used to it. But then, years later, she still felt the shame; but she also felt the love, too.

She remembers waiting for Todd to come out of his tiny classroom one day when he was five or six, feeling like she had just downed a glass of champagne. Fizzy with the excitement of just . . . seeing him, little him.

The love, true love, it should have eclipsed the shame, but there is so much judgment involved in parenthood that it never did. The shame is so easy to access, at the school gates, at the doctor's, on fucking Mumsnet. She can't let it go. And nor should she. *You don't usually pay attention to my stuff.*

"Let's head?" he says now. He jerks a thumb toward the door, motioning to leave.

"I'm sorry about Dad," she says to him.

A frown crosses his face like a cloud in front of the sun. "No – I said it's fine," he says, genuinely baffled, but not getting up.

"And I'm sorry if I haven't been . . . you know. The mum of your dreams."

"Oh, please, Mother." Todd flicks his hand on the table, a throwaway gesture. Already, at sixteen, he's learned to deflect.

"Let's just say –" she stops, not knowing how to word it.

"What?" Todd says, his expression softening, lowering.

"I had this dream . . ." Jen says. A dream is the easiest way into this mess. "About the future."

"Okay," Todd says, but it isn't imbued with his usual sarcasm. He looks curious, concerned, maybe. He fiddles with the fork from his chocolate pudding.

"You want a tea?"

He shrugs. "Sure."

They order from an irritated waitress who brings them over quickly, bags still bobbing in the liquid. Todd pokes at his with a wooden stick.

"The dream," she says carefully, "was that you were older, and we'd grown apart."

"Right," Todd says, his hand creeping across the table toward hers, the way it used to, yes, yes, yes, like this, when he was still half-child.

"You'd committed a crime," she says. "And it left me wondering . . ."

"I would never do that!" he says, his body making such a violent move as he laughs chaotically in that teenage way of his.

"I know. But – things can change. So it kind of made me want to ask . . . if you wanted anything to change – between us?"

"No?" Todd screws his face up again in that way that he does. He first made that face when he ate a strawberry when he was eight months old. Jen had known, somewhere deep inside her, that it came from her. She hadn't known she made it until she saw him do it. *That's my face!* she'd thought in wonder. She had seen it in candid photographs sometimes, but she only recognized it truly when he did it; her reflection.

The overhead lights, on some sort of sensor, begin to go off, leaving their bench spotlit in the middle, alone, like they're in a play. Just the two of them, in the basement of a shopping mall, out for his birthday. His later actions must start here: with her, his mother.

"No?"

"You're human." He says it so simply something deep within Jen's body seems to turn over, exactly the same way she used to feel when he was yet to be born, her baby, tucked up away in her, rolling like a little barrel, warm and safe and happy.

"I wouldn't have you any other way, Mother," he says. He puts his hands on the table, motioning to leave. The conversation closed. Not, Jen thinks, looking closely at him, because he wants to end the discussion, but because he doesn't think that a meaningful discussion has even taken place.

They get to the car and Jen almost tells him, then. That it wasn't a dream. That it's real, that it's the future, and that she's doing her best to save him, her baby boy, from that grizzly fate, that crime, that knife, that blood, that murder charge. But he wouldn't believe her. Nobody would. Just look at him. Pink-cheeked in the cold, the hint of a chocolate smear rimmed around his lips just like when he was tiny and she weaned him on all sorts, but mostly on his and her favorite: Bourbon biscuits. They ate so many of them.

She almost hopes she can go back to then, even further. Perhaps it is not directly about Kelly, but about how Todd reacts to whatever his father has done.

"Mad that I used to be able to carry you, and now look," she says, looking up at him.

"I bet *I* could carry *you* now."

"I bet you could." His arm is still across her shoulders, hers around his waist. It occurs to her, as they walk to her car, that this might be the last time they embrace.

She's pretty sure Todd gives it up after this age. Becomes too cool for it. The first time she walked with him on his birthday, here, tonight, she didn't know. She didn't know it might be the last time.

A voice downstairs. Jen was almost asleep but – clearly – not quite. She walks soundlessly past the picture window, down, down, down, into the house. Kelly is in the study, off the hallway, and Jen pauses, listening.

He's on the phone.

"Yeah, all right," he says. "Tell Joe I called as soon as you can get hold of him in the morning, yeah?"

Joe.

But it can't be the prison. It doesn't sound like he's talking to an organization. And it's so late. It must be a mutual acquaintance of some sort.

"Yeah, exactly," he says. "Wouldn't want him to think I don't care." He says it very carefully, slowly stumbling over the words like an amateur picking a guitar. "Wouldn't want to ruin a twenty-year business partnership."

Jen sits down on their bottom step. Twenty years.

Those two words are doubly significant. A betrayal, but also a prophecy of how far back she may have to go.

Day Minus One Thousand
and Ninety-Five, 06:55

Jen has an iPhone XR, she thinks. It feels like a big rect-angular block in her hand. She stares down at it in shock where it rests against the duvet. She upgraded it – she remembers it so clearly – because it stopped connecting with her car's Bluetooth and she couldn't check up on her neediest clients on the way home from work.

She checks the date now. The thirtieth of October 2019. A Wednesday. Three years before. Almost *exactly* three years before.

She makes a cup of tea downstairs, the house silent and empty. Todd isn't up yet. Kelly isn't here, even though it's so early.

Their oak tree out the back is in all its autumn splen-dor. Three mushrooms poke out of the base of the tree. She opens the door. The ground has that smoked-damp smell, winter revving its engine softly.

She sips her tea, standing with cold bare feet on the patio, wondering if she will ever see November 2022. The steam curls upward, obscuring her vision.

Jen is angry, and now fixated on what it is that she is supposed to uncover about her husband or her son.

Kelly has been a natural father. Kelly is a natural everything, never plagued by a surplus of thoughts, by resentment, by guilt. He loved the baby they made, and that was that. Jen had watched his transformation with interest. "That smile makes it all worth it," Kelly had said one morning at four o'clock, the moon out, only the owls and the babies of the world awake.

But sacrifice is a different notion for men and women. Worth what, exactly? Kelly did not have his body change, his nipples crack right across the center like smashed dishes. Jen now agrees it is *worth it all,* but she sometimes wonders if that is because some of the things she lost have been given back to her. Sleep. Time.

That is where the damage might live, she thinks, if she has somehow caused something to happen within Todd, which she is sure she must. Never a confident parent, Jen feels certain, deep inside herself, that something must have happened. Maybe in Todd's early years. When Todd was four, she clean forgot to collect him from nursery, thought Kelly had done it. Todd had been waiting with his key worker outside a locked-up nursery. She winces as she thinks of it now, standing here in the mildewing autumn. Is it that sort of thing that would lead him to think, much, much later in life, that he must solve whatever his father is mixed up in? It isn't about Kelly, perhaps, but Todd's response to it.

"Hope you're ready," Todd shouts from upstairs, his voice wobbling, still breaking. "It's finally here."

Anxiety fires off in Jen's stomach. She has no idea what today is, and she has no idea what to expect her son to be like. He'll be fifteen. Jesus Christ.

He arrives, and a stranger is in Jen's kitchen. A ghost. The past, her history. Todd's a child, he looks barely older than ten. He developed late. She'd forgotten. All the worrying she did about it, gone, into the ether, as soon as it corrected itself. Everything in parenthood feels so endless until it ceases. He shot up sometime before his sixteenth, seemed to lengthen in his sleep. Hormones, growing pains, his voice broke, his arms became spindly and elongated before they filled out. But here he is, before it happened. Her little Todd.

"It is today," she says, her mind idling like a spinning wheel. October, October, October. She has no idea. It isn't his birthday. It isn't a significant date in any way. But clearly, it is. To him.

"Get dressed then," he says. Then adds happily, "I will, too." Jen knows that she can't ask where they're going: can't let on that she has forgotten.

He turns to her as he always used t . Jen encircles his bony shoulders with her arm in the hallway, hope firing down her spine like somebody's struck a match. This is it. This must be it. Significant outings with her son are where she is being led.

Staying in Wagamama's with Todd on that chilly autumn birthday night was the right thing to do. No child can be loved too much. And so Jen is really getting what she has always most wanted: a do-over in parenting.

"What do you think I should wear?" she asks him, hoping for clues.

"Definitely smart-cas," Todd says, like a child actor. She follows him up the stairs. His walk is different, the awkward lope of the child who isn't yet comfortable in his own body.

"Smart casual, okay," she echoes.

Todd follows her into her bedroom and ambles through to use their en suite shower. Oh yes, that's right, he went through a phase of preferring that one, for no reason at all. Just the rhythm of family life, like the way Henry VIII finds a favored spot to sleep in and changes it every few months. Todd didn't care too much, when he was fifteen, about privacy. Didn't reach the teenage self-consciousness until late, too. She remembers being troubled by the open door to the en suite, but not knowing quite how to address it. Soon enough, like many things, it had addressed itself, and he had begun to use the main bathroom, door firmly locked into place.

"Using this towel," Todd calls.

"Okay," Jen shouts back softly. "Sure."

She heads out on to the landing, hoping to find Kelly, but there's no evidence of him around. His car isn't on the drive. His trainers are gone. It's so early. Is he at work – or . . . ? He was gone before she woke this morning, no opportunity to put the tracker on his phone.

Jen's fingers brush the paintwork of her bedroom. It's still magnolia, the way it was before they painted over it, gray, then got the new carpets; she lives their renovation in reverse.

There's nothing in her phone to mark this date. She searches her emails, but there's nothing there either. She's about to go and check the fridge for tickets stuck up with magnets when Todd speaks.

"Although," he calls, his voice small over the running shower, "the NEC is huge, so maybe trainers?"

Right. The science fair at the NEC. A good day out. Sweets on the motorway, laughs, hot chocolates on the way home. Jen had been bored by the science, but she hopes she hid it well. Evidently not.

"Really, that is totally expected," Todd says, watching a smoking test tube dispassionately. Big feet, big hair, a hidden smile. He's pretending not to enjoy himself, but he's buzzing. "What did they expect from solid CO_2?"

"Well, it looks like magic to me," Jen says.

Todd shrugs. They cross over the blue-carpeted hall, browsing the stands. It's crowded in here, the high ceiling doing nothing to offset the claustrophobia, the artificial heat, the dichotomy of the people who want to be there inevitably paired with people who do not, who are indulging them, who love them.

Jen's lower back is aching, just as it did the first time she lived this day. She'd wanted to go to the shop, the café, had looked at her phone too much instead of at the science exhibits and her son. She determinedly hasn't looked at anything else, today.

"That one looks good," Todd says now, pointing. A small marquee has been set up along the edge of the exhibition hall. An official-looking man in a hi-vis jacket is manning it. Through the throngs of people walking slowly, stopping to fiddle with things, buying cans of Coke at the various stalls, Jen can see its name: THE SCIENCE OF THE WORLD AROUND US.

Todd strides off ahead of her, and she follows. He goes toward a space exhibit, Jen toward a section called THINGS TO PLAY WITH.

"Anything catch your interest?" a woman in a blue

T-shirt behind a glossy white counter says. Various science gadgets litter the desk in front of her. Something that looks like a crystal ball that calls itself a radiometer. Newton's Cradle. A giant clock that has all of the world's time zones on it.

Jen is hot, the veins in her hands swollen. There are too many people in here, in this all-white space. She feels like Mike Teavee. She looks around for Todd. He's still in the headset, his shoulders shaking with laughter. He has a tote bag slung over his shoulder with various pamphlets and freebies in it. Soon, he will pick up some free mints. They eat them for months afterward.

"No, thanks," she says to the woman, moving away from the weird science toys.

She turns around in a slow circle, looking at the exhibitions. Surely, surely, surely, she could learn something here.

And that's when she sees him. At a busy stand called WRONG PLACE WRONG TIME. Andy. It's Andy, younger Andy, lither, and – very interestingly – more smiley, too. He's handing out pieces of paper. "It's part of my research into memory," he is telling a woman there with her twin boys.

Jen takes one. As his eyes meet hers, there's nothing. Not even a flicker. Of course there isn't.

"Memory?" she says.

"Yes – specifically, the storage of it. How, in people with good memories, that storage is very organized."

"Do you study subconscious memory?" she asks. She had no idea he had started out like this. He never said. She never asked. "Or" – she gestures to the sign – "time?"

"Same thing, aren't they?" he says with a small smile. "The past is memory, is it not?"

Suddenly, alone in a crowd, here in the past, Jen feels like she is almost at the end. Feels, instinctively, that this is the last time she will see Andy. The gruesome past is rushing toward her.

She takes one of his questionnaires, then leans her elbows on the counter in front of Andy. "We've met," she says.

Confusion flickers across his features. "Sorry – I . . . ?"

"It is in the future that we've met," she says. But then, actually, she thinks that is unlikely to be true. On the day she figures it all out, whenever that is, Andy seems to think it will play through from there, erasing everything, erasing all this backward stuff, which really has just been research into the past, hasn't it? So it's truer to say that they have never met. How funny. Their truths are the same, here in the NEC, years back.

She holds a hand out to placate him. "I always ask you the same questions, but I'm hoping sometimes your answers will be different."

He blinks at her, then slowly pulls the piece of paper back from her grasp. He's still looking at her. His beard is darker and fuller. He's slimmer. No wedding ring. Jen thinks of all the things she could tell him; the scant, few details she knows about his life in the future. Perhaps he wouldn't go on to study time loops. Perhaps she'd change his future entirely, though she couldn't make that change stick.

And that's when she plays her trump card.

"You told me – in the future . . . to tell you that your imaginary friend was called George."

Before she's finished speaking, he has interrupted her with a sharp inhale. "George," he says, his voice full of wonder. "That's what I tell the –"

"The time travelers. I know," she whispers, the hairs on her arms standing up. Magic. This is magic.

"How can I help?"

Jen tells him again. She's lost count of the number of times she has told this story. Andy listens intently, his face less lined than before, his demeanor less grumpy, too.

"Sometimes," he says gently, when she's finished, "the emotions of living something the first time prevent us from seeing the true picture, don't they?" He rubs at his beard. "If I could go back – the things in my life that I would just stand and truly, fully witness, if I knew how they were going to turn out . . ."

Jen stares at Andy, this younger, less jaded, more sentimental version of him.

"Maybe it's that . . ." she says. Watchfulness. Witnessing her life, and all its minutiae, from a distance, in a way.

And maybe that's all she needs to know.

"I have to wonder, though," he says, "how you would be able to create enough force to enter a time loop? It would have to be –"

"I know," she says quickly. "A superhuman kind of strength. That one remains a mystery."

She raises a hand to him, then turns and walks back to her son, and the path they are on together. Here, deep in the past, she feels almost ready.

Todd takes the headset off and beckons her over, offering her a mint. "$C_{10}H_{20}O$," he says, crunching one. "The chemical formula for menthol."

"How do you know that?" she says. God, she loves him. She drapes an arm around his shoulders. He glances at her in surprise. Oh, just let them stay here, in his boyhood, together, without anything else.

"Just do. I mean – it's only two oxygen molecules different from decanoic acid," he says happily, as though that is an explanation.

This is exactly the sort of sentence Jen would've laughed at. "Thanks for the clarification," she would have said. She *might* have said. But she doesn't today. Banter can hide the worst sins. Some people laugh to hide their shame, they laugh instead of saying *I feel embarrassed and small.* She suddenly thinks of Kelly. The easy humor they've always had. But when has Kelly ever told her how he felt? If she observes him dispassionately, what might she see?

Anyway, even if this knowledge about Todd, this compassion, doesn't stop the crime, Jen is glad she has it anyway. Glad her son spoke his truth to her that night in their kitchen when he said he cared about physics.

"What're your thoughts on time travel?" she asks him.

"Totally possible," he says.

"Yeah?"

"They say time is only linear because of cause and effect."

"You're going to have to come down a level or two . . ."

"A way of us thinking – well . . ." he glances at her face. He raises his eyebrows at a doughnut stand. She nods, and they queue there. "Never mind," he says.

"No, what?"

"You'll find it boring. I can tell. Your eyes glaze over."

"I won't," she says hurriedly. "I'm never bored by you. You explain things so well."

He comes to life. "All right then. Time is just a way of us thinking we are free agents. That our actions have cause and effect. That's what makes us think that time flows in one direction, like a river."

"But it doesn't?"

Todd shrugs, looking at her. "Nobody knows," he says, and Jen instantly feels very sorry for past-Jen, and even more so for past-Todd. That she felt – that she decided – that this relationship with her son, this intellectual relationship, wasn't accessible to her. As it goes, she now knows more about non-linear time than anyone.

"Like the hindsight paradox," he continues, when he's bought the doughnuts. "Everyone thinks they knew what was going to happen. They said, *I knew it all along!* but, actually, they would say that no matter what the outcome. Because our brains are so good at considering every possibility. We've known whenever *anything* was going to happen."

Jen thinks about that. Tries to digest it. Todd would be able to solve his own crime in five seconds flat. He's so smart. And here he is, still a kid, his mind unmuddied by convention. He's the perfect person to have this chat with, out of everybody in the whole world. What are the chances of that?

She decides, eventually, to say just that. "You're so smart, Toddy," she says.

They walk past a medical stand, diabetes tests, ECGs, a stand about the importance of abdominal aortic scanning. "Want your aorta scanned?" he jokes, but she knows he heard her, knows he took in the compliment. Sure enough, he says: "When I discover some new chemical compound, you'll say, *I knew it all along!*"

Jen laughs. "Probably."

Todd opens the doughnuts. "Want a whole one or a bite?" he offers.

And, for some reason, Jen remembers this exact, exact, exact moment. She had said no. She was on a diet. That's right. And, God, she's in fucking size twelve jeans. *Not* what she is in in 2022.

"A bite, please," she says, standing in a crowded corridor of the NEC, with her son, who thrusts a sugared piece toward her. People huff past them, annoyed, but they don't care. She bites it off the end of his finger, like an animal, and he laughs, eyebrows up, smile wide, suspended, suspended in animation, in her gaze.

Ryan

Ryan delivers the third car in as many weeks to Ezra. It's the dead of the night, between three and four. He's knackered. He's never been able to lie in, so he's hardly getting any sleep. His arms and legs feel heavy and he's cold, his body trembling.

"Thanks very much," Ezra says to him.

Just as he's about to leave, his colleague, Angela, arrives. "Ah ha," Ezra says.

Angela smiles at Ryan. It's a careful smile. One that says *familiar, but not in cahoots.* She's wearing tracksuit bottoms, no makeup, hair scraped back into a ponytail, ashy roots showing. "I have a Merc for you," she says to Ezra. "Bit tricky as the key was just out of reach, so I had to go in. Broke the little window above the toilet with the hammer."

Ezra rubs a hand over his beard. "Right – right. But the owners were out, though?" He checks this like a friendly office manager, not a criminal, then dutifully ticks the car off on his clipboard. "Plated?"

"Yep," Angela says. "No alarm."

It's a chilly night. March, but still frosty, the air ice-rink cold. Ryan's eyes feel gritty. It's slowly dawning on him that being undercover is – like most jobs – sometimes tedious, sometimes irritating, and very tiring.

"Yeah, amazing how many people don't turn it on

when they go on holiday," Ezra says, but his tone goes down at the end, is dark, ironic somehow. Like he's making a private joke with himself.

Angela is not an idiot so changes tack, though Ryan wants to press him, to just ask the question: So how do you know they're away? "Anyway – should be a good one," she says. "It's pretty new."

"The Middle East like a Merc," Ezra says. He's a man of few words. Ryan recognizes just his type. Kelly was similar. Cards close to his chest. His explanations credible enough so as not to invite any questions, but absolutely nothing more than necessary given away. You didn't even know he had evaded you most of the time, came away with no answers, usually laughing, then thought: *Hang on.* You can learn a lot from him.

"You got your texts for tomorrow?" Ezra says. This is another thing about undercover: the lines between work and play become so blurred. Ryan isn't supposed to be on shift tomorrow but, really, what can he say? "Sorry – not down to work?"

"Yep."

"You're good kids, you two," Ezra says. And Ryan thinks how funny it is that, underneath it all, this statement is completely true, only not quite in the way Ezra thinks.

"I love it," Ryan says. "Easiest money I ever made. Imagine having a fucking normal job where you give half to the taxman?"

Ezra makes a noise that sits somewhere between a grunt and a laugh. "Yeah, clock in, clock out. National insurance. No second homes in Marbella," he says.

Marbella. More intel. They can try to trace the money that he bought that asset with.

"Exactly."

"These rich twats don't need their second cars, anyway," Ezra adds. Ryan scuffs the ground with his foot. He has learned, during his time in the police, of the power of silence, and he exerts that, now, for the first time. He can tell Ezra is about to say something significant. "But it was such a fucking circus with the baby."

Ryan keeps his face completely expressionless, though his body has begun to sing with anticipation.

"Too right," Angela says delicately. "Bad eggs, were they?"

"Ha. Eggs," Ezra says. "You talk weird sometimes, you do."

Ryan winces, barely detectable to Ezra, Ryan hopes.

"Two fucking pagans," Ezra says.

Pagans. Gang-speak for disloyal foot soldiers. It's all information that might lead Ryan upward, toward the big guy. And, more importantly – to Ryan, anyway – to the baby. If he could get the baby and let the gang go, he would. He can't sleep for thinking about her. Alone, scared. In God-knows-whose custody. Missing her mother. He cannot, he cannot think about it.

They start walking toward the cars so that Ezra can check them in. The forecourt is littered with broken glass and cigarette butts. Ryan thinks idly again of the risk he's taking. Of the notion that he has consented to this danger. He wonders suddenly, from nowhere, what the fatality rate for undercover police officers is, how often they get rumbled. How often they overstep the line in the quest for information.

"How did they not even see a baby, though?" he says. Angela scratches her nose, an agreed cue to rein it in, but Ryan ignores her.

"Fucking jokers, right?" Ezra says, becoming more animated. "Think they just didn't care." He holds his hands up. "And I didn't care about no fucking baby. But I do care about the fucking jacks from the Major Crime Unit being on to us."

Angela's nose must be really itchy, but Ryan continues asking questions. He can't stop. "The baby just head on to the ship, in the end, then?"

They're at the cars, now, and Ezra leans a hand against the bonnet. He turns his head to look properly at Ryan, a slow, animalistic rotation. Eventually, their eyes meet, and Ryan sees flint and thinks he's fucked it.

But he hasn't.

"Are you joking?" Ezra says. "Of course I didn't let them put that baby on the ship."

Ryan pauses, holding his breath. They're teetering now, on the edge of something. Just as he's about to ask, Angela reaches her hand out. You'd never know what it meant unless you *knew*.

"Yeah, I mean – good call," Ryan says. His instincts agree with Angela, this time. But look where they got him first. He can tell his handler, who can tell the CID, that the baby is in this country. Not shipped out to the Middle East. Thank God.

Evidently, stopping was the right decision, because Ezra says: "I'm heading to see the boss tomorrow night."

"The mastermind," Ryan says. He is even starting to sound different. Phasing out the Welsh accent he inherited from his father. How easy it would be to lose yourself for ever in this life. To live — literally — the life of another identity so much that you might become it.

Ezra points at Ryan. It's so cold that his jaw is trembling, the air that chalk-dust dry of snow.

"You should come." He looks at Angela, then uses her undercover alias: "You, too, Nicola."

Day Minus One Thousand Six Hundred and Seventy-Two, 21:25

Todd is thirteen.

He's four and a half feet of thirteen-year-old boy. He smells of biscuits and the great outdoors. He's currently in the back of their old car that they trade in for a better model in a few years' time, kicking Jen's chair in the way he did that she hated and is now nostalgic for. Sort of.

It is the first of April. As soon as Jen woke up this morning, the sun a yellow melted pool on their hallway floor, she remembered this day, this weekend. It is Easter Sunday.

They are on their way back now from a village fair, followed by dinner. Simple things, family things. Jen has forgotten herself for some of the day, laughing at her son's banter, her husband's quick remarks.

It was a perfect weekend, the first time around. The weather had made it. They'd spent almost all of it outside, with friends, barbecuing, a small party with their inner circle. And, on the Sunday, in this exact car ride, Jen remembers so vividly Kelly looking at her and saying, *And we've still got a whole bank holiday tomorrow, too.*

She wonders curiously why she remembers that exact phrase so well. Some days, she supposes, are brighter than others, more memorable. Some days, even the great ones, like their wedding, fade away into history.

And now here they are again. Jen remembers spending a portion of this car journey worrying she had upset her father at the office on the Thursday night about a directions hearing on a case. She wishes she could stretch an arm back into the past and shake that Jen. Life is so short. It rushes by. He'll be dead one day, she would tell her, but she can't. Jen *is* that Jen, today.

The car is dark and quiet, the radio on low, the heater on high, just the way she likes it. Her skin feels stretched. She had forgotten that they both got burnt, today, the first time, and they made exactly the same mistake today. That deceptive British springtime sun, the air refrigerated, the sun molten.

The sun set about five minutes ago. The sky beyond the motorway is rosewater pink.

They've been discussing Brexit. "They just need to get on with it, now," Todd adds, a view he will later retract. *They should have been more considered*, he will say, when the queues stack up at the ports.

It's been the nicest day in the sun, and Jen can't work out why she's here. On every other day, she's been able to find at least something, a small, confusing clue, something to change. A piece of the mystery. But this day has played out exactly as it did then.

Fuck it. She leans her temple against the passenger window and closes her eyes. Kelly is driving. In the present day, he drives much less. She had forgotten that he almost always used to drive. His left hand rests casually on her knee.

She will just enjoy the rest of the day. Maybe if she stops trying to learn from it, something will happen.

"Can I stay up when we get in?" Todd asks from the back.

Jen opens her eyes and checks her watch. It's just gone half past seven. She has no idea what time Todd went to bed when he was thirteen. It became a blur, that creep toward adulthood. She looks across at Kelly, raising her eyebrows.

He shrugs. "Yeah, why not?" he says.

"Can we play *Tomb Raider*?"

"For sure."

Todd laughs, a happy sigh. Kelly looks at Jen. "You just like Lara Croft," she says in a low voice to him.

"Oh yeah, you know how I love computerized tits."

"What?" Todd calls from the back.

Kelly flashes her a grin. "I said, we've still got a whole bank holiday tomorrow, too."

Jen smiles back at him, in the darkness of the car, just as he takes the exit ramp. "Too right," she says softly, hoping he can't hear the nostalgia and grief in her voice. And something else, too. This banter of theirs . . . perhaps it does more than it purports to. Perhaps it evades the deeper issues, somehow. Jen thinks sometimes that Kelly is so busy laughing that he never does anything else. Like show how he feels. What's the bedrock, underneath the banter? Their family has always been so full of charm, exactly what she wanted after her repressed upbringing. But isn't humor a different kind of repression?

Lights appear in the rear-view mirror, a halo of blue. Kelly's eyes dart to them, and become illuminated, his navy gaze turning aquamarine just for one second. That's right . . . something is coming back to Jen. What is it? Is there an accident or . . . no, no . . . they get pulled over. That's right. Nothing comes of it, she knows that; that's why it had faded into the past so easily. She remembers being so panicked at the time. And now, look: it's just like Andy said. She can observe it.

Her gaze moves to the speedometer, but Kelly's doing thirty up the exit ramp. He never speeds. Never pays tax. Never travels. Never goes to parties. Never gets to know anyone. Sits quietly at dinner parties.

"It's the po po!" Todd says, laughing in the back seat, still so innocent. Jen's back feels uncomfortable, like there's a hostile gaze on it. She turns to look at Todd, who gets arrested in four and a half years' time for murder and doesn't seem to care, has jaded, old, un-focused eyes as they handcuff him. She reaches to squeeze his knee, which fits in her palm perfectly.

The police turn their lights off, then flick them on again. Jen looks in the mirror. An officer in the driver's seat in a black vest is pointing very obviously to the left.

"Pull over, I guess?" she says to Kelly.

The police start indicating. Blue lights meet orange.

"Yep, they want us," Kelly says, but his voice . . . Jen's gaze goes to his. Jaw set. Eyes on the mirror. His hand withdrawn from her knee. His tone: furious. Not about a speeding ticket or whatever, but about something else. Something bigger. She never would have noticed it the first time: she was feeling anxious too. But, now that she is calm, she notices. That anger that sometimes seems to simmer beneath the surface of her husband's caustic wit.

Kelly wrenches the wheel at the top of the exit ramp. He takes a left, to the services, and pulls over onto the shoulder, two wheels on, two wheels off, at an angle which seems somehow hostile, like a teenager who won't cooperate.

A male officer appears at the driver's side. He's got a completely round head, bald, shining under the bright lights of the service-station entryway. There's something satisfying about the symmetry of it, like a football. He has a chain around his neck, a big, thick one like a fighting dog would wear. "All right," he says, when Kelly winds the window down. Spring air drifts in.

"Just doing some random breathalyzing on the bank holiday. Happy to participate?" He has an expectant smile on his face, but it isn't a question.

Kelly's eyes go to the dashboard, the windshield, and then to the policeman. Jen watches every single movement he makes. "Sure," he says, unfolding himself from the car. As he does so, Jen watches him remove his wallet from the back pocket of his jeans and drop it. A completely fluid movement. It falls and skitters on to the seat like a beetle, unnoticed in the darkness of the car. Except to her.

"You going to bag me, then?" Kelly says, Jen thinks impatiently.

The policeman obliges, and Kelly blows into the breathalyzer, standing there by the side of the road as the cars whip by, his hands on his hips. He doesn't ever drink when he's driving, not even a pint. This is why Jen didn't worry. This is why Jen didn't remember. But look: she's here. There must be a reason why. Once again, everything points to her husband.

"Why would they breathalyze people randomly?" Todd asks.

"Oh, because some idiots like to drink on bank holidays and then drive."

Kelly gets back in the car and winds the window up. He must be sitting on the wallet. It can't be comfortable, but his face gives nothing away. Absolutely nothing.

He flashes Jen a quick, easy look. "Jesus, does he know this isn't LAPD?" he says.

"Wasn't it a bit scary, to be pulled over?" she asks. "I'd always be terrified I'd done something wrong."

"Not at all," Kelly says mildly.

Jen bites her lip, there in the front seat, a spectator on her own marriage. When was the last time Kelly *did* tell her something had bothered him? Has he ever? She goes hot, suddenly, in the car. What keeps this man awake at night? What makes him mad? What will he regret on his deathbed? She suddenly finds, in the passenger seat next to the man she has pledged to love for ever, that she can't answer a single one of these questions.

Jen is sitting in pajamas, cross-legged, on the velvet sofa. An old lamp is lit, one they get rid of in a few years. Tonight, Jen is glad to be back here, in the past, in the comfortable surroundings she didn't quite know she had missed.

Kelly's wallet is in her hands. It's brown leather, worn at the edges like a dog-eared novel. He has their joint-account card. That's it – no credit cards, no debit cards of his own. He has three pound coins, his locker token for the gym and his driving license.

Jen stares at them, spread across her lap. They're

totally normal. What she would expect to find. What illegal item could anybody possibly keep in their wallet, anyway?

She squints down at the ID. The hologram . . . she isn't sure. She vaults off the sofa to get her own driving license, setting them down side by side. Are the holograms the same? She holds them up to the light. No. They're not exactly the same, no. His is . . . flatter, somehow.

She googles *counterfeited driving licenses* on her phone.

"The best way to tell," an article says, "is to look at the hologram. It cannot be successfully replicated." Accompanying it are two photographs: one of a real driving license, and one of a fake.

The fake hologram looks exactly like the one on Kelly's.

She can't deal with this. Finding and finding and finding things which she wishes she could forget. She turns the lamp out, just sitting there in the darkness of the living room, on the comfort of their old sofa, her husband's forged identity held in her hands.

Day Minus Five Thousand Four Hundred and Twenty-Six, 07:00

Jen is in a different bed. She knows it the same way she knows it's roughly seven o'clock in the morning, the same way she knows when somebody has been discussing her just before she enters a room, or that a car is about to pull out in front of her. Micro-emotions, are they called that? The abilities humans have to detect small changes. You can't explain it. You just know. Todd would call it the hindsight paradox, she supposes.

The light looks different. That's the first tell. No blinds at the bay window. Instead, the room is cast in a gray light, filtered fuzzily through curtains.

It must be the winter. A radiator nearby is on; she can smell the hot metal of it, feel the artificial heat mingling with the chill in the air above the bed.

The mattress feels different. Old and lumpy, from when they had less money. Funny how you get used to having money. It seems easy. You forget what it's like to live without it, to sleep on shitty mattresses and save up for takeaways.

She's alone. She lies there in the gray light, just blinking and exhaling a long breath, afraid to look.

She runs a hand down her side, underneath the covers. Yep. Prominent hip bones. She is *much* younger.

Right. She steels herself, then gets out of bed. The carpet. She knows it instantly. The carpet orients her straight away. She is in her favorite house. The tiny house that sits alone in the valley. She's chilled by this. To be alone with a man whose identity is fake.

She reaches down to find a mobile phone and is at least glad there is one there waiting for her. She breathes, then checks the date. It is fifteen years prior. It is 2007. December the twenty-first. Jen feels like she might be sick. This is fucked up. This is completely and utterly fucked up. She has a three-year-old. She's twenty-eight. A giant leap back, skipping aged thirteen to *three*?

Jen is suddenly so angry that this has happened to her. She strides to the window, wanting to wrench it up, to scream out into the country air, to do something, anything, and – oh. There it is. Her favorite, favorite view. Still in their nomadic, off-grid phase with Kelly, before Todd needed to be settled at a school. In the little house in the valley, a Monopoly hotel of a house, where they never saw anybody.

Maybe it's that? Maybe this life was damaging for him. Too isolated. She rests her head on the window instead of screaming out of it. How the fuck should she know? There are no fucking clues. Her angry breath mists up the window. Give me a tell, she thinks, staring at the vapor. It clears off, and she looks out. The beauty of the stark landscape, sepia-brown in the winter wilderness. The hills look old, tatty. Proper, untended, wild countryside, long, blond, beachy grasses. She had loved it here, and now she's back.

She pulls a dressing gown around her, over a pair of tartan pajamas she doesn't remember even owning. She can hear Todd and Kelly in the living room. Loud chatter. She isn't ready yet to go and see them.

Her body remembers the layout of the bungalow. She heads right, into the bathroom, before going through to see them. She needs to see herself first. To know what to expect.

She looks at the miniature striplight above the mirror. Her hand instinctively reaches to tug hard on it. She knows it will resist, that it is stiff, that, later, it breaks entirely. With a *ping*, she is illuminated.

It's Jen from photographs. It's Jen from her wedding day. Jen has looked back at *this* Jen often, thought wistfully that she didn't know how great she looked. She'd focused on her strong nose, her wild hair, but, look: bright, clear skin. Cheekbones. Youth. You can't fake it. There isn't a single line on her face while it is at rest. She brings a hand to her skin, which yields like bread dough, springy and full of collagen, not the crêpe paper that awaits her at forty.

Jen turns to the door. She can still hear them. She knows that she will find them in the living room, in the December half-light.

"Jen?" Kelly calls.

"Yeah," she says, and her voice is higher and lighter than it is in 2022.

"He wants you!" Kelly calls, his voice imbued with a harassed tone she remembers well. They were so swept up in it, in the demands of parenting a small child. The Jen of now can hardly remember why it was so difficult, can't recall the exact details. Only that it was. Only the way her calf muscles ached in bed at night. Only the evidence that remained: toast still in the toaster, uneaten, forgotten in the chaos. Washing hung out at midnight, smelling of damp from too much time in the machine. Weird botch jobs to make life easier: one time, they put a playpen up around the television to stop Todd turning it off all the time . . . things they knew to be kind of mad, but did anyway. Things they did just to get by.

"I'm here," she says, turning the light out in the bathroom and stepping into the hallway.

There they are. Jen's eyes track to Todd, the Todd from her memories. Her son, three years old, barely a foot and a half high, Jen's face, Kelly's eyes, fat little hands outstretched toward her. "Todd the toddler," she says, his nickname rolling easily off her tongue, "you're up!"

"He's been up since five," Kelly says, pulling his hair back from his hairline. He raises his eyebrows to her. She's shocked by how much it's receded in the present day. Shocked by other things, too. His face is boyish. She finds him less attractive in his twenties than in his forties, she is surprised to find. He's fatter here, too. They had a lot of takeaways, didn't exercise. Any time to themselves was hard won, so precious that they spent it in blissful, sitting silence.

"Go back to bed, if you want," she offers. She walks down the hallway to the door. Cold is seeping in from underneath it, an icy backwash. She wants to see the view properly. Her hands – so young, so unlined – remember the knack for opening the Yale lock and pressing the handle at the same time, and she pulls it open and – ah! – finds her valley.

"It's your day for a lie-in," Kelly says automatically

from behind her. Yes, that's right. They alternated the lie-ins religiously.

"It's fine," she says with a wave of her hand, with all the concern of somebody only here for the day; a babysitter, a nanny, somebody who can give the baby back.

It's frosty out. They have a wreath on their door which she fingers absentmindedly. Wellies outside, a stone porch. Milk bottles – they had an old-fashioned milkman. And then: the valley. Two hills meeting in an X. Dusted with the cold, like icing sugar. It smells delicious out here. Smoke and pine and frost, menthol, like the air itself has been cleaned.

Satisfied, she closes the door and turns back to Todd, who is walking toward her. When he reaches her, she bends to him, and he moves his face into her shoulder, and it is as seamless a motion as a long-forgotten dance. Her body remembers him, her baby, in all of his guises. Three, fifteen, seventeen and a criminal. She loves them all. "Go back to bed," she says, looking at Kelly.

He gives her a warm half-smile. "I feel like I've been shot out of a cannon, not just woken up," he says, yawning and stretching.

He doesn't go, though. Like with most things in parenthood, he wanted support, to be understood, rather than for her to take over. He sinks on to the sofa.

She turns back to her son. With this person who, today, on the shortest day of the year, 2007, she has got to fix so that, as the clocks go back, in 2022, he doesn't kill somebody.

The room is littered with toys she had forgotten

about. The little yellow ice-cream truck. The Fisher Price garage, inherited from her parents. A Christmas tree sparkles in the corner. An old, artificial one that might still sit in their loft in Crosby to this day. The living room is dim, lit only by the fairy lights.

"Now," Jen says, drawing back from Todd and looking at him in his tiny dungarees. He stares back at her wordlessly in that soulful way that he used to. Inky eyes, snub nose, pink cheeks, a studious expression on his face. She holds up a wooden block and he takes it very seriously from her, then drops it on to the floor. "Shall we pile them up?" Jen says.

Todd stretches his hand out very, very slowly.

"As tense as a hostage negotiation," Kelly says.

"What is it they say – toddlers don't play, they go to work?"

"Ha, yeah."

"I was obsessed with blocks when I was a kid."

"Oh?" Kelly leans back on the sofa, putting his legs up over one arm. He closes his eyes. "Would've thought you'd be – I don't know. On the flashcards. You know. Always learning."

"Really not," Jen says. "It took ages for me to read."

"I don't believe that. You wordy lawyers . . . you're all the same," he drawls, and Jen smiles in surprise. He *was* more acerbic like this. In 2022, he's still dry but, here, Kelly comes complete with a chip on his shoulder. She'd forgotten. How much he used to moan about work, come up with various business ideas and abandon them. He seemed to want to succeed, then chicken out.

"What's on these flashcards, then?" she says.

"Definition of jurisprudence, for starters . . . one should know this by aged two at the latest."

"Of course. And what *is* that, Kelly – age . . ." Jen hesitates. "Twenty-eight?"

"Good at English, less so at maths," Kelly says, quick as a flash. "Twenty-nine. Forgotten my age already?"

"You know me."

Todd laughs suddenly, out of nowhere, and claps at Kelly. "Yes, yes," he says to him.

"What was yours?" Jen asks him, thinking of how she felt in the back of the car with him as they got pulled over, trying to reach that part of him that perhaps she never has.

"My what?"

"Favorite toy."

"Can't remember." Kelly shifts on the sofa, eyes still closed.

"What did you want to be when you grew up?"

Kelly sits up on an elbow, looking at her sardonically, emotional unavailability colored across his features. How can Jen have missed this? "Why?"

"Just wondering. I've never known. And we're so far from where you grew up . . . you know, I don't think I've ever met anyone who used to know you."

"They're all so far away. My mum always wanted me to be a manager," he says, changing the topic. "Isn't that funny?"

"A manager of what?" Jen is stacking the blocks up in front of Todd, who has his hands clasped in anticipation, but, really, she is thinking how evasive Kelly can be.

"Literally anything. That's what she wanted. After our

dad piss— disappeared," he corrects himself, glancing at Todd, "all she wanted for us was stability. To her – a boring office job. One holiday a year. A mortgage on a little place."

"And you did the opposite," Jen says, but internally she is thinking: *Our dad.* Our dad. The man in the photograph with Kelly's eyes. She *knew* she hadn't imagined the resemblance. She blinks, shocked.

He avoids her gaze. "Yeah."

"You said *our dad?*"

"No – my?"

"You said *our.*"

"I didn't."

Jen sighs. He will stonewall her if she asks further. She'll have to try something else. "I wish he could've met your mum," she says softly to him. "And mine."

"Oh, same."

"How old were you when she died, again?" Jen asks, wondering why this feels dangerous, tentative. This man is her fucking husband, for God's sake.

"Twenty."

"And you last saw your dad when you were . . ."

"God knows. Three? Five?"

"It must have been so . . . to be an only child, and then no parents."

"Yeah."

"Do you think she'd have liked me – and Todd?"

"Of course. Look. Going to take you up on that offer," he says. "Bed calls." He leans down and kisses her, full on the lips, the only thing that hasn't changed between 2007 and now, and then saunters off to bed, leaving Jen alone with Todd.

Something makes Jen leave Todd in the living room
with the blocks and follow Kelly down the drab, brown-
carpeted hallway.

She reaches their bedroom, one ear still listening out
for Todd, and stops by the door.

Kelly isn't in the bedroom. Not that she can see,
anyway. She edges the door open in the half-light and
creeps in. Nothing.

Well, where is he, then?

She moves forward across the room. The striplight is
on in the bathroom. Did she leave it on? Just as she's
standing there, wondering what to do, she hears a sound.
A quiet, anguished sort of sound, like somebody trying
to keep something in.

He's in there. She moves toward the bathroom door
and peers inside. And there is her husband of twenty
years sitting on the toilet lid, his head in his hands, sob-
bing. The only time Jen has ever seen him cry.

"Kelly?" she says.

He jumps, wiping hurriedly at his eyes with his fists.
The backs of his hands come away wet. He looks so like
Todd when he cries. Bottom lip going and all. Jen's whole
body feels heavy and sad as she watches him try to cover
it up.

"I've got this cold, it's making my eyes stream," Kelly
says. It's a ridiculous lie. Jen wonders how many of them
he's told. And why.

But look at him, now, she thinks sadly. It's the same
look. It's the same look he gives her in fifteen years' time
when their son kills somebody. Heartbreak.

"What's the matter?"

"No, nothing, honestly, it's this bloody cold. I hope it's gone for Christmas."

"Is this about your mum?" Jen says, her voice low.

"Is Todd all right – is he . . ."

"He's in the living room, he's fine." Jen moves across the tiny bathroom to Kelly. He stays where he is, on the toilet lid, but Jen moves in alongside him, putting her hand across his back and guiding him toward her. To her surprise, he lets her, his arm coming around the back of her legs, his head resting against her chest.

"It's okay," she says gently to him, the way she would to Todd. "It's okay to be upset."

"It's just this –"

"Your Christmas cold, I know," Jen says, letting him live the lie, whatever it is. Letting him believe it. Something he said to her in 2022 comes to her, about a divorcing couple. *Avoiding pain is priceless to some.*

After a few minutes, Kelly releases her. He looks across at Jen as she leaves to go and check on Todd and says one single sentence to her: "I just miss her – my mum." It seems to cost him a lot; his body convulses as he says it.

Jen nods quickly. And there it is. Something her husband – for some reason – has not ever been able to show her.

"I know," she says. And she does know, motherless herself. "Thank you for telling me," she says.

Kelly gives her a watery smile, his black hair everywhere. His eyes look especially blue. And, here, back in the past, something passes between them. Something more substantial than what has gone before. Something

Gillian McAllister

Jen can't even name, but something which goes some way toward igniting some hope within her that Kelly isn't what he appears to be. Please let that be so.

Jen walks back to Todd in the living room. It is old-fashioned. Green, worn carpet, dark-wood furniture. It has a specific smell to it. A comforting, homely sort of smell: cinnamon sugar, cookies, a blown-out candle somewhere. Jen guesses that, somewhere or other, an alternative version of her was baking last night. Funny how those things felt so important then. Go and see the Christmas lights, bake and assemble the gingerbread house. And – *poof.* They disappear into history, causing only stress and leaving no imprint, like a footstep on sand that gets washed away too swiftly. Her entire life, she's been so concerned with how things *seem to be.* Keeping up appearances. Having it all, the house with the carved pumpkin so everybody knew they'd done it. And yet. What was it all for?

Todd plays with his cars for a few minutes, then toddles over to the other side of the room.

"No, Toddy, not that," she says as he dives suddenly into the bin. He ignores her, pulling out two balls of tin foil from what was perhaps a KitKat. Jen is disappointed that irritation flares up so easily on just a single day with him.

"Mine," Todd says. His hurt little eyes gaze at her across the room. "More," he adds. He turns to the bin again.

He's practically upside down, his head at the bottom of the bin, his feet almost rising off the floor.

"Sorry, Todd, come here," she says. "Come to Mummy."

Todd turns to her the second he hears the very first syllable fall from her lips, like a flower to his sun, and looks at her. And suddenly, just like that, like a light going on, she knows. She knows deep in her stomach, deep inside her.

She knows because of the way his eyes catch the early-morning blue winter light.

It isn't her fault.

It isn't his fault.

She knows that she mothered him well enough. She knows because of his eyes. They are lit with love. They are lit with love for her. She deflates right there on the sofa.

She tried her best. And, even when she didn't, the guilt is as much evidence as anything else: she wanted to do her best for him, her baby boy.

The hindsight paradox that this very person here teaches her about in a decade's time: she thought she knew it would happen, self-blamed. Thought he'd killed because of a poor relationship with her. But he doesn't. It was an illusion. And so this is the moment, the moment Jen realizes that it isn't about this. It's not about Todd's childhood, at all.

"Come here, Toddy," she says. Immediately, he drops the balls of foil from the bin, and he comes to her, his mother.

Ryan

Ryan is finally about to meet him, the man in charge of the operation. The big guy. He will have hundreds of foot soldiers, of associates, multiple ops. The car thefts, the drugs, the stolen baby – they're only a tiny part of it.

Ryan doesn't know how the houses he targets are always empty, and he doesn't yet know where baby Eve has gone, but he's working it all out: and look. Here, walking in the cold to a warehouse in Birkenhead, he's infiltrated all the way to the top.

Angela and Ryan have been instructed by Ezra to meet him here, eight o'clock at night. After you meet the boss, you get given better jobs, more important jobs. And, crucially, better intel. Ryan's gone in wired, for the first time, on a wing and a prayer that the big boss won't check him over. Leo says he won't, says you don't meet the boss without trust. "If he even intimates it," Leo said last night on the phone, "you act so fucking offended he's quaking."

"Too right," Ryan had said. Not the sort of sentence he would usually say. Sometimes, he feels like he is becoming the person he is pretending to be. Darker, more volatile.

Ryan and Angela walk in silence for a few minutes more, watching cars being loaded and unloaded on to ships, people coming and going. As they near the warehouse, their body language changes. Angela becomes Nicola, Ryan watches it happen; her walk becomes a swagger, her mannerisms change.

Ryan doesn't know how his own body language changes, only that it does.

The warehouse has no sign up above it. It's closed down, the perfect place for these sorts of dealings. Ryan hopes it has good acoustics for the team who are listening in, gathering evidence with which to incriminate.

Ryan knocks twice on the dark green roller-shuttered door, as directed, then waits. Angela is trembling. She isn't as together as she first appears. Ryan thinks she is just as shit scared as he is. Of course, it has occurred to him that this could be it: a sting. They could be rumbled. They could be done for. Somehow, Ryan doesn't care. And, when he feels he does, he thinks of her, baby Eve, lost and alone, not at sea, but as good as.

"In," says a voice from around the side. Ryan and Angela move around the edge of the building and find a door, propped open, allowing the outside security light to illuminate a shaft of the warehouse.

It's otherwise empty, rows and rows and rows of floor-to-ceiling shelving, containing nothing. In the expanse of the huge room stands a tall man, younger than Ryan expected. He isn't moving at all, just standing, arms folded, wearing all black clothes. He has dark hair and a goatee.

"The two musketeers," he says. He tosses the end of a cigarette which embers at his feet for a few seconds before fizzling to nothing. "Got a job for you – need you to collect a list of empty properties. Going to send you an address now."

Almost instantaneously, Ryan's burner phone beeps with a single line of text from – yes! – an actual number. It's an address on a high street in Liverpool.

This is it. This man in charge of it all is going to trust them with how he gets his intel about which cars to steal.

"You await further instructions," he says to them.

"Cool, thanks, mate," Ryan says, altering the cadence of his natural voice.

The man tilts his head back. "Where you from?"

"Manchester."

He makes an impatient gesture. "Before that."

"Always Manchester, but got a Welsh dad," he says. It's the truth; they decided he should stick to this rather than try out an accent.

"You?" the man asks Angela.

"Yeah, round here," she says, in perfect Scouse, even though she is from Leigh. Undercover officers are not often local. Too much chance someone would know them, blow their cover.

The man crosses the warehouse to them, black boots crunching the grit and grime on the floor. "It's Joseph," he says, extending a hand to Ryan, then to Angela.

"Nicola," she says.

Joseph holds his hands up. "My standard warning. If you double-cross me. If you dob me in. If you're DS. If you slip up. I will do the time. And then – I will fucking come and kill you. Okay?"

"Likewise," Ryan says.

"Let's shake on it then," Joseph says.

"Kelly," Ryan says as he grasps Joseph's hand. "Good to meet you."

Kelly. The alias Ryan had to choose for himself. "Something you'd turn your head to," Leo advised. "Something familiar. That's the first test they do to check you're not coppers. Call your name in a bar, see if your head swivels."

"I'd always answer to my brother's name," Ryan had said in a low voice, thinking of the night, the night his brother got in too deep, owed so much money, so many favors. The night his brother tied the noose. They'd found him too late, by about half an hour, the coroner later said. He'd done it in the loft. He hadn't wanted to be found.

Day Minus Six Thousand Nine Hundred and Ninety-Eight, 08:00

Jen is in a two-up-two-down terrace. She and Kelly rented it for a year. They had no emotional connection to it at all. Jen hardly remembers it. It is only now, looking up at the ceiling marbled with damp, that she recalls living here at all.

Jen is not yet pregnant, and so Todd is not yet born. Which leaves only one person this mystery can be about.

"Lopez?" Kelly calls up the stairs. Emotion moves up through her. She'd forgotten he went through a phase of calling her that. Jen became Jenny became Jenny from the Block, after that song, then became Lopez.

"Kelly?" she says.

"You're up!"

"I am."

"Look," he says, in that way that he does, that authoritative, guarded way. "I have a thing today."

"What's that?"

"An all-day conference."

Something vague is stirring in Jen's mind. What kind of painter/decorator goes to a last-minute conference? One she trusted, she supposes.

"Sure," she says, but the ground underfoot as she rises from bed feels unstable, like it's made of quicksand.

"You'll be gone all day?"

"Yeah," Kelly says distractedly.

"Okay."

"You look like you've seen a ghost." Kelly's eyes are the same, but not much else. He's so slim. Elegant, almost.

"I'm fine," Jen says weakly, looking up at him. "Don't worry – you go."

"You sure?"

"Sure as sure can be."

Jen doesn't hesitate at all in following Kelly. They're rushing toward the moment she cracks it open, she can tell.

She's here, in the back of a cab. It was much harder to call a taxi this far back in the past. She has a mobile, but it's an old brick whose numbers illuminate green neon and sing as she touches them. A children's toy of a phone.

"Can we stop here?" Jen says.

Kelly has parked illegally right in the center of Liverpool, on double yellows. His car is a 2001: Jen hadn't realized quite how much cars had changed. It's boxy, looks too big. She can't stop looking at it, or him. She feels like an alien.

Kelly looks left and right as he unfolds his long legs out of the driver's seat. The checking seems habitual, a tic. Blue eyes flick up and down the street.

She remains in her black cab. She will be almost invisible to Kelly here, sheltered in the back, behind a grimy window.

"Got to get a move on soon," the cabbie says.

"Just five – just five minutes, please, I just need to watch something," she says.

The taxi driver doesn't answer her, instead pointedly gets a novel out. John Grisham, the pages folded down. He leaves the engine idling. Oh, the days when people read novels to pass the time.

"Sorry, won't be long," she adds, thinking of all the things she could tell this man about the future. Brexit. The pandemic. Nobody would believe her. It's mind-blowing. A whole two decades squashed here into a taxi with them.

Kelly moves around to the back of his car. He scans the horizon in that way he sometimes still does in the present day. She'd never thought about it much until forced to observe her husband in this way. His hair is gelled carefully, coiffed at the front.

Another driver honks at them, gesturing at the taxi as he drives past. He winds his window down. "Move!" he yells.

Jen's driver puts the car into gear. "One sec, please, please," she says. If she gets out now, Kelly will see her, and it will all be for nothing.

Kelly opens the trunk with one hand and pulls something out. It's large and burgundy, some folded material — curtains, maybe? Jen rests her forehead against the mucky window of the taxi, squinting. It's a suit bag. Jen recognizes it from years ago. He wore suits very occasionally. To funerals, to weddings. It hung on a hook in the back of their wardrobe.

"Any time, love," the taxi driver says, but Jen just nods.

Kelly disappears up a side road, his stride a study in casual walking that Jen knows to be false. She's going to lose him. "I need to go," she says.

She starts to gather her bag and purse, trying not to lose sight of him. As she's counting out the money she got out of the drawer in the kitchen – different drawer, different kitchen, different notes – another car honks their horn.

"Hang on," the taxi driver says.

"I'll go, I need to go," Jen says, almost shouting.

"We're blocking a bus route."

"I need to get out!" Jen yells. She fiddles with the car door handle as the honking continues, wondering what will happen if she just cuts and runs without paying. It's only a taxi. It's barely a crime.

She thrusts too many notes into the silver tray that has actual cigarette ash in – God, yes, people used to smoke everywhere! – and leaps out.

She dashes to the side-street. Kelly has almost reached the end of it. He stands out to her in a crowd the same way Todd does, the same way her own name does on a list.

He turns abruptly left and goes into a pub called the Sundance. He's holding his suit bag still, over his arm, so Jen hedges her bets and waits nearby, on the pavement.

She stands outside Woolworths, the red-and-white sign so familiar to her. It goes bust in just five years' time. The recent past, really, but it doesn't feel it. Inside: the sealed plasticky floors, the stationery. She could stay here for ever, just looking in through the window, marveling at times gone by, Christmases buying games and pic 'n' mix, just staring at the changes that have overtaken the world over the last twenty years, the things lost and gained. She raises a palm to the glass, just as she did right at the very beginning of this, and waits.

Reflected behind her, she sees Kelly emerge from the pub. He's now wearing the suit, the bag slung back over his arm. Hair freshly gelled. Black, shiny shoes on.

A woman seems to come out of nowhere, perhaps another pub, perhaps an alleyway. Jen watches her approach Kelly. She squints. It's Nicola.

"How was it?" Kelly says to her.

"Yeah, all right. Tough – they want to know all the methods."

Kelly guffaws. "We can't say those."

"I know. I said that. Judge didn't much like it. Listen – good luck. And call me, you know? If . . . in the future. You ever want to come back."

Nicola leaves Kelly there, in the street, without another word.

Jen gazes at him, unseen now in the crowds, thinking of the texts he sends Nicola in twenty years' time, asking for help. Of the fact that she asks for something in return from him.

Jen follows Kelly at a distance, grateful that it's Liverpool and not Crosby. She marvels at the fashions – flared jeans, boho tops exposing skin to the last of the summer sun, in September – and the old cars and shops, the world filtered vintage. Kelly walks with purpose but also with anxiety, Jen thinks. His head upright, a deer being pursued, or a lion in pursuit, she isn't sure which.

Down a cobbled street, past brands that have and haven't survived the last twenty years, Debenhams, Blockbusters. Into a striplit-bright mall full of jewelers, out the other side. Left, right. Up a side-street lined with industrial-sized bins. Jen drops even further back.

His pace slows on a wide, pedestrianized swathe of gray paving slabs. He's surrounded by tall buildings. His body turns completely toward one of them, and then he walks forward, pulls the door open, and disappears.

Jen doesn't need to look at a map or read the signs. She, a lawyer, knows this building well. How could she not? It's Liverpool crown court.

Outside, there are old-fashioned streetlamps, the bulbs spherical and white, like pearls. The building is no different back here in 2003. A large seventies cuboid sprawl, dark brown cladding, tinted windows. An embossed crest on the front. For once, she's glad of the justice system that never changes, creaking and ancient and fusty.

She waits in the sun for a few minutes, then follows Kelly inside, pulling open the glass double door to the courthouse.

She heads straight to the listings, glad of the legal knowledge that she has. They're pinned on a corkboard in the foyer, four scraps of paper fluttering together, held by a single drawing pin that's probably still in use today.

She knows what she's looking for. She knows what she will find.

The dates align. She didn't realize it, as she traveled back. The archived news story. The list of charges against him.

And there it is. She barely has to scan down at all.

R v. Joseph Jones. Courtroom One.

So this is a life lived in reverse. Things happened that

Jen had no idea about, that passed her by as innocuously as cars.

She heads into courtroom one and sits in the public gallery. It smells of stale teapots, ancient books, dust and polish. It is busy; a high-profile trial that she had no idea about at the time. And why would she?

She's lost Kelly. She has no idea in which capacity he is attending. As a friend of Joseph Jones, she assumes with a wince; an accomplice.

The benches in the public gallery are laid out like pews. "All rise," a clerk says. He has reading glasses perched on the end of his nose, robes that sweep the cheap-carpeted floors. Jen is embarrassed by the pomp and circumstance of the justice system that she's dedicated her life to. She gets to her feet as the judge arrives. She bows her head reflexively.

The defendant, in handcuffs, is led in by a security guard with one delicate hoop earring in his ear, and put in the dock.

Joseph Jones. Young, thirty-year-old Joseph. How strange it is to look at him and know the date on which – as things stand – he will die, Jen thinks, looking at those distinctive elfin ears, his goatee, his narrower shoulders, almost boy-like. He could be anyone's son. He could be Todd.

The judge addresses the court. "Earlier, we finished hearing from the second witness for the prosecution, Witness A, and now, we call the third," he says simply.

The court is already in session. Jen works it through in her mind. So Kelly's last-minute "conference" must have been a witness summons. Trials never know which day they will need their witnesses on, until the previous one finishes.

"Thank you, Your Honor," a barrister says. A woman with retro thick glasses. Her wig just covers their pale stems. Jen had forgotten it was the past until she saw those NHS glasses. They look almost like the ones kids wear today: funny how fashion works. "We heard yesterday from Grace Elincourt, HSBC employee, who confirmed that Joseph Jones regularly deposited and withdrew large sums of money into a company bank account." She looks pointedly at the jury. "We heard earlier from Witness A that he also regularly instructed his foot soldiers to steal cars. And to corroborate this, the state now calls the next witness to the stand and, for this, we must ask again that the jury and the public gallery temporarily depart."

Jen's mind is whirring. The public gallery and jury out only indicates a few things: evidential issues, matters of law and procedure, admissibility arguments.

And anonymous witnesses.

Everybody except the lawyers leaves. Jen loiters, watching people who presumably have as much vested in this as she does, drinking vending-machine coffee, talking. The same way they always have in courthouses. The only difference is fewer mobile phones.

She pops outside, stands on the courthouse steps, wanting to witness the world here in its 2003 snapshot. She watches the cars, brand-new-looking but old, too, 1996, 1997. A lawyer stands nearby, smoking, just thinking. The buildings are the same. Same sky, same sun. She met Kelly only the preceding March; their relationship is hardly six months old.

She spins in a slow circle. You wouldn't know. You wouldn't know. The world doesn't know how much it's changing.

"Jury back to courtroom one," an usher says from the foyer, and Jen heads inside, her eyes lingering on the city horizon for just a second. She's about to find something out. Something she can never un-know.

In the courtroom, her eyes take a second to adjust after the glare of the September sun, but after a moment she sees what she expects: the witness box has changed. It is secured by a black curtain.

"Witness B," the female barrister says, her voice as crisp and clear as a natural spring, "is a serving undercover police officer. His anonymity," she addresses the jury, "is to preserve his and the police's methods and working arrangements and his safety. So, now, to Witness B. You do not need to state your name for the record. How would you like to swear your oath?"

Whoever is behind the curtains says nothing. The barrister waits, then approaches the curtains after the silence throbs in the courtroom for too long. Jen holds her breath. Surely, surely, surely this is not her husband.

The barrister re-emerges after a second and approaches the bench. Jen hears it, then, a murmured discussion. "He wants his voice anonymized. He's got an accent. We did make a formal application," the barrister is saying.

Jen can't catch it all. She can only hear snatched phrases. She can only understand because she's a lawyer.

"But Your Honor, in the interests of open justice . . ." the other barrister says. Their debates continue in mumbled prose that Jen strains to hear.

"It's important in open court to be heard as you are," the judge announces after a few minutes more.

"Witness B, the oath?" the barrister prompts. Wait . . . this witness is a witness for the prosecution, not the defense. So . . .

Jen hears a sigh. A very, very distinctive, pissed-off sigh. And then a single word: "Secular."

Three syllables. And there it is. What Jen perhaps already knew: Kelly is Witness B.

She had it all wrong. Kelly isn't involved in crime. He had been trying to stop it.

Day Minus Six Thousand Nine Hundred and Ninety-Eight, 11:00

"I worked with him, yes," Kelly's voice says, "for several months last year." He has disguised his Welsh accent, smoothed it out like planing wood. Jen is fairly sure only she would know this was him. The verbal cues you pick up only through twenty years of marriage.

"And what was your role?" The questions continue even though Jen's mind is still trying to process it. The fact keeps repeating on her like shock waves after an earthquake. He's a police officer. He *was* a police officer?

Her eyes trail upward to the tiny windows at the top of the courtroom.

He never told her. He never told her, he never told her, he never told her. Her life is a lie.

Thoughts gather around her like a crowd of reporters asking questions. How could he have kept this from her? *Kelly?* Her happy-go-lucky, trustworthy husband, Kelly? It doesn't even explain anything. Why are they seeing the repercussions of this lie twenty years later? Why is Todd involved?

He never told her. He never told her.

Jen puts her forehead in her hands.

But then, isn't this truth more palatable than the other? Maybe, but being damned if you do and damned if you don't is still damned.

"I was assigned to infiltrate the organized-crime gang

the defendant was running," Kelly says dispassionately. God, it's mad. It's mad.

"And at what point were you dispatched?"

Kelly clears his throat. "When the baby was stolen."

"Your Honor," the defense barrister, an elderly man, says immediately, rising to his feet. "Please stick to the points in issue."

"When two foot soldiers stole a baby as part of the workings of the defendant's supply chain," Kelly clarifies acerbically.

"Your Honor —" the barrister says again.

"Witness B, we respectfully ask that you stick to the facts at issue. This is not a kidnapping trial."

"We never found the perpetrators," Kelly says. "But the defendant knows."

"Your Honor —"

"*Witness B*," the judge says, clearly exasperated now.

"Fine," Kelly says. Jen knows his teeth are gritted, hollows appearing underneath his cheekbones. He pauses, and she knows, too, that he will now be running a hand through his hair. Even this Kelly, whom she hasn't seen for twenty years. Even this Kelly, whom she has at this point loved for only six months. This Kelly, who's been a liar from day one. A painter/decorator since aged sixteen. Both parents dead. Never been to college, left school after GCSEs. How true is any of it? How can he be police? *Why didn't he tell her?*

She would've understood. It's hardly a crime, to have been an undercover police officer.

She shifts uncomfortably in the public gallery, wishing she could cross-examine along with the barristers.

317

"I was instructed to find out the defendant's identity," Kelly says. "And I did so by going in at the very bottom level of his gang. For reasons relating to my anonymity, I can't explain any further than that what my role was."

"What sort of tasks did you undertake for the defendant?"

"For reasons relating to my anonymity, I can't explain any further than that what my role was."

"What did you witness the defendant – directly – doing?"

"For reasons –"

The barrister sighs, clearly irritated. She takes off her glasses, cleans them theatrically on her robes, then puts them back on. For quite whose benefit, Jen isn't sure.

"I can tell you what I didn't do," Kelly says, in a tone of voice Jen knows to precede something unhelpful.

"Yes?" the barrister says.

"I didn't ever find the people who Joseph instructed to commit crimes. Instructions that resulted in the kidnap of baby Eve."

"Right." The defense barrister jumps to his feet. The judge waves them over, casting a look to the trouble-making black curtains. "Jury out," he says.

They filter back out into the foyer and, after ten minutes, an usher confirms the case is adjourned until tomorrow. Jen stands there, open-mouthed. "What?" she says.

"We're resuming again tomorrow," an usher says to her, a dismissal. Jen stands in the foyer, people milling around her like a school of fish.

318

She doesn't have a tomorrow, she thinks desperately. It won't come.

Kelly goes white when he sees Jen standing by his car.

His cheeks sink. His lips blanch. His eyes dart left and right, then he smiles at her. Trying to style it out. Jen watches him, this man who becomes her husband, lying to her. His suit is already rumpled, the jacket slung over his arm. He looks ill, pale and young, almost like a child, very much like Todd.

"I saw your testimony," she says simply. "I was in the public gallery." Her body immediately wants to cry and to be comforted by this man she's loved for over half her life. The man she would always turn to.

"I . . ." He looks up the high street, into the sun, then gestures to his car.

"Is that it?" she says to him. In the pause in which he considers which truths to tell and which to conceal, Jen tries to move the events in her brain so that they run forward, not backward, but she can't think, her mind a sea of disparate facts. Maybe it will end here, she thinks. She could break up with Kelly. But so many questions remain unanswered. She knows somehow, thanks to Andy maybe, that it isn't yet time.

They get inside the car. The air outside is soupy, the seats warm against their thighs. He guns the engine and drives, fast, out of Liverpool. He still hasn't spoken.

"Kelly?" she says. She hates that she has to prompt him. "I mean . . ." She tries to remember that they have only been in a relationship for six months. That he doesn't know the future, that they make it. They make it twenty happy years and counting. Somehow. He doesn't know the importance of what he is toying with, of what is at stake.

Kelly says nothing. He navigates a one-way junction, eyes flicking to the rear-view mirror.

"You're undercover police."

He nods, just once, a downward bob of his head. "Yeah."

"Is . . . were you undercover when you met me?"

"Yes."

"Is your name Kelly?"

He waits a beat. "No." He swallows, Adam's apple sliding up and down.

"How is this – how could you?" Jen's mind is spinning, spinning, spinning in space, in the blackness. She can't string a sentence together.

"You've lied to me . . ." Jen says slowly.

"It's confidential."

Jen has so many questions she doesn't know where to start. She is trying to marry up two things that simply do not go together.

Kelly looks like he's going to cry. Eyes red-rimmed. Gaze scanning the horizon. She knows him. She knows when he's unhappy. "My real name is Ryan," he says quietly. "Kelly was . . . someone I knew."

Ryan. Things begin to fall into place. "How . . ." Jen starts to say, trying to frame it correctly. "How do you intend to just – live as Kelly?"

He shifts, uncomfortable. "I – I don't know."

"Kill Ryan off? Fake his death?"

320

He turns to her in surprise. "No, what? I don't know . . . I don't know what I'm going to do about it."

Jen looks away from him, out of the window. Classic, evasive Kelly. Ignore the problem. Then – when it crops up . . . damage control. The abandoned house, Sandalwood, makes more sense to her now. Gina thought Ryan Hiles was dead because it passed to the Crown, the same thing Rakesh found. But there was no other record of Ryan Hiles's death. It seems obvious now. A fake death certificate, bought for the sole purpose of showing it to the Land Registry to ensure the property didn't pass to him and make him traceable, blowing his cover. But he didn't do anything else, didn't register his own death in any other way which would have attracted scrutiny, required more documents, more things he couldn't produce: a body, for one. It was a sticking plaster over a huge wound.

His mother must have died only recently. Sandalwood was only just beginning to fall into disrepair. Jen supposes that, when he cried in the bathroom when Todd was three, his mother might have been alive, and he missed her.

He looks at her. "I left the police," he says. "Last year. I stayed as Kelly because . . ."

"Why?" she says.

"Because I met you."

"But you could have – couldn't you have told me? Or just chosen a new name?"

"Joseph Jones believes I am a criminal called Kelly," he says quietly, so softly she has to strain to hear. "If I change anything, or if I tell anyone – word would get back to him that I was never Kelly. It would be the most obvious tell of all that I am undercover. So I – I have stayed."

"You stayed a criminal?"

"So he thinks, but I'm not. I'm not doing anything. I decided I had better hide in plain sight. It'll be better when he's convicted," he says ruefully, but Jen knows that it isn't. Every prison sentence has an end and, by then, it's too late. Ryan has truly become Kelly.

"What would the police do if they knew?"

"Arrest me, probably, because I haven't been acting on their authority. For fraud by false representation. Maybe sue me, too. Say I was impersonating a police officer, get me on charges for misconduct in a public office."

Jen is hot and panicked. This is so, so much bigger than she thought it would be. She closes her eyes. They'd arrest him not only for fraud but also for those crimes he commits in 2022 to keep his cover. He will not be protected by immunity for those. He will be regarded as a criminal.

"When we went traveling. You didn't want to come back. You wanted to stay in the cottage – in the middle of nowhere. Because of him?"

"Yes. He knew . . . he knew two of his soldiers dobbed him in. A woman and a man."

Nicola.

"Why didn't you ever tell me?" she asks.

Kelly's gaze moves off hers. "Confidential," he says, his voice low.

"But . . . I mean." She can't say the things she wants to say: does confidentiality apply between lovers? Why did he think it was acceptable to keep this from her for ever? Because he hasn't lived for ever yet, with her.

"Were you ever going to tell me?" she says.

"Of course I was," Kelly says. "I am." Jen marvels at their different tenses. Hers past. His future.

But it's a lie. Jen's lived it.

The last piece of the puzzle finally drifts into place now, in the correct order, front to back, as it should be. Jen stares at it in her mind. "Can I ask . . ." she says, thinking of what Kelly just said about Joseph.

"Yeah?"

"When Joseph gets out of prison, if he found out you were the copper who sent him down, what do you think he would do?"

"He won't find out. The curtain . . . they disguised my voice. There were so many of us – working for him. The scale of it . . ."

"But say – somehow . . . he does. What then?"

Kelly waits a beat, then speaks. "He'd come and kill me."

Day Minus Six Thousand Nine Hundred and Ninety-Eight, 23:00

It's late. Jen is in the bath. She can't wait to go to sleep and wake up someplace else, tomorrow.

A hot pool of confusion gathers in her stomach.

Undercover. Undercover. The word, ugly and huge, thrums underneath Jen's breastbone like a heartbeat. So this is why. No pay-as-you-earn job. No social media. No parties.

Kelly has been living under an assumed identity for twenty years.

But *why* did he never tell her?

She thinks she has pieced it together into the right order. She wishes she could ask Andy, but he won't even have finished his degree yet. Not even he can help her now.

She stares at the frosted window, thinking it through.

Kelly went undercover. His evidence sent Joseph to prison. Twenty years later, Joseph is released, comes looking – at the law firm – for Kelly, trying to start up his crime ring once again, with all the old players in it. If Kelly refused to obey Joseph, Joseph would suspect he was the undercover officer. If he complied, he became a criminal, proper. Kelly couldn't win. And, since Joseph served twenty years for the crimes he committed with many of his foot soldiers, he had a hold over all of them if they didn't comply: he could hand them in. Only, over

Kelly, he had an even greater hold, so great he didn't even know it: if he reported Kelly for his past crimes, then the police would come looking and find out Kelly was still living under his assumed identity. Illegally. Or, worse, that he was committing offenses now, without the authority of the police.

Hence the package passed, containing the stolen car key. Kelly was forced to comply. Todd was there when they met again, as was Clio, and they fell in love. Kelly told Todd not to tell Jen about him knowing Joseph, and he also, later, told Todd to finish it with Clio. He must have confessed all that night in the garden, told Todd who he really was. The most fucked-up thing Todd had ever had happen to him, he had said. He must have shown him his old badge, the poster. Jen can just imagine it now, the conversation taking place in Todd's room. Todd hiding the badge, phone and poster from her.

Kelly began working for Joseph again, but at the moment he thought Joseph might know he was the policeman who put him in prison, he desperately contacted Nicola for help. Who is not, as it turned out, a criminal, but somebody who had been undercover back then. Police. He must have felt between a rock and a hard place. In fear for his life, coming clean to Nicola must have been the least bad option.

In return for her silence, and because of the risk of Joseph finding them, she asked Kelly for a favor. This must have been for Kelly to pass information to the police about Joseph's ongoing crimes. Maybe she arranged protection for Kelly and that's why Jen saw the police cars circulating. Maybe that's why they arrived so soon on that night, way before the ambulance. They were waiting to intervene, but just too late, too late.

Nicola must have been harmed *by Joseph* two nights before Todd commits his crime. The section 18 wounding with intent Jen overheard in the police station. Joseph must have worked her out. Now out of prison, he would have been watching every single contact of his for signs they were not who they said. It would have been easier to work her out as police, given she never left. That's why Nicola looked so different in Wagamama's: she wasn't in her undercover role.

And figuring out Nicola will have led Joseph to Kelly.

So Joseph finds out, and comes for Kelly in the middle of the night at the end of October. And wasn't he armed? Didn't he reach into his pocket for a weapon?

The police appeared almost immediately after the murder. They probably already knew something was brewing.

And then they betrayed Kelly: they arrested Todd. Even though Kelly had asked Nicola for help. No wonder he was furious at the station.

And what of Todd? Well, it seems so simple now that Jen knows. He wanted to protect his father. So, on hearing about Nicola, he bought a knife. On his way home, he recognized Joseph, saw he was armed, and panicked. Then he did the only thing he could: protected his dad, at all costs.

Ryan

718 Welbeck Street.

That's the address Joseph has given Ryan and Angela. They're ready to go. Angela's going to keep a watch outside, and Ryan's going in. And, afterward, the rest of the squad is going to arrest Joseph now that Angela and Ryan can identify him. He's trusted Ryan and Angela, and as a result there's enough to incriminate him. The text message, Ryan and Angela's evidence . . . it will be enough to demonstrate he was running a crime ring, enough to send him down for decades.

The only thing missing is the baby. Still lost.

As they're walking over, another message appears.

> Go into the address in the previous text and say you're here to do painter/decorating. Once you get to the proprietor's office, say I sent you. JJ.

Ryan turns to Angela. "This is it," he says. "This is how he gets the addresses of the empty houses. This office. We've got him. We've fucking got him."

"I know," Angela says, buzzing. "I know."

Ryan and Angela walk along the rainy March streets, Ryan thinking of his brother and of Old Sandy, too. Thinking about how he kind of *has* changed the world. Just a little bit. In his own small way.

Ryan blinks back some emotion or other that he can't

name. They reach the address. Nicola walks away from him, perfectly in character, leaving Ryan to enter the building. A law firm, apparently. Looks well-to-do.

A woman is sitting in reception. She's pretty. Cascades of dark hair, big eyes.

"Need any painting or decorating done?" he says, a big, fixed, hopeful smile in place.

"What, just – spontaneous decorating?" she says with a dry laugh. Something turns over in his stomach at that laugh. He didn't expect this. He thought she'd be in on it. He'd thought she'd understand the code.

"Er, yeah?" he says.

"Sure, we'll just pull all the furniture away from the walls right now then, shall we? Do the legal work while you paint?"

"Okay, I'm game if you are," he says easily.

"We're all right, thanks," she says. "But if we ever want some unplanned decorating done – you're our man."

She ignores him, turning her gaze back to her computer.

"Can I just check with the owner?" he asks.

"How do you know I'm not the owner?"

"Well, are you?"

". . . No."

They hold each other's gazes for a second, then explode into laughter. "Well, pleased to meet you, not-the-owner," he says.

"Likewise, spontaneous decorator."

She smiles at him, like they know each other, and shouts over her shoulder. "Dad?" she says. "Someone here for you." She glances at Ryan just as he heads into her father's office. "I'm Jen."

"Kelly."

Day Minus Seven Thousand One Hundred and Fifty-Seven, 11:00

Jen's eyes open. Please be 2022. But she knows it isn't.

Hip bones. An old phone. A really, really old bed, God, it's that low one that had the wooden sides. Air rushes out of her lungs. It isn't over.

She sits up and rubs her eyes. Yes. Her flat, her first flat. The one she bought when she'd just started work. She'd put down a three-thousand-pound deposit; laughable in 2022.

It has one bedroom. She gets up and follows the worn path in the tattered brown carpet into the hallway and then into the living room. It's been made boho by her soft furnishings: a chintzy curtain separates the sitting room from the kitchen, purple cushions line a deep windowsill to disguise the damp. She gazes at it now, in wonder. She'd forgotten almost all of this.

Morning light filters in at the grimy windows.

She checks her phone, but it doesn't have the date on it. She turns the television on, goes to the news, then to Ceefax. Fucking hell, is this what they used to do to work out the date? It's March the twenty-sixth, 2003, eleven o'clock in the morning.

It's six months earlier, and it's the day after she met Kelly for the first time. Today is the day of their first official date.

She looks at her phone, though she can hardly use it. It

can send texts, make calls and she can play Snake on it. She navigates to SMS. Kelly's last message is right here, in the thread of conversation with a man listed in her contacts as Hot Painter/Decorator? The man who she didn't know was going to become her husband. *Cafe Taco, 5.30pm? From work? xx* he wrote, the text blocky and old-fashioned, the screen illuminated a neon calculator-green.

Her reply must be in a separate box, the messages unthreaded. Ancient.

She goes to the sent items. *Sure,* she'd said, a study in casual language. She doesn't remember obsessing over it, but she's sure she will have.

It's late. She used to binge drink and binge sleep. She feels hung over. She doesn't remember what she did the night after she first met Kelly, but she presumes it involved alcohol. She runs a finger over the kitchen counters — fake marble — and gazes at her possessions: legal textbooks, but lots of paperbacks with high-heeled women on, too. Candles in jars and stuck in the tops of wine bottles. Two pairs of suit trousers balled up on the floor, pants and socks still visible in them.

She takes a long shower, marveling at the dirt between the tiles. Funny how we get used to things. She's sure she never gave it more than a passing thought when she lived here. Just put up with the mold on the windowsills, the constant noise outside, that she had to budget for every penny.

When she's out, in her towel, she heads to her desktop computer. Something occurred to her in the hot, scented steam and she wants to look it up now.

She presses the spongy button on the front of the

machine and waits for it to power up, shower water dripping from the end of her nose and on to her carpet as she sits.

She watches the monitor spring to life and thinks. She had a best friend when she was a trainee, called Alison. Jen wonders if this is why that alias tripped off her tongue so easily, weeks ago. Alison worked at a nearby corporate firm. They used to meet every lunchtime, buy a Pret lunch. Alison would slag off the law. Later, she cross-qualified as a company secretary, and Jen had stayed where she was, divorcing couples, and they had lost touch, the way you sometimes do when a friendship is born out of a common interest only.

It's so strange to be here again. To know she could dial Alison's number, now, and catch up. How segmented life is. It splits so easily into friendships and addresses and life phases that feel endless but never, never last. Wearing suits. Dragging a changing bag around. Falling in love.

She blinks as Windows XP loads in front of her. Jesus Christ, it looks like something from an ancient hacker movie. She finds Explorer with difficulty. Her internet is dial-up, and she has to connect. Finally, she goes to Ask Jeeves and types it in: *Missing baby, Liverpool.*

And there it is. Eve Green. Taken in the back of a stolen car a couple of months ago. So this is why the personal investigator couldn't find her: she was missing twenty years in the past. Kelly was involved in catching the ring that stole her, but they never found the baby. Kelly kept the poster. He must have shown Todd when he told him about it. That's why the burner phone, the poster and the badge ended up in Todd's room. And Kelly discussed it with Nicola, that she was never found.

Jen's stomach rolls over. A lost baby, lost for twenty years.

She gazes out of the window at Liverpool, hazy in the low, winter-morning sun, trying to understand it. Her father is alive. Her best friend is Alison. In the future, she marries Kelly, the man she will have her first date with tonight and will have a child with, named Todd.

She thinks about the missing baby, Todd, Kelly, a crime ring made up of bad people and undercover people who are sometimes both. And, more than all that: she thinks about how to stop it.

The puzzle isn't yet complete. Clearly, it isn't over yet. She's still here, in the deep past, still with things to do, to solve, and to understand.

In need of some light relief, Jen heads to the mirror and drops her towel, unable to resist looking at her twenty-four-year-old body. Damn, she thinks, two decades too late. She was a ten! But, like everyone, she didn't appreciate it until it was too late.

At five forty, fashionably late, Kelly arrives in the café. Jen can tell, now that she has known him for twenty years, that he is nervous. He is wearing double denim, light and dark, effortlessly cool, the way he's always been, that hair turned up at the front. But his gaze is skittish, like a deer's, and he wipes his hand on his jeans before he comes over.

She stands to greet him. Her body is so slim, it's so lightweight, like she's been underwater and just got out.

She bumps into fewer things. There is just . . . less of her. And she's so supple, so boundlessly energetic, the hangover burned off in minutes, cured with coffee and sunshine.

Kelly leans to kiss her cheek. He smells of tree sap. That smell, that smell, that smell. She'd forgotten. An old aftershave, deodorant, laundry detergent – something. She'd forgotten his smell, and suddenly, she is here, in 2003, in a café, with him, the man she falls in love with.

She looks at him, her young eyes meeting his, and she finds she has to cover up a wave of tears. *We do it*, she wants to say. *Once. In one universe, we make it all the way to 2022, still having sex, still having dates. We have a wonderful, funny, nerdy kid called Todd.*

But, first, you lie to me.

Kelly says nothing in greeting to her. Typically him. She understands, now, the need to be guarded. Because he is a liar. But his eyes flick up and down her body and, nevertheless, her stomach rolls over.

"Coffee?"

"Sure."

She messes with the sugar packets on the table. Pink Sweet 'n Lows. The menu contains coffee, tea, peppermint tea and orange squash. Nothing like 2022's macchiatos. The front window is illuminated with fairy lights, even though it's late March. The rest is pretty mundane. Formica tables, linoleum floors. The smell of fried food and cigarettes, the sound of a till ringing up. People signing receipts for card payments. Two thousand and three lacks the flair of 2022. There's nothing, except the fairy lights, that is there just because it's nice. No picture walls or hanging plants. Just these tables and those blank walls, and him.

He's in the queue, weight on one hip, slim frame, his face inscrutable, an enigma.

"Sorry," he says, bringing over two old-fashioned cups and saucers. He sits down opposite her and, bold as that, her future husband knocks his knee against hers, as if by accident, but then lets it settle there. It has exactly the same effect on her the second time as the first, even though she knows in precise detail what it's like to kiss him, to love him, to fuck him, to make a child with him. Kelly has never failed to turn her on.

"So," he says to her, a sentence as loaded as a gun. "Who is Jen?" His knee is warm against hers, his elegant hands plucking at the same sugar packets she was just messing with. He's always done this to her. She can't think clearly around him.

She stares down at the table. He is undercover. His name isn't Kelly. Why does he never, ever tell her, not in twenty years? That's what she can't figure out. The answer must be out there, somewhere, beyond those fairy lights, but she can't yet find it. She wonders if, when she does, the time loop will end. And, if not, what it'll take to stop it.

"Not much to tell," she says, still looking at the street outside, at the 2003 world. Thinking, too, about the glaring truth that she's been trying to ignore: unless Jen and Kelly fall in love, Todd won't exist at all.

"Who is Kelly?" she says back. She thinks, out of nowhere, of the way he bought that pumpkin for her, because she wanted it. The Belfast sink he got her. The lack of fucks he gives to the whole world, in the future. Both inspirational and slightly dangerous. He excites her. They were good together. They *are* good together. But the foundation of it is this: lies. A crumbling cliff edge.

He lets his smile spread across his features as he looks at her, biting his bottom lip. "Kelly is a pretty boring guy on a date with a pretty hot woman."

"Only pretty hot."

"Trying to keep my cool."

"Failing."

He holds his hands up and laughs. "True. I left my cool at the law-firm door."

"The painting then – it was a ruse."

Something dark passes across his expression. "No . . . but I don't give a fuck about decorating your dad's law firm any more."

"How did you get into that then?"

"You know, I just never wanted to be of the establishment," he says, and Jen remembers this exact sentence, the effect it had on her, on of-the-establishment her. She'd found it thrilling. Now, she's jaded by it, confused. She doesn't understand where Ryan ends and Kelly begins. Whether the things she fell in love with are the real him.

"Which area of law do you practice?"

"I'm a trainee – so everything. Dogsbody stuff."

Kelly nods, just once. "Photocopying?"

"Photocopying. Tea-making. Form-filling."

Another sip of his coffee, yet more eye contact. "You like it?"

"I like the people. I want to help people."

His eyes catch the light at that. "Me too," he says softly. Something seems to shift between them. "I like that," he adds. "You have much to do with the running of it or . . . ?"

"Hardly anything." Jen remembers being flattered by these questions, at his ability to sit and listen, unusual among young men, but she feels differently about it, today.

Kelly crosses his legs at the ankles, his knee leaving hers. She's cold with the absence of it, despite everything. "That's good," he says quietly.

She looks across at him. Sparks fly between them, like embers spitting out from a fire that only they can see.

"I never wanted the big job, big house, all that," he adds.

She glances down at the table, smiling. It is such a Kelly thing to say, the attitude, the confidence, the edge, she finds herself tumbling. And, for much of their marriage, they were poor but happy.

"Tell me about the most interesting case you have on," he says. And she remembers this, too. She'd confided in him about some divorce or another. He'd listened for so long, genuinely interested. So she'd thought.

"Oh, I won't bore you with that."

"Okay – tell me where you want to be in ten years."

She looks at him, hypnotized by him. *With you*, she thinks simply. *The old you.*

But hasn't he always – God, what is she thinking? – but hasn't he always been a good husband to her? Loyal, straight-up, sexy, funny, attentive. He *has*.

The knee is back again. He rolls up through his foot, moving his knee against hers. Jen's stomach is set on fire immediately, like a match struck with only the merest touch to the box.

As the evening air gets blacker and blacker outside, the rain heavier, the café steamier, they talk about everything. The media. They briefly touch on Kelly's childhood – "only child, both parents dead, just me and my paintbrush" – and where Jen lives. They talk about their favorite animals – his are otters – and if they believe in marriage.

They talk about politics and religion and cats and dogs and that he is a morning person and she a night owl. "The best things happen at night," she says.

"The best thing is a 6 a.m. cup of coffee. I will not be taking any arguments."

"Six o'clock is the middle of the night."

"So stay up then. With me."

They get closer and closer, as close as the table will allow them. She tells him she wants a fat cat called Henry VIII, Kelly having no idea that they do get one, and he laughs so much he shakes the table. "And then what's his heir called? Henry IX?"

They talk about their favorite holidays – Cornwall for him, hates flying – and their death-row meals – they both want a Chinese takeaway.

"Oh, well," he says, around ten o'clock. "Just a rough upbringing, I guess. I want to give my kids better."

"Kids, hey?" And there it is. A layer of Kelly that Jen knows to be true.

"I mean – yeah?" he says. "I don't know – just something about raising the next generation, isn't there? Teach them the stuff our parents didn't teach us . . ."

"Well, I'm glad we've skipped the small talk."

"I like big talk."

"Did you come in yesterday just – on the off chance? Of work?" she asks, wanting to understand, fully, their origin story. He'd gone in to check with her dad, then come out only five minutes later.

"No. You know," he says, seeming to be wanting something from her, his expression expectant, "your dad and I have a mutual acquaintance. Joseph Jones? You might've met him."

A bomb explodes somewhere, or that's how it feels, at least. Dad knew Joseph fucking Jones? The world seems to stop, for Jen, for just a blink.

"No, I haven't," she says, almost a whisper. "Dad deals with everyone."

It's as though she's popped a balloon. Kelly's shoulders drop, perhaps in relief. He reaches for her hand. She lets him take it automatically. But her mind is whirring. Her *father* knew Joseph Jones? So – what? Her father is . . . Is what? If Jen were a cartoon, a burst of question marks would appear above her head.

Kelly's fingers are playing piano on her wrist. "Shall we get out of here?" he asks.

They leave the café and stand outside in the March rain. The streets are washed with it, the spotlights of the high street reflected, the pavement a wet gold. He draws her to him, right outside the café, a hand on the small of her back, his lips right next to hers.

This time, she doesn't kiss Kelly. She doesn't ask him back to hers, where they would talk all night on her bed.

Instead, she makes her excuses. His brows lower in disappointment.

He walks off down the street, a backward wave behind his head, because he knows she will still be looking.

Jen stands on the street, alone, as she has a thousand times since this all began. She draws her arms across her body, thinking of how to save her son and thinking, too, about how nobody will save her, nobody can, not even her father, and especially not her husband.

Ryan

He's in too deep.

Ryan is standing in Jen's bedroom. It's the very early morning. She's sleeping, hair splayed across the pillow like a mermaid's. It's the second night in a row that he's spent with her, hasn't been back to his bedsit since he met her at the café, the day before yesterday.

And he doesn't ever want to leave.

That is the problem.

Joseph has texted him today, asking how he got on. The fact that he went home with Jen will get back to Joseph. Ryan's mind spins, trying to work out what to do. Damage control. That's what he is focused on.

"You weren't joking when you said you were a lark," Jen mumbles, turning on to her side. She's naked. Her breasts roll together, and she covers them with the duvet.

"Sorry," he says, his voice hoarse-sounding. He's investigating her father. He's investigating her father. She thinks he is called Kelly. *This can never, never work.*

Her eyes fly open and meet his. She props herself up in bed then smiles at him, a slow, happy smile, like she can't believe he's there. "Don't go," she says to him, bold as that, across the room. She naked, he dressed.

"I . . ."

This can never, never work.

"Stay here with me." She folds back the corner of the duvet, inviting him back in.

This has to work.

"I should go . . ."

"Kelly," she says, and he loves the sound of that name on him. Something old and something new, all at once. "Life's too long for work."

Life's too long. That's so clever. He puts his head in his hands, standing up, like a madman. He loves her. He fucking loves her.

Life's too long for work.

She's right.

She's so fucking right. His clothes are off, and he's back in the bed within a minute, with her. "Do you like mornings yet?" he says.

"I like them with you."

Ryan's been up all night, for the third night in a row. He's finally back home, at his bedsit. He tore his body away from hers today, at almost midnight, feigning tiredness, and came back here, where he has spent the entire night in his kitchen, sitting at the MDF table, making coffee after coffee after coffee.

Jen is all he can think about. Jen – and what to do about Jen. *Sleeping with the enemy, I see?* Joseph texted him earlier. A crass, reductive text that removed the heart of it all, made it sound like only sex. Ryan stared at it before he replied, trying to figure out what to do.

At 00:59 this morning, he made his decision. He'd forgotten that the clocks were going forward. 01:00 becomes 02:00, and he has decided.

Quit the police, or lose her.

In the end, he thought, in his shitty little bedsit, fake ID on the table, it wasn't a decision at all.

He's waiting underneath the streetlight on the corner of Cross Street, stepping from foot to foot, telling himself he has no choice. None at all. He's freezing cold, and his hands are shaking with too much adrenaline.

Ryan is in love.

Ryan no longer wants to change the world. Ryan wants to be with Jen. Jen, whose father is a facilitator of the organized-crime group he's investigating.

Jen, who thinks he's called Kelly, both parents dead, left school at aged sixteen.

Jen, whose eyes shine like she's been crying-laughing.

Jen, who said to him, on their first date, that she thought otters were dicks, that she wanted kids, too, that she's only ever wanted to help people, whose body fits into his like it's always been there, like it's part of him. Jen, who says she eats too much, who kisses like she was invented only to kiss him.

Her fucking father. Her father has been supplying Joseph Jones with a list of empty properties which he has used to dispatch foot soldiers to steal the cars. He acted on conveyances of timeshare properties and kept a log of whose week was whose. That is how he knew when people would likely be away, leaving their first home vacant. Such a simple crime, born out of the day-to-day information lawyers have access to.

And now. Ryan drags both hands through his hair, looking up at the sky. He wants to scream, but he can't.

The man appears. An associate of an associate of an associate. Hopefully far enough removed from Joseph, but who knows.

The stranger is stocky, short, balding. "Bag there," he says. Ryan might be back on Cross Street, but he's here for a different reason this time. He passes the stranger the bag of cash.

The man counts the money, then gives him a wolfish smile, passes him a small, crumpled envelope from the back pocket of his jeans. Ryan takes it, and leaves, fueled only by panic. No backward glance.

Ryan lets himself into the law firm when he knows Jen is out. Kenneth is there, in his office, and looks up, startled, when Kelly arrives.

"I need to tell you something and I need you to listen."

Kenneth swallows, just once. He looks like Jen. The fine bone structure.

"It never leaves this room," Ryan says.

"Okay." Kenneth's hands shake as he discards the contract he's reading, turning his attention fully to Ryan. Ryan leans over the desk to shake Kenneth's hand. His grasp is firm and dry.

"I'm police. There is going to be an arrest of Joseph any day now. He forms part of a much wider organized-crime ring, but he sits at the top of it, as I'm sure you know."

"No – I . . ."

"If you tip him off, I will get you banged up." Ryan's never spoken like this before, but needs must. He has to do everything he can to extricate himself.

Kenneth looks at him. "What do you want?"

"Tell me how you came to be involved."

"Kelly, I – I never . . . it started out so easy."

"How?" Ryan folds his arms.

"I couldn't pay the bills," Kenneth says quietly. "I literally couldn't. We were going to go under. I defended Joseph, years ago, on the civil element of a fraud case. He came in to settle his retainer and he saw the overdue bills. Said he could help. We cooked it up together. I'd act on the sale and purchase of timeshare properties for clients and keep the list of whose week was whose. Then I'd put in a calendar when all these various owners would be at the timeshare, and so not in their houses. It almost always worked. Most of them had two cars, so left one behind: usually the expensive impractical sports car. Only occasionally did they skip their timeshare slot, or give it to someone else. And, if they did, we'd bail. I got ten percent of the value of the car."

"Your actions resulted in a baby being stolen."

"I wasn't – I didn't know they'd try the next house, too," he stutters.

"You took the proceeds of crime happily."

"To pay the bills."

"Does Jen know?"

"God, no," Kenneth says, and Ryan thinks he's telling the truth.

"She can never know," Ryan says. "She can never know about you."

"No. Agreed," Kenneth says crisply.

"Or about me. I want to – I want to be with her."

Kenneth blinks in surprise, and Ryan waits, saying

344

nothing. He has a trump card. "If you comply, I'll get you off."

"Okay," Kenneth whispers. "Okay. How do I . . ."

"Get rid of your accounts. Burn them. Drown them. Whatever."

"I . . . okay."

"Any word – you're dead to me."

"Okay."

"Good."

"Before you go to be with my daughter," Kenneth says, holding his own trump card up, as clear as day. "Tell me about you. The real you. And tell me why you want to be with her. Because, if you don't, I'm happy to fess up, and go down for it. For her."

"Just isn't for me," Ryan says in Leo's office. He's only seen it a handful of times, was always in his cupboard. Leo's office, as it turns out, is offensively large. Room enough for two.

"You know," he continues, "the lies, the deception. The police generally. I hated Response, and I hate this," he says. His voice cracks on the last word, because it isn't true at all. This is the biggest lie he has told since he lied to Jen about his name. His name and his career, so new, already feel bound together. His total, authentic self, kissed goodbye to. He wonders, if he told Leo the truth, what he'd say. But he can't risk it. They wouldn't permit him to live as Kelly. It is their identity, created by them in order to embed Ryan in criminality. These fake identities are destroyed as soon as their purpose is up. To keep it would be to leave the police open to lawsuits, to criminal charges, to retribution from the criminals themselves.

They'd make him come clean. The risk to himself, and to Jen, be damned.

He has no choice. He's got to get out of the police. He's got to, before she finds out. She's become more important than him. That's love, Ryan supposes. He always knew he'd fall hard one day – he's that sort of person, isn't he? He just didn't think it would happen like this. He has to stay as Kelly.

He looks at his mentor and friend, and winces at the lies he's telling.

"I have to say, I'm so disappointed," Leo says sincerely.

"I know. Thank you," Ryan says. He hesitates, just for a second, wondering if he's doing the right thing. But it's the police – or it's her. His resolve crystallizes like hardened clay. There is no contest.

"Right, well, you know . . ." Leo pauses, and Ryan thinks he's going to elaborate, but maybe he changes his mind, because he just looks at him and says, "Yeah. I get it. Effective immediately – it has to be, with UC work."

"I know."

"I'm sorry it didn't work out, Ryan."

"Me too."

"Any idea what you'll go and do?"

Ryan stares at Leo's immaculate desk. The question is enough to crack his features with an ironic smile. He guesses he will have to go and be a painter/decorator, like he said he is.

"Nah, I'll figure it out, I guess."

"Will you still come to give your evidence? Your work was – invaluable."

Ryan glances at Leo. He can feel his gaze is cold. "I know," Leo says. "I know we didn't find Eve."

"Yeah," Ryan says. That cuts him up. Maybe if he hadn't met Jen. Maybe it wouldn't have happened like this. Maybe he could've stayed longer. But he wouldn't choose it. Not now he's met her. He's a goner, for ever. Happily so.

"The daughter – at the law firm," he says quickly. "I'm pretty sure she doesn't know. And the dad . . . honestly, he's just a small-town idiot."

"Is he?"

"Concentrate on Joseph. Not even sure the dad knew the significance of passing the addresses," Ryan lies.

"Your evidence will be useful . . ."

"I'll do it – if you don't go after the dad. Just Joseph. The other foot soldiers."

"I'll talk to those on the top landing," Leo says slowly, seeming to understand that Ryan is negotiating, even if he doesn't know why.

"Okay."

One problem solved. He might get away with this. All he needs to do now is become somebody else.

"But hey – we'll get the main man, you know? He'll go down for twenty."

"Yeah. Well," Ryan says sadly, standing there in front of Leo's desk. "Doesn't seem worth it, somehow. Not without the baby."

"I get that," Leo says amiably. This must happen all the time, especially in undercover. He holds his hand out, and

Ryan slaps the legend into his palm. The police-issued passport and driving license in Kelly's name. All gone.

"Yeah. You know, Ry, I don't think I'd do it if I had my chance again," Leo says, taking the documents.

This stops Ryan. "Really?" he says.

"Yeah, I mean – it's no way to live. What's the difference, really, between pretending to be a criminal and being one?"

Ryan doesn't answer the rhetorical question, just looks at Leo, who shows him the door after a few seconds. "Adieu," Leo says softly as he leaves.

Ryan always wanted to change the world, but it doesn't matter any more. Maybe he's bitter but, suddenly, Ryan feels chewed up by a system he hadn't even thought twice about getting involved with. From here on, Ryan vows, he will not give a fuck what anyone thinks of him: society, employers – anyone. He won't let anybody get to know him. He will only let one person in: her.

He goes to his cupboard to say goodbye to it. He leaves most things here, at the station. The only things he takes are the talismans he can't bear to part with. His badge and the missing-person poster with the baby on it. They are too precious to lose.

He'll keep them with him, for ever. Whoever he is.

As he leaves, he thinks of the Jiffy bag sitting underneath the passenger seat of his car, containing a new fake ID, purchased from a criminal last night. He has no choice but to become Kelly. Anything else would tip people off. Joseph knows he likes Jen. He can't be with her but become somebody else. There is no way back:

he's stepped into an identity as Kelly, petty career criminal, and now he's got to live it.

Kelly Brotherhood: that's the surname he chose when he elected to go undercover as Kelly, the criminal.

Brotherhood. To honor the real Kelly.

He thinks about what Leo said about the heads of organized-crime gangs. How they stay under the radar. No travel, don't pay tax.

So he won't go abroad, won't get through airport scanners, shouldn't ever get pulled over. But he can live. Love. Get married.

He tells his mother through tears. Then he tells a couple of Joseph's associates that he'll call them up when he's back in the game but he's staying under the radar for a while since Joseph's arrest. After all this, he gets a tattoo. His skin scratches and burns, hot, as the needle scars his skin for ever. His wrist is marred, branded with his decision, made in haste in the middle of the night as the clocks went forward, but which he knows he will never regret. The date he fell in love with her, and the date he became himself.

Day Minus Seven Thousand One Hundred and Fifty-Eight, 12:00

It's the day Jen meets Kelly. She's always known this date, when the handsome stranger walked into the law firm. But, today, sitting at her desk working on the enormous 2003 desktop computer, she waits to meet him for the first time.

She has that March feeling. Fun in the sun and laughing with him. She will always feel that way – whatever happens. Whoever he is. Whatever his reasons for his betrayal, his secrets, his lies.

She never liked working in the reception area of her father's law firm – people always thought she was a secretary – but today, she likes the vantage point. The plate-glass windows. The bleak March high street outside. The silence of the reception, ancient and sweeping and hers.

"Jen," her father says, walking into the foyer. She turns her gaze to him. He's forty-five. Strapping. Big, happy, healthy. She can't bear it. His youth and his betrayal. His connection to Joseph. When she visited him in 2021, had the garlic bread with him – he must have known . . . he must have known what Kelly had been up to. Surely?

"We need to file the Part 8 by four o'clock," he says.

"Sure, sure," she says, no idea what he's talking about. As she's pretending to type, clicking around on the

350

fucking enormous and antiquated computer, she notices movement outside.

And there he is. It's Kelly. Trying to look inconspicuous but, because she knows him, she sees him. He sticks out.

And he's watching her. Trying to look like he isn't. In a hoodie, the same denim jacket he wears tomorrow on their date. That hair . . .

"Jen?" her father says. "Part 8?"

But Kelly's coming in. A head poked around the propped-open door. A March gust whooshes in. They never liked the door closed, didn't want to deter patrons.

"All right," Kelly says. Her husband, who doesn't yet know her name. Whose motivations she doesn't yet know. "Just wondering if you want any painting and decorating done?"

They're walking back from the pub lunch. The shared umbrella. Kelly has brushed his shoulder against hers several times.

"We're so late," she laughs.

"I'm a bad influence."

It's quiet in the reception, only the noise of her computer whirring and, in the depths of the building, her father on the phone. "Tea?" she says to Kelly.

He blinks, not expecting it, but nods anyway. "Sure."

She disappears into the tiny kitchen off the reception, but this time she waits, watching him. And that's when he does it: the thing she now knows he will do but that breaks her heart regardless. He slowly begins to root around on her desk. He's good. His head bowed. Hands barely moving as his fingers sift gently. Unless you were looking at his hands, you'd never know.

Jen allows it to continue. Just watching, taking her time with the tea. He inches a drawer open and – God. All these years ago, he was doing just this. Her heart is pounding.

He pulls a piece of paper out of her drawer, then slides it back in again after he's looked at it.

Her father emerges from his office just as Jen thinks she's been far too long making the teas. He nods to Kelly and Jen stops herself joining them, just listens.

"Thanks for the list earlier," Kelly says in a low voice to her father. "I wondered about this timeshare – this number here, is that an eight or a six?"

"Ah," her father says, perfectly politely, unsurprised. He pats his suit uselessly, looking for his glasses. "A six."

"Okay – thanks," Kelly says. He is scanning the piece of paper.

Jen swallows. The timeshare conveyances her father pretended not to remember. Her father, facilitating organized crime. Her husband, investigating.

It was her father who was bad. The world seems to tilt and spin. Her father. A crooked lawyer.

And it was Kelly who was investigating him. All those questions on their first date. His intensity, part of their origin story, the way they fell in love.

Only it wasn't.

"What was that about?" Jen has been to run some documents over to another law firm to cool down, to think things through. And now she's back, and ready to ask her father while she can.

"Nothing."

"No – what was on that paper you looked at? Was it addresses?"

Her father avoids her gaze. "Of unoccupied houses?" she prompts.

"It's a small side project." His eyes shift to the side. But he's no idiot. He can tell what's coming, and he walks over to the window to close the blind, then brushes past her to close the door.

"Of what? Selling data? To – criminals? Don't lie," she says to him. "I'll ask Kelly if you won't tell me."

Her father turns away from inspecting a filing cabinet and looks at her. "I . . ." he starts to say. "I doubt Kelly would tell you," he says eventually.

Jen sits down in the chair in the corner of the room.

"We couldn't make rent," her father stammers. "I thought – it was just information. Like people who sell whiplash claims."

"But this isn't whiplash claims."

"No."

"I thought you were as straight as they come."

"I was."

"But – until . . ."

"Money, Jen." The force of this sentence makes him spin, just slightly, on the chair. "It was a bad decision. But, by the time you're working with someone like that . . . you can't extricate yourself. I regret it every day."

"So you should."

Her father's eyes flick toward her. This conversation is excruciating for him. Perhaps the strangest thing about traveling back through the past is the changes people themselves undergo. Kelly going from dark in 2022 to lightness and naïveté in 2003. Her father from openness to repression.

"Do you remember before you started out here when we couldn't meet the rent? We organized a longer payment window. You drafted the deed while you were at uni."

Her first-ever contract. Of course she remembers. "Yeah."

"Well, after that, an old client came in. And – Jen, he made me an offer I couldn't refuse. Passing those names and addresses kept us afloat for years. It paid for your LPC. It's paying for your training."

"People being robbed."

"How did you find out?"

"That doesn't matter," she says.

She almost wishes she hadn't found this out, she thinks, looking at her father, thinking about how she can never un-know it. But finding out that Kelly discovered this dark secret right in the center of her family and never told her . . . it is a kindness. Kelly kept his identity, his transformation, secret from her.

Because he loves her. And because he walked into the law firm one day in 2003, fell head over heels in love with her and didn't want to look back.

Day Minus Seven Thousand Two Hundred and Thirty, 08:00

Jen is back in the flat when she wakes. She blinks, looking at the sash window and the purple cushions below it. She flings an arm across her eyes.

She's here.

She rolls over in her single bed. Still in the past.

He did it because he loved her.

He has been lying to her for twenty years.

What else was he supposed to do?

He isn't who he says he is.

He gave up everything. For her.

He never told her her father was bent.

Why is she here? She pads out of her bedroom and into her kitchenette. It's full of early-morning January sun. She hasn't yet met Kelly. His number isn't yet in her phone.

He's undercover. Investigating her father. That's why he never tells her.

That's why he warns her, in the future, about looking into it.

That is why Joseph comes to the law firm, to find Kelly, to start things up again – and to notice which of his old associates may not be who they said. This is why Kelly says, in 2022, that she is in danger, that she should stop looking: Joseph assumed she knew what her father was doing. He said as much in the prison when they met.

She goes to the sash window that overlooks the crowded streets, already full of commuters in suits. Her husband-to-be is out there, somewhere, working as a police officer, yet to meet her.

She turns away from the sunlight. January the twelfth.

The date from the news story she saw after her shower.

Today is the day Eve goes missing.

Tonight is the night she is stolen.

Jen takes the bus to Merseyside Police in Birkenhead.

It's so like Crosby police station from the outside. A sixties building. A revolving door lets her into a bright foyer. Bigger than Crosby, but still as tired, the same kind of chairs bolted to each other. She thinks about how they sat in them on that first night, all those weeks ago but years into the future, Kelly vibrating with fury.

She supposes it is easy to disappear. Quit the police, go traveling in a camper van with the woman you love. Re-settle out of Liverpool. Never travel. Get married using a fake passport that nobody ever checks. Thousands of people must do it, for reasons both more and less honorable than Kelly's. Jen has never once in Crosby bumped into somebody she grew up with. She wonders if Kelly had any near misses. The world's a big place.

A receptionist with thin, plucked eyebrows and her waterline penciled in the way that everybody did in 2003 types at a boxy computer.

"I need to speak to a police officer," Jen says. "He will go by the name of Ryan or Kelly."

"Why?"

"I have a tip-off. About the crime-ring operation that he is working undercover on," Jen says. As she says it, a man pushes the door open. He's old, maybe fifty, and has feathering gray hair at his temples.

His face arranges itself into an expression of surprise. "Kelly?" he says to her.

"I need to speak to Kelly. I know he's undercover."

"You'd better come in," he says. He reaches to shake her hand. "I'm Leo."

Kelly is sitting opposite Jen in an interviewing suite and he doesn't know who she is. It's crazy, but it's true. To him, they have never met.

"Look," Jen is explaining patiently. "I can't say how I know. But the house they intend to burgle tonight . . . they intend to take two cars." She dutifully gives the address of Eve Green, taken from the news story, which Leo and Kelly write down.

It's the same address – only one digit different – from the one on her father's piece of paper. 125 Greenwood Avenue.

"Thanks," Kelly says professionally to her. His blue eyes linger on hers. "No intel at all on where it came from?"

Jen's gaze meets his. "Sorry – can't say."

"Sure, okay. Well," he says, dismissing her as though she is a stranger, "we will be sure to check it out." A fixed, careful smile.

She looks at him, wondering where the join is between him – this Ryan – and her Kelly. Whether he became the latter, or always was, deep inside. Suddenly, there in the police station, looking at this man that she has loved for twenty years, she wonders if it matters. Does anyone care how or why we are forged into who we are? Dark, guarded, funny. Whatever. Or does it only matter that we *are*?

"You will look into it?"

"Yeah – 'course," he says lightly. "Life's too long not to follow a lead."

Jen waits on the road where it all happens that evening. She is sitting in an old banger of a car, wondering how come her father could do it: supply information to criminals, keep it from her, let her marry somebody undercover . . .

It begins to rain, spring drops that fall irregularly on the roof of her car. She thinks, too, of what her father said the night he died. That Kelly was straight-up. Why would he say that, if he didn't believe Kelly to be good? Perhaps he knew. Perhaps Kelly told him.

Something pops into her head, as if from nowhere. The sign she saw at the NEC but didn't realize the significance of. Abdominal aortic scanning. You could scan for the illness that killed her father. She wonders if that technology exists yet. If it does, she could do that – call him, now, tell him to get a scan. Save more than one life tonight.

She rests her elbow on the window and her face in her palm. She knows, somewhere deep inside her, that it isn't the right thing to do.

She thinks of him asking her to make that garlic bread.

Content as anything. She thinks, too, of her mother, long gone before him. Perhaps it was his time to go. You can't save everyone. You just can't.

She must have woken up on the day he died so that she would go and speak to him and learn something about the timeshares. That must be what it was for. Nothing else, but something still feels unfinished about it, to Jen.

The police have 123 Greenwood Avenue surrounded with unmarked cars.

Eventually, around eleven thirty, they arrive. Two teenagers, just boys really, barely Todd's age. They get out of the car, wearing all black, their bodies like spiders', and she watches them go in.

She knows it'll happen but is still awed when it does. That she, forty-three-year-old Jen, is still here, in a much younger Jen's body, watching the things happen that she knew would, the things she's worked out, despite never believing that she could, that she was capable of it.

She watches them fish keys out of the letterbox. She knows things are coming to a close. She knows that this is the last day, however it will end.

Like clockwork, a tired-looking woman emerges out of the house next door to 125, carrying a baby. She lowers the baby, crying, into a car seat, then stops, patting her pockets. She hesitates, looking at the quiet street. Not seeing the car parked wonkily. Not seeing the careful letterbox crime happening next door, the two boys dressed in black, camouflaged in the shadows of the house.

At that moment: blue. An explosion of light so blue it's as though the saturation is turned up.

Police everywhere, emerging from cars and shrubs and behind buildings, arresting the teenagers.

She hears somebody read the caution out. She thinks of Kelly, absent for his own protection. He hasn't yet done anything that will require undercover testimony. He hasn't yet become Witness B, and everyone he will become after that. He hasn't yet met Jen as he knows her.

The woman with the baby hasn't left her driveway, has just watched it all play out, holding Eve, with no idea of the bullet she's just dodged; there but for the . . . We only think of the bad things that happen, rather than those that, through fortune, pass us by.

Jen closes her eyes, leans her head on the steering wheel and wants to sleep. She's almost ready. There's a deep knowledge, sitting underneath everything, just like Andy said there would be. She'd lived her life once, and missed it all, but her wise mind, her subconscious, it knew things.

She's almost ready.

Almost one o'clock in the morning and the police pull back up at Merseyside station, where Jen is waiting. And so, too, is Kelly. Just as Jen hoped.

The moon is out, the sky high and clear, and Jen is almost gone. She knows it.

Kelly and Leo get out of an unmarked car. Leo goes immediately to his own car, but Kelly loiters. He walks slowly toward the station, his breath puffing out into the cold winter air. He pulls a mobile phone out, presumably to call a taxi home.

She gets out of her car before he can dial. They only met once, earlier today, and uncertainty crosses his features. Confusion blended with amusement: he is all Todd.

"Hi. We met earlier," Jen says, hurrying over to her husband of twenty years.

"All right," Kelly says, his frown deepening. "You okay?"

"Yes," she says breathlessly. She's so far back now, an arrow aimed at the future: the slightest, slightest tweak, and she will miss. "I just wanted to know – the burglars – my tip-off – you got them?"

"We did," he says carefully. He puts his phone back in his pocket but turns his slim body away from her.

The remoteness stops her in her tracks, there in the January drizzle, almost identical to the October mist. He doesn't know, she thinks, looking at him. This man she's loved and laughed with, got pregnant by, said vows to, shared a bed with. He doesn't know. He doesn't know her. She is seeing wary Kelly, the way he greets strangers. He has nothing to be wary of, now, in the past, but he still is. He is still him. She was right. He is still himself. The man she loves.

"I'm so glad you got them."

Curiosity gets the better of him. "How did you know?"

"I can never reveal my sources," she says, the exact kind of banter he likes.

His face eases into a grin. "You asked for me. You said you wanted to speak to Ryan or Kelly."

"Yeah. I know."

"Nobody is supposed to know the connection between those two names. I mean – *I* barely knew that . . ."

Jen shrugs, holding her hands out by their sides. "Like I said. No sources." She's getting wet, out here in the cold drizzle.

"Ha, well. You know, we intervened so early. The main guy got away, we think. Our arrest of his foot soldiers tipped him off."

Joseph. Joseph got away. Jen shivers with something more than the cold. Shouldn't she be wary of one thing: unintended consequences? But didn't she do the right thing, whenever she could? She didn't play the lottery. She didn't even save her father, not this time, though she had the opportunity. She let those things go. She draws her coat further around herself and moves closer to Kelly, hoping it'll be okay.

"I think you did the right thing," she says softly, sadly, thinking of baby Eve. Thinking about how we never see the near misses that slide past us, just missing us, arrows just grazing our skin.

He hasn't called the taxi yet. His gaze lights on hers. And she knows, she knows, she knows that look.

He raises an eyebrow. And then he says it, the sentence which changes everything: "I know this is a fucking cliché, but: do I know you? From before today?"

Jen can't help but laugh. "Not yet," she says, the banter with her husband flowing as easily as ever.

She meets his eyes in the car park. He fell in love with her so deeply that he gave up his life for her. His name. His mother. His *identity*. She doesn't think he has been pretending all of their marriage. She thinks he was try-ing *not* to.

"I'm Ryan, anyway. You?"

"I'm Jen."

And this is the moment. Jen knows. She's ready. She closes her eyes, as if falling asleep. And she's gone. And everything that has been is wiped, just as she suspected.

Day Zero

01:59 becomes 01:00. Jen Hiles is on the landing.

The pumpkin is there. Everything is there. On her skin, she can still feel the phantom mist of the January night, still feel her husband's eyes on hers.

Her husband emerges from the bedroom. "All right?" he says.

"Tell me about the day we met," she says to him, stepping into his warm embrace.

"Huh?" he says sleepily.

"Tell me," she says, with all the urgency of somebody with everything on the line.

"Er . . . you came into the station . . ." Jen gapes in disbelief. She's done it. She's lived it, these whole twenty years, with him, with Ryan.

"Am I a lawyer?" she asks him.

"Er – yes? I need to sleep. I'm on shift tomorrow."

He's a policeman. Jen closes her eyes in pleasure. He will be happier. No longer so unfulfilled, no longer found wanting.

"It's so fucking late," he moans.

But still him.

"Is my dad alive?" she says.

"What's happened to you?"

"Please – just tell me."

". . . No," he says, and that's when Jen understands it.

The papercut, saving her father. Neither of them lasted. Andy was right: events played through from that rainy day in January almost twenty years ago, erasing all the other changes she made along the way. Changes she only made because they gave her the information to go back to the right place, the right time, and solve it.

"Hello?" Todd calls.

Something lifts in Jen's heart like a sunrise, dawn breaking over their lives. It's Todd. He's home. Home, calling up the stairs, not walking along the street, knife in hand.

"You're still up?" Todd calls. "You're in the window like a fucking rude picture!"

Kelly laughs loudly.

"Hey – Ryan?" Jen says.

"Hmm?" he says, as though it's nothing at all, but, to her, his name confirms everything. Jen stares at him. Same navy eyes. Same slim frame. A tattoo that says only *Jen*.

So Joseph didn't get caught, but the baby never got stolen, either. Jen reflects on this, just for a second, in the picture window. Well, you win some, you lose some. Criminals will always trade in drugs, in arms, in information. They will always steal and lie. You can't catch everyone, but you can save the innocent. Did twenty years in prison teach Joseph anything, anyway?

She looks at her husband and at her son, coming up the stairs two at a time. Isn't it a price worth paying?

Something niggles in the back of her mind. Something about how she will account for this, this strange period of her life spent reliving it.

"All right?" Todd says, interrupting her thoughts.

"Where have you been – out with Clio?"

"Who's Clio?" Todd says, staring down at his phone.

Of course. Joseph never comes to find Kelly, so Todd never meets Clio. Jen stares at her son. She has denied him his first love. Is *that* a price worth paying, too?

"I had a dream you met somebody called Clio," she says, wanting to be sure.

"Eve wouldn't like that, would she?" Todd says.

"Eve?" Jen says sharply. "Who?"

"My . . ." Todd's eyes slide to Kelly, who shrugs. "Girlfriend?"

"What's her surname?"

"Green . . . ?"

The baby. The stolen baby that was never stolen. Jen is standing at the edge of a hurricane, feeling just the breeze of it beginning to waft her hairline.

"Can I see a photo?"

Todd looks at her like she is a total idiot and flicks through his camera roll on his phone. And there she is. It's Clio. It's fucking Clio. Clio was the stolen baby. No wonder she felt recognition when she saw the photo of the baby. Jen reaches, in a daze, to hold his phone in her grasp. He lets her do it easily, no secrecy here, not really. "Wow," Jen says, zooming in on her features.

"Never seen a woman before?" Todd remarks.

"Let me look in peace," Jen says, working it through.

So, now. Baby Eve was never stolen. Jen prevented it. She stayed with her mother, as Eve Green. Jen stopped them meeting in one way, but, look: they met in another. She fell in love with her son in 2022 the same way she did as Clio, when she was stolen and sent to live with a relative of Joseph's. Fate.

Jen looks up at her husband, and at her son. Clio. Ryan. Eve. Kelly. People whose names have changed but whose love has endured despite that.

Jen extends an arm to him and Todd steps into their embrace, and they stand there, in the picture window, just the three of them. Jen's breaths slow.

She goes downstairs after a few minutes, just to check, just to look. Her hand on the door knob.

A strange feeling descends around her, like a fine mist. Déjà vu. What was that? She shakes her head. Stolen babies and . . . gangs? She blinks, and it's gone. How strange. She never gets déjà vu.

And on such a normal evening, too.

Day Plus One

Jen wakes up. It's the thirtieth of October and, for whatever reason, she isn't sure, she feels as though she has her entire life ahead of her.

"All right?" Todd says to her on the landing as she pulls a dressing gown around her. "You okay?"

"Sure?" Jen says. She has a headache, but that's about it. She can smell cooking downstairs. Ryan must have started breakfast.

"You said some weird shit last night. Thought I had a girlfriend called Clio?"

"Who's Clio?" Jen says.

Epilogue:

Day Minus One
The Unintended Consequence

For the first few minutes after she wakes up, Pauline has forgotten.

And then she remembers. Dread descends as she does, and she shoots out of bed like a firework. *Connor.*

She'd known this was going to happen for months. He's been secretive, rude, sullen. She's been waiting up for him, all hours. There's been a series of escalating behaviors. And now this.

It began with the déjà vu. Last night. And then, right after that, Connor was arrested. The police said he'd committed all sorts of offenses: drugs, thefts, the lot. He's been involved recently, over the past few years, with somebody called Joseph. He's supposed to have the rest of his life in front of him, and here he is, ruining it.

She needs to call a solicitor. She needs to fix it. She needs to do so many things. She needs to get to the bottom of why he did this.

She heads out onto the landing, ready to fire up the computer and find a solicitor. But there he is, her boy, on the landing. "Er?" she says to him. "Did they let you go?"

"Who?"

"The police?"

"What police?" he says, with a laugh. And that's when Pauline sees it. The date, flashing up on BBC News, blaring from inside his room. It's October the thirtieth. Wasn't yesterday the thirtieth? She's sure of it.

HYSTERICAL STRENGTH

Hysterical strength is a display of extreme strength by humans, beyond what is believed to be normal, usually occurring in life-or-death situations, particularly involving mothers. Anecdotal reports are of women lifting cars to rescue newborn babies, sometimes creating a huge force field of energy. Indeed, more supernatural reports have also been noted, such as time loops, though none has been proven to date. Sufferers often report déjà vu alongside episodes of hysterical strength.

Acknowledgments

I remember the exact moment I had the idea for this novel. My text history with my author friend Holly tells me it was 27 November, 2019.

> Me, 18:32: I want to write a book like Russian Doll but about knife crime.

Holly Seddon, 18:37: OMG the dream.

Holly, 18:38: How would you do it?
Would someone keep
getting stabbed?

> Me, 18:38: Yes, I think so. And the guy has to go further and further back through when he joined a gang maybe, to the point where it doesn't begin. OMG so told backwards?

Holly, 18:38: OMG

> Me, 18:38: Have I just invented something?

Just like that.

I'd watched *Russian Doll* recently, then sat down to watch the news, and a section on knife crime caught my attention. This is how it happens for writers. Never at the desk, never at the right time, but always, inevitably, the ideas come, and I think this is my best one yet. It's been an honor to write it, to spend the year with Jen and Todd, and to fall in love with them as I hope you did too.

Of course, the idea changed so much in the planning and the writing of it, but here remains the core: a crime novel where you must stop the ending, told backward. It makes a simplistic kind of sense to me – doesn't every crime have its inception in the past, buried deep in history?

I wrote this book from July 2020 to May 2021, across two lockdowns, one lasting almost five months. It was all I did over the pandemic. I figured, if I could produce a great book, then something good came out of the gloom. (My boyfriend proposed during the January lock-down and I still hit my wordcount that day.)

I've dedicated this novel to my agents, Felicity Blunt and Lucy Morris. It's hard for an author to overstate the effect two great agents can have on their career. They counsel, they edit, they hand-hold, they sell and, most of all, they make me a better writer. They were never wor-ried by this idea, never thought it was too ambitious, and for that I am forever thankful.

It is not hyperbole, either, to say that my editors, Max-ine Hitchcock and Rebecca Hilsdon at Penguin Michael Joseph, have totally changed my life. I count this up in every acknowledgement, but that's because it's true: I have now written six bestsellers, and it's because of the dream team that is PMJ: Max, Rebecca, Ellie Hughes, Sriya Varadharajan, Jen Breslin (the genius) and all in Sales, plus my super copy-editor Sarah Day. Six *Sunday Times* bestsellers, one Richard and Judy pick, an eBook number-one bestseller . . . almost half a million sold: the list of the things they have achieved with my books goes on.

Thanks, too, to my brand-new US editor, Lyssa Keusch, and the team at William Morrow/HarperCollins. I can't wait to get started!

I consulted a few experts during my time writing this novel. Richard Price (who does indeed have a J. D. Salinger T-shirt), for his physics and closed timeline curve expertise. Neil Greenough for the ongoing police procedure help. I can't even tell you how valuable it is to know someone who can help with procedure, and Neil is endlessly generous with his time and my strange questions (any errors are my own, indeed, deliberately so: an undercover unit would never work out of the main station, of course).

Paul Wade, for talking multiverses with me. Tyler Thomas, for being so great and Todd-like. Thanks, too, to my Liverpool gurus, John Gibbons and Neil Atkinson.

And my father, of course, for the many chats, invaluable suggestions, and for being my first reader, always.

Thanks, too, to Jo Zamo for dedicating her name, and to Kenneth Eagles and Kacie for letting me borrow their family lore.

The deeper into my thirties I get, the more I realize I wouldn't be much of anything without my many and varied best friendships. For Lia Louis, Holly Seddon, Beth O'Leary, Lucy Blackburn, Phil Rolls and the Wades: you are my therapists, comedians and the holders of my dearest secrets.

And finally, thanks, too, to David. He is, as I write these acknowledgements, due to become my husband in twenty hours' time (ah, marrying writers: who else would do their acknowledgements on a Sunday afternoon when they're getting married tomorrow?). In whatever universe, whatever timeline, whatever your name, I will love you to Day Minus Five Thousand Three Hundred and Seventy-Two (and back).

Read on for a sneek peek at

JUST ANOTHER MISSING PERSON

the unmissable next thriller
from *Sunday Times* bestseller
GILLIAN McALLISTER

Prologue

Julia knew from the way Cal closed the front door that something was wrong. A hasty, chaotic kind of slam. She sat upright in bed, heart thrumming. She could feel her pulse right down through her arms and legs as she listened intently, like an animal in the wild.

And then she heard it. An intake of breath. All of Julia's instincts were trained on it, on him.

And then it came: a cry for help.

"Mum?" he called urgently up the stairs. "Mum? Something's happened."

First Day Missing

I

Julia

Julia has always been too soft to be a police officer. She is thinking this as she stands in the custody suite of the station, coat on, apparently ready to leave, but really staring at an old informant of hers who is sitting on one of the benches.

It's seven o'clock. The family WhatsApp group is trilling with dinner plans. Julia catches a glimpse of a message from her daughter saying, "Okay to Nando's. But know that I think it is passé." Julia smiles at her arch firstborn, then looks back at the informant, Price. She fails to resist the urge to ask him what he's doing here, even though she knows it'll keep her from that Nando's. She can't help it. Curiosity. It's shot through her, imprinted onto her body and mind. It's why she's here, double-checking on an arrest. Only she didn't expect to see Price.

He has his legs crossed at the ankles, an arm slung across the backs of the chairs, ostensibly casual, but Julia knows he will be afraid. So afraid he trades on information – the most dangerous of commodities.

She raises her eyebrows at him. Just as he opens his mouth, the custody sergeant speaks. "DCI Day, urgent call for you," he says.

Julia looks at Price, thinks of a busy, warm restaurant and her amusing kids, then sighs. "I'll take it out back," she says.

This is the job. This is the job. That has become her mantra, necessarily so after twenty years in the police, and all the collateral surrounding that. She shrugs her coat off and holds it over her arms. The custody sergeant puts it through, then stands and goes to the kitchenette. Julia glances at Price again, whose eyes self-consciously meet hers. "What're you in for?" she asks him, standing opposite him in the empty foyer.

"This and that," he says. He smiles up at her, a bombastic, swaggering teenager's smile.

"Meaning?" she asks. Price is hardly ever interviewed. Smart, slippery, and funny, too, but never under arrest. Almost all of Julia's dealings with him have been out there, in the world.

"Business." He meets her eyes, and the tension in his smile quivers his jaw, just once. Julia notices it immediately.

"Who arrested you?"

"Poole."

"What for?"

"Jesus, am I in the interview suite now? Dealing," he says, but, on that final word, the tightness of his jaw becomes a wobble.

Julia swallows. That bottom lip. It's exactly the same face her children have made at her hundreds of times over the years, and every single time floors her.

The custody sergeant arrives back with a cup of station coffee, just for himself. Julia flicks her gaze to it,

386

then back at Price. She sighs again as she walks toward the back office but stops at the kitchen. She makes a tea, three sugars, loads of milk. The cup warms her fingers. She's tempted to down it, hasn't had a drink all day, but she doesn't.

Price's hand is already extended out to her as she arrives back with it. "Ohhh, miss," he says to her, delighted. He sips it. "The sugars as well. I owe you a tip. What's ten percent of free?"

She smiles and avoids the gaze of the custody sergeant. Better to be judged by a colleague for overfamiliarity than to lie awake tonight thinking about Price and whether he'd had a hot drink yet that day. There is nothing Julia does better than obsess in the middle of the night. And, in fact, in the middle of the day, too.

"Good luck, okay?" she says to him. He raises the cup to her in a silent toast.

She leaves him there, in reception, and takes the call in her office.

Afterward, she stares around her, just for a couple of seconds as she processes it. She fires a text to the kids saying she will be late. They respond typically: Saskia issues a to-the-point "FFS." Cal quotes Saskia's message and says: "We don't need her to have fun, young Sask."

Julia tells them to be good. The call was a new case. A missing woman. No mental health history. Last seen on CCTV last night. Housemates have called her in missing. Those are the facts.

Julia sits still, the warm telephone receiver still in her hand, and thinks that, facts aside, she doesn't have a good feeling about the missing woman, twenty-two.

Something about it bothers her already, something that goes beyond the evidence. Some sinister fact, waiting in a dark shadow, hoping it isn't uncovered.

Julia sticks the polaroid photograph of Olivia onto the whiteboard in the briefing room. It's a tired, old room: suspended ceilings, awful carpets. For some reason, their cleaners don't vacuum it as often as the rest of the offices, and it houses preserved, old coffee cups, the smell of Portishead's ever-present damp, and the paperwork scraps of old investigations. The blinds have shut out the night sky and as Julia looks at them, she wonders if she has seen more evenings than mornings here, in the station. It isn't a bright Nando's with her kids, but, funnily enough, it is something almost more potent: to Julia, it is actually home.

Julia stares up at Olivia's photograph and thinks that nobody is truly missing, not to themselves. Only to those left behind. She doesn't know what Olivia's fate is, but she already knows her own. Insomnia. Discussing the confidential details too much at home. Saskia – already far too much like Julia – will start to fixate. Art will get annoyed. A small smile plays on Julia's features as she thinks about it. How inappropriate to say it, but the thrill of a new investigation – there really is nothing like it.

The rest of the team files in, looking tired. Some won't have left yet. Some will have been recalled from dinners, date nights, parents' evenings. There isn't a designated Major Investigation Unit here. It's been hastily assembled once the case was deemed high risk. Julia scans the mass of people, hoping it contains some of the best ones.

Two analysts are discussing a man who was arrested last night. "It was Buddhas," Jonathan is saying to the other, Brian.

"Buddhas . . ."

"He was putting them –"

"All right," Julia says, badly stifling a grin. She knows all about that arrest.

She turns back to the photograph. Olivia is tall and blonde, but with a strength around the nose that elevates her to striking. Julia reaches out to straighten the polaroid. A selfie on the estuary, a stone's throw from Julia's house. Vanilla ice cream shingle, the River Severn blue-gray. Olivia, off-center. Huge smile, crooked teeth. Perfect imperfection, that luminous quality that the young have.

What troubles Julia the most is the text to the house-mates. A single missive, one o'clock in the morning. *Please come x.* That text is a specifically female call to arms, sent with only one intention, Julia thinks: to be rescued. There are things you don't just know because you're police: you know them because you're a woman.

It's freezing in the briefing room. It's late April, but still cold, as cold as January. Nathan Best, one of her favorite Detective Sergeants, catches her looking out. "Going to snow tomorrow," he says. "Fucking joke."

"Snow is a great preservative," Jonathan shoots at him.

"Let's not talk preservatives," Julia exclaims. "Let's talk finding living people."

"Is this one similar to last year's? I can't do that again, honestly," Best says, gesturing with his tea so wildly he slops it on the carpet. The stain will never be cleaned, will probably be there forever.

Poole enters the room. "Sorry," he says. "Just let a dealer go for this, so it had better be good."

Julia smiles inwardly as she thinks of Price, going on his way, free tea and call.

"Similar-ish to last year's," Julia says. "It is a young woman." Julia still thinks of it often, the missing girl, aged nineteen. She was never found, despite Julia's very best efforts, which resulted not only in the missing woman's father accusing the police of laziness but Julia's husband accusing her of marital neglect.

She grabs a red marker pen and draws an arrow across the whiteboard. It squeaks as she does so, and the room falls as quiet as if she has clinked a glass.

She begins to speak. "Here's what we know. Olivia is twenty-two. She works in marketing. April twenty-ninth, she signs the lease for a house share. April thirtieth, yesterday, she moves into the house in Portishead. A firm of movers called Johnson's moved her things." She glances at her favorite analyst, Jonathan. As dogged as Julia herself, he seems able to magic up information in seconds. He asks and asks: phone companies, airlines, anyone. He simply repeats his request, then calls up again and again. His catchphrase is, "I don't mind holding."

"She spends that night in her room, unpacks a bit, then leaves the next morning for a job interview in Bristol City Centre at a marketing firm called Reflections. She sends a text to her housemates, late, one o'clock in the morning, saying, please come. Kiss. This morning, the housemates reported her missing. It's taken a while to work its way to us, and meantime the father's been interviewed on the phone, who was helpful."

She begins handing out tasks. Poole interrupts her before she can really start. "Why is she high risk?" he says. He's a contrary type, the sort of person who would argue against his own existence in the right circumstances.

"No past mental health problems that we know of, attractive woman walking alone late at night, text sent to housemates asking them to come to her. Probably worth looking into, isn't it?" Julia says, her tone sharp.

"All right," he says, holding his hands up. "No need to go loopy on me."

Julia talks over him, directing CCTV collection, phone records, interviewing the father formally, questioning the housemates, fingertip searches. Julia's strategy is to throw as much time – and budget – at a missing person's case as she can early on. She doesn't understand why anyone would work differently. Information, to Julia, is king, and they need it in abundance; she will feast on it. It will tell them if Olivia is hiding or dead: there is no other outcome.

Julia walks back to her office to begin her own set of tasks, thinking guiltily of her children at home, eating takeaway Nando's. They're both teenagers. Only a few years younger than Olivia.

Julia likes her team to report to her one-on-one, and she likes to look at the things they show her, too. You can't get a feel from an email and, anyway, you can tell a lot about a piece of information by the way it is relayed. Both by analysts and her own teenagers, as it goes.

She concentrates on Jonathan, sitting in her office. It's just after ten at night. He's taken his large, black-framed glasses off and is rubbing at his eyes. His wedding ring hits the desk as he reaches to put them back on.

His wife had a baby only a few months ago. Julia had to force him to take leave. He'd returned to work days early, his eyes bright, alive with the joys of his life having changed in an instant. He loves the baby, but he loves the job more. Julia remembers it so well, the faux-rueful glances exchanged with her husband, cradling a warm sugarloaf of a baby. She got a nanny and returned here, to this very station, so fast and, looking back, sometimes wishes she hadn't.

"Alrighty, Instagram," Jonathan says. He's sitting on Julia's spare chair, which is designated for exactly this, nicknamed the Interrogation Chair by – well, everyone.

"Twenty-four hours missing now," Jonathan says in a low voice.

"I know."

Julia looks at the colored, filtered boxes that comprise Olivia's Instagram grid. Selfies, flowers, stacks of books. Witty captions. "Can you print them all for me?" she asks. "Go through them anyway, but can I have them? And anything else: her emails, Tweets, whatever."

"Already done it," he says, lifting the file up to show a duplicate. "In anticipation of you saying just that."

Julia smiles a half-smile. "Thanks."

"Sure. So. Right. This last photo, on her grid – clearly taken in the Portishead Starbucks, yesterday, yeah? Same window. She used a VCSO filter and an iPhone to upload." Jonathan is a middle-aged analyst who is now an expert, thanks to his job, in the detailed machinations of the way Gen-Z-ers live their lives online.

"Right."

He zooms in on it. The photograph is of a distinctive lemon-yellow coat folded onto a stool, a laptop open in the window, and a coffee. Caption: *Pretending it's summer*.

"We have CCTV of a woman in a coat like this," he says.

CCTV. Julia blinks. Since last summer, CCTV will forever remind her of Cal. More specifically, of what Cal did.

"The uniformed officers have watched all the CCTV from Starbucks yesterday. They've got this, from outside the estate agents. Yellow coat, right? Walks up the alleyway."

It's grainy footage from up above, but it is in color, and it is – to Julia, anyway – clearly Olivia. The same distinctively fair hair, a natural blonde, no roots. And the same coat from the photograph. Julia tries to forget Cal, for just a second, and be moved, the way she has always been, by the last-seen footage of a missing person. She pauses it, zooms in. Did she know, then? Did she want it to happen – to disappear? Or was she taken?

"Agreed. That's her," she says.

"Right. Goes into the alley. Nine thirty last night. Here's the weird bit." Jonathan presses play again. Olivia turns right off the high street, up to an alleyway. He leaves the tape running for five minutes, people coming and going, late-night shoppers, the dribs and drabs of commuters, a handful of evening drinkers. As he often does, he allows his evidence to speak for itself, the silence to breathe.

"Okay?" Julia says.

He opens Google Maps on his phone – he uses his personal phone, which Julia has always liked. "Here is that alley," he says. "Blindman's Lane, it's called."

It's off the High Street in Portishead. Jonathan places his phone down on the desk and angles Street View up to the alley. As she's looking, a text from his wife comes up, a photograph icon and the message: *bedtime*, Julia presumes of their baby.

"It's blocked up," he says, flicking the photograph away. "Dead end."

"Dead end?"

"She doesn't come out. I have watched five hours of footage."

"Is it still blocked up? Is Google Maps up to date?"

"Five uniformed officers have confirmed it. And I went myself – it's only –" he jerks his thumb – "down there."

"No ladder? No fire door? A shaft down to a basement?" Julia says, zooming in on Google.

"No, no, no," Jonathan says. He closes Google Maps and opens the text from his wife. It is indeed a photograph of her, and their baby, maybe four months now. Something soft and doughy exhales inside Julia, releases a puff of longing for those days, those distant-past days. Both the marriage and the babies. The babies consigned to teenagehood. And the marriage . . .

"I need to look at this alleyway," she says to Jonathan.

He gestures, as he often does – economically – to the door, like, be my guest.

It's a quarter of a mile down the road to the alleyway. Julia's passed it thousands of times, but of course has never looked at it properly until now. She walks there quickly, her mind fizzing the way it always does. "Never once does the inner monologue stop," Art, her husband – is he still, technically? – once said to her, a sentence that for some reason she has remembered for all of these years.

It's freezing out, the air dry-ice cold, the streets quiet. Portishead's nightlife hasn't yet recovered from the pandemic, Julia thinks, or perhaps nobody's has. The silent street ahead is frosted, the pavement tactile underfoot. She slows her steps. She has learned, after this long in the job, to relax in these pockets of time. Nobody enjoys a two-minute walk to run an errand more than her.

As soon as she reaches the correct alleyway, it's obvious: sealed off with police tape, two PCSOs manning it. Olivia's house will be the same. Everything is a crime scene until it isn't. Julia's surprised they could get two: Portishead is small, underfunded, like everything, ill-equipped, each big case requiring a team cobbled together from Bristol, Avon and Somerset.

She stands and looks at the alleyway. The PCSOs acknowledge her with raised eyebrows, but nothing more. They will not be surprised by her sudden appearance here. None of the force would be.

It truly is blocked up. Completely and utterly. On the left an estate agents. Old stone, stained with years of water damage. On the right a pub, red brick, new-ish, but still probably forty years old.

It is a complete dead end. The back of the alleyway is bricked up. Julia walks a slow circle around until she understands. At the very end of the alleyway, a new build set of flats has been erected onto the back of both the estate agents and the pub.

Julia, back at the entrance, puts on protective clothing – some officers aren't fastidious at this, but Julia is. *By the book, by the book, by the book.* It's another of her mantras. Somebody guilty will never walk free because of an error on Julia's part. And neither will somebody innocent be convicted, either.

She enters the alleyway, stooping under the police tape, and runs a gloved hand across the back wall. The seam where the buildings meet. It's faultless. Not a single way out. No windows into here. The first window of the flats is at least twenty feet in the air. Julia looks around it, her mind spinning.

There's nothing. No marks where a ladder would be. No manhole covers. No drains. Nothing. Olivia wasn't carrying anything. No vehicle entered the alley.

The only items in the alley are two industrial blue bins. Julia remembers a case on the news, years ago, where the Scottish police didn't check the bins, to catastrophic results. They contained an unconscious drunken lad, who was taken to a landfill. Discovered two days too late.

"The bins been emptied?" she calls to the PCSOs.

"Nobody has been let in or out since we found the CCTV," one of them, Ed, replies. He's young, barely twenty, is gym-obsessed, drinks tea with protein powder in it, which Julia finds incredibly endearing.

"Don't," she says. "Nobody comes in or out."

She tugs at one of the bins with a gloved hand. It moves easily. She opens both bins, then stares in. Nothing. One pristine, looks never used. It doesn't smell of cleaning fluid. The other has a single can of Carling in it, but the stain that's dribbled out of it is ancient, a dark brown fuzz.

She adds it to her mental list: fingertip searchers and forensics on the bins. This skill is now a living, breathing thing. The way tasks leap up the priority list. A mystical but methodical sort of sifting, the larger items naturally rising to the surface, the finer grains falling to the bottom. She gets it right most times. But not enough.

She casts a gaze across the ground. Old chewing gum. She's looking for blood. A weapon. Signs of a struggle. But there's nothing.

"Right," she says, taking another look before she leaves. She's freezing. There's so much to do, and none of it here. She gets her phone out. "I need every single bit of CCTV on this alleyway," she says to Jonathan.

"Mad, isn't it?"

"Completely and utterly," Julia says, looking at the walls, looking for tiny holes. Could somebody have used a ladder, then taken it off the wall . . . ? She scans again, but sees nothing but clear bricks, mortar, nothing.

"Maybe it wasn't her," Jonathan says.

"If it wasn't, whoever it was still went in and never left," Julia replies.

"Yeah," he says slowly. "Yeah. I'll send it. But I have watched it. I promise, she doesn't come back out."

It's after midnight, and Julia leaves the station with gritty eyes that have watched four videos at a time on her monitor, followed by another four. She has covered every single camera, and every single minute. She has barely blinked.

It can't be true, but it is: Olivia goes into the alleyway and doesn't leave. Nobody else walks in there. The bins do not go in or out. At two o'clock in the morning, a fox enters then exits. And that's it. No cars, no people. Nothing. She's called both the estate agents and the pub, and both have confirmed the bins aren't used. "Why are they there then?" Julia asked, and neither could give a satisfactory answer. They're on Julia's list, somewhere in the middle, troubling her like a couple of nuisance summer flies. Think, she implores herself. Think outside of the box.

She is now walking to her car. She's parked half a mile away, due to a lack of police parking spaces. The younger guys steal them, getting in earlier and earlier, and she lets them. She rubs at her forehead. This morning feels a hundred years ago. Another day that's passed without her seeing her children. Perhaps Art was right.

Out of guilt, she checks Saskia's last seen. Two minutes ago. "You up?" she texts.

Saskia calls immediately, just as Julia wanted her to. "Always," she says. She has inherited Julia's insomnia.

"Same," Julia says with a smile. How amazing that Saskia, her posing toddler, once a fan of wearing sunglasses and a volatile expression, is now an adult she can call up for a late-night chat.

"We made dinner, in the end," Saskia says. "We've saved Nando's for tomorrow. How are the criminals?"

"We have a missing person, actually, not much older than you."

"Ooh. Color me intrigued. Cal is still up, too," Saskia says. "Want him on?"

"Sure," Julia says, her voice high and light. Her two children's voices chorus down the phone to her, and she closes her eyes. It's okay. They're okay. She's okay.

"Saskia is doing last-minute cramming," Cal says to her in his low, amused drawl. Julia's children are as opposite as can be. Saskia may be sardonic, but she is also a conformist. Happy to work hard and get a good job, finds life easy. Cal is on the fringes, awkward, emotional, intense.

Julia's breath makes cirrus clouds in the cold April air as she walks. She cuts through a park, the iron gate singing behind her, the sky dark blueberry beyond. There's nobody around, except her; except them.

"I'm just looking it over," Saskia says.

"Where are you?" Cal asks. Julia is glad he's at home. Wholesome, fifteen, and with his older sibling. She closes her eyes. She doesn't regret it.

"Almost at the car, now," she says.

"Is it juicy?" Saskia asks. "The misper?"

"Very."

"Oh – how so?"

"Disappeared into an alleyway – only it's blocked up. No escape. Riddle me that," Julia says.

"Wow," Saskia says. "That's so weird. You need the TikTok detectives on the case."

Julia has to laugh. "Maybe I actually do."

"What's that saying? You can't hide one body, but you can hide a body in a hundred pieces?"

"Jesus, Saskia," Cal says.

"I know," Julia says. "Right – home in ten. Love to you both." She hangs up. It isn't even a ten-minute drive to home, new home, anyway. After everything with Art, they moved, even though it felt like the wrong thing to do, to move house together, still as a family, while she and Art sleep in separate bedrooms and ruminate (Julia can only speak for herself here).

But now they have a new semi-detached house for which they paid a huge premium: it's overlooking the beach at Portishead. During winter storms, the sand glasses the windows and blows in the cracks. Julia finds it everywhere. It is unimaginably romantic.

She emerges from the park. It's surrounded by black iron railings that blend into the dark air.

Footsteps.

Julia doesn't react, has trained herself not to. She isn't worried. She always feels somehow armed, even though she isn't. The power the police hold. To arrest, to flash a badge. Julia feels untouchable, even in a deserted city park at dusk.

She keeps her pace measured. Lets her phone glow bright. If they want to mug her, let them, make the target bright and obvious. She looks casually over her shoulder. A man in a hoody. A kid, really, maybe sixteen, seventeen. Has a mother, somewhere. She looks closely. She doesn't know him. Has never arrested him, and so she immediately relaxes.

Everything about his body language says that he has a problem with the world. Arms criss-crossing in front of and behind his body as he walks. Hood pulled down, obscuring his face completely. Pace slow, like he has all the time in the world. Julia has met many men like him. Has arrested them, pressed them for information. Has taken victim impact statements from them, too. Has met their parents, has met their sons.

She takes a quick left, just to see what he does. He smiles a half-smile, then walks on past her. Julia watches him go. Hoping he has a home to go to with somebody who cares enough about that walk, and what it might mean.

Julia reaches for her car keys, and only unlocks the door when she's as close to it as can be. She lets a sigh out as she gets in. It smells of her children's McDonald's. Saskia steers with her knees while eating Big Macs, much to Julia's shame. She once said, "Oh sure, so you're going to arrest me for it, then, are you?" while Julia gaped, thinking, well, maybe?

The fabric of the seat is cold against Julia's skin. She allows her heartbeat to slow, thinking of Olivia and where she could be. That distinctively female fear she must've felt, that text to her housemates. Is that what Julia would send, if she were in real trouble?

She starts the engine, turns her lights on, then turns the heat up. Her phone vibrates in the cup holder, but she ignores it. She knows it will be Saskia, having thought of another question and fired it off in that way that she does.

As soon as her phone stops, she feels it. A presence. Or, rather, a lack of absence.

She tells herself she always gets like this when working on missing persons cases, that it is because a young, attractive woman has disappeared, that it's because it's late, unseasonably cold, it's because Art both is and isn't at home, waiting for her.

But then the back of her neck shivers with something more than just anxiety: instead, a deep, limbic part of her brain fires up a warning flare into the night. She isn't alone. She counts to three, then raises her eyes to the rear view mirror.

In the back is a man wearing a balaclava. He says only one word: "Drive."